Scaramouche

A ROMANCE OF THE
FRENCH REVOLUTION

Scaramouche

A ROMANCE OF THE
FRENCH REVOLUTION

RAFAEL SABATINI

A COMMON READER EDITION
THE AKADINE PRESS

Scaramouche

This COMMON READER EDITION copyright © 1999 by The Akadine Press, Inc.

Book design by Chris Carruth.

A COMMON READER EDITION and fountain colophon are trademarks of The Akadine Press, Inc.

ISBN 1-888173-58-0

2 4 6 8 10 9 7 5 3 1

Hommes sensibles qui pleurez sur les maux de la Révolution, versez donc aussi quelques larmes sur les maux qui l'ont amené.

—Michelet

Table of Contents

Book I

THE ROBE

Book II

THE BUSKIN

CHAPTER I

The Republican

He was born with a gift of laughter and a sense that the world was mad. And that was all his patrimony. His very paternity was obscure, although the village of Gavrillac had long since dispelled the cloud of mystery that hung about it. Those simple Brittany folk were not so simple as to be deceived by a pretended relationship which did not even possess the virtue of originality. When a nobleman, for no apparent reason, announces himself the godfather of an infant fetched no man knew whence, and thereafter cares for the lad's rearing and education, the most unsophisticated of country folk perfectly understand the situation. And so the good people of Gavrillac permitted themselves no illusions on the score of the real relationship between André-Louis Moreau—as the lad had been named—and Quintin de Kercadiou, Lord of Gavrillac, who dwelt in the big grey house that dominated from its eminence the village clustering below.

André-Louis had learnt his letters at the village school, lodged the while with old Rabouillet, the attorney, who in the capacity of fiscal intendant, looked after the affairs of M. de Kercadiou. Thereafter, at the age of fifteen, he had been packed off to Paris, to the Lycée of Louis le Grand, to study the law which he was now returned to practise in conjunction with Rabouillet. All this at the charges of his godfather, M. de Kercadiou, who by placing him once more under the tutelage of Rabouillet would seem thereby quite clearly to be making provision for his future.

André-Louis, on his side, had made the most of his opportunities. You behold him at the age of four-and-twenty stuffed with learning enough to produce an intellectual indigestion in an ordinary mind. Out of his zestful study of Man, from Thucydides to the Encyclopædists, from Seneca to Rousseau, he had confirmed into an unassailable conviction his earliest conscious impressions of the general insanity of his own species. Nor can I discover that anything in his eventful life ever afterwards caused him to waver in that opinion.

In body he was a slight wisp of a fellow, scarcely above middle height, with a lean, astute countenance, prominent of nose and cheek-bones, and with lank, black hair that reached almost to his shoulders. His mouth was long, thin-lipped, and humorous. He was only just redeemed from ugliness by the splendour of a pair of ever-questing, luminous eyes, so dark as to be almost black. Of the whimsical quality of his mind and his rare gift of graceful expression, his writings—unfortunately but too scanty—and particularly his *Confessions*, afford us very ample evidence. Of his gift of oratory he was hardly conscious yet, although he had already achieved a certain fame for it in the Literary Chamber of

Rennes—one of those clubs by now ubiquitous in the land, in which the intellectual youth of France foregathered to study and discuss the new philosophies that were permeating social life. But the fame he had acquired there was hardly enviable. He was too impish, too caustic, too much disposed—so thought his colleagues—to ridicule their sublime theories for the regeneration of mankind. Himself he protested that he merely held them up to the mirror of truth, and that it was not his fault if when reflected there they looked ridiculous.

All that he achieved by this was to exasperate; and his expulsion from a society grown mistrustful of him must already have followed but for his friend, Philippe de Vilmorin, a divinity student of Rennes, who, himself, was one of the most popular members of the Literary Chamber.

Coming to Gavrillac on a November morning, laden with news of the political storms which were then gathering over France, Philippe found in that sleepy Breton village matter to quicken his already lively indignation. A peasant of Gavrillac, named Mabey, had been shot dead that morning in the woods of Meupont, across the river, by a gamekeeper of the Marquis de La Tour d'Azyr. The unfortunate fellow had been caught in the act of taking a pheasant from a snare, and the gamekeeper had acted under explicit orders from his master.

Infuriated by an act of tyranny so absolute and merciless, M. de Vilmorin proposed to lay the matter before M. de Kercadiou. Mabey was a vassal of Gavrillac, and Vilmorin hoped to move the Lord of Gavrillac to demand at least some measure of reparation for the widow and the three orphans which that brutal deed had made.

But because André-Louis was Philippe's dearest friend—indeed, his almost brother—the young seminarist sought him out in the first instance. He found him at breakfast alone in the long, low-ceilinged, white-panelled dining-room at Rabouillet's—the only home that André-Louis had ever known—and after embracing him, deafened him with his denunciation of M. de La Tour d'Azyr.

"I have heard of it already," said André-Louis.

"You speak as if the thing had not surprised you," his friend reproached him.

"Nothing beastly can surprise me when done by a beast. And La Tour d'Azyr is a beast, as all the world knows. The more fool Mabey for stealing his pheasants. He should have stolen somebody else's."

"Is that all you have to say about it?"

"What more is there to say? I've a practical mind, I hope."

"What more there is to say I propose to say to your godfather, M. de Kercadiou. I shall appeal to him for justice."

"Against M. de La Tour d'Azyr?" André-Louis raised his eyebrows.

"Why not?"

"My dear ingenuous Philippe, dog doesn't eat dog."

"You are unjust to your godfather. He is a humane man."

"Oh, as humane as you please. But this isn't a question of humanity. It's a question of game-laws."

M. de Vilmorin tossed his long arms to Heaven in disgust. He was a tall, slender young gentleman, a year or two younger than André-Louis. He was very soberly dressed in black, as became a seminarist, with white bands at wrists and throat and silver buckles to his shoes. His neatly clubbed brown hair was innocent of powder.

"You talk like a lawyer," he exploded.

"Naturally. But don't waste anger on me on that account. Tell me what you want me to do."

"I want you to come to M. de Kercadiou with me, and to use your influence to obtain justice. I suppose I am asking too much."

"My dear Philippe, I exist to serve you. I warn you that it is a futile quest; but give me leave to finish my breakfast, and I am at your orders."

M. de Vilmorin dropped into a winged armchair by the well-swept hearth, on which a piled-up fire of pine logs was burning cheerily. And whilst he waited now he gave his friend the latest news of the events in Rennes. Young, ardent, enthusiastic, and inspired by Utopian ideals, he passionately denounced the rebellious attitude of the privileged.

André-Louis, already fully aware of the trend of feeling in the ranks of an order in whose deliberations he took part as the representative of a nobleman, was not at all surprised by what he heard. M. de Vilmorin found it exasperating that his friend should apparently decline to share his own indignation.

"Don't you see what it means?" he cried. "The nobles, by disobeying the King, are striking at the very foundations of the throne. Don't they perceive that their very existence depends upon it; that if the throne falls over, it is they who stand nearest to it who will be crushed? Don't they see that?"

"Evidently not. They are just governing classes, and I never heard of governing classes that had eyes for anything but their own profit."

"That is our grievance. That is what we are going to change."

"You are going to abolish governing classes? An interesting experiment. I believe it was the original plan of creation, and it might have succeeded but for Cain."

"What we are going to do," said M. de Vilmorin, curbing his exasperation, "is to transfer the government to other hands."

"And you think that will make a difference?"

"I know it will."

"Ah! I take it that being now in minor orders, you already possess the confidence of the Almighty. He will have confided to you His intention of changing the pattern of mankind."

M. de Vilmorin's fine ascetic face grew overcast.

"You are profane, André," he reproved his friend.

"I assure you that I am quite serious. To do what you imply would require nothing short of divine intervention. You must change man, not systems. Can you and our vapouring friends of the Literary Chamber of Rennes, or any other learned society of France, devise a system of government that has never yet been tried? Surely not. And can they say of any system tried that it proved other than a failure in the end? My dear Philippe, the future is to be read with certainty only in the past. *Ab actu ad posse valet consecutio.* Man never changes. He is always greedy, always acquisitive, always vile. I am speaking of Man in the bulk."

"Do you pretend that it is impossible to ameliorate the lot of the people?" M. de Vilmorin challenged him.

"When you say the people you mean, of course, the populace. Will you abolish it? That is the only way to ameliorate its lot, for as long as it remains populace its lot will be damnation."

"You argue, of course, for the side that employs you. That is

8

natural, I suppose." M. de Vilmorin spoke between sorrow and indignation.

"On the contrary, I seek to argue with absolute detachment. Let us test these ideas of yours. To what form of government do you aspire? A republic, it is to be inferred from what you have said. Well, you have it already. France in reality is a republic today."

Philippe stared at him. "You are being paradoxical, I think. What of the King?"

"The King? All the world knows there has been no king in France since Louis XIV. There is an obese gentleman at Versailles who wears the crown, but the very news you bring shows for how little he really counts. It is the nobles and clergy who sit in the high places, with the people of France harnessed under their feet, who are the real rulers. That is why I say that France is a republic; she is a republic built on the best pattern—the Roman pattern. Then, as now, there were great patrician families in luxury, preserving for themselves power and wealth, and what else is accounted worth possessing; and there was the populace crushed and groaning, sweating, bleeding, starving, and perishing in the Roman kennels. That was a republic; the mightiest we have seen."

Philippe strove with his impatience. "At least you will admit—you have, in fact, admitted it—that we could not be worse governed than we are?"

"That is not the point. The point is should we be better governed if we replaced the present ruling class by another? Without some guarantee of that I should be the last to lift a finger to effect a change. And what guarantees can you give? What is the class that aims at government? I will tell you. The bourgeoisie."

9

"What?"

"That startles you, eh? Truth is so often disconcerting. You hadn't thought of it? Well, think of it now. Look well into this Nantes manifesto. Who are the authors of it?"

"I can tell you who it was constrained the municipality of Nantes to send it to the King. Some ten thousand workmen—shipwrights, weavers, labourers, and artisans of every kind."

"Stimulated to it, driven to it, by their employers, the wealthy traders and shipowners of that city," André-Louis replied. "I have a habit of observing things at close quarters, which is why our colleagues of the Literary Chamber dislike me so cordially in debate. Where I delve they but skim. Behind those labourers and artisans of Nantes, counselling them, urging on these poor, stupid, ignorant toilers to shed their blood in pursuit of the will o' the wisp of freedom, are the sailmakers, the spinners, the shipowners and the slave-traders. The slave-traders! The men who live and grow rich by a traffic in human flesh and blood in the colonies, are conducting at home a campaign in the sacred name of liberty! Don't you see that the whole movement is a movement of hucksters and traders and peddling vassals swollen by wealth into envy of the power that lies in birth alone? The money-changers in Paris who hold the bonds in the national debt, seeing the parlous financial condition of the State, tremble at the thought that it may lie in the power of a single man to cancel the debt by bankruptcy. To secure themselves they are burrowing underground to overthrow a state and build upon its ruins a new one in which they shall be the masters. And to accomplish this they inflame the people. Already in Dauphiny we have seen blood run like water—the blood of the populace, always the blood of the populace. Now in Brittany we may see the like. And if in the end the new ideas prevail? If the seigneurial rule is overthrown, what then? You will have exchanged an aristocracy for a plutocracy. Is that worth while? Do you think that under money-changers and slave-traders and men who have waxed rich in other ways by the ignoble arts of buying and selling, the lot of the people will be any better than under their priests and nobles? Has it ever occurred to you, Philippe, what it is that makes the rule of the nobles so intolerable? Acquisitiveness. Acquisitiveness is the curse of mankind. And shall you expect less acquisitiveness in men who have built themselves up by acquisitiveness? Oh, I am ready to admit that the present government is execrable, unjust, tyrannical—what you will; but I beg you to look ahead, and to see that the government for which it is aimed at exchanging it may be infinitely worse."

Philippe sat thoughtful a moment. Then he returned to the attack.

"You do not speak of the abuses, the horrible, intolerable abuses of power under which we labour at present."

"Where there is power there will always be the abuse of it."

"Not if the tenure of power is dependent upon its equitable administration."

"The tenure of power is power. We cannot dictate to those who hold it."

"The people can—the people in its might."

"Again I ask you, when you say the people do you mean the populace? You do. What power can the populace wield? It can run wild. It can burn and slay for a time. But enduring power it cannot wield, because power demands qualities which the populace does not possess, or it would not be populace. The inevitable, tragic corollary of civilization is populace. For the rest, abuses can be corrected by equity; and equity, if it is not found in the enlightened, is not to be found at all. M. Necker is to set about correcting abuses, and limiting privileges. That is decided. To that end the States General are to assemble."

"And a promising beginning we have made in Brittany, as Heaven hears me!" cried Philippe.

"Pooh! That is nothing. Naturally the nobles will not yield without a struggle. It is a futile and ridiculous struggle—but then . . . it is human nature, I suppose, to be futile and ridiculous."

M. de Vilmorin became witheringly sarcastic. "Probably you will also qualify the shooting of Mabey as futile and ridiculous. I should even be prepared to hear you argue in defence of the Marquis de La Tour d'Azyr that his gamekeeper was merciful in shooting Mabey, since the alternative would have been a life-sentence to the galleys."

André-Louis drank the remainder of his chocolate; set down his cup, and pushed back his chair, his breakfast done.

"I confess that I have not your big charity, my dear Philippe. I am touched by Mabey's fate. But, having conquered the shock of this news to my emotions, I do not forget that, after all, Mabey was thieving when he met his death."

M. de Vilmorin heaved himself up in his indignation.

"That is the point of view to be expected in one who is the assistant fiscal intendant of a nobleman, and the delegate of a nobleman to the States of Brittany."

"Philippe, is that just? You are angry with me!" he cried, in real solicitude.

"I am hurt," Vilmorin admitted. "I am deeply hurt by your attitude. And I am not alone in resenting your reactionary tendencies. Do you know that the Literary Chamber is seriously considering your expulsion?"

André-Louis shrugged. "That neither surprises nor troubles me."

M. de Vilmorin swept on, passionately: "Sometimes I think that you have no heart. With you it is always the law, never equity. It occurs to me, André, that I was mistaken in coming to you. You are not likely to be of assistance to me in my interview with M. de Kercadiou." He took up his hat, clearly with the intention of departing.

André-Louis sprang up and caught him by the arm.

"I vow," said he, "that this is the last time ever I shall consent to talk law or politics with you, Philippe. I love you too well to quarrel with you over other men's affairs."

"But I make them my own," Philippe insisted vehemently.

"Of course you do, and I love you for it. It is right that you should. You are to be a priest; and everybody's business is a priest's business. Whereas I am a lawyer—the fiscal intendant of a nobleman, as you say—and a lawyer's business is the business of his client. That is the difference between us. Nevertheless, you are not going to shake me off."

"But I tell you frankly, now that I come to think of it, that I should prefer you did not see M. de Kercadiou with me. Your duty to your client cannot be a help to me." His wrath had passed; but his determination remained firm, based upon the reason he gave.

"Very well," said André-Louis. "It shall be as you please. But nothing shall prevent me at least from walking with you as far as the château, and waiting for you while you make your appeal to M. de Kercadiou."

And so they left the house good friends, for the sweetness of M. de Vilmorin's nature did not admit of rancour, and together they took their way up the steep main street of Gavrillac.

CHAPTER II

The Aristocrat

The sleepy village of Gavrillac, a half-league removed from the main road to Rennes, and therefore undisturbed by the world's traffic, lay in a curve of the River Meu, at the foot, and straggling halfway up the slope, of the shallow hill that was crowned by the squat manor. By the time Gavrillac had paid tribute to its seigneur—partly in money and partly in service—tithes to the Church, and imposts to the King, it was hard put to it to keep body and soul together with what remained. Yet, hard as conditions were in Gavrillac, they were not so hard as in many other parts of France, not half so hard, for instance, as with the wretched feudatories of the great Lord of La Tour d'Azyr, whose vast possessions were at one point separated from this little village by the waters of the Meu.

The Château de Gavrillac owed such seigneurial airs as might be claimed for it to its dominant position above the village rather than to any feature of its own. Built of granite, like all the rest of Gavrillac, though mellowed by some three centuries of existence, it was a squat, flat-fronted edifice of two stories, each lighted by four windows with external wooden shutters, and flanked at either end by two square towers or pavilions under extinguisher roofs. Standing well back in a garden, denuded now, but very pleasant in summer, and immediately fronted by a fine sweep of balustraded terrace, it looked what indeed it was, and always had been, the residence of unpretentious folk who found more interest in husbandry than in adventure.

Quintin de Kercadiou, Lord of Gavrillac—Seigneur de Gavrillac was all the vague title that he bore, as his forefathers had borne before him, derived no man knew whence or how—confirmed the impression that his house conveyed. Rude as the granite itself, he had never sought the experience of courts, had not even taken service in the armies of his King. He left it to his younger brother, Étienne, to represent the family in those exalted spheres. His own interests from earliest years had been centred in his woods and pastures. He hunted, and he cultivated his acres, and superficially he appeared to be little better than any of his rustic *métayers*. He kept no state, or at least no state commensurate with his position or with the tastes of his niece Aline de Kercadiou. Aline, having spent some two years in the court atmosphere of Versailles under the ægis of her uncle Étienne, had ideas very different from those of her uncle Quintin of what was befitting seigneurial dignity. But though this only child of a third Kercadiou had exercised, ever since she was left an orphan at the early age of four, a tyrannical rule over the Lord of Gavrillac, who had been father and mother to her, she had never yet succeeded in beating down his stubbornness on that score.

She did not yet despair—persistence being a dominant note in her character—although she had been assiduously and fruitlessly at work since her return from the great world of Versailles, some three months ago.

She was walking on the terrace when André-Louis and M. de Vilmorin arrived. Her slight body was wrapped against the chill air in a white pélisse; her head was encased in a close-fitting bonnet, edged with white fur. It was caught tight in a knot of pale-blue ribbon on the right of her chin; on the left a long ringlet of corn-coloured hair had been permitted to escape. The keen air had whipped so much of her cheeks as was presented to it, and seemed to have added sparkle to eyes that were of darkest blue.

André-Louis and M. de Vilmorin had been known to her from childhood. The three had been playmates once, and André-Louis—in view of his spiritual relationship with her uncle—she called her cousin. The cousinly relations had persisted between these two long after Philippe de Vilmorin had outgrown the earlier intimacy, and had become to her Monsieur de Vilmorin.

She waved her hand to them in greeting as they advanced, and stood—an entrancing picture, and fully conscious of it—to await them at the end of the terrace nearest the short avenue by which they approached.

"If you come to see monsieur my uncle, you come inopportunely, messieurs," she told them, a certain feverishness in her air. "He is closely—oh, so very closely—engaged."

"We will wait, mademoiselle," said M. de Vilmorin, bowing gallantly over the hand she extended to him. "Indeed, who would haste to the uncle that may tarry a moment with the niece?"

"M. l'abbé," she teased him, "when you are in orders I shall take you for my confessor. You have so ready and sympathetic an understanding."

"But no curiosity," said André-Louis. "You haven't thought of that."

"I wonder what you mean, Cousin André."

"Well you may," laughed Philippe. "For no one ever knows." And then, his glance straying across the terrace settled upon a carriage that was drawn up before the door of the château. It was a vehicle such as was often to be seen in the streets of a great city, but rarely in the country. It was a beautifully sprung two-horse cabriolet of walnut, with a varnish upon it like a sheet of glass and little pastoral scenes exquisitely painted on the panels of the door. It was built to carry two persons, with a box in front for the coachman, and a stand behind for the footman. This stand was empty, but the footman paced before the door, and as he emerged now from behind the vehicle into the range of M. de Vilmorin's vision, he displayed the resplendent blue-and-gold livery of the Marquis de La Tour d'Azyr.

"Why!" he exclaimed. "Is it M. de La Tour d'Azyr who is with your uncle?"

"It is, monsieur," said she, a world of mystery in voice and eyes, of which M. de Vilmorin observed nothing.

"Ah, pardon!" He bowed low, hat in hand. "Serviteur, mademoiselle," and he turned to depart towards the house.

"Shall I come with you, Philippe?" André-Louis called after him.

"It would be ungallant to assume that you would prefer it," said M. de Vilmorin, with a glance at mademoiselle. "Nor do I think it would serve. If you will wait . . ."

M. de Vilmorin strode off. Mademoiselle, after a moment's blank pause, laughed ripplingly. "Now where is he going in such a hurry?"

"To see M. de La Tour d'Azyr as well as your uncle, I should say."

"But he cannot. They cannot see him. Did I not say that they are very closely engaged? You don't ask me why, André." There was an arch mysteriousness about her, a latent something that may have been elation or amusement, or perhaps both. André-Louis could not determine it.

"Since obviously you are all eagerness to tell, why should I ask?" quoth he.

"If you are caustic I shall not tell you even if you ask. Oh, yes, I will. It will teach you to treat me with the respect that is my due."

"I hope I shall never fail in that."

"Less than ever when you learn that I am very closely concerned in the visit of M. de La Tour d'Azyr. I am the object of this visit." And she looked at him with sparkling eyes and lips parted in laughter.

"The rest, you would seem to imply, is obvious. But I am a dolt, if you please; for it is not obvious to me."

"Why, stupid, he comes to ask my hand in marriage."

"Good God!" said André-Louis, and stared at her, chapfallen.

She drew back from him a little with a frown and an upward tilt of her chin. "It surprises you?"

"It disgusts me," said he, bluntly. "In fact, I don't believe it. You are amusing yourself with me."

For a moment she put aside her visible annoyance to remove his doubts. "I am quite serious, monsieur. There came a formal letter to my uncle this morning from M. de La Tour d'Azyr, announcing the visit and its object. I will not say that it did not surprise us a little . . ."

"Oh, I see," cried André-Louis, in relief. "I understand. For a moment I had almost feared . . ." He broke off, looked at her, and shrugged.

"Why do you stop? You had almost feared that Versailles had been wasted upon me. That I should permit the courtship of me to be conducted like that of any village wench. It was stupid of you. I am being sought in proper form, at my uncle's hands."

"Is his consent, then, all that matters, according to Versailles?"

"What else?"

"There is your own."

She laughed. "I am a dutiful niece . . . when it suits me."

"And will it suit you to be dutiful if your uncle accepts this monstrous proposal?"

"Monstrous!" She bridled. "And why monstrous, if you please?"

"For a score of reasons," he answered, irritably.

"Give me one," she challenged him.

"He is twice your age."

"Hardly so much," said she.

"He is forty-five, at least."

"But he looks no more than thirty. He is very handsome—so much you will admit; nor will you deny that he is very wealthy and very powerful; the greatest nobleman in Brittany. He will make me a great lady."

"God made you that, Aline."

"Come, that's better. Sometimes you can almost be polite." And she moved along the terrace, André-Louis pacing beside her.

"I can be more than that to show reason why you should not let this beast befoul the beautiful thing that God has made."

She frowned, and her lips tightened. "You are speaking of my future husband," she reproved him.

His lips tightened too; his pale face grew paler.

"And is it so? It is settled, then? Your uncle is to agree? You are to be sold thus, lovelessly, into bondage to a man you do not know. I had dreamed of better things for you, Aline."

"Better than to be Marquise de La Tour d'Azyr?"

He made a gesture of exasperation. "Are men and women nothing more than names? Do the souls of them count for nothing? Is there no joy in life, no happiness, that wealth and pleasure and empty, high-sounding titles are to be its only aims? I had set you high—so high, Aline—a thing scarce earthly. There is joy in your heart, intelligence in your mind; and, as I thought, the vision that pierces husks and shams to claim the core of reality for its own. Yet you will surrender all for a parcel of make-believe. You will sell your soul and your body to be Marquise de La Tour d'Azyr."

"You are indelicate," said she, and though she frowned her eyes laughed. "And you go headlong to conclusions. My uncle will not consent to more than to allow my consent to be sought. We understand each other, my uncle and I. I am not to be bartered like a turnip."

He stood still to face her, his eyes glowing, a flush creeping into his pale cheeks.

"You have been torturing me to amuse yourself!" he cried. "Ah, well, I forgive you out of my relief."

"Again you go too fast, Cousin André. I have permitted my uncle to consent that M. le Marquis shall make his court to me. I like the look of the gentleman. I am flattered by his preference when I consider his eminence. It is an eminence that I may find it desirable to share. M. le Marquis does not look as if he were a dullard. It should be interesting to be wooed by him. It may be more interesting still to marry him, and I think, when all is considered, that I shall probably—very probably—decide to do so."

He looked at her, looked at the sweet, challenging loveliness of that childlike face so tightly framed in the oval of white fur, and all the life seemed to go out of his own countenance.

"God help you, Aline!" he groaned.

She stamped her foot. He was really very exasperating, and something presumptuous too, she thought.

"You are insolent, monsieur."

"It is never insolent to pray, Aline. And I did no more than pray, as I shall continue to do. You'll need my prayers, I think."

"You are insufferable!" She was growing angry, as he saw by the deepening frown, the heightened colour.

"That is because I suffer. Oh, Aline, little cousin, think well of what you do; think well of the realities you will be bartering for these shams—the realities that you will never know, because these cursed shams will block your way to them. When M. de La Tour d'Azyr comes to make his court, study him well; consult your fine instincts; leave your own noble nature free to judge this animal by its intuitions. Consider that . . ."

"I consider, monsieur, that you presume upon the kindness I

have always shown you. You abuse the position of toleration in which you stand. Who are you? What are you, that you should have the insolence to take this tone with me?"

He bowed, instantly his cold, detached self again, and resumed the mockery that was his natural habit.

"My congratulations, mademoiselle, upon the readiness with which you begin to adapt yourself to the great rôle you are to play."

"Do you adapt yourself also, monsieur," she retorted angrily, and turned her shoulder to him.

"To be as the dust beneath the haughty feet of Madame la Marquise. I hope I shall know my place in future."

The phrase arrested her. She turned to him again, and he perceived that her eyes were shining now suspiciously. In an instant the mockery in him was quenched in contrition.

"Lord, what a beast I am, Aline!" he cried, as he advanced. "Forgive me if you can."

Almost had she turned to sue forgiveness from him. But his contrition removed the need.

"I'll try," said she, "provided that you undertake not to offend again."

"But I shall," said he. "I am like that. I will fight to save you, from yourself if need be, whether you forgive me or not."

They were standing so, confronting each other a little breathlessly, a little defiantly, when the others issued from the porch.

First came the Marquis of La Tour d'Azyr, Count of Solz, Knight of the Orders of the Holy Ghost and Saint Louis, and Brigadier in the armies of the King. He was a tall, graceful man, upright and soldierly of carriage, with his head disdainfully set upon his shoulders. He was magnificently dressed in a full-skirted coat of mulberry velvet that was laced with gold. His waistcoat, of velvet too, was of a golden apricot colour; his breeches and stockings were of black silk, and his lacquered, red-heeled shoes were buckled in diamonds. His powdered hair was tied behind in a broad ribbon of watered silk; he carried a little three-cornered hat under his arm, and a gold-hilted slender dress-sword hung at his side.

Considering him now in complete detachment, observing the magnificence of him, the elegance of his movements, the great air, blending in so extraordinary a manner disdain and graciousness, André-Louis trembled for Aline. Here was a practised, irresistible wooer, whose *bonnes fortunes* were become a by-word, a man who had hitherto been the despair of dowagers with marriageable daughters, and the desolation of husbands with attractive wives.

He was immediately followed by M. de Kercadiou, in completest contrast. On legs of the shortest, the Lord of Gavrillac carried a body that at forty-five was beginning to incline to corpulence and an enormous head containing an indifferent allotment of intelligence. His countenance was pink and blotchy, liberally branded by the smallpox which had almost extinguished him in youth. In dress he was careless to the point of untidiness, and to this and to the fact that he had never married— disregarding the first duty of a gentleman to provide himself with an heir—he owed the character of misogynist attributed to him by the countryside.

After M. de Kercadiou came M. de Vilmorin, very pale and self-contained, with tight lips and an overcast brow.

24

To meet them, there stepped from the carriage a very elegant young gentleman, the Chevalier de Chabrillane, M. de La Tour d'Azyr's cousin, who whilst awaiting his return had watched with considerable interest—his own presence unsuspected—the perambulations of André-Louis and mademoiselle.

Perceiving Aline, M. de La Tour d'Azyr detached himself from the others, and lengthening his stride came straight across the terrace to her.

To André-Louis the Marquis inclined his head with that mixture of courtliness and condescension which he used. Socially, the young lawyer stood in a curious position. By virtue of the theory of his birth, he ranked neither as noble nor as simple, but stood somewhere between the two classes, and whilst claimed by neither he was used familiarly by both. Coldly now he returned M. de La Tour d'Azyr's greeting, and discreetly removed himself to go and join his friend.

The Marquis took the hand that mademoiselle extended to him, and bowing over it, bore it to his lips.

"Mademoiselle," he said, looking into the blue depths of her eyes, that met his gaze smiling and untroubled, "monsieur your uncle does me the honour to permit that I pay my homage to you. Will you, mademoiselle, do me the honour to receive me when I come tomorrow? I shall have something of great importance for your ear."

"Of importance, M. le Marquis? You almost frighten me." But there was no fear on the serene little face in its furred hood. It was not for nothing that she had graduated in the Versailles school of artificialities.

"That," said he, "is very far from my design."

"But of importance to yourself, monsieur, or to me?"

"To us both, I hope," he answered her, a world of meaning in his fine, ardent eyes.

"You whet my curiosity, monsieur; and, of course, I am a dutiful niece. It follows that I shall be honoured to receive you."

"Not honoured, mademoiselle; you will confer the honour. Tomorrow at this hour, then, I shall have the felicity to wait upon you."

He bowed again; and again he bore her fingers to his lips, what time she curtsied. Thereupon, with no more than this formal breaking of the ice, they parted.

She was a little breathless now, a little dazzled by the beauty of the man, his princely air, and the confidence of power he seemed to radiate. Involuntarily almost, she contrasted him with his critic—the lean and impudent André-Louis in his plain brown coat and steel-buckled shoes—and she felt guilty of an unpardonable offence in having permitted even one word of that presumptuous criticism. Tomorrow M. le Marquis would come to offer her a great position, a great rank. And already she had derogated from the increase of dignity accruing to her from his very intention to translate her to so great an eminence. Not again would she suffer it; not again would she be so weak and childish as to permit André-Louis to utter his ribald comments upon a man by comparison with whom he was no better than a lackey.

Thus argued vanity and ambition with her better self; and to her vast annoyance her better self would not admit entire conviction.

Meanwhile, M. de La Tour d'Azyr was climbing into his carriage. He had spoken a word of farewell to M. de Kercadiou, and he had also had a word for M. de Vilmorin in reply to which M. de Vilmorin had bowed in assenting silence.

The carriage rolled away, the powdered footman in blue-and-gold very stiff behind it, M. de La Tour d'Azyr bowing to mademoiselle, who waved to him in answer.

Then M. de Vilmorin put his arm through that of André-Louis, and said to him, "Come, André."

"But you'll stay to dine, both of you!" cried the hospitable Lord of Gavrillac. "We'll drink a certain toast," he added, winking an eye that strayed towards mademoiselle, who was approaching. He had no subtleties, good soul that he was.

M. de Vilmorin deplored an appointment that prevented him doing himself the honour. He was very stiff and formal.

"And you, André?"

"I? Oh, I share the appointment, godfather," he lied, "and I have a superstition against toasts." He had no wish to remain. He was angry with Aline for her smiling reception of M. de La Tour d'Azyr and the sordid bargain he saw her set on making. He was suffering from the loss of an illusion.

CHAPTER III

The Eloquence
of M. de Vilmorin

As they walked down the hill together, it was now M. de
Vilmorin who was silent and preoccupied, André-Louis who
was talkative. He had chosen Woman as a subject for his present
discourse. He claimed—quite unjustifiably—to have discovered
Woman that morning and the things he had to say of the sex
were unflattering, and occasionally almost gross. M. de Vilmorin,
having ascertained the subject, did not listen. Singular though it
may seem in a young French abbé of his day, M. de Vilmorin
was not interested in Woman. Poor Philippe was in several ways
exceptional.

Opposite the Breton Armé—the inn and posting-house at
the entrance of the village of Gavrillac—M. de Vilmorin interrupted his companion just as he was soaring to the dizziest heights
of caustic invective, and André-Louis, restored thereby to actu-
alities, observed the carriage of M. de La Tour d'Azyr standing

before the door of the hostelry.

"I don't believe you've been listening to me," said he.

"Had you been less interested in what you were saying, you might have observed it sooner and spared your breath. The fact is, you disappoint me, André. You seem to have forgotten what we went for. I have an appointment here with M. le Marquis. He desires to hear me further in the matter. Up there at Gavrillac I could accomplish nothing. The time was ill-chosen as it happened. But I have hopes of M. le Marquis."

"Hopes of what?"

"That he will make what reparation lies in his power. Provide for the widow and the orphans. Why else should he desire to hear me further?"

"Unusual condescension," said André-Louis, and quoted: *"Timeo Danaos et dona ferentes."*

"Why?" asked Philippe.

"Let us go and discover—unless you consider that I shall be in the way."

Into a room on the right, rendered private to M. le Marquis for so long as he should elect to honour it, the young men were ushered by the host. A fire of logs was burning brightly at the room's far end, and by this sat now M. de La Tour d'Azyr and his cousin, the Chevalier de Chabrillane. Both rose as M. de Vilmorin came in. André-Louis following, paused to close the door.

"You oblige me by your prompt courtesy, M. de Vilmorin," said the Marquis, but in a tone so cold as to belie the politeness of his words. "A chair, I beg. Ah, Moreau?" The note was frigidly interrogative. "He accompanies you, monsieur?" he asked.

"If you please, M. le Marquis."

"Why not? Find yourself a seat, Moreau." He spoke over his shoulder as to a lackey.

"It is good of you, monsieur," said Philippe, "to have offered me this opportunity of continuing the subject that took me so fruitlessly, as it happens, to Gavrillac."

The Marquis crossed his legs, and held one of his fine hands to the blaze. He replied, without troubling to turn to the young man, who was slightly behind him.

"The goodness of my request we will leave out of question for the moment," said he, darkly, and M. de Chabrillane laughed. André-Louis thought him easily moved to mirth, and almost envied him the faculty.

"But I am grateful," Philippe insisted, "that you should condescend to hear me plead their cause."

The Marquis stared at him over his shoulder. "Whose cause?" quoth he.

"Why, the cause of the widow and orphans of this unfortunate Mabey."

The Marquis looked from Vilmorin to the Chevalier, and again the Chevalier laughed, slapping his leg this time.

"I think," said M. de La Tour d'Azyr, slowly, "that we are at cross-purposes. I asked you to come here because the Château de Gavrillac was hardly a suitable place in which to carry our discussion further, and because I hesitated to incommode you by suggesting that you should come all the way to Azyr. But my object is connected with certain expressions that you let fall up there. It is on the subject of those expressions, monsieur, that I would hear you further—if you will honour me."

André-Louis began to apprehend that there was something

sinister in the air. He was a man of quick intuitions, quicker far than those of M. de Vilmorin, who evinced no more than a mild surprise.

"I am at a loss, monsieur," said he. "To what expressions does monsieur allude?"

"It seems, monsieur, that I must refresh your memory. The Marquis crossed his legs, and swung sideways on his chair, so that at last he directly faced M. de Vilmorin. "You spoke, monsieur—and however mistaken you may have been, you spoke very eloquently, too eloquently almost, it seemed to me—of the infamy of such a deed as the act of summary justice upon this thieving fellow Mabey, or whatever his name may be. *Infamy* was the precise word you used. You did not retract that word when I had the honour to inform you that it was by my orders that my gamekeeper Benet proceeded as he did."

"If," said M. de Vilmorin, "the deed was infamous, its infamy is not modified by the rank, however exalted, of the person responsible. Rather is it aggravated."

"Ah!" said M. le Marquis, and drew a gold snuffbox from his pocket. "You say, 'if the deed was infamous,' monsieur. Am I to understand that you are no longer as convinced as you appeared to be of its infamy?"

M. de Vilmorin's fine face wore a look of perplexity. He did not understand the drift of this.

"It occurs to me, M. le Marquis, in view of your readiness to assume responsibility, that you must believe in some justification for the deed which is not apparent to myself."

"That is better. That is distinctly better." The Marquis took snuff delicately, dusting the fragments from the fine lace at his throat. "You realize that with an imperfect understanding of these matters, not being yourself a landowner, you may have rushed to unjustifiable conclusions. That is indeed the case. May it be a warning to you, monsieur. When I tell you that for months past I have been annoyed by similar depredations, you will perhaps understand that it had become necessary to employ a deterrent sufficiently strong to put an end to them. Now that the risk is known, I do not think there will be any more prowling in my coverts. And there is more in it than that, M. de Vilmorin. It is not the poaching that annoys me so much as the contempt for my absolute and inviolable rights. There is, monsieur, as you cannot fail to have observed, an evil spirit of insubordination in the air, and there is only one way in which to meet it. To tolerate it, in however slight a degree, to show leniency, however leniently disposed, would entail having recourse to still harsher measures tomorrow. You understand me, I am sure, and you will also, I am sure, appreciate the condescension of what amounts to an explanation from me where I cannot admit that any explanations were due. If anything in what I have said is still obscure to you, I refer you to the game laws, which your lawyer friend there will expound for you at need."

With that the gentleman swung round again to face the fire. It appeared to convey the intimation that the interview was at an end. And yet this was not by any means the intimation that it conveyed to the watchful, puzzled, vaguely uneasy André-Louis. It was, thought he, a very curious, a very suspicious oration. It affected to explain, with a politeness of terms and a calculated insolence of tone; whilst in fact it could only serve to stimulate and goad a man of M. de Vilmorin's opinions. And that is precisely what it did. He rose.

"Are there in the world no laws but game laws?" he demanded, angrily. "Have you never by any chance heard of the laws of humanity?"

The Marquis sighed wearily. "What have I to do with the laws of humanity?" he wondered.

M. de Vilmorin looked at him a moment in speechless amazement.

"Nothing, M. le Marquis. That is—alas!—too obvious. I hope you will remember it in the hour when you may wish to appeal to those laws which you now deride."

M. de La Tour d'Azyr threw back his head sharply, his high-bred face imperious.

"Now what precisely shall that mean? It is not the first time today that you have made use of dark sayings that I could almost believe to veil the presumption of a threat."

"Not a threat, M. le Marquis—a warning. A warning that such deeds as these against God's creatures . . . Oh, you may sneer, monsieur, but they are God's creatures, even as you or I— neither more nor less, deeply though the reflection may wound your pride. In His eyes . . ."

"Of your charity, spare me a sermon, M. l'abbe!"

"You mock, monsieur. You laugh. Will you laugh, I wonder, when God presents His reckoning to you for the blood and plunder with which your hands are full?"

"Monsieur!" The word, sharp as the crack of a whip, was from M. de Chabrillane, who bounded to his feet. But instantly the Marquis repressed him.

"Sit down, Chevalier. You are interrupting M. l'abbé, and I

should like to hear him further. He interests me profoundly."

In the background André-Louis, too, had risen, brought to his feet by alarm, by the evil that he saw written on the handsome face of M. de La Tour d'Azyr. He approached, and touched his friend upon the arm.

"Better be going, Philippe," said he.

But M. de Vilmorin, caught in the relentless grip of passions long repressed, was being hurried by them recklessly along.

"Oh, monsieur," said he, "consider what you are and what you will be. Consider how you and your kind live by abuses, and consider the harvest that abuses must ultimately bring."

"Revolutionist!" said M. le Marquis, contemptuously. "You have the effrontery to stand before my face and offer me this stinking cant of your modern so-called intellectuals!"

"Is it cant, monsieur? Do you think—do you believe in your soul—that it is cant? Is it cant that the feudal grip is on all things that live, crushing them like grapes in the press, to its own profit? Does it not exercise its rights upon the waters of the river, the fire that bakes the poor man's bread of grass and barley, on the wind that turns the mill? The peasant cannot take a step upon the road, cross a crazy bridge over a river, buy an ell of cloth in the village market, without meeting feudal rapacity, without being taxed in feudal dues. Is not that enough, M. le Marquis? Must you also demand his wretched life in payment for the least infringement of your sacred privileges, careless of what widows or orphans you dedicate to woe? Will naught content you but that your shadow must lie like a curse upon the land? And do you think in your pride that France, this Job among the nations, will suffer it forever?"

He paused as if for a reply. But none came. The Marquis considered him, strangely silent, a half smile of disdain at the corners of his lips, an ominous hardness in his eyes.

Again André-Louis tugged at his friend's sleeve.

"Philippe."

Philippe shook him off, and plunged on, fanatically.

"Do you see nothing of the gathering clouds that herald the coming of the storm? You imagine, perhaps, that these States General summoned by M. Necker, and promised for next year, are to do nothing but devise fresh means of extortion to liquidate the bankruptcy of the State? You delude yourselves, as you shall find. The Third Estate, which you despise, will prove itself the preponderating force, and it will find a way to make an end of this canker of privilege that is devouring the vitals of this unfortunate country."

M. le Marquis shifted in his chair, and spoke at last.

"You have, monsieur," said he, "a very dangerous gift of eloquence. And it is of yourself rather than of your subject. For after all, what do you offer me? A *réchauffé* of the dishes served to out-at-elbow enthusiasts in the provincial literary chambers, compounded of the effusions of your Voltaires and Jean-Jacques and such dirty-fingered scribblers. You have not among all your philosophers one with the wit to understand that we are an order consecrated by antiquity, that for our rights and privileges we have behind us the authority of centuries."

"Humanity, monsieur," Philippe replied, "is more ancient than nobility. Human rights are contemporary with man."

The Marquis laughed and shrugged.

"That is the answer I might have expected. It has the right

note of cant that distinguishes the philosophers."

And then M. de Chabrillane spoke.

"You go a long way round," he criticized his cousin, on a note of impatience.

"But I am getting there," he was answered. "I desired to make quite certain first."

"Faith, you should have no doubt by now."

"I have none." The Marquis rose, and turned again to M. de Vilmorin, who had understood nothing of that brief exchange. "M. l'abbé," said he once more, "you have a very dangerous gift of eloquence. I can conceive of men being swayed by it. Had you been born a gentleman, you would not so easily have acquired these false views that you express."

M. de Vilmorin stared blankly, uncomprehending.

"Had I been born a gentleman, do you say?" quoth he, in a slow, bewildered voice. "But I was born a gentleman. My race is as old, my blood as good as yours, monsieur."

From M. le Marquis there was a slight play of eyebrows, a vague, indulgent smile. His dark, liquid eyes looked squarely into the face of M. de Vilmorin.

"You have been deceived in that, I fear."

"Deceived?"

"Your sentiments betray the indiscretion of which madame your mother must have been guilty."

The brutally affronting words were sped beyond recall, and the lips that had uttered them, coldly, as if they had been the merest commonplace, remained calm and faintly sneering.

A dead silence followed. André-Louis' wits were numbed. He stood aghast, all thought suspended in him, what time M. de

Vilmorin's eyes continued fixed upon M. de La Tour d'Azyr's, as if searching there for a meaning that eluded him. Quite suddenly he understood the vile affront. The blood leapt to his face, fire blazed in his gentle eyes. A convulsive quiver shook him. Then, with an inarticulate cry, he leaned forward, and with his open hand struck M. le Marquis full and hard upon his sneering face.

In a flash M. de Chabrillane was on his feet, between the two men.

Too late André-Louis had seen the trap. La Tour d'Azyr's words were but as a move in a game of chess, calculated to exasperate his opponent into some such countermove as this—a countermove that left him entirely at the other's mercy.

M. le Marquis looked on, very white save where M. de Vilmorin's finger-prints began slowly to colour his face; but he said nothing more. Instead, it was M. de Chabrillane who now did the talking, taking up his preconcerted part in this vile game.

"You realize, monsieur, what you have done," said he, coldly, to Philippe. "And you realize, of course, what must inevitably follow."

M. de Vilmorin had realized nothing. The poor young man had acted upon impulse, upon the instinct of decency and honour, never counting the consequences. But he realized them now at the sinister invitation of M. de Chabrillane, and if he desired to avoid these consequences, it was out of respect for his priestly vocation, which strictly forbade such adjustments of disputes as M. de Chabrillane was clearly thrusting upon him.

He drew back. "Let one affront wipe out the other," said he, in a dull voice. "The balance is still in M. le Marquis's favour. Let that content him."

"Impossible." The Chevalier's lips came together tightly. Thereafter he was suavity itself, but very firm. "A blow has been struck, monsieur. I think I am correct in saying that such a thing has never happened before to M. le Marquis in all his life. If you felt yourself affronted, you had but to ask the satisfaction due from one gentleman to another. Your action would seem to confirm the assumption that you found so offensive. But it does not on that account render you immune from the consequences."

It was, you see, M. de Chabrillane's part to heap coals upon this fire, to make quite sure that their victim should not escape them.

"I desire no immunity," flashed back the young seminarist, stung by this fresh goad. After all, he was nobly born, and the traditions of his class were strong upon him—stronger far than the seminarist schooling in humility. He owed it to himself, to his honour, to be killed rather than avoid the consequences of the thing he had done.

"But he does not wear a sword, messieurs!" cried André-Louis, aghast.

"That is easily amended. He may have the loan of mine."

"I mean, messieurs," André-Louis insisted, between fear for his friend and indignation, "that it is not his habit to wear a sword, that he has never worn one, that he is untutored in its uses. He is a seminarist—a postulant for holy orders, already half a priest, and so forbidden from such an engagement as you propose."

"All that he should have remembered before he struck a blow," said M. de Chabrillane, politely.

"The blow was deliberately provoked," raged André-Louis.

Then he recovered himself, though the other's haughty stare had no part in that recovery. "O my God, I talk in vain! How is one to argue against a purpose formed! Come away, Philippe. Don't you see the trap . . ."

M. de Vilmorin cut him short, and flung him off. "Be quiet, André. M. le Marquis is entirely in the right."

"M. le Marquis is in the right?" André-Louis let his arms fall helplessly. This man he loved above all other living men was caught in the snare of the world's insanity. He was baring his breast to the knife for the sake of a vague, distorted sense of the honour due to himself. It was not that he did not see the trap. It was that his honour compelled him to disdain consideration of it. To André-Louis in that moment he seemed a singularly tragic figure. Noble, perhaps, but very pitiful.

CHAPTER IV

The Heritage

It was M. de Vilmorin's desire that the matter should be settled out of hand. In this he was at once objective and subjective. A prey to emotions sadly at conflict with his priestly vocation, he was above all in haste to have done, so that he might resume a frame of mind more proper to it. Also he feared himself a little; by which I mean that his honour feared his nature. The circumstances of his education, and the goal that for some years now he had kept in view, had robbed him of much of that spirited brutality that is the birthright of the male. He had grown timid and gentle as a woman. Aware of it, he feared that once the heat of his passion was spent he might betray a dishonouring weakness in the ordeal.

M. le Marquis, on his side, was no less eager for an immediate settlement; and since they had M. de Chabrillane to act for his cousin, and André-Louis to serve as witness for M. de Vilmorin, there was nothing to delay them.

And so, within a few minutes, all arrangements were concluded, and you behold that sinisterly intentioned little group of four assembled in the afternoon sunshine on the bowling-green behind the inn. They were entirely private, screened more or less from the windows of the house by a ramage of trees, which, if leafless now, was at least dense enough to provide an effective lattice.

There were no formalities over measurements of blades or selection of ground. M. le Marquis removed his sword-belt and scabbard, but declined—not considering it worth while for the sake of so negligible an opponent—to divest himself either of his shoes or his coat. Tall, lithe, and athletic, he stood to face the no less tall, but very delicate and frail, M. de Vilmorin. The latter also disdained to make any of the usual preparations. Since he recognized that it could avail him nothing to strip, he came on guard fully dressed, two hectic spots above the cheek-bones burning on his otherwise grey face.

M. de Chabrillane, leaning upon a cane—for he had relinquished his sword to M. de Vilmorin—looked on with quiet interest. Facing him on the other side of the combatants stood André-Louis, the palest of the four, staring from fevered eyes, twisting and untwisting clammy hands.

His every instinct was to fling himself between the antagonists, to protest against and frustrate this meeting. That sane impulse was curbed, however, by the consciousness of its futility. To calm him, he clung to the conviction that the issue could not really be very serious. If the obligations of Philippe's honour compelled him to cross swords with the man he had struck, M. de La

Tour d'Azyr's birth compelled him no less to do no serious hurt to the unfledged lad he had so grievously provoked. M. le Marquis, after all, was a man of honour. He could intend no more than to administer a lesson; sharp, perhaps, but one by which his opponent must live to profit. André-Louis clung obstinately to that for comfort.

Steel beat on steel, and the men engaged. The Marquis presented to his opponent the narrow edge of his upright body, his knees slightly flexed and converted into living springs, whilst M. de Vilmorin stood squarely, a full target, his knees wooden. Honour and the spirit of fair play alike cried out against such a match.

The encounter was very short, of course. In youth, Philippe had received the tutoring in sword-play that was given to every boy born into his station of life. And so he knew at least the rudiments of what was now expected of him. But what could rudiments avail him here? Three disengages completed the exchanges, and then without any haste the Marquis slid his right foot along the moist turf, his long, graceful body extending itself in a lunge that went under M. de Vilmorin's clumsy guard, and with the utmost deliberation he drove his blade through the young man's vitals.

André-Louis sprang forward just in time to catch his friend's body under the armpits as it sank. Then, his own legs bending beneath the weight of it, he went down with his burden until he was kneeling on the damp turf. Philippe's limp head lay against André-Louis' left shoulder; Philippe's relaxed arms trailed at his sides; the blood welled and bubbled from the ghastly wound to saturate the poor lad's garments.

With white face and twitching lips, André-Louis looked up at M. de La Tour d'Azyr, who stood surveying his work with a countenance of grave but remorseless interest.

"You have killed him!" cried André-Louis.

"Of course."

The Marquis ran a lace handkerchief along his blade to wipe it. As he let the dainty fabric fall, he explained himself. "He had, as I told him, a too dangerous gift of eloquence."

And he turned away, leaving completest understanding with André-Louis. Still supporting the limp, draining body, the young man called to him.

"Come back, you cowardly murderer, and make yourself quite safe by killing me too!"

The Marquis half turned, his face dark with anger. Then M. de Chabrillane set a restraining hand upon his arm. Although a party throughout to the deed, the Chevalier was a little appalled now that it was done. He had not the high stomach of M. de La Tour d'Azyr, and he was a good deal younger.

"Come away," he said. "The lad is raving. They were friends."

"You heard what he said?" quoth the Marquis.

"Nor can he, or you, or any man deny it," flung back André-Louis. "Yourself, monsieur, you made confession when you gave me now the reason why you killed him. You did it because you feared him."

"If that were true—what, then?" asked the great gentleman.

"Do you ask? Do you understand of life and humanity nothing but how to wear a coat and dress your hair—oh, yes, and to handle weapons against boys and priests? Have you no mind to think, no soul into which you can turn its vision? Must you be told that it is a coward's part to kill the thing he fears, and doubly a coward's part to kill in this way? Had you stabbed him in the back with a knife, you would have shown the courage of your vileness. It would have been a vileness undisguised. But you feared the consequences of that, powerful as you are; and so you shelter your cowardice under the pretext of a duel."

The Marquis shook off his cousin's hand, and took a step forward, holding now his sword like a whip. But again the Chevalier caught and held him.

"No, no, Gervais! Let be, in God's name!"

"Let him come, monsieur," raved André-Louis, his voice thick and concentrated. "Let him complete his coward's work on me, and thus make himself safe from a coward's wages."

M. de Chabrillane let his cousin go. He came white to the lips, his eyes glaring at the lad who so recklessly insulted him. And then he checked. It may be that he remembered suddenly the relationship in which this young man was popularly believed to stand to the Seigneur de Gavrillac, and the well-known affection in which the Seigneur held him. And so he may have realized that if he pushed this matter further, he might find himself upon the horns of a dilemma. He would be confronted with the alternatives of shedding more blood, and so embroiling himself with the Lord of Gavrillac at a time when that gentleman's friendship was of the first importance to him, or else of withdrawing with such hurt to his dignity as must impair his authority in the countryside hereafter.

Be it so or otherwise, the fact remains that he stopped short; then, with an incoherent ejaculation, between anger and contempt, he tossed his arms, turned on his heel and strode off quickly with his cousin.

When the landlord and his people came, they found André-Louis, his arms about the body of his dead friend, murmuring passionately into the deaf ear that rested almost against his lips:

"Philippe! Speak to me, Philippe! Philippe . . . Don't you hear me? O God of Heaven! Philippe!"

At a glance they saw that here neither priest nor doctor could avail. The cheek that lay against André-Louis' was leaden-hued, the half-open eyes were glazed, and there was a little froth of blood upon the vacuously parted lips.

Half blinded by tears André-Louis stumbled after them when they bore the body into the inn. Upstairs in the little room to which they conveyed it, he knelt by the bed, and holding the dead man's hand in both his own, he swore to him out of his impotent rage that M. de La Tour d'Azyr should pay a bitter price for this.

"It was your eloquence he feared, Philippe," he said. "Then if I can get no justice for this deed, at least it shall be fruitless to him. The thing he feared in you, he shall fear in me. He feared that men might be swayed by your eloquence to the undoing of such things as himself. Men shall be swayed by it still. For your eloquence and your arguments shall be my heritage from you. I will make them my own. It matters nothing that I do not believe in your gospel of freedom. I know it—every word of it; that is all that matters to our purpose, yours and mine. If all else fails, your thoughts shall find expression in my living tongue. Thus at least we shall have frustrated his vile aim to still the voice he feared. It shall profit him nothing to have your blood upon his soul. That voice in you would never half so relentlessly have hounded him

45

and his as it shall in me—if all else fails."

It was an exulting thought. It calmed him; it soothed his grief, and he began very softly to pray. And then his heart trembled as he considered that Philippe, a man of peace, almost a priest, an apostle of Christianity, had gone to his Maker with the sin of anger on his soul. It was horrible. Yet God would see the righteousness of that anger. And in no case—be man's interpretation of Divinity what it might—could that one sin outweigh the loving good that Philippe had ever practised, the noble purity of his great heart. God, after all, reflected André-Louis, was not a grand-seigneur.

CHAPTER V

The Lord of Gavrillac

For the second time that day André-Louis set out for the château, walking briskly, and heeding not at all the curious eyes that followed him through the village, and the whisperings that marked his passage through the people, all agog by now with that day's event in which he had been an actor.

He was ushered by Bénoît, the elderly body-servant, rather grandiloquently called the seneschal, into the ground-floor room known traditionally as the library. It still contained several shelves of neglected volumes, from which it derived its title, but implements of the chase—fowling-pieces, powder-horns, hunting-bags, sheath-knives—obtruded far more prominently than those of study. The furniture was massive, of oak richly carved, and belonging to another age. Great massive oak beams crossed the rather lofty whitewashed ceiling.

Here the squat Seigneur de Gavrillac was restlessly pacing

when André-Louis was introduced. He was already informed, as he announced at once, of what had taken place at the Breton Armé. M. de Chabrillane had just left him, and he confessed himself deeply grieved and deeply perplexed.

"The pity of it!" he said. "The pity of it!" He bowed his enormous head. "So estimable a young man, and so full of promise. Ah, this La Tour d'Azyr is a hard man, and he feels very strongly in these matters. He may be right. I don't know. I have never killed a man for holding different views from mine. In fact, I have never killed a man at all. It isn't in my nature. I shouldn't sleep of nights if I did. But men are differently made."

"The question, monsieur my godfather," said André-Louis, "is what is to be done." He was quite calm and self-possessed, but very white.

M. de Kercadiou stared at him blankly out of his pale eyes.

"Why, what the devil is there to do? From what I am told, Vilmorin went so far as to strike M. le Marquis."

"Under the very grossest provocation."

"Which he himself provoked by his revolutionary language. The poor lad's head was full of this encyclopædist trash. It comes of too much reading. I have never set much store by books, André; and I have never known anything but trouble to come out of learning. It unsettles a man. It complicates his views of life, destroys the simplicity which makes for peace of mind and happiness. Let this miserable affair be a warning to you, André. You are, yourself, too prone to these new-fashioned speculations upon a different constitution of the social order. You see what comes of it. A fine, estimable young man, the only prop of his widowed mother too, forgets himself, his position, his duty to that mother—

48

everything; and goes and gets himself killed like this. It is infernally sad. On my soul it is sad." He produced a handkerchief, and blew his nose with vehemence.

André-Louis felt a tightening of his heart, a lessening of the hopes, never too sanguine, which he had founded upon his godfather.

"Your criticisms," he said, "are all for the conduct of the dead, and none for that of the murderer. It does not seem possible that you should be in sympathy with such a crime."

"Crime?" shrilled M. de Kercadiou. "My God, boy, you are speaking of M. de La Tour d'Azyr."

"I am, and of the abominable murder he has committed . . ."

"Stop!" M. de Kercadiou was very emphatic. "I cannot permit that you apply such terms to him. I cannot permit it. M. le Marquis is my friend, and is likely very soon to stand in a still closer relationship."

"Notwithstanding this?" asked André-Louis.

M. de Kercadiou was frankly impatient.

"Why, what has this to do with it? I may deplore it. But I have no right to condemn it. It is a common way of adjusting differences between gentlemen."

"You really believe that?"

"What the devil do you imply, André? Should I say a thing that I don't believe? You begin to make me angry."

"'Thou shalt not kill,' is the King's law as well as God's."

"You are determined to quarrel with me, I think. It was a duel . . ."

André-Louis interrupted him. "It is no more a duel than if it had been fought with pistols of which only M. le Marquis' was loaded. He invited Philippe to discuss the matter further, with the deliberate intent of forcing a quarrel upon him and killing him. Be patient with me, monsieur my godfather. I am not telling you of what I imagine but what M. le Marquis himself admitted to me."

Dominated a little by the young man's earnestness, M. de Kercadiou's pale eyes fell away. He turned with a shrug, and sauntered over to the window.

"It would need a court of honour to decide such an issue. And we have no courts of honour," he said.

"But we have courts of justice."

With returning testiness the seigneur swung round to face him again. "And what court of justice, do you think, would listen to such a plea as you appear to have in mind?"

"There is the court of the King's Lieutenant at Rennes."

"And do you think the King's Lieutenant would listen to you?"

"Not to me, perhaps, monsieur. But if you were to bring the plaint . . ."

"I bring the plaint?" M. de Kercadiou's pale eyes were wide with horror of the suggestion.

"The thing happened here on your domain."

"I bring a plaint against M. de La Tour d'Azyr! You are out of your senses, I think. Oh, you are mad; as mad as that poor friend of yours who has come to this end through meddling in what did not concern him. The language he used here to M. le Marquis on the score of Mabey was of the most offensive. Perhaps you didn't know that. It does not at all surprise me that the Marquis should have desired satisfaction."

"I see," said André-Louis, on a note of hopelessness.

"You see? What the devil do you see?"

"That I shall have to depend upon myself alone."

"And what the devil do you propose to do, if you please?"

"I shall go to Rennes, and lay the facts before the King's Lieutenant."

"He'll be too busy to see you." And M. de Kercadiou's mind swung a trifle inconsequently, as weak minds will. "There is trouble enough in Rennes already on the score of these crazy States General, with which the wonderful M. Necker is to repair the finances of the kingdom. As if a peddling Swiss bank-clerk, who is also a damned Protestant, could succeed where such men as Calonne and Brienne have failed."

"Good afternoon, monsieur my godfather," said André-Louis.

"Where are you going?" was the querulous demand.

"Home at present. To Rennes in the morning."

"Wait, boy, wait!" The squat little man rolled forward, affectionate concern on his great ugly face, and he set one of his podgy hands on his godson's shoulder. "Now listen to me, André," he reasoned. "This is sheer knight-errantry—moonshine, lunacy. You'll come to no good by it if you persist. You've read *Don Quixote,* and what happened to him when he went tilting against windmills. It's what will happen to you, neither more nor less. Leave things as they are, my boy. I wouldn't have a mischief happen to you."

André-Louis looked at him, smiling wanly.

"I swore an oath today which it would damn my soul to break."

"You mean that you'll go in spite of anything that I may say?" Impetuous as he was inconsequent, M. de Kercadiou was bristling again. "Very well, then, go . . . Go to the devil!"

"I will begin with the King's Lieutenant."

"And if you get into the trouble you are seeking, don't come whimpering to me for assistance," the seigneur stormed. He was very angry now. "Since you choose to disobey me, you can break your empty head against the windmill, and be damned to you."

André-Louis bowed with a touch of irony, and reached the door.

"If the windmill should prove too formidable," said he, from the threshold, "I may see what can be done with the wind. Goodbye, monsieur my godfather."

He was gone, and M. de Kercadiou was alone, purple in the face, puzzling out that last cryptic utterance, and not at all happy in his mind, either on the score of his godson or of M. de La Tour d'Azyr. He was disposed to be angry with them both. He found these headstrong, wilful men who relentlessly followed their own impulses very disturbing and irritating. Himself he loved his ease, and to be at peace with his neighbours; and that seemed to him so obviously the supreme good of life that he was disposed to brand them as fools who troubled to seek other things.

CHAPTER VI

The Windmill

There was between Nantes and Rennes an established service of three stage-coaches weekly in each direction, which for a sum of twenty-four livres—roughly, the equivalent of an English guinea—would carry you the seventy and odd miles of the journey in some fourteen hours. Once a week one of the diligences going in each direction would swerve aside from the highroad to call at Gavrillac, to bring and take letters, newspapers, and sometimes passengers. It was usually by this coach that André-Louis came and went when the occasion offered. At present, however, he was too much in haste to lose a day awaiting the passing of that diligence. So it was on a horse hired from the Breton Armé that he set out next morning; and an hour's brisk ride under a grey wintry sky, by a half-ruined road through ten miles of flat, uninteresting country, brought him to the city of Rennes.

He rode across the main bridge over the Vilaine, and so into the upper and principal part of that important city of some thirty thousand souls, most of whom, he opined from the seething, clamant crowds that everywhere blocked his way, must on this day have taken to the streets. Clearly Philippe had not overstated the excitement prevailing there.

He pushed on as best he could, and so came at last to the Place Royale, where he found the crowd to be most dense. From the plinth of the equestrian statue of Louis XV, a white-faced young man was excitedly addressing the multitude. His youth and dress proclaimed the student, and a group of his fellows, acting as a guard of honour to him, kept the immediate precincts of the statue.

Over the heads of the crowd André-Louis caught a few of the phrases flung forth by that eager voice.

"It was the promise of the King . . . It is the King's authority they flout . . . They arrogate to themselves the whole sovereignty in Brittany. The King has dissolved them . . . These insolent nobles defying their sovereign and the people . . ."

Had he not known already, from what Philippe had told him, of the events which had brought the Third Estate to the point of active revolt, those few phrases would fully have informed him. This popular display of temper was most opportune to his need, he thought. And in the hope that it might serve his turn by disposing to reasonableness the mind of the King's Lieutenant, he pushed on up the wide and well-paved Rue Royale, where the concourse of people began to diminish. He put up his hired horse at the Corne de Cerf, and set out again, on foot, to the Palais de Justice.

There was a brawling mob by the framework of poles and

scaffoldings about the building cathedral, upon which work had been commenced a year ago. But he did not pause to ascertain the particular cause of that gathering. He strode on, and thus came presently to the handsome Italianate palace that was one of the few public edifices that had survived the devastating fire of sixty years ago.

He won through with difficulty to the great hall, known as the Salle des Pas Perdus, where he was left to cool his heels for a full half-hour after he had found an usher so condescending as to inform the god who presided over that shrine of Justice that a lawyer from Gavrillac humbly begged an audience on an affair of gravity.

That the god condescended to see him at all was probably due to the grave complexion of the hour. At long length he was escorted up the broad stone staircase, and ushered into a spacious, meagrely furnished anteroom, to make one of a waiting crowd of clients, mostly men.

There he spent another half-hour, and employed the time in considering exactly what he should say. This consideration made him realize the weakness of the case he proposed to set before a man whose views of law and morality were coloured by his social rank.

At last he was ushered through a narrow but very massive and richly decorated door into a fine, well-lighted room furnished with enough gilt and satin to have supplied the boudoir of a lady of fashion.

It was a trivial setting for a King's Lieutenant, but about the King's Lieutenant there was—at least to ordinary eyes—nothing trivial. At the far end of the chamber, to the right of one of the tall windows that looked out over the inner court, before a goat-legged writing-table with Watteau panels, heavily encrusted with ormolu, sat that exalted being. Above a scarlet coat with an order flaming on its breast, and a billow of lace in which diamonds sparkled like drops of water, sprouted the massive powdered head of M. de Lesdiguières. It was thrown back to scowl upon this visitor with an expectant arrogance that made André-Louis wonder almost was a genuflexion awaited from him.

Perceiving a lean, lantern-jawed young man, with straight, lank black hair, in a caped riding-coat of brown cloth, and yellow buckskin breeches, his knee-boots splashed with mud, the scowl upon that august visage deepened until it brought together the thick black eyebrows above the great hooked nose.

"You announce yourself as a lawyer of Gavrillac with an important communication," he growled. It was a peremptory command to make this communication without wasting the valuable time of a King's Lieutenant, of whose immense importance it conveyed something more than a hint. M. de Lesdiguières accounted himself an imposing personality, and he had every reason to do so, for in his time he had seen many a poor devil scared out of all his senses by the thunder of his voice.

He waited now to see the same thing happen to this youthful lawyer from Gavrillac. But he waited in vain.

André-Louis found him ridiculous. He knew pretentiousness for the mask of worthlessness and weakness. And here he beheld pretentiousness incarnate. It was to be read in that arrogant poise of the head, that scowling brow, the inflexion of that reverberating voice. Even more difficult than it is for a man to be a hero to his valet—who has witnessed the dispersal of the parts that make up the imposing whole—is it for a man to be a hero to the student of Man who has witnessed the same in a different sense.

André-Louis stood forward boldly—impudently, thought M. de Lesdiguières.

"You are His Majesty's Lieutenant here in Brittany," he said— and it almost seemed to the august lord of life and death that this fellow had the incredible effrontery to address him as one man speaking to another. "You are the dispenser of the King's high justice in this province."

Surprise spread on that handsome, sallow face under the heavily powdered wig.

"Is your business concerned with this infernal insubordination of the *canaille*?" he asked.

"It is not, monsieur."

The black eyebrows rose. "Then what the devil do you mean by intruding upon me at a time when all my attention is being claimed by the obvious urgency of this disgraceful affair?"

"The affair that brings me is no less disgraceful and no less urgent."

"It will have to wait!" thundered the great man in a passion, and tossing back a cloud of lace from his hand, he reached for the little silver bell upon his table.

"A moment, monsieur!" André-Louis' tone was peremptory. M. de Lesdiguières checked in sheer amazement at its impudence. "I can state it very briefly . . ."

"Haven't I said already . . ."

"And when you have heard it," André-Louis went on, relentlessly, interrupting the interruption, "you will agree with me as to its character."

M. de Lesdiguières considered him very sternly.

"What is your name?" he asked.

"André-Louis Moreau."

"Well, André-Louis Moreau, if you can state your plea briefly, I will hear you. But I warn you that I shall be very angry if you fail to justify the impertinence of this insistence at so inopportune a moment."

"You shall be the judge of that, monsieur," said André-Louis, and he proceeded at once to state his case, beginning with the shooting of Mabey, and passing thence to the killing of M. de Vilmorin. But he withheld until the end the name of the great gentleman against whom he demanded justice, persuaded that did he introduce it earlier he would not be allowed to proceed.

He had a gift of oratory of whose full powers he was himself hardly conscious yet, though destined very soon to become so. He told his story well, without exaggeration, yet with a force of simple appeal that was irresistible. Gradually the great man's face relaxed from its forbidding severity. Interest, warming almost to sympathy, came to be reflected on it.

"And who, sir, is the man you charge with this?"

"The Marquis de La Tour d'Azyr."

The effect of that formidable name was immediate. Dismayed anger, and an arrogance more utter than before, took the place of the sympathy he had been betrayed into displaying.

"Who?" he shouted, and without waiting for an answer, "Why, here's impudence," he stormed on, "to come before me with such a charge against a gentleman of M. de La Tour d'Azyr's eminence! How dare you speak of him as a coward . . ."

"I speak of him as a murderer," the young man corrected.

"And I demand justice against him."

"You demand it, do you? My God, what next?"

"That is for you to say, monsieur."

It surprised the great gentleman into a more or less successful effort of self-control.

"Let me warn you," said he, acidly, "that it is not wise to make wild accusations against a nobleman. That, in itself, is a punishable offence, as you may learn. Now listen to me. In this matter of Mabey—assuming your statement of it to be exact—the gamekeeper may have exceeded his duty; but by so little that it is hardly worth comment. Consider, however, that in any case it is not a matter for the King's Lieutenant, or for any court but the seigneurial court of M. de La Tour d'Azyr himself. It is before the magistrates of his own appointing that such a matter must be laid, since it is matter strictly concerning his own seigneurial jurisdiction. As a lawyer you should not need to be told so much."

"As a lawyer, I am prepared to argue the point. But, as a lawyer I also realize that if that case were prosecuted, it could only end in the unjust punishment of a wretched gamekeeper, who did no more than carry out his orders, but who none the less would now be made a scapegoat, if scapegoat were necessary. I am not concerned to hang Benet on the gallows earned by M. de La Tour d'Azyr."

M. de Lesdiguières smote the table violently. "My God!" he cried out, to add more quietly, on a note of menace, "You are singularly insolent, my man."

"That is not my intention, sir, I assure you. I am a lawyer, pleading a case—the case of M. de Vilmorin. It is for his assassination that I have come to beg the King's justice."

"But you yourself have said that it was a duel!" cried the Lieutenant, between anger and bewilderment.

"I have said that it was made to appear a duel. There is a distinction, as I shall show, if you will condescend to hear me out."

"Take your own time, sir!" said the ironical M. de Lesdiguières, whose tenure of office had never yet held anything that remotely resembled this experience.

André-Louis took him literally. "I thank you, sir," he answered, solemnly, and submitted his argument. "It can be shown that M. de Vilmorin never practised fencing in all his life, and it is notorious that M. de La Tour d'Azyr is an exceptional swordsman. Is it a duel, monsieur, where one of the combatants alone is armed? For it amounts to that on a comparison of their measures of respective skill."

"There has scarcely been a duel fought on which the same trumpery argument might not be advanced."

"But not always with equal justice. And in one case, at least, it was advanced successfully."

"Successfully? When was that?"

"Ten years ago, in Dauphiny. I refer to the case of M. de Gesvres, a gentleman of that province, who forced a duel upon M. de La Roche Jeannine, and killed him. M. de Jeannine was a member of a powerful family, which exerted itself to obtain justice. It put forward just such arguments as now obtain against M. de La Tour d'Azyr. As you will remember, the judges held that the provocation had proceeded of intent from M. de Gesvres; they found him guilty of premeditated murder, and he was hanged."

M. de Lesdiguières exploded yet again. "Death of my life!" he cried. "Have you the effrontery to suggest that M. de La Tour d'Azyr should be hanged? Have you?"

"But why not, monsieur, if it is the law, and there is precedent for it, as I have shown you, and if it can be established that what I state is the truth—as established it can be without difficulty?"

"Do you ask me, why not? Have you temerity to ask me that?"

"I have, monsieur. Can you answer me? If you cannot, monsieur, I shall understand that whilst it is possible for a powerful family like that of La Roche Jeannine to set the law in motion, the law must remain inert for the obscure and uninfluential, however brutally wronged by a great nobleman."

M. de Lesdiguières perceived that in argument he would accomplish nothing against this impassive, resolute young man. The menace of him grew more fierce.

"I should advise you to take yourself off at once, and to be thankful for the opportunity to depart unscathed."

"I am, then, to understand, monsieur, that there will be no inquiry into this case? That nothing that I can say will move you?"

"You are to understand that if you are still there in two minutes it will be very much the worse for you." And M. de Lesdiguières tinkled the silver hand-bell upon his table.

"I have informed you, monsieur, that a duel—so-called—has been fought, and a man killed. It seems that I must remind you, the administrator of the King's justice, that duels are against the law, and that it is your duty to hold an inquiry. I come as the legal representative of the bereaved mother of M. de Vilmorin to demand of you the inquiry that is due."

The door behind André-Louis opened softly. M. de Lesdiguières, pale with anger, contained himself with difficulty.

"You seek to compel us, do you, you impudent rascal?" he growled. "You think the King's justice is to be driven headlong by the voice of any impudent *roturier*? I marvel at my own patience with you. But I give you a last warning, master lawyer; keep a closer guard over that insolent tongue of yours, or you will have cause very bitterly to regret its glibness." He waved a jewelled, contemptuous hand, and spoke to the usher standing behind André. "To the door!" he said, shortly.

André-Louis hesitated a second. Then with a shrug he turned. This was the windmill, indeed, and he a poor knight of rueful countenance. To attack it at closer quarters would mean being dashed to pieces. Yet on the threshold he turned again.

"M. de Lesdiguières," said he, "may I recite to you an interesting fact in natural history? The tiger is a great lord in the jungle, and was for centuries the terror of lesser beasts, including the wolf. The wolf, himself a hunter, wearied of being hunted. He took to associating with other wolves, and then the wolves, driven to form packs for self-protection, discovered the power of the pack, and took to hunting the tiger, with disastrous results to him. You should study Buffon, M. de Lesdiguières."

"I have studied a buffoon this morning, I think," was the punning sneer with which M. de Lesdiguières replied. But that he conceived himself witty, it is probable he would not have condescended to reply at all. "I don't understand you," he added.

"But you will, M. de Lesdiguières. You will," said André-Louis, and so departed.

CHAPTER VII

The Wind

He had broken his futile lance with the windmill—the image suggested by M. de Kercadiou persisted in his mind—and it was, he perceived, by sheer good fortune that he had escaped without hurt. There remained the wind itself—the whirlwind. And the events in Rennes, reflex of the graver events in Nantes, had set that wind blowing in his favour.

He set out briskly to retrace his steps towards the Place Royale, where the gathering of the populace was greatest, where, as he judged, lay the heart and brain of this commotion that was exciting the city.

But the commotion that he had left there was as nothing to the commotion which he found on his return. Then there had been a comparative hush to listen to the voice of a speaker who denounced the First and Second Estates from the pedestal of the statue of Louis XV. Now the air was vibrant with the voice of the multitude itself, raised in anger. Here and there men were fighting with canes and fists; everywhere a fierce excitement raged, and the gendarmes sent thither by the King's Lieutenant to restore and maintain order were so much helpless flotsam in that tempestuous human ocean.

There were cries of "To the Palais! To the Palais! Down with the assassins! Down with the nobles! To the Palais!"

An artisan who stood shoulder to shoulder with him in the press enlightened André-Louis on the score of the increased excitement.

"They've shot him dead. His body is lying there where it fell at the foot of the statue. And there was another student killed not an hour ago over there by the cathedral works. Pardi! If they can't prevail in one way they'll prevail in another." The man was fiercely emphatic. "They'll stop at nothing. If they can't overawe us, by God, they'll assassinate us. They are determined to conduct these States of Brittany in their own way. No interests but their own shall be considered."

André-Louis left him still talking, and clove himself a way through that human press.

At the statue's base he came upon a little cluster of students about the body of the murdered lad, all stricken with fear and helplessness.

"You here, Moreau!" said a voice.

He looked round to find himself confronted by a slight, swarthy man of little more than thirty, firm of mouth and impertinent of nose, who considered him with disapproval. It was Le Chapelier, a lawyer of Rennes, a prominent member of the Literary Chamber of that city, a forceful man, fertile in revolutionary ideas and of an exceptional gift of eloquence.

"Ah, it is you, Chapelier! Why don't you speak to them? Why don't you tell them what to do? Up with you, man!" And he pointed to the plinth.

Le Chapelier's dark, restless eyes searched the other's impassive face for some trace of the irony he suspected. They were as wide asunder as the poles, these two, in their political views; and mistrusted as André-Louis was by all his colleagues of the Literary Chamber of Rennes, he was by none mistrusted so thoroughly as by this vigorous republican. Indeed, had Le Chapelier been able to prevail against the influence of the seminarist Vilmorin, André-Louis would long since have found himself excluded from that assembly of the intellectual youth of Rennes, which he exasperated by his eternal mockery of their ideals.

So now Le Chapelier suspected mockery in that invitation, suspected it even when he failed to find traces of it on André-Louis' face, for he had learnt by experience that it was a face not often to be trusted for an indication of the real thoughts that moved behind it.

"Your notions and mine on that score can hardly coincide," said he.

"Can there be two opinions?" quoth André-Louis.

"There are usually two opinions whenever you and I are together, Moreau—more than ever now that you are the appointed delegate of a nobleman. You see what your friends have done. No doubt you approve their methods." He was coldly hostile.

André-Louis looked at him without surprise. So invariably opposed to each other in academic debates, how should Le Chapelier suspect his present intentions?

"If you won't tell them what is to be done, I will," said he.

"Nom de Dieu! If you want to invite a bullet from the other side, I shall not hinder you. It may help to square the account."

Scarcely were the words out than he repented them; for as if in answer to that challenge André-Louis sprang up on to the plinth. Alarmed now, for he could only suppose it to be André-Louis' intention to speak on behalf of Privilege, of which he was a publicly appointed representative, Le Chapelier clutched him by the leg to pull him down again.

"Ah, that, no!" he was shouting. "Come down, you fool. Do you think we will let you ruin everything by your clowning? Come down!"

André-Louis, maintaining his position by clutching one of the legs of the bronze horse, flung his voice like a bugle-note over the heads of that seething mob.

"Citizens of Rennes, the motherland is in danger!"

The effect was electric. A stir ran, like a ripple over water, across that froth of upturned human faces, and completest silence followed. In that great silence they looked at this slim young man, hatless, long wisps of his black hair fluttering in the breeze, his neckcloth in disorder, his face white, his eyes on fire.

André-Louis felt a sudden surge of exaltation as he realized by instinct that at one grip he had seized that crowd, and that he held it fast in the spell of his cry and his audacity.

Even Le Chapelier, though still clinging to his ankle, had ceased to tug. The reformer, though unshaken in his assumption of André-Louis' intentions, was for a moment bewildered by the first note of his appeal.

And then, slowly, impressively, in a voice that travelled clear to the ends of the square, the young lawyer of Gavrillac began to speak.

"Shuddering in horror of the vile deed here perpetrated, my voice demands to be heard by you. You have seen murder done under your eyes—the murder of one who nobly, without any thought of self, gave voice to the wrongs by which we are all oppressed. Fearing that voice, shunning the truth as foul things shun the light, our oppressors sent their agents to silence him in death."

Le Chapelier released at last his hold of André-Louis' ankle, staring up at him the while in sheer amazement. It seemed that the fellow was in earnest; serious for once; and for once on the right side. What had come to him?

"Of assassins what shall you look for but assassination? I have a tale to tell which will show that this is no new thing that you have witnessed here today; it will reveal to you the forces with which you have to deal. Yesterday . . ."

There was an interruption. A voice in the crowd, some twenty paces, perhaps, was raised to shout:

"Yet another of them!"

Immediately after the voice came a pistol-shot, and a bullet flattened itself against the bronze figure just behind André-Louis.

Instantly there was turmoil in the crowd, most intense about the spot whence the shot had been fired. The assailant was one of a considerable group of the opposition, a group that found itself at once beset on every side, and hard put to it to defend him.

From the foot of the plinth rang the voice of the students making chorus to Le Chapelier, who was bidding André-Louis to seek shelter.

"Come down! Come down at once! They'll murder you as they murdered La Rivière."

"Let them!" He flung wide his arms in a gesture supremely theatrical, and laughed. "I stand here at their mercy. Let them, if they will, add mine to the blood that will presently rise up to choke them. Let them assassinate me. It is a trade they understand. But until they do so, they shall not prevent me from speaking to you, from telling you what is to be looked for in them." And again he laughed, not merely in exaltation as they supposed who watched him from below, but also in amusement. And his amusement had two sources. One was to discover how glibly he uttered the phrases proper to whip up the emotions of a crowd: the other was in the remembrance of how the crafty Cardinal de Retz, for the purpose of inflaming popular sympathy on his behalf, had been in the habit of hiring fellows to fire upon his carriage. He was in just such case as that arch-politician. True, he had not hired the fellow to fire that pistol-shot; but he was none the less obliged to him, and ready to derive the fullest advantage from the act.

The group that sought to protect that man was battling on, seeking to hew a way out of that angry, heaving press.

"Let them go!" André-Louis called down. "What matters one assassin more or less? Let them go, and listen to me, my countrymen!"

And presently, when some measure of order was restored, he began his tale. In simple language now, yet with a vehemence and directness that drove home every point, he tore their hearts with the story of yesterday's happenings at Gavrillac. He drew tears from them with the pathos of his picture of the bereaved widow Mabey and her three starving, destitute children—"orphaned to avenge the death of a pheasant"—and the bereaved mother of that M. de Vilmorin, a student of Rennes, known here to many of them, who had met his death in a noble endeavour to champion the cause of an esurient member of their afflicted order.

"The Marquis de La Tour d'Azyr said of him that he had too dangerous a gift of eloquence. It was to silence his brave voice that he killed him. But he has failed of his object. For I, poor Philippe de Vilmorin's friend, have assumed the mantle of his apostleship, and I speak to you with his voice today."

It was a statement that helped Le Chapelier at last to understand, at least in part, this bewildering change in André-Louis, which rendered him faithless to the side that employed him.

"I am not here," continued André-Louis, "merely to demand at your hands vengeance upon Philippe de Vilmorin's murderers. I am here to tell you the things he would today have told you had he lived."

So far at least he was frank. But he did not add that they were things he did not himself believe, things that he accounted the cant by which an ambitious bourgeoisie—speaking through the mouths of the lawyers, who were its articulate part—sought to overthrow to its own advantage the present state of things. He left his audience in the natural belief that the views he expressed were the views he held.

And now in a terrible voice, with an eloquence that amazed himself, he denounced the inertia of the royal justice where the great are the offenders. It was with bitter sarcasm that he spoke of their King's Lieutenant, M. de Lesdiguières.

"Do you wonder," he asked them, "that M. de Lesdiguières

should administer the law so that it shall ever be favourable to our great nobles? Would it be just, would it be reasonable that he should otherwise administer it?"

He paused dramatically to let his sarcasm sink in. It had the effect of reawakening Le Chapelier's doubts, and checking his dawning conviction in André-Louis' sincerity. Whither was he going now?

He was not left long in doubt. Proceeding, André-Louis spoke as he conceived that Philippe de Vilmorin would have spoken. He had so often argued with him, so often attended the discussions of the Literary Chamber, that he had all the cant of the reformers—that was yet true in substance—at his fingers' ends.

"Consider, after all, the composition of this France of ours. A million of its inhabitants are members of the privileged classes. They compose France. They are France. For surely you cannot suppose the remainder to be anything that matters. It cannot be pretended that twenty-four million souls are of any account, that they can be representative of this great nation, or that they can exist for any purpose but that of servitude to the million elect."

Bitter laughter shook them now, as he desired it should.

"Seeing their privileges in danger of invasion by these twenty-four millions—mostly *canailles*; possibly created by God, it is true, but clearly so created to be the slaves of Privilege—does it surprise you that the dispensing of royal justice should be placed in the stout hands of these Lesdiguières, men without brains to think or hearts to be touched? Consider what it is that must be defended against the assault of us others—*canaille*. Consider a few of these feudal rights that are in danger of being swept away should the Privileged yield even to the commands of their sovereign, and admit the Third Estate to an equal vote with themselves.

"What would become of the right of *terrage* on the land, of *parcière* on the fruit-trees, of *carpot* on the vines? What of the *corvées* by which they command forced labour; of the *ban de vendage*, which gives them the first vintage, the *banvin* which enables them to control to their own advantage the sale of wine? What of their right of grinding the last *liard* of taxation out of the people to maintain their own opulent estate; the *cens*, the *lods-et-ventes*, which absorb a fifth of the value of the land, the *blairée*, which must be paid before herds can feed on communal lands, the *pulvérage* to indemnify them for the dust raised on their roads by the herds that go to market, the *sextelage* on every-thing offered for sale in the public markets, the *étalonnage*, and all the rest? What of their rights over men and animals for field labour, of ferries over rivers, and of bridges over streams, of sink-ing wells, of warren, of dovecot, and of fire, which last yields them a tax on every peasant hearth? What of their exclusive rights of fishing and of hunting, the violation of which is ranked as almost a capital offence?

"And what of other rights, unspeakable, abominable, over the lives and bodies of their people, rights which, if rarely exer-cised, have never been rescinded. To this day if a noble returning from the hunt were to slay two of his serfs to bathe and refresh his feet in their blood, he could still claim in his sufficient de-fence that it was his absolute feudal right to do so.

"Rough-shod, these million Privileged ride over the souls and bodies of twenty-four million contemptible *canaille* existing but for their own pleasure. Woe betide him who so much as raises his voice in protest in the name of humanity against an excess of these already excessive abuses. I have told you of one remorselessly slain in cold blood for doing no more than that. Your own eyes have witnessed the assassination of another here upon this plinth, of yet another over there by the cathedral works, and the attempt upon my own life.

"Between them and the justice due to them in such cases stand these Lesdiguières, these King's Lieutenants; not instruments of justice, but walls erected for the shelter of Privilege and Abuse whenever it exceeds its grotesquely excessive rights.

"Do you wonder that they will not yield an inch; that they will resist the election of a Third Estate with the voting power to sweep all these privileges away, to compel the Privileged to submit themselves to a just equality in the eyes of the law with the meanest of the *canaille* they trample underfoot, to provide that the moneys necessary to save this state from the bankruptcy into which they have all but plunged it shall be raised by taxation to be borne by themselves in the same proportion as by others?

"Sooner than yield to so much they prefer to resist even the royal command."

A phrase occurred to him used yesterday by Vilmorin, a phrase to which he had refused to attach importance when uttered then. He used it now. "In doing this they are striking at the very foundations of the throne. These fools do not perceive that if that throne falls over, it is they who stand nearest to it who will be crushed."

A terrific roar acclaimed that statement. Tense and quivering with the excitement that was flowing through him, and from him out into that great audience, he stood a moment smiling ironically. Then he waved them into silence, and saw by their ready obedience how completely he possessed them. For in the voice with which he spoke each now recognized the voice of himself, giving at last expression to the thoughts that for months and years had been inarticulately stirring in each simple mind.

Presently he resumed, speaking more quietly, that ironic smile about the corner of his mouth growing more marked:

"In taking my leave of M. de Lesdiguières I gave him warning out of a page of natural history. I told him that when the wolves, roaming singly through the jungle, were weary of being hunted by the tiger, they banded themselves into packs, and went a-hunting the tiger in their turn. M. de Lesdiguières contemptuously answered that he did not understand me. But your wits are better than his. You understand me, I think? Don't you?"

Again a great roar, mingled now with some approving laughter, was his answer. He had wrought them up to a pitch of dangerous passion, and they were ripe for any violence to which he urged them. If he had failed with the windmill, at least he was now master of the wind.

"To the Palais!" they shouted, waving their hands, brandishing canes, and—here and there—even a sword. "To the Palais! Down with M. de Lesdiguières! Death to the King's Lieutenant!"

He was master of the wind, indeed. His dangerous gift of oratory—a gift nowhere more powerful than in France, since nowhere else are men's emotions so quick to respond to the appeal of eloquence—had given him this mastery. At his bidding now the gale would sweep away the windmill against which he had flung himself in vain. But that, as he straightforwardly revealed it, was no part of his intent.

"Ah, wait!" he bade them. "Is this miserable instrument of a

73

corrupt system worth the attention of your noble indignation?"

He hoped his words would be reported to M. de Lesdiguières. He thought it would be good for the soul of M. de Lesdiguières to hear the undiluted truth about himself for once.

"It is the system itself you must attack and overthrow; not a mere instrument—a miserable painted lath such as this. And precipitancy will spoil everything. Above all, my children, no violence!"

My children! Could his godfather have heard him!

"You have seen often already the result of premature violence elsewhere in Brittany, and you have heard of it elsewhere in France. Violence on your part will call for violence on theirs. They will welcome the chance to assert their mastery by a firmer grip than heretofore. The military will be sent for. You will be faced by the bayonets of mercenaries. Do not provoke that, I implore you. Do not put it into their power, do not afford them the pretext they would welcome to crush you down into the mud of your own blood."

Out of the silence into which they had fallen anew broke now the cry of:

"What else, then? What else?"

"I will tell you," he answered them. "The wealth and strength of Brittany lies in Nantes—a bourgeois city, one of the most prosperous in this realm, rendered so by the energy of the bourgeoisie and the toil of the people. It was in Nantes that this movement had its beginning, and as a result of it the King issued his order dissolving the States as now constituted—an order which those who base their power on Privilege and Abuse do not hesitate to thwart. Let Nantes be informed of the precise situation, and let nothing be done here until Nantes shall have given us the lead.

She has the power—which we in Rennes have not—to make her will prevail, as we have seen already. Let her exert that power once more, and until she does so do you keep the peace in Rennes. Thus shall you triumph. Thus shall the outrages that are being perpetrated under your eyes be fully and finally avenged."

As abruptly as he had leapt upon the plinth did he now leap down from it. He had finished. He had said all—perhaps more than all—that could have been said by the dead friend with whose voice he spoke. But it was not their will that he should thus extinguish himself. The thunder of their acclamations rose deafeningly upon the air. He had played upon their emotions—each in turn—as a skilful harpist plays upon the strings of his instrument. And they were vibrant with the passions he had aroused, and the high note of hope on which he had brought his symphony to a close.

A dozen students caught him as he leapt down, and swung him to their shoulders, where again he came within view of all the acclaiming crowd.

The delicate Le Chapelier pressed alongside of him with flushed face and shining eyes.

"My lad," he said to him, "you have kindled a fire today that will sweep the face of France in a blaze of liberty." And then to the students he issued a sharp command. "To the Literary Chamber—at once. We must concert measures upon the instant, a delegate must be dispatched to Nantes forthwith, to convey to our friends there the message of the people of Rennes."

The crowd fell back, opening a lane through which the students bore the hero of the hour. Waving his hands to them, he called upon them to disperse to their homes, and await there in patience what must follow very soon.

"You have endured for centuries with a fortitude that is a pattern to the world," he flattered them. "Endure a little longer yet. The end, my friends, is well in sight at last."

They carried him out of the square and up the Rue Royale to an old house, one of the few old houses surviving in that city that had risen from its ashes, where in an upper chamber lighted by diamond-shaped panes of yellow glass the Literary Chamber usually held its meetings. Thither in his wake the members of that chamber came hurrying, summoned by the messages that Le Chapelier had issued during their progress.

Behind closed doors a flushed and excited group of some fifty men, the majority of whom were young, ardent, and afire with the illusion of liberty, hailed André-Louis as the strayed sheep who had returned to the fold, and smothered him in congratulations and thanks.

Then they settled down to deliberate upon immediate measures, whilst the doors below were kept by a guard of honour that had improvised itself from the masses. And very necessary was this. For no sooner had the Chamber assembled than the house was assailed by the gendarmerie of M. de Lesdiguières, dispatched in haste to arrest the firebrand who was inciting the people of Rennes to sedition. The force consisted of fifty men. Five hundred would have been too few. The mob broke their carbines, broke some of their heads, and would indeed have torn them into pieces had they not beaten a timely and well-advised retreat before a form of horseplay to which they were not at all accustomed.

And whilst that was taking place in the street below, in the room abovestairs the eloquent Le Chapelier was addressing his colleagues of the Literary Chamber. Here, with no bullets to fear, and no one to report his words to the authorities, Le Chapelier could permit his oratory a full, unintimidated flow. And that considerable oratory was as direct and brutal as the man himself was delicate and elegant.

He praised the vigour and the greatness of the speech they had heard from their colleague Moreau. Above all he praised its wisdom. Moreau's words had come as a surprise to them. Hitherto they had never known him as other than a bitter critic of their projects of reform and regeneration; and quite lately they had heard, not without misgivings, of his appointment as delegate for a nobleman in the States of Brittany. But they held the explanation of his conversion. The murder of their dear colleague Vilmorin had produced this change. In that brutal deed Moreau had beheld at last in true proportions the workings of that evil spirit which they were vowed to exorcise from France. And today he had proven himself the stoutest apostle among them of the new faith. He had pointed out to them the only sane and useful course. The illustration he had borrowed from natural history was most apt. Above all, let them pack like the wolves, and to ensure this uniformity of action in the people of all Brittany, let a delegate at once be sent to Nantes, which had already proved itself the real seat of Brittany's power. It but remained to appoint that delegate, and Le Chapelier invited them to elect him.

André-Louis, on a bench near the window, a prey now to some measure of reaction, listened in bewilderment to that flood of eloquence.

As the applause died down, he heard a voice exclaiming:

"I propose to you that we appoint our leader here, Le Chapelier, to be that delegate."

Le Chapelier reared his elegantly dressed head, which had been bowed in thought, and it was seen that his countenance was pale. Nervously he fingered a gold spy-glass.

"My friends," he said, slowly, "I am deeply sensible of the honour that you do me. But in accepting it I should be usurping an honour that rightly belongs elsewhere. Who could represent us better, who more deserving to be our representative, to speak to our friends of Nantes with the voice of Rennes, than the champion who once already today has so incomparably given utterance to the voice of this great city? Confer this honour of being your spokesman where it belongs—upon André-Louis Moreau."

Rising in response to the storm of applause that greeted the proposal, André-Louis bowed and forthwith yielded.

"Be it so," he said, simply. "It is perhaps fitting that I should carry out what I have begun, though I too am of the opinion that Le Chapelier would have been a worthier representative. I will set out tonight."

"You will set out at once, my lad," Le Chapelier informed him, and now revealed what an uncharitable mind might account the true source of his generosity. "It is not safe after what has happened for you to linger an hour in Rennes. And you must go secretly. Let none of you allow it to be known that he has gone. I would not have you come to harm over this, André-Louis. But you must see the risks you run, and if you are to be spared to help in this work of salvation of our afflicted motherland, you must use caution, move secretly, veil your identity even. Or else M. de Lesdiguières will have you laid by the heels, and it will be good-night for you."

CHAPTER VIII

Omnes Omnibus

André-Louis rode forth from Rennes committed to a deeper adventure than he had dreamed of when he left the sleepy village of Gavrillac. Lying the night at a roadside inn, and setting out again early in the morning, he reached Nantes soon after noon of the following day.

Through that long and lonely ride through the dull plains of Brittany, now at their dreariest in their winter garb, he had ample leisure in which to review his actions and his position. From one who had taken hitherto a purely academic and by no means friendly interest in the new philosophies of social life, exercising his wits upon these new ideas merely as a fencer exercises his eye and wrist with the foils, without ever suffering himself to be deluded into supposing the issue a real one, he found himself suddenly converted into a revolutionary firebrand, committed to revolutionary action of the most desperate kind. The representative and delegate of a nobleman in the States of Brittany, he found himself simultaneously and incongruously the representative and delegate of the whole Third Estate of Rennes.

It is difficult to determine to what extent, in the heat of passion and swept along by the torrent of his own oratory, he might yesterday have succeeded in deceiving himself. But it is at least certain that, looking back in cold blood now, he had no single delusion on the score of what he had done. Cynically he had presented to his audience one side only of the great question that he propounded.

But since the established order of things in France was such as to make a rampart for M. de La Tour d'Azyr, affording him complete immunity for this and any other crimes that it pleased him to commit, why, then the established order must take the consequences of its wrong-doing. Therein he perceived his clear justification.

And so it was without misgivings that he came on his errand of sedition into that beautiful city of Nantes, rendered by its spacious streets and splendid port the rival in prosperity of Bordeaux and Marseilles.

He found an inn on the Quai La Fosse, where he put up his horse, and where he dined in the embrasure of a window that looked out over the tree-bordered quay and the broad bosom of the Loire, on which argosies of all nations rode at anchor. The sun had again broken through the clouds, and shed its pale wintry light over the yellow waters and the tall-masted shipping.

Along the quays there was a stir of life as great as that to be seen on the quays of Paris. Foreign sailors in outlandish garments and of harsh-sounding, outlandish speech, stalwart fishwives with baskets of herrings on their heads, voluminous of petticoat above bare legs and bare feet, calling their wares shrilly and almost inarticulately, watermen in woollen caps and loose trousers rolled to the knees, peasants in goatskin coats, their wooden shoes clattering on the round kidney-stones, shipwrights and labourers from the dockyards, bellows-menders, rat-catchers, water-carriers, inksellers, and other itinerant pedlars. And, sprinkled through this proletariat mass that came and went in constant movement, André-Louis beheld tradesmen in sober garments, merchants in long, fur-lined coats; occasionally a merchant-prince rolling along in his two-horse cabriolet to the whip-crackings and shouts of "Gare!" from his coachman; occasionally a dainty lady carried past in her sedan-chair, with perhaps a mincing abbé from the episcopal court tripping along in attendance; occasionally an officer in scarlet riding disdainfully; and once the great carriage of a nobleman, with escutcheoned panels and a pair of white-stockinged, powdered footmen in gorgeous liveries hanging on behind. And there were Capuchins in brown and Benedictines in black, and secular priests in plenty—for God was well served in the sixteen parishes of Nantes—and by way of contrast there were lean-jawed, out-at-elbow adventurers, and gendarmes in blue coats and gaitered legs, sauntering guardians of the peace.

Representatives of every class that went to make up the seventy thousand inhabitants of that wealthy, industrious city were to be seen in the human stream that ebbed and flowed beneath the window from which André-Louis observed it.

Of the waiter who ministered to his humble wants with soup and bouilli, and a measure of *vin gris*, André-Louis enquired into the state of public feeling in the city. The waiter, a staunch supporter of the privileged orders, admitted regretfully that an uneasiness prevailed. Much would depend upon what happened at Rennes. If it was true that the King had dissolved the States of Brittany, then all should be well, and the malcontents would have no pretext for further disturbances. There had been trouble and to spare in Nantes already. They wanted no repetition of it. All manner of rumours were abroad, and since early morning there had been crowds besieging the portals of the Chamber of Commerce for definite news. But definite news was yet to come. It was not even known for a fact that His Majesty actually had dissolved the States.

It was striking two, the busiest hour of the day upon the Bourse, when André-Louis reached the Place du Commerce. The square, dominated by the imposing classical building of the Exchange, was so crowded that he was compelled almost to fight his way through to the steps of the magnificent Ionic porch. A word would have sufficed to have opened a way for him at once. But guile moved him to keep silent. He would come upon that waiting multitude as a thunderclap, precisely as yesterday he had come upon the mob at Rennes. He would lose nothing of the surprise effect of his entrance.

The precincts of that house of commerce were jealously kept by a line of ushers armed with staves, a guard as hurriedly assembled by the merchants as it was evidently necessary. One of these now effectively barred the young lawyer's passage as he attempted to mount the steps.

André-Louis announced himself in a whisper.

The stave was instantly raised from the horizontal, and he passed and went up the steps in the wake of the usher. At the top, on the threshold of the chamber, he paused, and stayed his guide.

"I will wait here," he announced. "Bring the president to me."

"Your name, monsieur?"

Almost had André-Louis answered him when he remembered Le Chapelier's warning of the danger with which his mission was fraught, and Le Chapelier's parting admonition to conceal his identity.

"My name is unknown to him; it matters nothing; I am the mouthpiece of a people, no more. Go."

The usher went, and in the shadow of that lofty, pillared portico André-Louis waited, his eyes straying out ever and anon to survey that spread of upturned faces immediately below him.

Soon the president came, others following, crowding out into the portico, jostling one another in their eagerness to hear the news.

"You are a messenger from Rennes?"

"I am the delegate sent by the Literary Chamber of that city to inform you here in Nantes of what is taking place."

"Your name?"

André-Louis paused. "The less we mention names perhaps the better."

The president's eyes grew big with gravity. He was a corpulent, florid man, purse-proud, and self-sufficient.

He hesitated a moment. Then—"Come into the Chamber," said he.

"By your leave, monsieur, I will deliver my message from here—from these steps."

"From here?" The great merchant frowned.

"My message is for the people of Nantes, and from here I can speak at once to the greatest number of Nantais of all ranks, and it is my desire—and the desire of those whom I represent—that as great a number as possible should hear my message at first hand."

"Tell me, sir, is it true that the King has dissolved the States?"

André-Louis looked at him. He smiled apologetically, and waved a hand towards the crowd, which by now was straining for a glimpse of this slim young man who had brought forth the president and more than half the members of the Chamber, guessing already, with that curious instinct of crowds, that he was the awaited bearer of tidings.

"Summon the gentlemen of your Chamber, monsieur," said he, "and you shall hear all."

"So be it."

A word, and forth they came to crowd upon the steps, but leaving clear the topmost step and a half-moon space in the middle.

To the spot so indicated, André-Louis now advanced very deliberately. He took his stand there, dominating the entire assembly. He removed his hat, and launched the opening bombshell of that address which is historic, marking as it does one of the great stages of France's progress towards revolution.

"People of this great city of Nantes, I have come to summon you to arms!"

In the amazed and rather scared silence that followed he surveyed them for a moment before resuming.

"I am a delegate of the people of Rennes, charged to announce to you what is taking place, and to invite you in this dreadful hour of our country's peril to rise and march to her defence."

"Name! Your name!" a voice shouted, and instantly the

cry was taken up by others, until the multitude rang with the question.

He could not answer that excited mob as he had answered the president. It was necessary to compromise, and he did so, happily. "My name," said he, "is *Omnes Omnibus*—all for all. Let that suffice you now. I am a herald, a mouthpiece, a voice; no more. I come to announce to you that since the privileged orders, assembled for the States of Brittany in Rennes, resisted your will—our will—despite the King's plain hint to them, His Majesty has dissolved the States."

There was a burst of delirious applause. Men laughed and shouted, and cries of "Vive le Roi!" rolled forth like thunder. André-Louis waited, and gradually the preternatural gravity of his countenance came to be observed, and to beget the suspicion that there might be more to follow. Gradually silence was restored, and at last André-Louis was able to proceed.

"You rejoice too soon. Unfortunately, the nobles, in their insolent arrogance, have elected to ignore the royal dissolution, and in despite of it persist in sitting and in conducting matters as seems good to them."

A silence of utter dismay greeted that disconcerting epilogue to the announcement that had been so rapturously received. André-Louis continued after a moment's pause:

"So that these men who were already rebels against the people, rebels against justice and equity, rebels against humanity itself, are now also rebels against their King. Sooner than yield an inch of the unconscionable privileges by which too long already they have flourished, to the misery of a whole nation, they will make a mock of royal authority, hold up the King himself to contempt.

They are determined to prove that there is no real sovereignty in France but the sovereignty of their own parasitic *fainéantise*."

There was a faint splutter of applause, but the majority of the audience remained silent, waiting.

"This is no new thing. Always has it been the same. No minister in the last ten years, who, seeing the needs and perils of the State, counselled the measures that we now demand as the only means of arresting our motherland in its ever-quickening progress to the abyss, but found himself as a consequence cast out of office by the influence which Privilege brought to bear against him. Twice already has M. Necker been called to the ministry, to be twice dismissed when his insistent counsels of reform threatened the privileges of clergy and nobility. For the third time now has he been called to office, and at last it seems we are to have States General in spite of Privilege. But what the privileged orders can no longer prevent, they are determined to stultify. Since it is now a settled thing that these States General are to meet, at least the nobles and the clergy will see to it—unless we take measures to prevent them—by packing the Third Estate with their own creatures, and denying it all effective representation, that they convert the States General into an instrument of their own will for the perpetuation of the abuses by which they live. To achieve this end they will stop at nothing. They have flouted the authority of the King, and they are silencing by assassination those who raise their voices to condemn them. Yesterday in Rennes two young men who addressed the people as I am addressing you were done to death in the streets by assassins at the instigation of the nobility. Their blood cries out for vengeance."

Beginning in a sullen mutter, the indignation that moved his hearers swelled up to express itself in a roar of anger.

"Citizens of Nantes, the motherland is in peril. Let us march to her defence. Let us proclaim it to the world that we recognize that the measures to liberate the Third Estate from the slavery in which for centuries it has groaned find only obstacles in those orders whose phrenetic egotism sees in the tears and suffering of the unfortunate an odious tribute which they would pass on to their generations still unborn. Realizing from the barbarity of the means employed by our enemies to perpetuate our oppression that we have everything to fear from the aristocracy they would set up as a constitutional principle for the governing of France, let us declare ourselves at once enfranchised from it.

"The establishment of liberty and equality should be the aim of every citizen member of the Third Estate; and to this end we should stand indivisibly united, especially the young and vigorous, especially those who have had the good fortune to be born late enough to be able to gather for themselves the precious fruits of the philosophy of this eighteenth century."

Acclamations broke out unstintedly now. He had caught them in the snare of his oratory. And he pressed his advantage instantly.

"Let us all swear," he cried in a great voice, "to raise up in the name of humanity and of liberty a rampart against our enemies, to oppose to their bloodthirsty covetousness the calm perseverance of men whose cause is just. And let us protest here and in advance against any tyrannical decrees that should declare us seditious when we have none but pure and just intentions. Let us make oath upon the honour of our motherland that should any of us be seized by an unjust tribunal, intending against us one of those acts termed of political expediency—which are, in effect, but acts of despotism—let us swear, I say, to give a full expression to the strength that is in us and do that in self-defence which nature, courage, and despair dictate to us."

Loud and long rolled the applause that greeted his conclusion, and he observed with satisfaction and even some inward grim amusement that the wealthy merchants who had been congregated upon the steps, and who now came crowding about him to shake him by the hand and to acclaim him, were not merely participants in, but the actual leaders of, this delirium of enthusiasm.

It confirmed him, had he needed confirmation, in his conviction that just as the philosophies upon which this new movement was based had their source in thinkers extracted from the bourgeoisie, so the need to adopt those philosophies to the practical purposes of life was most acutely felt at present by those bourgeois who found themselves debarred by Privilege from the expansion their wealth permitted them. If it might be said of André-Louis that he had that day lighted the torch of the Revolution in Nantes, it might with even greater truth be said that the torch itself was supplied by the opulent bourgeoisie.

I need not dwell at any length upon the sequel. It is a matter of history how that oath which Omnes Omnibus administered to the citizens of Nantes formed the backbone of the formal protest which they drew up and signed in their thousands. Nor were the results of that powerful protest—which, after all, might already be said to harmonize with the expressed will of the sovereign himself—long delayed. Who shall say how far it may have strengthened the hand of Necker, when on the 27th of that same month of November he compelled the Council to adopt the most significant and comprehensive of all those measures to which clergy and nobility had refused their consent? On that date was published the royal decree ordaining that the deputies to be elected to the States General should number at least one thousand, and that the deputies of the Third Estate should be fully representative by numbering as many as the deputies of clergy and nobility together.

Chapter IX

The Aftermath

Dusk of the following day was falling when the homing André-Louis approached Gavrillac. Realizing fully what a hue and cry there would presently be for the apostle of revolution who had summoned the people of Nantes to arms, he desired as far as possible to conceal the fact that he had been in that maritime city. Therefore he made a wide détour, crossing the river at Bruz, and recrossing it a little above Chavagne, so as to approach Gavrillac from the north, and create the impression that he was returning from Rennes, whither he was known to have gone two days ago.

Within a mile or so of the village he caught in the fading light his first glimpse of a figure on horseback pacing slowly towards him. But it was not until they had come within a few yards of each other, and he observed that this cloaked figure was leaning forward to peer at him, that he took much notice of it. And then he found himself challenged almost at once by a woman's voice.

"It is you, André—at last!"

He drew rein, mildly surprised, to be assailed by another question, impatiently, anxiously asked.

"Where have you been?"

"Where have I been, Cousin Aline? Oh . . . seeing the world."

"I have been patrolling this road since noon today, waiting for you." She spoke breathlessly, in haste to explain. "A troop of the *maréchaussée* from Rennes descended upon Gavrillac this morning in quest of you. They turned the château and the village inside out, and at last discovered that you were due to return with a horse hired from the Breton Armé. So they have taken up their quarters at the inn to wait for you. I have been here all the afternoon on the lookout to warn you against walking into that trap."

"My dear Aline! That I should have been the cause of so much concern and trouble!"

"Never mind that. It is not important."

"On the contrary; it is the most important part of what you tell me. It is the rest that is unimportant."

"Do you realize that they have come to arrest you?" she asked him, with increasing impatience. "You are wanted for sedition, and upon a warrant from M. de Lesdiguières."

"Sedition?" quoth he, and his thoughts flew to that business at Nantes. It was impossible they could have had news of it in Rennes and acted upon it in so short a time.

"Yes, sedition. The sedition of that wicked speech of yours at Rennes on Wednesday."

"Oh, that!" said he. "Pooh!" His note of relief might have

told her, had she been more attentive, that he had to fear the consequences of a greater wickedness committed since. "Why, that was nothing."

"Nothing?"

"I almost suspect that the real intentions of these gentlemen of the *maréchaussée* have been misunderstood. Most probably they have come to thank me on M. de Lesdiguières' behalf. I restrained the people when they would have burnt the Palais and himself inside it."

"After you had first incited them to do it. I suppose you were afraid of your work. You drew back at the last moment. But you said things of M. de Lesdiguières, if you are correctly reported, which he will never forgive."

"I see," said André-Louis, and he fell into thought.

But Mlle. de Kercadiou had already done what thinking was necessary, and her alert young mind had settled all that was to be done.

"You must not go into Gavrillac," she told him, "and you must get down from your horse, and let me take it. I will stable it at the château tonight. And sometime tomorrow afternoon, by when you should be well away, I will return it to the Breton Armé."

"Oh, but that is impossible."

"Impossible? Why?"

"For several reasons. One of them is that you haven't considered what will happen to you if you do such a thing."

"To me? Do you suppose I am afraid of that pack of oafs sent by M. Lesdiguières? I have committed no sedition."

"But it is almost as bad to give aid to one who is wanted for the crime. That is the law."

"What do I care for the law? Do you imagine that the law will presume to touch me?"

"Of course there is that. You are sheltered by one of the abuses I complained of at Rennes. I was forgetting."

"Complain of it as much as you please, but meanwhile profit by it. Come, André, do as I tell you. Get down from your horse." And then, as he still hesitated, she stretched out and caught him by the arm. Her voice was vibrant with earnestness. "André, you don't realize how serious is your position. If these people take you, it is almost certain that you will be hanged. Don't you realize it? You must not go to Gavrillac. You must go away at once, and lie completely lost for a time until this blows over. Indeed, until my uncle can bring influence to bear to obtain your pardon, you must keep in hiding."

"That will be a long time, then," said André-Louis. "M. de Kercadiou has never cultivated friends at court."

"There is M. de La Tour d'Azyr," she reminded him, to his astonishment.

"That man!" he cried, and then he laughed. "But it was chiefly against him that I aroused the resentment of the people of Rennes. I should have known that all my speech was not reported to you."

"It was, and that part of it among the rest."

"Ah! And yet you are concerned to save me, the man who seeks the life of your future husband at the hands either of the law or of the people? Or is it, perhaps, that since you have seen his true nature revealed in the murder of poor Philippe, you have changed your views on the subject of becoming Marquise de La Tour d'Azyr?"

93

"You often show yourself without any faculty of deductive reasoning."

"Perhaps. But hardly to the extent of imagining that M. de La Tour d'Azyr will ever lift a finger to do as you suggest."

"In which, as usual, you are wrong. He will certainly do so if I ask him."

"If you ask him?" Sheer horror rang in his voice.

"Why, yes. You see, I have not yet said that I will be Marquise de La Tour d'Azyr. I am still considering. It is a position that has its advantages. One of them is that it ensures a suitor's complete obedience."

"So, so. I see the crooked logic of your mind. You might go so far as to say to him: 'Refuse me this, and I shall refuse to be your marquise.' You would go so far as that?"

"At need, I might."

"And do you not see the converse implication? Do you not see that your hands would then be tied, that you would be wanting in honour if afterwards you refused him? And do you think that I would consent to anything that could so tie your hands? Do you think I want to see you damned, Aline?"

Her hand fell away from his arm.

"Oh, you are mad!" she exclaimed, quite out of patience.

"Possibly. But I like my madness. There is a thrill in it unknown to such sanity as yours. By your leave, Aline, I think I will ride on to Gavrillac."

"André, you must not! It is death to you!" In her alarm she backed her horse, and pulled it across the road to bar his way.

It was almost completely night by now; but from behind the wrack of clouds overhead a crescent moon sailed out to alleviate the darkness.

"Come, now," she enjoined him. "Be reasonable. Do as I bid you. See, there is a carriage coming up behind you. Do not let us be found here together thus."

He made up his mind quickly. He was not the man to be actuated by false heroics about dying, and he had no fancy whatever for the gallows of M. de Lesdiguières' providing. The immediate task that he had set himself might be accomplished. He had made heard—and ringingly—the voice that M. de La Tour d'Azyr imagined he had silenced. But he was very far from having done with life.

"Aline, on one condition only."

"And that?"

"That you swear to me you will never seek the aid of M. de La Tour d'Azyr on my behalf."

"Since you insist, and as time presses, I consent. And now ride on with me as far as the lane. There is that carriage coming up."

The lane to which she referred was one that branched off the road some three hundred yards nearer the village and led straight up the hill to the château itself. In silence they rode together towards it, and together they turned into that thickly hedged and narrow bypath. At a depth of fifty yards she halted him.

"Now!" she bade him.

Obediently he swung down from his horse, and surrendered the reins to her.

"Aline," he said, "I haven't words in which to thank you."

"It isn't necessary," said she.

"But I shall hope to repay you some day."

"Nor is that necessary. Could I do less than I am doing? I do not want to hear of you hanged, André; nor does my uncle, though he is very angry with you."

"I suppose he is."

"And you can hardly be surprised. You were his delegate, his representative. He depended upon you, and you have turned your coat. He is rightly indignant, calls you a traitor, and swears that he will never speak to you again. But he doesn't want you hanged, André."

"Then we are agreed on that at least, for I don't want it myself."

"I'll make your peace with him. And now—goodbye, André. Send me a word when you are safe."

She held out a hand that looked ghostly in the faint light. He took it and bore it to his lips.

"God bless you, Aline."

She was gone, and he stood listening to the receding clopper-clop of hooves until it grew faint in the distance. Then slowly, with shoulders hunched and head sunk on his breast, he retraced his steps to the main road, cogitating whither he should go. Quite suddenly he checked, remembering with dismay that he was almost entirely without money. In Brittany itself he knew of no dependable hiding-place, and as long as he was in Brittany his peril must remain imminent. Yet to leave the province, and to leave it as quickly as prudence dictated, horses would be necessary. And how was he to procure horses, having no money beyond a single *louis d'or* and a few pieces of silver?

There was also the fact that he was very weary. He had had little sleep since Tuesday night, and not very much then; and much of the time had been spent in the saddle, a wearing thing to one so little accustomed to long rides. Worn as he was, it was unthinkable that he should go far tonight. He might get as far as Chavagne, perhaps. But there he must sup and sleep; and what, then, of tomorrow?

Had he but thought of it before, perhaps Aline might have been able to assist him with the loan of a few *louis*. His first impulse now was to follow her to the château. But prudence dismissed the notion. Before he could reach her, he must be seen by servants, and word of his presence would go forth.

There was no choice for him; he must tramp as far as Chavagne, find a bed there, and leave tomorrow until it dawned. On the resolve he set his face in the direction whence he had come. But again he paused. Chavagne lay on the road to Rennes. To go that way was to plunge further into danger. He would strike south again. At the foot of some meadows on this side of the village there was a ferry that would put him across the river. Thus he would avoid the village; and by placing the river between himself and the immediate danger, he would obtain an added sense of security.

A lane, turning out of the highroad, a quarter of a mile this side of Gavrillac, led down to that ferry. By this lane some twenty minutes later came André-Louis with dragging feet. He avoided the little cottage of the ferryman, whose window was alight, and in the dark crept down to the boat, intending if possible to put himself across. He felt for the chain by which the boat was moored, and ran his fingers along this to the point where it was fastened. Here to his dismay he found a padlock.

He stood up in the gloom and laughed silently. Of course he might have known it. The ferry was the property of M. de La

Tour d'Azyr, and not likely to be left unfastened so that poor devils might cheat him of seigneurial dues.

There being no possible alternative, he walked back to the cottage, and rapped on the door. When it opened, he stood well back, and aside, out of the shaft of light that issued thence.

"Ferry!" he rapped out, laconically.

The ferryman, a burly scoundrel well known to him, turned aside to pick up a lantern, and came forth as he was bidden. As he stepped from the little porch, he levelled the lantern so that its light fell on the face of this traveller.

"My God!" he ejaculated.

"You realize, I see, that I am pressed," said André-Louis, his eyes on the fellow's startled countenance.

"And well you may be with the gallows waiting for you at Rennes," growled the ferryman. "Since you've been so foolish as to come back to Gavrillac, you had better go again as quickly as you can. I will say nothing of having seen you."

"I thank you, Fresnel. Your advice accords with my intention. That is why I need the boat."

"Ah, that, no," said Fresnel, with determination. "I'll hold my peace, but it's as much as my skin is worth to help you."

"You need not have seen my face. Forget that you have seen it."

"I'll do that, monsieur. But that is all I will do. I cannot put you across the river."

"Then give me the key of the boat, and I will put myself across."

"That is the same thing. I cannot. I'll hold my tongue, but I will not—I dare not—help you."

André-Louis looked a moment into that sullen, resolute face, and understood. This man, living under the shadow of La Tour d'Azyr, dared exercise no will that might be in conflict with the will of his dread lord.

"Fresnel," he said, quietly, "if, as you say, the gallows claim me, the thing that has brought me to this extremity arises out of the shooting of Mabey. Had not Mabey been murdered there would have been no need for me to have raised my voice as I have done. Mabey was your friend, I think. Will you for his sake lend me the little help I need to save my neck?"

The man kept his glance averted, and the cloud of sullenness deepened on his face.

"I would if I dared, but I dare not." Then, quite suddenly he became angry. It was as if in anger he sought support. "Don't you understand that I dare not? Would you have a poor man risk his life for you? What have you or yours ever done for me that you should ask that? You do not cross tonight in my ferry. Understand that, monsieur, and go at once—go before I remember that it may be dangerous even to have talked to you and not give information. Go!"

He turned on his heel to reënter his cottage, and a wave of hopelessness swept over André-Louis.

But in a second it was gone. The man must be compelled, and he had the means. He bethought him of a pistol pressed upon him by Le Chapelier at the moment of his leaving Rennes, a gift which at the time he had almost disdained. True, it was not loaded, and he had no ammunition. But how was Fresnel to know that?

He acted quickly. As with his right hand he pulled it from his pocket, with his left he caught the ferryman by the shoulder, and swung him round.

"What do you want now?" Fresnel demanded angrily. "Haven't I told you that I . . ."

He broke off short. The muzzle of the pistol was within a foot of his eyes.

"I want the key of the boat. That is all, Fresnel. And you can either give it me at once, or I'll take it after I have burnt your brains. I should regret to kill you, but I shall not hesitate. It is your life against mine, Fresnel; and you'll not find it strange that if one of us must die I prefer that it shall be you."

Fresnel dipped a hand into his pocket, and fetched thence a key. He held it out to André-Louis in fingers that shook more in anger than in fear.

"I yield to violence," he said, showing his teeth like a snarling dog. "But don't imagine that it will greatly profit you."

André-Louis took the key. His pistol remained levelled.

"You threaten me, I think," he said. "It is not difficult to read your threat. The moment I am gone, you will run to inform against me. You will set the *maréchaussée* on my heels to overtake me."

"No, no!" cried the other. He perceived his peril. He read his doom in the cold, sinister note on which André-Louis addressed him, and grew afraid. "I swear to you, monsieur, that I have no such intention."

"I think I had better make quite sure of you."

"O my God! Have mercy, monsieur!" The knave was in a palsy of terror. "I mean you no harm—I swear to Heaven I mean you no harm. I will not say a word. I will not . . ."

"I would rather depend upon your silence than your assurances. Still, you shall have your chance. I am a fool, perhaps, but I have a reluctance to shed blood. Go into the house, Fresnel. Go, man. I follow you."

In the shabby main room of that dwelling, André-Louis halted him again. "Get me a length of rope," he commanded, and was readily obeyed.

Five minutes later Fresnel was securely bound to a chair, and effectively silenced by a very uncomfortable gag improvised out of a block of wood and a muffler.

On the threshold the departing André-Louis turned.

"Goodnight, Fresnel," he said. Fierce eyes glared mute hatred at him. "It is unlikely that your ferry will be required again tonight. But some one is sure to come to your relief quite early in the morning. Until then bear your discomfort with what fortitude you can, remembering that you have brought it entirely upon yourself by your uncharitableness. If you spend the night considering that, the lesson should not be lost upon you. By morning you may even have grown so charitable as not to know who it was that tied you up. Goodnight."

He stepped out and closed the door.

To unlock the ferry, and pull himself across the swift-running waters, on which the faint moonlight was making a silver ripple, were matters that engaged not more than six or seven minutes. He drove the nose of the boat through the decaying sedges that fringed the southern bank of the stream, sprang ashore, and made the little craft secure. Then, missing the footpath in the dark, he struck out across a sodden meadow in quest of the road.

BOOK II

THE BUSKIN

CHAPTER I

The Trespassers

Coming presently upon the Rédon road, André-Louis, obey-ing instinct rather than reason, turned his face to the south, and plodded wearily and mechanically forward. He had no clear idea of whither he was going, or of whither he should go. All that imported at the moment was to put as great a distance as possible between Gavrillac and himself.

He had a vague, half-formed notion of returning to Nantes; and there, by employing the newly found weapon of his oratory, excite the people into sheltering him as the first victim of the persecution he had foreseen, and against which he had sworn them to take up arms. But the idea was one which he entertained merely as an indefinite possibility upon which he felt no real impulse to act.

Meanwhile he chuckled at the thought of Fresnel as he had last seen him, with his muffled face and glaring eyeballs. "For one who was anything but a man of action," he writes, "I felt that I had acquitted myself none so badly." It is a phrase that recurs at intervals in his sketchy *Confessions*. Constantly is he reminding you that he is a man of mental and not physical activities, and apologizing when dire necessity drives him into acts of violence. I suspect this insistence upon his philosophic detachment—for which I confess he had justification enough—to betray his besetting vanity.

With increasing fatigue came depression and self-criticism. He had stupidly overshot his mark in insultingly denouncing M. de Lesdiguières. "It is much better," he says somewhere, "to be wicked than to be stupid. Most of this world's misery is the fruit not as priests tell us of wickedness, but of stupidity." And we know that of all stupidities he considered anger the most deplorable. Yet he had permitted himself to be angry with a creature like M. de Lesdiguières—a lackey, a fribble, a nothing, despite his potentialities for evil. He could perfectly have discharged his self-imposed mission without arousing the vindicative resentment of the King's Lieutenant.

He beheld himself vaguely launched upon life with the riding-suit in which he stood, a single *louis d'or* and a few pieces of silver for all capital, and a knowledge of law which had been inadequate to preserve him from the consequences of infringing it.

He had, in addition—but these things that were to be the real salvation of him he did not reckon—his gift of laughter, sadly repressed of late, and the philosophic outlook and mercurial temperament which are the stock-in-trade of your adventurer in all ages.

Meanwhile he tramped mechanically on through the night,

until he felt that he could tramp no more. He had skirted the little township of Guichen, and now within a half-mile of Guignen, and with Gavrillac a good seven miles behind him, his legs refused to carry him any farther.

He was midway across the vast common to the north of Guignen when he came to a halt. He had left the road, and taken heedlessly to the footpath that struck across the waste of indifferent pasture interspersed with clumps of gorse. A stone's throw away on his right the common was bordered by a thorn hedge. Beyond this loomed a tall building which he knew to be an open barn, standing on the edge of a long stretch of meadowland. That dark, silent shadow it may have been that had brought him to a standstill, suggesting shelter to his subconsciousness. A moment he hesitated; then he struck across towards a spot where a gap in the hedge was closed by a five-barred gate. He pushed the gate open, went through the gap, and stood now before the barn. It was as big as a house, yet consisted of no more than a roof carried upon half a dozen tall, brick pillars. But densely packed under that roof was a great stack of hay that promised a warm couch on so cold a night. Stout timbers had been built into the brick pillars, with projecting ends to serve as ladders by which the labourer might climb to pack or withdraw hay. With what little strength remained him, André-Louis climbed by one of these and landed safely at the top, where he was forced to kneel, for lack of room to stand upright. Arrived there, he removed his coat and neckcloth, his sodden boots and stockings. Next he cleared a trough for his body, and lying down in it, covered himself to the neck with the hay he had removed. Within five minutes he was lost to all worldly cares and soundly asleep.

When next he awakened, the sun was already high in the heavens, from which he concluded that the morning was well advanced; and this before he realized quite where he was or how he came there. Then to his awakening senses came a drone of voices close at hand, to which at first he paid little heed. He was deliciously refreshed, luxuriously drowsy and luxuriously warm.

But as consciousness and memory grew more full, he raised his head clear of the hay that he might free both ears to listen, his pulses faintly quickened by the nascent fear that those voices might bode him no good. Then he caught the reassuring accents of a woman, musical and silvery, though laden with alarm.

"Ah, mon Dieu, Léandre, let us separate at once. If it should be my father . . ."

And upon this a man's voice broke in, calm and reassuring:

"No, no, Climène; you are mistaken. There is no one coming. We are quite safe. Why do you start at shadows?"

"Ah, Léandre, if he should find us here together! I tremble at the very thought."

More was not needed to reassure André-Louis. He had overheard enough to know that this was but the case of a pair of lovers who, with less to fear of life, were yet—after the manner of their kind—more timid of heart than he. Curiosity drew him from his warm trough to the edge of the hay. Lying prone, he advanced his head and peered down.

In the space of cropped meadow between the barn and the hedge stood a man and a woman, both young. The man was a well-set-up, comely fellow, with a fine head of chestnut hair tied in a queue by a broad bow of black satin. He was dressed with certain tawdry attempts at ostentatious embellishments, which did not prepossess one at first glance in his favour. His coat of a fashionable cut was of faded plum-coloured velvet edged with silver lace, whose glory had long since departed. He affected ruffles, but for want of starch they hung like weeping willows over hands that were fine and delicate. His breeches were of plain black cloth, and his black stockings were of cotton—matters entirely out of harmony with his magnificent coat. His shoes, stout and serviceable, were decked with buckles of cheap, lacklustre paste. But for his engaging and ingenuous countenance, André-Louis must have set him down as a knight of that order which lives dishonestly by its wits. As it was, he suspended judgment whilst pushing investigation further by a study of the girl. At the outset, be it confessed that it was a study that attracted him prodigiously. And this notwithstanding the fact that, bookish and studious as were his ways, and in despite of his years, it was far from his habit to waste consideration on femininity.

The child—she was no more than that, perhaps twenty at the most—possessed, in addition to the allurements of face and shape that went very near perfection, a sparkling vivacity and a grace of movement the like of which André-Louis did not remember ever before to have beheld assembled in one person. And her voice too—that musical, silvery voice that had awakened him—possessed in its exquisite modulations an allurement of its own that must have been irresistible, he thought, in the ugliest of her sex. She wore a hooded mantle of green cloth, and the hood being thrown back, her dainty head was all revealed to him. There were glints of gold struck by the morning sun from her light nut-brown hair that hung in a cluster of curls about her oval face. Her complexion was of a delicacy that he could compare only with a rose petal. He could not at that distance discern the colour of her eyes, but he guessed them blue, as he admired the sparkle of them under the fine, dark line of eyebrows.

He could not have told you why, but he was conscious that it aggrieved him to find her so intimate with this pretty young fellow, who was partly clad, as it appeared, in the cast-offs of a nobleman. He could not guess her station, but the speech that reached him was cultured in tone and word. He strained to listen.

"I shall know no peace, Léandre, until we are safely wedded," she was saying. "Not until then shall I count myself beyond his reach. And yet if we marry without his consent, we but make trouble for ourselves, and of gaining his consent I almost despair."

Evidently, thought André-Louis, her father was a man of sense, who saw through the shabby finery of M. Léandre, and was not to be dazzled by cheap paste buckles.

"My dear Climène," the young man was answering her, standing squarely before her, and holding both her hands, "you are wrong to despond. If I do not reveal to you all the stratagem that I have prepared to win the consent of your unnatural parent, it is because I am loath to rob you of the pleasure of the surprise that is in store. But place your faith in me, and in that ingenious friend of whom I have spoken, and who should be here at any moment."

The stilted ass! Had he learnt that speech by heart in advance, or was he by nature a pedantic idiot who expressed himself in this set and formal manner? How came so sweet a blossom to waste her perfumes on such a prig? And what a ridiculous name the creature owned!

Thus André-Louis to himself from his observatory. Meanwhile, she was speaking.

"That is what my heart desires, Léandre, but I am beset by fears lest your stratagem should be too late. I am to marry this horrible Marquis of Sbrufadelli this very day. He arrives by noon. He comes to sign the contract—to make me the Marchioness of Sbrufadelli. Oh!" It was a cry of pain from that tender young heart. "The very name burns my lips. If it were mine I could never utter it—never! The man is so detestable. Save me, Léandre. Save me! You are my only hope."

André-Louis was conscious of a pang of disappointment. She failed to soar to the heights he had expected of her. She was evidently infected by the stilted manner of her ridiculous lover. There was an atrocious lack of sincerity about her words. They touched his mind, but left his heart unmoved. Perhaps this was because of his antipathy to M. Léandre and to the issue involved.

So her father was marrying her to a marquis! That implied birth on her side. And yet she was content to pair off with this dull young adventurer in the tarnished lace! It was, he supposed, the sort of thing to be expected of a sex that all philosophy had taught him to regard as the maddest part of a mad species.

"It shall never be!" M. Léandre was storming passionately. "Never! I swear it!" And he shook his puny fist at the blue vault of heaven—Ajax defying Jupiter. "Ah, but here comes our subtle friend . . ." (André-Louis did not catch the name, M. Léandre having at that moment turned to face the gap in the hedge.) "He will bring us news, I know."

André-Louis looked also in the direction of the gap. Through it emerged a lean, slight man in a rusty cloak and a three-cornered hat worn well down over his nose so as to shade his face. And when presently he doffed this hat and made a sweeping bow to the young lovers, André-Louis confessed to himself that had he been cursed with such a hangdog countenance he would have worn his hat in precisely such a manner, so as to conceal as much of it as possible. If M. Léandre appeared to be wearing, in part at least, the cast-offs of a nobleman, the newcomer appeared to be wearing the cast-offs of M. Léandre. Yet despite his vile clothes and viler face, with its three days' growth of beard, the fellow carried himself with a certain air; he positively strutted as he advanced, and he made a leg in a manner that was courtly and practised.

"Monsieur," said he, with the air of a conspirator, "the time for action has arrived, and so has the Marquis. That is why."

The young lovers sprang apart in consternation; Climène with clasped hands, parted lips, and a bosom that raced distractingly under its white *fichu-menteur*; M. Léandre agape, the very picture of foolishness and dismay.

Meanwhile the newcomer rattled on. "I was at the inn an hour ago when he descended there, and I studied him attentively whilst he was at breakfast. Having done so, not a single doubt remains me of our success. As for what he looks like, I could entertain you at length upon the fashion in which nature has designed his gross fatuity. But that is no matter. We are concerned with what he is, with the wit of him. And I tell you confidently that I find him so dull and stupid that you may be confident he will tumble headlong into each and all of the traps I have so cunningly prepared for him."

"Tell me, tell me! Speak!" Climène implored him, holding out her hands in a supplication no man of sensibility could have resisted. And then on the instant she caught her breath on a faint scream. "My father!" she exclaimed, turning distractedly from one to the other of those two. "He is coming! We are lost!"

"You must fly, Climène!" said M. Léandre.

"Too late!" she sobbed. "Too late! He is here."

"Calm, mademoiselle, calm!" the subtle friend was urging her. "Keep calm and trust to me. I promise you that all shall be well."

"Oh!" cried M. Léandre, limply. "Say what you will, my friend, this is ruin—the end of all our hopes. Your wits will never extricate us from this. Never!"

Through the gap strode now an enormous man with an inflamed moon face and a great nose, decently dressed after the fashion of a solid bourgeois. There was no mistaking his anger, but the expression that it found was an amazement to Andre-Louis.

"Léandre, you're an imbecile! Too much phlegm, too much phlegm! Your words wouldn't convince a plough boy! Have you considered what they mean at all? Thus," he cried, and casting his round hat from him in a broad gesture, he took his stand at M. Léandre's side, and repeated the very words that Léandre had lately uttered, what time the three observed him coolly and attentively.

"Oh, say what you will, my friend, this is ruin—the end of all our hopes. Your wits will never extricate us from this. Never!"

A frenzy of despair vibrated in his accents. He swung again to face M. Léandre. "Thus," he bade him contemptuously. "Let the passion of your hopelessness express itself in your voice. Consider that you are not asking Scaramouche here whether he has put a patch in your breeches. You are a despairing lover expressing . . ."

He checked abruptly, startled. André-Louis, suddenly realizing what was afoot, and how duped he had been, had loosed his laughter. The sound of it pealing and booming uncannily under the great roof that so immediately confined him was startling to those below.

The fat man was the first to recover, and he announced it after his own fashion in one of the ready sarcasms in which he habitually dealt.

"Hark!" he cried, "the very gods laugh at you, Léandre." Then he addressed the roof of the barn and its invisible tenant. "Hi! You there!"

André-Louis revealed himself by a further protrusion of his tousled head.

"Good-morning," said he, pleasantly. Rising now on his knees, his horizon was suddenly extended to include the broad common beyond the hedge. He beheld there an enormous and very battered travelling chaise, a cart piled up with timbers partly visible under the sheet of oiled canvas that covered them, and a sort of house on wheels equipped with a tin chimney, from which the smoke was slowly curling. Three heavy Flemish horses and a couple of donkeys—all of them hobbled—were contentedly cropping the grass in the neighbourhood of these vehicles. These, had he perceived them sooner, must have given him the clue to the queer scene that had been played under his eyes. Beyond the hedge other figures were moving. Three at that moment came crowding into the gap—a saucy-faced girl with a tip-tilted nose, whom he supposed to be Columbine, the soubrette; a lean, active youngster, who must be the lackey Harlequin; and another rather loutish youth who might be a zany or an apothecary.

All this he took in at a comprehensive glance that consumed no more time than it had taken him to say good-morning. To that good-morning Pantaloon replied in a bellow—

"What the devil are you doing up there?"

"Precisely the same thing that you are doing down there," was the answer. "I am trespassing."

"Eh?" said Pantaloon, and looked at his companions, some of the assurance beaten out of his big red face. Although the thing was one that they did habitually, to hear it called by its proper name was disconcerting.

"Whose land is this?" he asked, with diminishing assurance.

André-Louis answered, whilst drawing on his stockings. "I believe it to be the property of the Marquis de La Tour d'Azyr."

"That's a high-sounding name. Is the gentleman severe?"

"The gentleman," said André-Louis, "is the devil; or rather, I should prefer to say upon reflection, that the devil is a gentleman by comparison."

"And yet," interposed the villainous-looking fellow who played Scaramouche, "by your own confessing you don't hesitate, yourself, to trespass upon his property."

"Ah, but then, you see, I am a lawyer. And lawyers are notoriously unable to observe the law, just as actors are notoriously unable to act. Moreover, sir, Nature imposes her limits upon us, and Nature conquers respect for law as she conquers all else. Nature conquered me last night when I had got as far as this. And so I slept here without regard for the very high and puissant

115

Marquis de La Tour d'Azyr. At the same time, M. Scaramouche, you'll observe that I did not flaunt my trespass quite as openly as you and your companions."

Having donned his boots, André-Louis came nimbly to the ground in his shirt-sleeves, his riding-coat over his arm. As he stood there to don it, the little cunning eyes of the heavy father conned him in detail. Observing that his clothes, if plain, were of a good fashion, that his shirt was of fine cambric, and that he expressed himself like a man of culture, such as he claimed to be, M. Pantaloon was disposed to be civil.

"I am very grateful to you for the warning, sir . . ." he was beginning.

"Act upon it, my friend. The *gardes-champêtres* of M. d'Azyr have orders to fire on trespassers. Imitate me, and decamp."

They followed him upon the instant through that gap in the hedge to the encampment on the common. There André-Louis took his leave of them. But as he was turning away he perceived a young man of the company performing his morning toilet at a bucket placed upon one of the wooden steps at the tail of the house on wheels. A moment he hesitated, then he turned frankly to M. Pantaloon, who was still at his elbow.

"If it were not unconscionable to encroach so far upon your hospitality, monsieur," said he, "I would beg leave to imitate that very excellent young gentleman before I leave you."

"But, my dear sir!" Good-nature oozed out of every pore of the fat body of the master player. "It is nothing at all. But, by all means. Rhodomont will provide what you require. He is the dandy of the company in real life, though a fire-eater on the stage. Hi, Rhodomont!"

116

The young ablutionist straightened his long body from the right angle in which it had been bent over the bucket, and looked out through a foam of soapsuds. Pantaloon issued an order, and Rhodomont, who was indeed as gentle and amiable off the stage as he was formidable and terrible upon it, made the stranger free of the bucket in the friendliest manner.

So André-Louis once more removed his neckcloth and his coat, and rolled up the sleeves of his fine shirt, whilst Rhodomont procured him soap, a towel, and presently a broken comb, and even a greasy hair-ribbon, in case the gentleman should have lost his own. This last André-Louis declined, but the comb he gratefully accepted, and having presently washed himself clean, stood, with the towel flung over his left shoulder, restoring order to his dishevelled locks before a broken piece of mirror affixed to the door of the travelling house.

He was standing thus, what time the gentle Rhodomont babbled aimlessly at his side, when his ears caught the sound of hooves. He looked over his shoulder carelessly, and then stood frozen, with uplifted comb and loosened mouth. Away across the common, on the road that bordered it, he beheld a party of seven horsemen in the blue coats with red facings of the *maréchaussée*.

Not for a moment did he doubt what was the quarry of this prowling *gendarmerie*. It was as if the chill shadow of the gallows had fallen suddenly upon him.

And then the troop halted, abreast with them, and the sergeant leading it sent his bawling voice across the common.

"Hi, there! Hi!" His tone rang with menace.

Every member of the company—and there were some twelve

in all—stood at gaze. Pantaloon advanced a step or two, stalking, his head thrown back, his manner that of a King's Lieutenant.

"Now, what the devil's this?" quoth he, but whether of Fate or Heaven or the sergeant, was not clear.

There was a brief colloquy among the horsemen, then they came trotting across the common straight towards the players' encampment.

André-Louis had remained standing at the tail of the travelling house. He was still passing the comb through his straggling hair, but mechanically and unconsciously. His mind was all intent upon the advancing troop, his wits alert and gathered together for a leap in whatever direction should be indicated.

Still in the distance, but evidently impatient, the sergeant bawled a question.

"Who gave you leave to encamp here?"

It was a question that reassured André-Louis not at all. He was not deceived by it into supposing or even hoping that the business of these men was merely to round up vagrants and trespassers. That was no part of their real duty; it was something done in passing—done, perhaps, in the hope of levying a tax of their own. It was very long odds that they were from Rennes, and that their real business was the hunting down of a young lawyer charged with sedition. Meanwhile Pantaloon was shouting back.

"Who gave us leave, do you say? What leave? This is communal land, free to all."

The sergeant laughed unpleasantly, and came on, his troop following.

"There is," said a voice at Pantaloon's elbow, "no such thing as communal land in the proper sense in all M. de La Tour d'Azyr's vast domain. This is a *terre censive,* and his bailiffs collect his dues from all who send their beasts to graze here."

Pantaloon turned to behold at his side André-Louis in his shirt-sleeves, and without a neckcloth, the towel still trailing over his left shoulder, a comb in his hand, his hair half dressed.

"God of God!" swore Pantaloon. "But it is an ogre, this Marquis de La Tour d'Azyr!"

"I have told you already what I think of him," said André-Louis. "As for these fellows you had better let me deal with them. I have experience of their kind." And without waiting for Pantaloon's consent, André-Louis stepped forward to meet the advancing men of the *maréchaussée.* He had realized that here boldness alone could save him.

When a moment later the sergeant pulled up his horse alongside of this half-dressed young man, André-Louis combed his hair what time he looked up with a half smile, intended to be friendly, ingenuous, and disarming.

In spite of it the sergeant hailed him gruffly: "Are you the leader of this troop of vagabonds?"

"Yes . . . that is to say, my father, there, is really the leader." And he jerked a thumb in the direction of M. Pantaloon, who stood at gaze out of earshot in the background. "What is your pleasure, captain?"

"My pleasure is to tell you that you are very likely to be gaoled for this, all the pack of you." His voice was loud and bullying. It carried across the common to the ears of every member of the company, and brought them all to stricken attention where they stood. The lot of strolling players was hard enough without the addition of gaolings.

"But how so, my captain? This is communal land—free to all."

"It is nothing of the kind."

"Where are the fences?" quoth André-Louis, waving the hand that held the comb, as if to indicate the openness of the place.

"Fences!" snorted the sergeant. "What have fences to do with the matter? This is *terre censive*. There is no grazing here save by payment of dues to the Marquis de La Tour d'Azyr."

"But we are not grazing," quoth the innocent André-Louis.

"To the devil with you, zany! You are not grazing! But your beasts are grazing!"

"They eat so little," André-Louis apologized, and again essayed his ingratiating smile.

The sergeant grew more terrible than ever. "That is not the point. The point is that you are committing what amounts to a theft, and there's the gaol for thieves."

"Technically, I suppose you are right," sighed André-Louis, and fell to combing his hair again, still looking up into the sergeant's face. "But we have sinned in ignorance. We are grateful to you for the warning." He passed the comb into his left hand, and with his right fumbled in his breeches' pocket, whence there came a faint jingle of coins. "We are desolated to have brought you out of your way. Perhaps for their trouble your men would honour us by stopping at the next inn to drink the health of . . . of . . . this M. de La Tour d' Azyr, or any other health that they think proper."

Some of the clouds lifted from the sergeant's brow. But not yet all.

"Well, well," said he, gruffly. "But you must decamp, you

understand." He leaned from the saddle to bring his recipient hand to a convenient distance. André-Louis placed in it a three-livre piece.

"In half an hour," said André-Louis.

"Why in half an hour? Why not at once?"

"Oh, but time to break our fast."

They looked at each other. The sergeant next considered the broad piece of silver in his palm. Then at last his features relaxed from their sternness.

"After all," said he, "it is none of our business to play the tipstaves for M. de La Tour d'Azyr. We are of the *maréchaussée* from Rennes." André-Louis' eyelids played him false by flickering. "But if you linger, look out for the *gardes-champêtres* of the Marquis. You'll find them not at all accommodating. Well, well—a good appetite to you, monsieur," said he, in valediction.

"A pleasant ride, my captain," answered André-Louis.

The sergeant wheeled his horse about, his troop wheeled with him. They were starting off, when he reined up again.

"You, monsieur!" he called over his shoulder. In a bound André-Louis was beside his stirrup. "We are in quest of a scoundrel named André-Louis Moreau, from Gavrillac, a fugitive from justice wanted for the gallows on a matter of sedition. You've seen nothing, I suppose, of a man whose movements seemed to you suspicious?"

"Indeed, we have," said Andre-Louis, very boldly, his face eager with consciousness of the ability to oblige.

"You have?" cried the sergeant, in a ringing voice. "Where? When?"

"Yesterday evening in the neighbourhood of Guignen . . ."

121

"Yes, yes," the sergeant felt himself hot upon the trail.

"There was a fellow who seemed very fearful of being recognized . . . a man of fifty or thereabouts . . ."

"Fifty!" cried the sergeant, and his face fell. "Bah! This man of ours is no older than yourself, a thin wisp of a fellow of about your own height and of black hair, just like your own, by the description. Keep a lookout on your travels, master player. The King's Lieutenant in Rennes has sent us word this morning that he will pay ten *louis* to any one giving information that will lead to this scoundrel's arrest. So there's ten *louis* to be earned by keeping your eyes open, and sending word to the nearest justices. It would be a fine windfall for you, that."

"A fine windfall, indeed, captain," answered André-Louis, laughing.

But the sergeant had touched his horse with the spur, and was already trotting off in the wake of his men. André-Louis continued to laugh, quite silently, as he sometimes did when the humour of a jest was peculiarly keen.

Then he turned slowly about, and came back towards Pantaloon and the rest of the company, who were now all grouped together, at gaze.

Pantaloon advanced to meet him with both hands outheld. For a moment André-Louis thought he was about to be embraced.

"We hail you our saviour!" the big man declaimed. "Already the shadow of the gaol was creeping over us, chilling us to the very marrow. For though we be poor, yet are we all honest folk and not one of us has ever suffered the indignity of prison. Nor is there one of us would survive it. But for you, my friend, it might have happened. What magic did you work?"

"The magic that is to be worked in France with a King's portrait. The French are a very loyal nation, as you will have observed. They love their King—and his portrait even better than himself, especially when it is wrought in gold. But even in silver it is respected. The sergeant was so overcome by the sight of that noble visage—on a three-*livre* piece—that his anger vanished, and he has gone his ways leaving us to depart in peace."

"Ah, true! He said we must decamp. About it, my lads! Come, come . . ."

"But not until after breakfast," said André-Louis. "A half-hour for breakfast was conceded us by that loyal fellow, so deeply was he touched. True, he spoke of possible *gardes-champêtres*. But he knows as well as I do that they are not seriously to be feared, and that if they came, again the King's portrait—wrought in copper this time—would produce the same melting effect upon them. So, my dear M. Pantaloon, break your fast at your ease. I can smell your cooking from here, and from the smell I argue that there is no need to wish you a good appetite."

"My friend, my saviour!" Pantaloon flung a great arm about the young man's shoulders. "You shall stay to breakfast with us."

"I confess to a hope that you would ask me," said André-Louis.

Chapter II

The Service of Thespis

They were, thought André-Louis, as he sat down to breakfast with them behind the itinerant house, in the bright sunshine that tempered the cold breath of that November morning, an odd and yet an attractive crew. An air of gaiety pervaded them. They affected to have no cares, and made merry over the trials and tribulations of their nomadic life. They were curiously, yet amiably, artificial; histrionic in their manner of discharging the most commonplace of functions; exaggerated in their gestures; stilted and affected in their speech. They seemed, indeed, to belong to a world apart, a world of unreality which became real only on the planks of their stage, in the glare of their footlights. Good-fellowship bound them one to another; and André-Louis reflected cynically that this harmony amongst them might be the cause of their apparent unreality. In the real world, greedy striving and the emulation of acquisitiveness preclude such amity as was present here.

They numbered exactly eleven, three women and eight men; and they addressed each other by their stage names: names which denoted their several types, and never—or only very slightly—varied, no matter what might be the play that they performed.

"We are," Pantaloon informed him, "one of those few remaining staunch bands of real players, who uphold the traditions of the old Italian Commedia dell' Arte. Not for us to vex our memories and stultify our wit with the stilted phrases that are the fruit of a wretched author's lucubrations. Each of us is in detail his own author in a measure as he develops the part assigned to him. We are improvisers—improvisers of the old and noble Italian school."

"I had guessed as much," said André-Louis, "when I discovered you rehearsing your improvisations."

Pantaloon frowned.

"I have observed, young sir, that your humour inclines to the pungent, not to say the acrid. It is very well. It is, I suppose, the humour that should go with such a countenance. But it may lead you astray, as in this instance. That rehearsal—a most unusual thing with us—was necessitated by the histrionic rawness of our Léandre. We are seeking to inculcate into him by training an art with which Nature neglected to endow him against his present needs. Should he continue to fail in doing justice to our schooling . . . But we will not disturb our present harmony with the unpleasant anticipation of misfortunes which we still hope to avert. We love our Léandre, for all his faults. Let me make you acquainted with our company."

And he proceeded to introduction in detail. He pointed out

the long and amiable Rhodomont, whom André-Louis already knew.

"His length of limb and hooked nose were his superficial qualifications to play roaring captains," Pantaloon explained. "His lungs have justified our choice. You should hear him roar. At first we called him Spavento or Épouvante. But that was unworthy of so great an artist. Not since the superb Mondor amazed the world has so thrasonical a bully been seen upon the stage. So we conferred upon him the name of Rhodomont that Mondor made famous; and I give you my word, as an actor and a gentleman—for I am a gentleman, monsieur, or was—that he has justified us."

His little eyes beamed in his great swollen face as he turned their gaze upon the object of his encomium. The terrible Rhodomont, confused by so much praise, blushed like a schoolgirl as he met the solemn scrutiny of André-Louis.

"Then here we have Scaramouche, whom also you already know. Sometimes he is Scapin and sometimes Coviello, but in the main Scaramouche, to which let me tell you he is best suited—sometimes too well suited, I think. For he is Scaramouche not only on the stage, but also in the world. He has a gift of sly intrigue, an art of setting folk by the ears, combined with an impudent aggressiveness upon occasion when he considers himself safe from reprisals. He is Scaramouche, the little skirmisher, to the very life. I could say more. But I am by disposition charitable and loving to all mankind."

"As the priest said when he kissed the serving-wench," snarled Scaramouche, and went on eating.

"His humour, like your own, you will observe, is acrid," said Pantaloon. He passed on. "Then that rascal with the lumpy nose and the grinning bucolic countenance is, of course, Pierrot. Could he be aught else?"

"I could play lovers a deal better," said the rustic cherub.

"That is the delusion proper to Pierrot," said Pantaloon, contemptuously. "This heavy, beetle-browed ruffian, who has grown old in sin, and whose appetite increases with his years, is Polichinelle. Each one, as you perceive, is designed by Nature for the part he plays. This nimble, freckled jackanapes is Harlequin; not your spangled Harlequin into which modern degeneracy has debased that first-born of Momus, but the genuine original zany of the Commedia, ragged and patched, an impudent, cowardly, blackguardly clown."

"Each one of us, as you perceive," said Harlequin, mimicking the leader of the troupe, "is designed by Nature for the part he plays."

"Physically, my friend, physically only, else we should not have so much trouble in teaching this beautiful Léandre to become a lover. Then we have Pasquariel here, who is sometimes an apothecary, sometimes a notary, sometimes a lackey—an amiable, accommodating fellow. He is also an excellent cook, being a child of Italy, that land of gluttons. And finally, you have myself, who as the father of the company very properly play as Pantaloon the rôles of father. Sometimes, it is true, I am a deluded husband, and sometimes an ignorant, self-sufficient doctor. But it is rarely that I find it necessary to call myself other than Pantaloon. For the rest, I am the only one who has a name—a real name. It is Binet, monsieur.

"And now for the ladies. First in order of seniority we have Madame there." He waved one of his great hands towards a buxom, smiling blonde of five-and-forty, who was seated on the lowest of the steps of the travelling house. "She is our Duègne, or Mother, or Nurse, as the case requires. She is known quite simply and royally as Madame. If she ever had a name in the world, she has long since forgotten it, which is perhaps as well. Then we have this pert jade with the tip-tilted nose and the wide mouth, who is of course our soubrette Columbine, and lastly, my daughter Climène, an amoureuse of talents not to be matched outside the Comédie Francaise, of which she has the bad taste to aspire to become a member."

The lovely Climène—and lovely indeed she was—tossed her nut-brown curls and laughed as she looked across at André-Louis. Her eyes, he had perceived by now, were not blue, but hazel.

"Do not believe him, monsieur. Here I am queen, and I prefer to be queen here rather than a slave in Paris."

"Mademoiselle," said André-Louis, quite solemnly, "will be queen wherever she condescends to reign."

Her only answer was a timid—timid and yet alluring—glance from under fluttering lids. Meanwhile her father was bawling at the comely young man who played lovers—"You hear, Léandre! That is the sort of speech you should practise."

Léandre raised languid eyebrows. "That?" quoth he, and shrugged. "The merest commonplace."

André-Louis laughed approval. "M. Léandre is of a readier wit than you concede. There is subtlety in pronouncing it a commonplace to call Mlle. Climène a queen."

Some laughed, M. Binet amongst them, with good-humoured mockery.

"You think he has the wit to mean it thus? Bah! His subtleties are all unconscious."

The conversation becoming general, André-Louis soon learnt what yet there was to learn of this strolling band. They were on their way to Guichen, where they hoped to prosper at the fair that was to open on Monday next. They would make their triumphal entry into the town at noon, and setting up their stage in the old market, they would give their first performance that same Saturday night, in a new *canevas*—or scenario—of M. Binet's own, which should set the rustics gaping. And then M. Binet fetched a sigh, and addressed himself to the elderly, swarthy, beetle-browed Polichinelle, who sat on his left.

"But we shall miss Félicien," said he. "Indeed, I do not know what we shall do without him."

"Oh, we shall contrive," said Polichinelle, with his mouth full.

"So you always say, whatever happens, knowing that in any case the contriving will not fall upon yourself."

"He should not be difficult to replace," said Harlequin.

"True, if we were in a civilized land. But where among the rustics of Brittany are we to find a fellow of even his poor parts?" M. Binet turned to André-Louis. "He was our property-man, our machinist, our stage-carpenter, our man of affairs, and occasionally he acted."

"The part of Figaro, I presume," said André-Louis, which elicited a laugh.

"So you are acquainted with Beaumarchais!" Binet eyed the young man with fresh interest.

"He is tolerably well known, I think."

"In Paris, to be sure. But I had not dreamt his fame had

reached the wilds of Brittany."

"But then I was some years in Paris—at the Lycée of Louis le Grand. It was there I made acquaintance with his work."

"A dangerous man," said Polichinelle, sententiously.

"Indeed, and you are right," Pantaloon agreed. "Clever—I do not deny him that, although myself I find little use for authors. But of a sinister cleverness responsible for the dissemination of many of these subversive new ideas. I think such writers should be suppressed."

"M. de La Tour d'Azyr would probably agree with you—the gentleman who by the simple exertion of his will turns this communal land into his own property." And André-Louis drained his cup, which had been filled with the poor *vin gris* that was the players' drink.

It was a remark that might have precipitated an argument had it not also reminded M. Binet of the terms on which they were encamped there, and of the fact that the half-hour was more than past. In a moment he was on his feet, leaping up with an agility surprising in so corpulent a man, issuing his commands like a marshal on a field of battle.

"Come, come, my lads! Are we to sit guzzling here all day? Time flees, and there's a deal to be done if we are to make our entry into Guichen at noon. Go, get you dressed. We strike camp in twenty minutes. Bestir, ladies! To your chaise, and see that you contrive to look your best. Soon the eyes of Guichen will be upon you, and the condition of your interior tomorrow will depend upon the impression made by your exterior today. Away! Away!"

The implicit obedience this autocrat commanded set them

in a whirl. Baskets and boxes were dragged forth to receive the platters and remains of their meagre feast. In an instant the ground was cleared, and the three ladies had taken their departure to the chaise, which was set apart for their use. The men were already climbing into the house on wheels, when Binet turned to André-Louis.

"We part here, sir," said he, dramatically, "the richer by your acquaintance; your debtors and your friends." He put forth his podgy hand.

Slowly André-Louis took it in his own. He had been thinking swiftly in the last few moments. And remembering the safety he had found from his pursuers in the bosom of this company, it occurred to him that nowhere could he be better hidden for the present, until the quest for him should have died down.

"Sir," he said, "the indebtedness is on my side. It is not every day one has the felicity to sit down with so illustrious and engaging a company."

Binet's little eyes peered suspiciously at the young man, in quest of irony. He found nothing but candour and simple good faith.

"I part from you reluctantly," André-Louis continued. "The more reluctantly since I do not perceive the absolute necessity for parting."

"How?" quoth Binet, frowning, and slowly withdrawing the hand which the other had already retained rather longer than was necessary.

"Thus," André-Louis explained himself. "You may set me down as a sort of knight of rueful countenance in quest of adventure, with no fixed purpose in life at present. You will not marvel

131

that what I have seen of yourself and your distinguished troupe should inspire me to desire your better acquaintance. On your side you tell me that you are in need of some one to replace your Figaro—your Félicien, I think you called him. Whilst it may be presumptuous of me to hope that I could discharge an office so varied and so onerous . . ."

"You are indulging that acrid humour of yours again, my friend," Binet interrupted him. "Excepting for that," he added, slowly, meditatively, his little eyes screwed up, "we might discuss this proposal that you seem to be making."

"Alas! we can except nothing. If you take me, you take me as I am. What else is possible? As for this humour—such as it is— which you decry, you might turn it to profitable account."

"How so?"

"In several ways. I might, for instance, teach Léandre to make love."

Pantaloon burst into laughter. "You do not lack confidence in your powers. Modesty does not afflict you."

"Therefore I evince the first quality necessary in an actor."

"Can you act?"

"Upon occasion, I think," said André-Louis, his thoughts upon his performance at Rennes and Nantes, and wondering when in all his histrionic career Pantaloon's improvisations had so rent the heart of mobs.

M. Binet was musing. "Do you know much of the theatre?" quoth he.

"Everything," said André-Louis.

"I said that modesty will prove no obstacle in your career."

"But consider. I know the work of Beaumarchais, Églantine,

132

Mercier, Chénier, and many others of our contemporaries. Then I have read, of course, Molière, Racine, Corneille, besides many other lesser French writers. Of foreign authors, I am intimate with the works of Gozzi, Goldoni, Guarini, Bibbiena, Machiavelli, Secchi, Tasso, Ariosto, and Fedini. Whilst of those of antiquity I know most of the work of Euripides, Aristophanes, Terence, Plautus . . ."

"Enough!" roared Pantaloon.

"I am not nearly through with my list," said André-Louis.

"You may keep the rest for another day. In Heaven's name, what can have induced you to read so many dramatic authors?"

"In my humble way I am a student of man, and some years ago I made the discovery that he is most intimately to be studied in the reflections of him provided for the theatre."

"That is a very original and profound discovery," said Pantaloon, quite seriously. "It had never occurred to me. Yet is it true. Sir, it is a truth that dignifies our art. You are a man of parts, that is clear to me. It has been clear since first I met you. I can read a man. I knew you from the moment that you said 'good morning.' Tell me, now: Do you think you could assist me upon occasion in the preparation of a scenario? My mind, fully engaged as it is with a thousand details of organization, is not always as clear as I would have it for such work. Could you assist me there, do you think?"

"I am quite sure I could."

"Hum, yes. I was sure you would be. The other duties that were Félicien's you would soon learn. Well, well, if you are willing, you may come along with us. You'd want some salary, I suppose?"

"If it is usual," said André-Louis.

"What should you say to ten livres a month?"

"I should say that it isn't exactly the riches of Peru."

"I might go as far as fifteen," said Binet, reluctantly. "But times are bad."

"I'll make them better for you."

"I've no doubt you believe it. Then we understand each other?"

"Perfectly," said André-Louis, dryly, and was thus committed to the service of Thespis.

CHAPTER III

The Comic Muse

The company's entrance into the township of Guichen, if not exactly triumphal, as Binet had expressed the desire that it should be, was at least sufficiently startling and cacophonous to set the rustics gaping. To them these fantastic creatures appeared—as indeed they were—beings from another world.

First went the great travelling chaise, creaking and groaning on its way, drawn by two of the Flemish horses. It was Pantaloon who drove it, an obese and massive Pantaloon in a tight-fitting suit of scarlet under a long brown bedgown, his countenance adorned by a colossal cardboard nose. Beside him on the box sat Pierrot in a white smock, with sleeves that completely covered his hands, loose white trousers, and a black skull-cap. He had whitened his face with flour, and he made hideous noises with a trumpet.

On the roof of the coach were assembled Polichinelle,

Scaramouche, Harlequin, and Pasquariel. Polichinelle in black
and white, his doublet cut in the fashion of a century ago, with
humps before and behind, a white frill round his neck and a
black mask upon the upper half of his face, stood in the middle,
his feet planted wide to steady him, solemnly and viciously banging a big drum. The other three were seated each at one of the
corners of the roof, their legs dangling over. Scaramouche, all in
black in the Spanish fashion of the seventeenth century, his face
adorned with a pair of moustachios, jangled a guitar discordantly.
Harlequin, ragged and patched in every colour of the rainbow,
with his leather girdle and sword of lath, the upper half of his
face smeared in soot, clashed a pair of cymbals intermittently.
Pasquariel, as an apothecary in skull-cap and white apron, excited the hilarity of the onlookers by his enormous tin clyster,
which emitted when pumped a dolorous squeak.

Within the chaise itself, but showing themselves freely at the
windows, and exchanging quips with the townsfolk, sat the three
ladies of the company. Climène, the *amoureuse*, beautifully
gowned in flowered satin, her own clustering ringlets concealed
under a pumpkin-shaped wig, looked so much the lady of fashion that you might have wondered what she was doing in that
fantastic rabble. Madame, as the mother, was also dressed with
splendour, but exaggerated to achieve the ridiculous. Her headdress was a monstrous structure adorned with flowers, and su-
perimposed by little ostrich plumes. Columbine sat facing them,
her back to the horses, falsely demure, in milkmaid bonnet of
white muslin, and a striped gown of green and blue.

The marvel was that the old chaise, which in its halcyon days
may have served to carry some dignitary of the Church, did not

founder instead of merely groaning under that excessive and ribald load.

Next came the house on wheels, led by the long, lean
Rhodomont, who had daubed his face red, and increased the
terror of it by a pair of formidable moustachios. He was in long
thigh-boots and leather jerkin, trailing an enormous sword from
a crimson baldrick. He wore a broad felt hat with a draggled
feather, and as he advanced he raised his great voice and roared
out defiance, and threats of blood-curdling butchery to be performed upon all and sundry. On the roof of this vehicle sat
Léandre alone. He was in blue satin, with ruffles, small sword,
powdered hair, patches and spy-glass, and red-heeled shoes; the
complete courtier, looking very handsome. The women of
Guichen ogled him coquettishly. He took the ogling as a proper
tribute to his personal endowments, and returned it with interest. Like Climène, he looked out of place amid the bandits who
composed the remainder of the company.

Bringing up the rear came André-Louis leading the two donkeys that dragged the property-cart. He had insisted upon assuming a false nose, representing as for embellishment that which
he intended for disguise. For the rest, he had retained his own
garments. No one paid any attention to him as he trudged along
beside his donkeys, an insignificant rear guard, which he was well
content to be.

They made the tour of the town, in which the activity was
already above the normal in preparation for next week's fair. At
intervals they halted, the cacophony would cease abruptly, and
Polichinelle would announce in a stentorian voice that at five
o'clock that evening in the old market, M. Binet's famous com-

pany of improvisers would perform a new comedy in four acts entitled, *The Heartless Father.*

Thus at last they came to the old market, which was the ground floor of the town hall, and open to the four winds by two archways on each side of its length, and one archway on each side of its breadth. These archways, with two exceptions, had been boarded up. Through those two, which gave admission to what presently would be the theatre, the ragamuffins of the town, and the niggards who were reluctant to spend the necessary *sous* to obtain proper admission, might catch furtive glimpses of the performance.

That afternoon was the most strenuous of André-Louis' life, unaccustomed as he was to any sort of manual labour. It was spent in erecting and preparing the stage at one end of the market-hall; and he began to realize how hard-earned were to be his monthly fifteen *livres*. At first there were four of them to the task—or really three, for Pantaloon did no more than bawl directions. Stripped of their finery, Rhodomont and Léandre assisted André-Louis in that carpentering. Meanwhile the other four were at dinner with the ladies. When a half-hour or so later they came to carry on the work, André-Louis and his companions went to dine in their turn, leaving Polichinelle to direct the operations as well as assist in them.

They crossed the square to the cheap little inn where they had taken up their quarters. In the narrow passage André-Louis came face to face with Climène, her fine feathers cast, and restored by now to her normal appearance.

"And how do you like it?" she asked him, pertly.

He looked her in the eyes. "It has its compensations," quoth he, in that curious cold tone of his that left one wondering whether he meant or not what he seemed to mean.

She knit her brows. "You . . . you feel the need of compensations already?"

"Faith, I felt it from the beginning," said he. "It was the perception of them allured me."

They were quite alone, the others having gone on into the room set apart for them, where food was spread. André-Louis, who was as unlearned in Woman as he was learned in Man, was not to know, upon feeling himself suddenly extraordinarily aware of her femininity, that it was she who in some subtle, imperceptible manner so rendered him.

"What," she asked him, with demurest innocence, "are these compensations?"

He caught himself upon the brink of the abyss.

"Fifteen *livres* a month," said he, abruptly.

A moment she stared at him bewildered. He was very disconcerting. Then she recovered.

"Oh, and bed and board," said she. "Don't be leaving that from the reckoning, as you seem to be doing; for your dinner will be going cold. Aren't you coming?"

"Haven't you dined?" he cried, and she wondered had she caught a note of eagerness.

"No," she answered, over her shoulder. "I waited."

"What for?" quoth his innocence, hopefully.

"I had to change, of course, zany," she answered, rudely. Having dragged him, as she imagined, to the chopping-block, she could not refrain from chopping. But then he was of those who must be chopping back.

"And you left your manners upstairs with your grand-lady clothes, mademoiselle. I understand."

A scarlet flame suffused her face. "You are very insolent," she said, lamely.

"I've often been told so. But I don't believe it." He thrust open the door for her, and bowing with an air which imposed upon her, although it was merely copied from Fleury of the Comédie Francaise, so often visited in the Louis le Grand days, he waved her in. "After you, ma demoiselle." For greater emphasis he deliberately broke the word into its two component parts.

"I thank you, monsieur," she answered, frostily, as near sneering as was possible to so charming a person, and went in, nor addressed him again throughout the meal. Instead, she devoted herself with an unusual and devastating assiduity to the suspiring Léandre, that poor devil who could not successfully play the lover with her on the stage because of his longing to play it in reality.

André-Louis ate his herrings and black bread with a good appetite nevertheless. It was poor fare, but then poor fare was the common lot of poor people in that winter of starvation, and since he had cast in his fortunes with a company whose affairs were not flourishing, he must accept the evils of the situation philosophically.

"Have you a name?" Binet asked him once in the course of that repast and during a pause in the conversation.

"It happens that I have," said he. "I think it is Parvissimus."

"Parvissimus?" quoth Binet. "Is that a family name?"

"In such a company, where only the leader enjoys the privilege of a family name, the like would be unbecoming its least member. So I take the name that best becomes me. And I think it is Parvissimus—the very least."

Binet was amused. It was droll; it showed a ready fancy. Oh, to be sure, they must get to work together on those scenarios.

"I shall prefer it to carpentering," said André-Louis.

Nevertheless he had to go back to it that afternoon, and to labour strenuously until four o'clock, when at last the autocratic Binet announced himself satisfied with the preparations, and proceeded, again with the help of André-Louis, to prepare the lights, which were supplied partly by tallow candles and partly by lamps burning fish-oil.

At five o'clock that evening the three knocks were sounded, and the curtain rose on *The Heartless Father*.

Among the duties inherited by André-Louis from the departed Félicien whom he replaced, was that of doorkeeper. This duty he discharged dressed in a Polichinelle costume, and wearing a pasteboard nose. It was an arrangement mutually agreeable to M. Binet and himself. M. Binet—who had taken the further precaution of retaining André-Louis' own garments—was thereby protected against the risk of his latest recruit absconding with the takings. André-Louis, without illusions on the score of Pantaloon's real object, agreed to it willingly enough, since it protected him from the chance of recognition by any acquaintance who might possibly be in Guichen.

The performance was in every sense unexciting; the audience meagre and unenthusiastic. The benches provided in the front half of the market contained some twenty-seven persons: eleven at twenty *sous* a head and sixteen at twelve. Behind these stood a rabble of some thirty others at six *sous* apiece. Thus the gross takings were two *louis*, ten *livres*, and two *sous*. By the time M.

Binet had paid for the use of the market, his lights, and the expenses of his company at the inn over Sunday, there was not likely to be very much left towards the wages of his players. It is not surprising, therefore, that M. Binet's bonhomie should have been a trifle overcast that evening.

"And what do you think of it?" he asked André-Louis, as they were walking back to the inn after the performance.

"Possibly it could have been worse; probably it could not," said he.

In sheer amazement M. Binet checked in his stride, and turned to look at his companion.

"Huh!" said he. "Dieu de Dieu! But you are frank."

"An unpopular form of service among fools, I know."

"Well, I am not a fool," said Binet.

"That is why I am frank. I pay you the compliment of assuming intelligence in you, M. Binet."

"Oh, you do?" quoth M. Binet. "And who the devil are you to assume anything? Your assumptions are presumptuous, sir." And with that he lapsed into silence and the gloomy business of mentally casting up his accounts.

But at table over supper a half-hour later he revived the topic.

"Our latest recruit, this excellent M. Parvissimus," he announced, "has the impudence to tell me that possibly our comedy could have been worse, but that probably it could not." And he blew out his great round cheeks to invite a laugh at the expense of that foolish critic.

"That's bad," said the swarthy and sardonic Polichinelle. He was grave as Rhadamanthus pronouncing judgment. "That's bad. But what is infinitely worse is that the audience had the impudence to be of the same mind."

"An ignorant pack of clods," sneered Léandre, with a toss of his handsome head.

"You are wrong," quoth Harlequin. "You were born for love, my dear, not criticism."

Léandre—a dull dog, as you will have conceived—looked contemptuously down upon the little man. "And you, what were you born for?" he wondered.

"Nobody knows," was the candid admission. "Nor yet why. It is the case of many of us, my dear, believe me."

"But why"—M. Binet took him up, and thus spoilt the beginnings of a very pretty quarrel—"why do you say that Léandre is wrong?"

"To be general, because he is always wrong. To be particular, because I judge the audience of Guichen to be too sophisticated for *The Heartless Father*."

"You would put it more happily," interposed André-Louis—who was the cause of this discussion—"if you said that *The Heartless Father* is too unsophisticated for the audience of Guichen."

"Why, what's the difference?" asked Léandre.

"I didn't imply a difference. I merely suggested that it is a happier way to express the fact."

"The gentleman is being subtle," sneered Binet.

"Why happier?" Harlequin demanded.

"Because it is easier to bring *The Heartless Father* to the sophistication of the Guichen audience, than the Guichen audience to the unsophistication of *The Heartless Father*."

"Let me think it out," groaned Polichinelle, and he took his head in his hands.

But from the tail of the table André-Louis was challenged by Climène who sat there between Columbine and Madame.

"You would alter the comedy, would you, M. Parvissimus?" she cried.

He turned to parry her malice.

"I would suggest that it be altered," he corrected, inclining his head.

"And how would you alter it, monsieur?"

"I? Oh, for the better."

"But of course!" She was sleekest sarcasm. "And how would you do it?"

"Aye, tell us that," roared M. Binet, and added: "Silence, I pray you, gentlemen and ladies. Silence for M. Parvissimus."

André-Louis looked from father to daughter, and smiled. "Pardi!" said he. "I am between bludgeon and dagger. If I escape with my life, I shall be fortunate. Why, then, since you pin me to the very wall, I'll tell you what I should do. I should go back to the original and help myself more freely from it."

"The original?" questioned M. Binet—the author.

"It is called, I believe, *Monsieur de Pourceaugnac,* and was written by Molière."

Somebody tittered, but that somebody was not M. Binet. He had been touched on the raw, and the look in his little eyes betrayed the fact that his bonhomme exterior covered anything but a bonhomme.

"You charge me with plagiarism," he said at last; "with filching the ideas of Molière."

"There is always, of course," said André-Louis, unruffled, "the alternative possibility of two great minds working upon parallel lines."

M. Binet studied the young man attentively a moment. He found him bland and inscrutable, and decided to pin him down.

"Then you do not imply that I have been stealing from Molière?"

"I advise you to do so, monsieur," was the disconcerting reply.

M. Binet was shocked.

"You advise me to do so! You advise me, me, Antoine Binet, to turn thief at my age!"

"He is outrageous," said mademoiselle, indignantly.

"Outrageous is the word. I thank you for it, my dear. I take you on trust, sir. You sit at my table, you have the honour to be included in my company, and to my face you have the audacity to advise me to become a thief—the worst kind of thief that is conceivable, a thief of spiritual things, a thief of ideas! It is insufferable, intolerable! I have been, I fear, deeply mistaken in you, monsieur; just as you appear to have been mistaken in me. I am not the scoundrel you suppose me, sir, and I will not number in my company a man who dares to suggest that I should become one. Outrageous!"

He was very angry. His voice boomed through the little room, and the company sat hushed and something scared, their eyes upon André-Louis, who was the only one entirely unmoved by this outburst of virtuous indignation.

"You realize, monsieur," he said, very quietly, "that you are insulting the memory of the illustrious dead?"

"Eh?" said Binet.

André-Louis developed his sophistries.

"You insult the memory of Molière, the greatest ornament of our stage, one of the greatest ornaments of our nation, when you suggest that there is vileness in doing that which he never hesitated to do, which no great author yet has hesitated to do. You cannot suppose that Molière ever troubled himself to be original in the matter of ideas. You cannot suppose that the stories he tells in his plays have never been told before. They were culled, as you very well know—though you seem momentarily to have forgotten it, and it is therefore necessary that I should remind you—they were culled, many of them, from the Italian authors, who themselves had culled them Heaven alone knows where. Molière took those old stories and retold them in his own language. That is precisely what I am suggesting that you should do. Your company is a company of improvisers. You supply the dialogue as you proceed, which is rather more than Molière ever attempted. You may, if you prefer it—though it would seem to me to be yielding to an excess of scruple—go straight to Boccaccio or Sacchetti. But even then you cannot be sure that you have reached the sources."

André-Louis came off with flying colours after that. You see what a debater was lost in him; how nimble he was in the art of making white look black. The company was impressed, and no one more that M. Binet, who found himself supplied with a crushing argument against those who in future might tax him with the impudent plagiarisms which he undoubtedly perpetrated. He retired in the best order he could from the position he had taken up at the outset.

"So that you think," he said, at the end of a long outburst of agreement, "you think that our story of *The Heartless Father* could be enriched by dipping into *Monsieur de Pourceaugnac*, to which I confess upon reflection that it may present certain superficial resemblances?"

"I do; most certainly I do—always provided that you do so judiciously. Times have changed since Molière."

It was as a consequence of this that Binet retired soon after, taking André-Louis with him. The pair sat together late that night, and were again in close communion throughout the whole of Sunday morning.

After dinner M. Binet read to the assembled company the amended and amplified *canevas* of *The Heartless Father*, which, acting upon the advice of M. Parvissimus, he had been at great pains to prepare. The company had few doubts as to the real authorship before he began to read; none at all when he had read. There was a verve, a grip about this story; and, what was more, those of them who knew their Molière realized that far from approaching the original more closely, this *canevas* had drawn farther away from it. Molière's original part—the title rôle—had dwindled into insignificance, to the great disgust of Polichinelle, to whom it fell. But the other parts had all been built up into importance, with the exception of Léandre, who remained as before. The two great rôles were now Scaramouche, in the character of the intriguing Sbrigandini, and Pantaloon the father. There was, too, a comical part for Rhodomont, as the roaring bully hired by Polichinelle to cut Léandre into ribbons. And in view of the importance now of Scaramouche, the play had been rechristened *Figaro-Scaramouche*.

This last had not been without a deal of opposition from M.

Binet. But his relentless collaborator, who was in reality the real author—drawing shamelessly, but practically at last upon his great store of reading—had overborne him.

"You must move with the times, monsieur. In Paris Beaumarchais is the rage. *Figaro* is known today throughout the world. Let us borrow a little of his glory. It will draw the people in. They will come to see half a *Figaro* when they will not come to see a dozen *Heartless Fathers*. Therefore let us cast the mantle of Figaro upon some one, and proclaim it in our title."

"But as I am the head of the company . . ." began M. Binet, weakly.

"If you will be blind to your interests, you will presently be a head without a body. And what use is that? Can the shoulders of Pantaloon carry the mantle of Figaro? You laugh. Of course you laugh. The notion is absurd. The proper person for the mantle of Figaro is Scaramouche, who is naturally Figaro's twin-brother."

Thus tyrannized, the tyrant Binet gave way, comforted by the reflection that if he understood anything at all about the theatre, he had for fifteen *livres* a month acquired something that would presently be earning him as many *louis*.

The company's reception of the *canevas* now confirmed him, if we except Polichinelle, who, annoyed at having lost half his part in the alterations, declared the new scenario fatuous.

"Ah! You call my work fatuous, do you?" M. Binet hectored him.

"Your work?" said Polichinelle, to add with his tongue in his cheek: "Ah, pardon. I had not realized that you were the author."

"Then realize it now."

"You were very close with M. Parvissimus over this authorship," said Polichinelle, with impudent suggestiveness.

"And what if I was? What do you imply?"

"That you took him to cut quills for you, of course."

"I'll cut your ears for you if you're not civil," stormed the infuriated Binet.

Polichinelle got up slowly, and stretched himself.

"Dieu de Dieu!" said he. "If Pantaloon is to play Rhodomont, I think I'll leave you. He is not amusing in the part." And he swaggered out before M. Binet had recovered from his speechlessness.

CHAPTER IV

Exit
Monsieur Parvissimus

At four o'clock on Monday afternoon the curtain rose on *Figaro-Scaramouche* to an audience that filled three quarters of the market-hall. M. Binet attributed this good attendance to the influx of people to Guichen for the fair, and to the magnificent parade of his company through the streets of the township at the busiest time of the day. André-Louis attributed it entirely to the title. It was the *Figaro* touch that had fetched in the better-class bourgeoisie, which filled more than half of the twenty-*sous* places and three quarters of the twelve-*sous* seats. The lure had drawn them. Whether it was to continue to do so would depend upon the manner in which the *canevas* over which he had laboured to the glory of Binet was interpreted by the company. Of the merits of the *canevas* itself he had no doubt. The authors upon whom he had drawn for the elements of it were sound, and he had taken of their best, which he claimed to be no more than the justice due to them.

The company excelled itself. The audience followed with relish the sly intriguings of Scaramouche, delighted in the beauty and freshness of Climène, was moved almost to tears by the hard fate which through four long acts kept her from the hungering arms of the so beautiful Léandre, howled its delight over the ignominy of Pantaloon, the buffooneries of his sprightly lackey Harlequin, and the thrasonical strut and bellowing fierceness of the cowardly Rhodomont.

The success of the Binet troupe in Guichen was assured. That night the company drank Burgundy at M. Binet's expense. The takings reached the sum of eight *louis*, which was as good business as M. Binet had ever done in all his career. He was very pleased. Gratification rose like steam from his fat body. He even condescended so far as to attribute a share of the credit for the success to M. Parvissimus.

"His suggestion," he was careful to say, by way of properly delimiting that share, "was most valuable, as I perceived at the time."

"And his cutting of quills," growled Polichinelle. "Don't forget that. It is most important to have by you a man who understands how to cut a quill, as I shall remember when I turn author."

But not even that gibe could stir M. Binet out of his lethargy of content.

On Tuesday the success was repeated artistically and augmented financially. Ten *louis* and seven *livres* was the enormous sum that André-Louis, the doorkeeper, counted over to M. Binet after the performance. Never yet had M. Binet made so much money in one evening—and a miserable little village like Guichen was certainly the last place in which he would have expected this windfall.

"Ah, but Guichen in time of fair," André-Louis reminded him. "There are people here from as far as Nantes and Rennes to buy and sell. Tomorrow, being the last day of the fair, the crowds will be greater than ever. We should better this evening's receipts."

"Better them? I shall be quite satisfied if we do as well, my friend."

"You can depend upon that," André-Louis assured him. "Are we to have Burgundy?"

And then the tragedy occurred. It announced itself in a succession of bumps and thuds, culminating in a crash outside the door that brought them all to their feet in alarm.

Pierrot sprang to open, and beheld the tumbled body of a man lying at the foot of the stairs. It emitted groans, therefore it was alive. Pierrot went forward to turn it over, and disclosed the fact that the body wore the wizened face of Scaramouche, a grimacing, groaning, twitching Scaramouche.

The whole company, pressing after Pierrot, abandoned itself to laughter.

"I always said you should change parts with me," cried Harlequin. "You're such an excellent tumbler. Have you been practising?"

"Fool!" Scaramouche snapped. "Must you be laughing when I've all but broken my neck?"

"You are right. We ought to be weeping because you didn't break it. Come, man, get up," and he held out a hand to the prostrate rogue.

Scaramouche took the hand, clutched it, heaved himself from the ground, then with a scream dropped back again.

"My foot!" he complained.

Binet rolled through the group of players, scattering them to right and left. Apprehension had been quick to seize him. Fate had played him such tricks before.

"What ails your foot?" quoth he, sourly.

"It's broken, I think," Scaramouche complained.

"Broken? Bah! Get up, man." He caught him under the arm-pits and hauled him up.

Scaramouche came howling to one foot; the other doubled under him when he attempted to set it down, and he must have collapsed again but that Binet supported him. He filled the place with his plaint, whilst Binet swore amazingly and variedly.

"Must you bellow like a calf, you fool? Be quiet. A chair here, some one."

A chair was thrust forward. He crushed Scaramouche down into it.

"Let us look at this foot of yours."

Heedless of Scaramouche's howls of pain, he swept away shoe and stocking.

"What ails it?" he asked, staring. "Nothing that I can see." He seized it, heel in one hand, instep in the other, and gyrated it. Scaramouche screamed in agony, until Climène caught Binet's arm and made him stop.

"My God, have you no feelings?" she reproved her father. "The lad has hurt his foot. Must you torture him? Will that cure it?"

"Hurt his foot!" said Binet. "I can see nothing the matter

with his foot—nothing to justify all this uproar. He has bruised it, maybe . . ."

"A man with a bruised foot doesn't scream like that," said Madame over Climène's shoulder. "Perhaps he has dislocated it."

"That is what I fear," whimpered Scaramouche. Binet heaved himself up in disgust. "Take him to bed," he bade them, "and fetch a doctor to see him."

It was done, and the doctor came. Having seen the patient, he reported that nothing very serious had happened, but that in falling he had evidently sprained his foot a little. A few days' rest and all would be well.

"A few days!" cried Binet. "God of God! Do you mean that he can't walk?"

"It would be unwise, indeed impossible for more than a few steps."

M. Binet paid the doctor's fee, and sat down to think. He filled himself a glass of Burgundy, tossed it off without a word, and sat thereafter staring into the empty glass.

"It is of course the sort of thing that must always be happening to me," he grumbled to no one in particular. The members of the company were all standing in silence before him, sharing his dismay. "I might have known that this—or something like it—would occur to spoil the first vein of luck that I have found in years. Ah, well, it is finished. Tomorrow we pack and depart. The best day of the fair, on the crest of the wave of our success— a good fifteen *louis* to be taken, and this happens! God of God!"

"Do you mean to abandon tomorrow's performance?"

All turned to stare with Binet at André-Louis.

"Are we to play *Figaro-Scaramouche* without Scaramouche?"

asked Binet, sneering.

"Of course not." André-Louis came forward. "But surely some rearrangement of the parts is possible. For instance, there is a fine actor in Polichinelle."

Polichinelle swept him a bow. "Overwhelmed," said he, ever sardonic.

"But he has a part of his own," objected Binet.

"A small part, which Pasquariel could play."

"And who will play Pasquariel?"

"Nobody. We delete it. The play need not suffer."

"He thinks of everything," sneered Polichinelle. "What a man!"

But Binet was far from agreement. "Are you suggesting that Polichinelle should play Scaramouche?" he asked, incredulously.

"Why not? He is able enough!"

"Overwhelmed again," interjected Polichinelle.

"Play Scaramouche with that figure?" Binet heaved himself up to point a denunciatory finger at Polichinelle's sturdy, thick-set shortness.

"For lack of a better," said André-Louis.

"Overwhelmed more than ever." Polichinelle's bow was superb this time. "Faith, I think I'll take the air to cool me after so much blushing."

"Go to the devil," Binet flung at him.

"Better and better." Polichinelle made for the door. On the threshold he halted and struck an attitude. "Understand me, Binet. I do not now play Scaramouche in any circumstances whatever." And he went out. On the whole, it was a very dignified exit.

André-Louis shrugged, threw out his arms, and let them fall to his sides again. "You have ruined everything," he told M. Binet. "The matter could easily have been arranged. Well, well, it is you are master here; and since you want us to pack and be off, that is what we will do, I suppose."

He went out, too. M. Binet stood in thought a moment, then followed him, his little eyes very cunning. He caught him up in the doorway. "Let us take a walk together, M. Parvissimus," said he, very affably.

He thrust his arm through André-Louis', and led him out into the street, where there was still considerable movement. Past the booths that ranged about the market they went, and down the hill towards the bridge.

"I don't think we shall pack tomorrow," said M. Binet, presently. "In fact, we shall play tomorrow night."

"Not if I know Polichinelle. You have . . ."

"I am not thinking of Polichinelle."

"Of whom, then?"

"Of yourself."

"I am flattered, sir. And in what capacity are you thinking of me?" There was something too sleek and oily in Binet's voice for André-Louis' taste.

"I am thinking of you in the part of Scaramouche."

"Day-dreams," said André-Louis. "You are amusing yourself, of course."

"Not in the least. I am quite serious."

"But I am not an actor."

"You told me that you could be."

"Oh, upon occasion . . . a small part, perhaps . . ."

"Well, here is a big part—the chance to arrive at a single stride. How many men have had such a chance?"

"It is a chance I do not covet, M. Binet. Shall we change the subject?" He was very frosty, as much perhaps because he scented in M. Binet's manner something that was vaguely menacing as for any other reason.

"We'll change the subject when I please," said M. Binet, allowing a glimpse of steel to glimmer through the silk of him. "Tomorrow night you play Scaramouche. You are ready enough in your wits, your figure is ideal, and you have just the kind of mordant humour for the part. You should be a great success."

"It is much more likely that I should be an egregious failure."

"That won't matter," said Binet, cynically, and explained himself. "The failure will be personal to yourself. The receipts will be safe by then."

"Much obliged," said André-Louis.

"We should take fifteen *louis* tomorrow night."

"It is unfortunate that you are without a Scaramouche," said André-Louis.

"It is fortunate that I have one, M. Parvissimus."

André-Louis disengaged his arm. "I begin to find you tiresome," said he. "I think I will return."

"A moment, M. Parvissimus. If I am to lose that fifteen *louis*, you'll not take it amiss that I compensate myself in other ways?"

"That is your own concern, M. Binet."

"Pardon, M. Parvissimus. It may possibly be also yours." Binet took his arm again. "Do me the kindness to step across the street with me. Just as far as the post-office there. I have something to show you."

André-Louis went. Before they reached that sheet of paper nailed upon the door, he knew exactly what it would say. And in effect it was, as he had supposed, that twenty *louis* would be paid for information leading to the apprehension of one André-Louis Moreau, lawyer of Gavrillac, who was wanted by the King's Lieutenant in Rennes upon a charge of sedition.

M. Binet watched him whilst he read. Their arms were linked, and Binet's grip was firm and powerful.

"Now, my friend," said he, "will you be M. Parvissimus and play Scaramouche tomorrow, or will you be André-Louis Moreau of Gavrillac and go to Rennes to satisfy the King's Lieutenant?"

"And if it should happen that you are mistaken?" quoth André-Louis, his face a mask.

"I'll take the risk of that," leered M. Binet. "You mentioned, I think, that you were a lawyer. An indiscretion, my dear. It is unlikely that two lawyers will be in hiding at the same time in the same district. You see it is not really clever of me. Well, M. André-Louis Moreau, lawyer of Gavrillac, what is it to be?"

"We will talk it over as we walk back," said André-Louis.

"What is there to talk over?"

"One or two things, I think. I must know where I stand. Come, sir, if you please."

"Very well," said M. Binet, and they turned up the street again, but M. Binet maintained a firm hold of his young friend's arm, and kept himself on the alert for any tricks that the young gentleman might be disposed to play. It was an unnecessary precaution. André-Louis was not the man to waste his energy futilely. He knew that in bodily strength he was no match at all for the heavy and powerful Pantaloon.

158

"If I yield to your most eloquent and seductive persuasions, M. Binet," said he, sweetly, "what guarantee do you give me that you will not sell me for twenty louis after I shall have served your turn?"

"You have my word of honour for that." M. Binet was emphatic.

André-Louis laughed. "Oh, we are to talk of honour, are we? Really, M. Binet? It is clear you think me a fool."

In the dark he did not see the flush that leapt to M. Binet's round face. It was some moments before he replied.

"Perhaps you are right," he growled. "What guarantee do you want?"

"I do not know what guarantee you can possibly give."

"I have said that I will keep faith with you."

"Until you find it more profitable to sell me."

"You have it in your power to make it more profitable always for me to keep faith with you. It is due to you that we have done so well in Guichen. Oh, I admit it frankly."

"In private," said André-Louis.

M. Binet left the sarcasm unheeded.

"What you have done for us here with *Figaro-Scaramouche*, you can do elsewhere with other things. Naturally, I shall not want to lose you. That is your guarantee."

"Yet tonight you would sell me for twenty *louis*."

"Because—name of God!—you enrage me by refusing me a service well within your powers. Don't you think, had I been entirely the rogue you think me, I could have sold you on Saturday last? I want you to understand me, my dear Parvissimus."

"I beg that you'll not apologize. You would be more tiresome

159

than ever."

"Of course you will be gibing. You never miss a chance to gibe. It'll bring you trouble before you're done with life. Come; here we are back at the inn, and you have not yet given me your decision."

André-Louis looked at him. "I must yield, of course. I can't help myself."

M. Binet released his arm at last, and slapped him heartily upon the back. "Well declared, my lad. You'll never regret it. If I know anything of the theatre, I know that you have made the great decision of your life. Tomorrow night you'll thank me."

André-Louis shrugged, and stepped out ahead towards the inn. But M. Binet called him back.

"M. Parvissimus!"

He turned. There stood the man's great bulk, the moonlight beating down upon that round fat face of his, and he was holding out his hand.

"M. Parvissimus, no rancour. It is a thing I do not admit into my life. You will shake hands with me, and we will forget all this."

André-Louis considered him a moment with disgust. He was growing angry. Then, realizing this, he conceived himself ridiculous, almost as ridiculous as that sly, scoundrelly Pantaloon. He laughed and took the outstretched hand.

"No rancour?" M. Binet insisted.

"Oh, no rancour," said André-Louis.

CHAPTER V

Enter Scaramouche

Dressed in the close-fitting suit of a bygone age, all black, from flat velvet cap to rosetted shoes, his face whitened and a slight up-curled moustache glued to his upper lip, a small-sword at his side and a guitar slung behind him, Scaramouche surveyed himself in a mirror, and was disposed to be sardonic—which was the proper mood for the part.

He reflected that his life, which until lately had been of a stagnant, contemplative quality, had suddenly become excessively active. In the course of one week he had been lawyer, mob-orator, outlaw, property-man, and finally buffoon. Last Wednesday he had been engaged in moving an audience of Rennes to anger; on this Wednesday he was to move an audience of Guichen to mirth. Then he had been concerned to draw tears; today it was his business to provoke laughter. There was a difference, and yet there was a parallel. Then as now he had been a comedian; and the part

161

that he had played then was, when you came to think of it, akin to the part he was to play this evening. For what had he been at Rennes but a sort of Scaramouche—the little skirmisher, the astute intriguer, scattering the seed of trouble with a sly hand? The only difference lay in the fact that today he went forth under the name that properly described his type, whereas last week he had been disguised as a respectable young provincial attorney.

He bowed to his reflection in the mirror.

"Buffoon!" he apostrophized it. "At last you have found yourself. At last you have come into your heritage. You should be a great success."

Hearing his new name called out by M. Binet, he went below to find the company assembled, and waiting in the entrance corridor of the inn.

He was, of course, an object of great interest to all the company. Most critically was he conned by M. Binet and mademoiselle; by the former with gravely searching eyes, by the latter with a curl of scornful lip.

"You'll do," M. Binet commended his make-up. "At least you look the part."

"Unfortunately men are not always what they look," said Climène, acidly.

"That is a truth that does not at present apply to me," said André-Louis. "For it is the first time in my life that I look what I am."

Mademoiselle curled her lip a little further, and turned her shoulder to him. But the others thought him very witty—probably because he was obscure. Columbine encouraged him with a friendly smile that displayed her large white teeth, and M. Binet swore yet once again that he would be a great success, since he threw himself with such spirit into the undertaking. Then in a voice that for the moment he appeared to have borrowed from the roaring captain, M. Binet marshalled them for the short parade across to the market-hall.

The new Scaramouche fell into place beside Rhodomont. The old one, hobbling on a crutch, had departed an hour ago to take the place of doorkeeper, vacated of necessity by André-Louis, so that the exchange between those two was a complete one.

Headed by Polichinelle banging his great drum and Pierrot blowing his trumpet, they set out, and were duly passed in review by the ragamuffins drawn up in files to enjoy so much of the spectacle as was to be obtained for nothing.

Ten minutes later the three knocks sounded, and the curtains were drawn aside to reveal a battered set that was partly garden, partly forest, in which Climène feverishly looked for the coming of Léandre. In the wings stood the beautiful, melancholy lover, awaiting his cue, and immediately behind him the unfledged Scaramouche, who was anon to follow him.

André-Louis was assailed with nausea in that dread moment. He attempted to take a lightning mental review of the first act of this scenario of which he was himself the author-in-chief; but found his mind a complete blank. With the perspiration starting from his skin, he stepped back to the wall, where above a dim lantern was pasted a sheet bearing the brief outline of the piece. He was still studying it, when his arm was clutched, and he was pulled violently towards the wings. He had a glimpse of Pantaloon's grotesque face, its eyes blazing, and he caught a raucous growl:

"Climène has spoken your cue three times already."

Before he realized it, he had been bundled on to the stage, and stood there foolishly, blinking in the glare of the footlights, with their tin reflectors. So utterly foolish and bewildered did he look that volley upon volley of laughter welcomed him from the audience, which this evening packed the hall from end to end. Trembling a little, his bewilderment at first increasing, he stood there to receive that rolling tribute to his absurdity. Climène was eyeing him with expectant mockery, savouring in advance his humiliation; Léandre regarded him in consternation, whilst behind the scenes, M. Binet was dancing in fury.

"Name of a name," he groaned to the rather scared members of the company assembled there, "what will happen when they discover that he isn't acting?"

But they never did discover it. Scaramouche's bewildered paralysis lasted but a few seconds. He realized that he was being laughed at, and remembered that his Scaramouche was a creature to be laughed with, and not at. He must save the situation; twist it to his own advantage as best he could. And now his real bewilderment and terror was succeeded by acted bewilderment and terror far more marked, but not quite so funny. He contrived to make it clearly appear that his terror was of some one off the stage. He took cover behind a painted shrub, and thence, the laughter at last beginning to subside, he addressed himself to Clemène and Léandre.

"Forgive me, beautiful lady, if the abrupt manner of my entrance startled you. The truth is that I have never been the same since that last affair of mine with Almaviva. My heart is not what it used to be. Down there at the end of the lane I came face to face with an elderly gentleman carrying a heavy cudgel, and the horrible thought entered my mind that it might be your father, and that our little stratagem to get you safely married might already have been betrayed to him. I think it was the cudgel put such a notion in my head. Not that I am afraid. I am not really afraid of anything. But I could not help reflecting that, if it should really have been your father, and he had broken my head with his cudgel, your hopes would have perished with me. For without me, what should you have done, my poor children?"

A ripple of laughter from the audience had been steadily enheartening him, and helping him to recover his natural impudence. It was clear they found him comical. They were to find him far more comical than ever he had intended, and this was largely due to a fortuitous circumstance upon which he had insufficiently reckoned. The fear of recognition by some one from Gavrillac or Rennes had been strong upon him. His face was sufficiently made up to baffle recognition; but there remained his voice. To dissemble this he had availed himself of the fact that Figaro was a Spaniard. He had known a Spaniard at Louis le Grand who spoke a fluent but most extraordinary French, with a grotesque excess of sibilant sounds. It was an accent that he had often imitated, as youths will imitate characteristics that excite their mirth. Opportunely he had bethought him of that Spanish student, and it was upon his speech that tonight he modelled his own. The audience of Guichen found it as laughable on his lips as he and his fellows had found it formerly on the lips of that derided Spaniard.

Meanwhile, behind the scenes, Binet—listening to that glib impromptu of which the scenario gave no indication—had recovered from his fears.

"Dieu de Dieu!" he whispered, grinning. "Did he do it, then, on purpose?"

It seemed to him impossible that a man who had been so terror-stricken as he had fancied André-Louis, could have recovered his wits so quickly and completely. Yet the doubt remained.

To resolve it after the curtain had fallen upon a first act that had gone with a verve unrivalled until this hour in the annals of the company, borne almost entirely upon the slim shoulders of the new Scaramouche, M. Binet bluntly questioned him.

They were standing in the space that did duty as greenroom, the company all assembled there, showering congratulations upon their new recruit. Scaramouche, a little exalted at the moment by his success, however trivial he might consider it tomorrow, took then a full revenge upon Climène for the malicious satisfaction with which she had regarded his momentary blank terror.

"I do not wonder that you ask," said he. "Faith, I should have warned you that I intended to do my best from the start to put the audience in a good humour with me. Mademoiselle very nearly ruined everything by refusing to reflect any of my terror. She was not even startled. Another time, mademoiselle, I shall give you full warning of my every intention."

She crimsoned under her grease-paint. But before she could find an answer of sufficient venom, her father was rating her soundly for her stupidity—the more soundly because himself he had been deceived by Scaramouche's supreme acting.

Scaramouche's success in the first act was more than confirmed as the performance proceeded. Completely master of himself by now, and stimulated as only success can stimulate, he warmed to his work. Impudent, alert, sly, graceful, he incarnated the very ideal of Scaramouche, and he helped out his own native wit by many a remembered line from Beaumarchais, thereby persuading the better informed among the audience that here indeed was something of the real Figaro, and bringing them, as it were, into touch with the great world of the capital.

When at last the curtain fell for the last time, it was Scaramouche who shared with Climène the honours of the evening, his name that was coupled with hers in the calls that summoned them before the curtains.

As they stepped back, and the curtains screened them again from the departing audience, M. Binet approached them, rubbing his fat hands softly together. This runagate young lawyer, whom chance had blown into his company, had evidently been sent by Fate to make his fortune for him. The sudden success at Guichen, hitherto unrivalled, should be repeated and augmented elsewhere. There would be no more sleeping under hedges and tightening of belts. Adversity was behind him. He placed a hand upon Scaramouche's shoulder, and surveyed him with a smile whose oiliness not even his red paint and colossal false nose could dissemble.

"And what have you to say to me now?" he asked him. "Was I wrong when I assured you that you would succeed? Do you think I have followed my fortunes in the theatre for a lifetime without knowing a born actor when I see one? You are my discovery, Scaramouche. I have discovered you to yourself. I have set your feet upon the road to fame and fortune. I await your thanks."

Scaramouche laughed at him, and his laugh was not altogether pleasant.

"Always Pantaloon!" said he.

The great countenance became overcast. "I see that you do not yet forgive me the little stratagem by which I forced you to do justice to yourself. Ungrateful dog! As if I could have had any purpose but to make you; and I have done so. Continue as you have begun, and you will end in Paris. You may yet tread the stage of the Comédie Française, the rival of Talma, Fleury, and Dugazon. When that happens to you perhaps you will feel the gratitude that is due to old Binet, for you will owe it all to this soft-hearted old fool."

"If you were as good an actor on the stage as you are in private," said Scaramouche, "you would yourself have won to the Comédie Française long since. But I bear no rancour, M. Binet." He laughed, and put out his hand.

Binet fell upon it and wrung it heartily.

"That, at least, is something," he declared. "My boy, I have great plans for you—for us. Tomorrow we go to Maure; there is a fair there to the end of this week. Then on Monday we take our chances at Pipriac, and after that we must consider. It may be that I am about to realize the dream of my life. There must have been upwards of fifteen *louis* taken tonight. Where the devil is that rascal Cordemais?"

Cordemais was the name of the original Scaramouche, who had so unfortunately twisted his ankle. That Binet should refer to him by his secular designation was a sign that in the Binet company at least he had fallen for ever from the lofty eminence of Scaramouche.

"Let us go and find him, and then we'll away to the inn and

168

crack a bottle of the best Burgundy, perhaps two bottles."

But Cordemais was not readily to be found. None of the company had seen him since the close of the performance. M. Binet went round to the entrance. Cordemais was not there. At first he was annoyed; then as he continued in vain to bawl the fellow's name, he began to grow uneasy; lastly, when Polichinelle, who was with them, discovered Cordemais' crutch standing discarded behind the door, M. Binet became alarmed. A dreadful suspicion entered his mind. He grew visibly pale under his paint.

"But this evening he couldn't walk without the crutch!" he exclaimed. "How then does he come to leave it there and take himself off?"

"Perhaps he has gone on to the inn," suggested someone.

"But he couldn't walk without his crutch," M. Binet insisted.

Nevertheless, since clearly he was not anywhere about the market-hall, to the inn they all trooped, and deafened the landlady with their inquiries.

"Oh, yes, M. Cordemais came in some time ago."

"Where is he now?"

"He went away again at once. He just came for his bag."

"For his bag!" Binet was on the point of an apoplexy. "How long ago was that?"

She glanced at the timepiece on the overmantel. "It would be about half an hour ago. It was a few minutes before the Rennes diligence passed through."

"The Rennes diligence!" M. Binet was almost inarticulate. "Could he . . . could he walk?" he asked, on a note of terrible anxiety.

"Walk? He ran like a hare when he left the inn. I thought,

myself, that his agility was suspicious, seeing how lame he had been since he fell downstairs yesterday. Is anything wrong?"

M. Binet had collapsed into a chair. He took his head in his hands, and groaned.

"The scoundrel was shamming all the time!" exclaimed Climène. "His fall downstairs was a trick. He was playing for this. He has swindled us."

"Fifteen *louis* at least—perhaps sixteen!" said M. Binet. "Oh, the heartless blackguard! To swindle me who have been as a father to him—and to swindle me in such a moment."

From the ranks of the silent, awe-stricken company, each member of which was wondering by how much of the loss his own meagre pay would be mulcted, there came a splutter of laughter.

M. Binet glared with blood-injected eyes.

"Who laughs?" he roared. "What heartless wretch has the audacity to laugh at my misfortune?"

André-Louis, still in the sable glories of Scaramouche, stood forward. He was laughing still.

"It is you, is it? You may laugh on another note, my friend, if I choose a way to recoup myself that I know of."

"Dullard!" Scaramouche scorned him. "Rabbit-brained elephant! What if Cordemais has gone with fifteen *louis*? Hasn't he left you something worth twenty times as much?"

M. Binet gaped uncomprehending.

"You are between two wines, I think. You've been drinking," he concluded.

"So I have—at the fountain of Thalia. Oh, don't you see? Don't you see the treasure that Cordemais has left behind him?"

"What has he left?"

"A unique idea for the groundwork of a scenario. It unfolds itself all before me. I'll borrow part of the title from Molière. We'll call it *Les Fourberies de Scaramouche,* and if we don't leave the audiences of Maure and Pipriac with sides aching from laughter I'll play the dullard Pantaloon in future."

Polichinelle smacked fist into palm. "Superb!" he said, fiercely. "To cull fortune from misfortune, to turn loss into profit, that is to have genius."

Scaramouche made a leg. "Polichinelle, you are a fellow after my own heart. I love a man who can discern my merit. If Pantaloon had half your wit, we should have Burgundy tonight in spite of the flight of Cordemais."

"Burgundy?" roared M. Binet, and before he could get farther Harlequin had clapped his hands together.

"That is the spirit, M. Binet. You heard him, landlady. He called for Burgundy."

"I called for nothing of the kind."

"But you heard him, dear madame. We all heard him."

The others made chorus, whilst Scaramouche smiled at him, and patted his shoulder.

"Up, man, a little courage. Did you not say that fortune awaits us? And have we not now the wherewithal to constrain fortune? Burgundy, then, to . . . to toast *Les Fourberies de Scaramouche.*"

And M. Binet, who was not blind to the force of the idea, yielded, took courage, and got drunk with the rest.

CHAPTER VI

Climène

Diligent search among the many scenarios of the improvisers which have survived their day, has failed to bring to light the scenario of *Les Fourberies de Scaramouche,* upon which we are told the fortunes of the Binet troupe came to be soundly established. They played it for the first time at Maure in the following week, with André-Louis—who was known by now as Scaramouche to all the company, and to the public alike—in the title-rôle. If he had acquitted himself well as Figaro-Scaramouche, he excelled himself in the new piece, the scenario of which would appear to be very much the better of the two.

After Maure came Pipriac, where four performances were given, two of each of the scenarios that now formed the backbone of the Binet repertoire. In both Scaramouche, who was beginning to find himself, materially improved his performances, so smoothly now did the two pieces run that Scaramouche actually suggested to Binet that after Fougeray, which they were to visit in the following week, they should tempt fortune in a real theatre in the important town of Rédon. The notion terrified Binet at first, but coming to think of it, and his ambition being fanned by André-Louis, he ended by allowing himself to succumb to the temptation.

It seemed to André-Louis in those days that he had found his real métier, and not only was he beginning to like it, but actually to look forward to a career as actor-author that might indeed lead him in the end to that Mecca of all comedians, the Comédie Française. And there were other possibilities. From the writing of skeleton scenarios for improvisers, he might presently pass to writing plays of dialogue, plays in the proper sense of the word, after the manner of Chénier, Églantine, and Beaumarchais.

The fact that he dreamed such dreams shows us how very kindly he had taken to the profession into which Chance and M. Binet between them had conspired to thrust him. That he had real talent both as author and as actor I do not doubt, and I am persuaded that had things fallen out differently he would have won for himself a lasting place among French dramatists, and thus fully have realized that dream of his.

Now, dream though it was, he did not neglect the practical side of it.

"You realize," he told M. Binet, "that I have it in my power to make your fortune for you."

He and Binet were sitting alone together in the parlour of the inn at Pipriac, drinking a very excellent bottle of Volnay. It was on the night after the fourth and last performance there of *Les Fourberies*. The business in Pipriac had been as excellent as in

173

Maure and Guichen. You will have gathered this from the fact that they drank Volnay.

"I will concede it, my dear Scaramouche, so that I may hear the sequel."

"I am disposed to exercise this power if the inducement is sufficient. You will realize that for fifteen *livres* a month a man does not sell such exceptional gifts as mine."

"There is an alternative," said M. Binet, darkly.

"There is no alternative. Don't be a fool, Binet."

Binet sat up as if he had been prodded. Members of his company did not take this tone of direct rebuke with him.

"Anyway, I make you a present of it," Scaramouche pursued, airily. "Exercise it if you please. Step outside and inform the police that they can lay hands upon one André-Louis Moreau. But that will be the end of your fine dreams of going to Rédon, and for the first time in your life playing in a real theatre. Without me, you can't do it, and you know it; and I am not going to Rédon or anywhere else, in fact I am not even going to Fougeray, until we have an equitable arrangement."

"But what heat!" complained Binet, "and all for what? Why must you assume that I have the soul of a usurer? When our little arrangement was made, I had no idea—how could I?—that you would prove as valuable to me as you are? You had but to remind me, my dear Scaramouche. I am a just man. As from today you shall have thirty *livres* a month. See, I double it at once. I am a generous man."

"But you are not ambitious. Now listen to me, a moment."

And he proceeded to unfold a scheme that filled Binet with a paralyzing terror.

"After Rédon, Nantes," he said. "Nantes and the Théâtre Feydau."

M. Binet choked in the act of drinking. The Théâtre Feydau was a sort of provincial Comédie Française. The great Fleury had played there to an audience as critical as any in France. The very thought of Rédon, cherished as it had come to be by M. Binet, gave him at moments a cramp in the stomach, so dangerously ambitious did it seem to him. And Rédon was a puppet-show by comparison with Nantes. Yet this raw lad whom he had picked up by chance three weeks ago, and who in that time had blossomed from a country attorney into author and actor, could talk of Nantes and the Théâtre Feydau without changing colour.

"But why not Paris and the Comédie Française?" wondered M. Binet, with sarcasm, when at last he had got his breath.

"That may come later," says impudence.

"Eh? You've been drinking, my friend."

But André-Louis detailed the plan that had been forming in his mind. Fougeray should be a training-ground for Rédon, and Rédon should be a training-ground for Nantes. They would stay in Rédon as long as Rédon would pay adequately to come and see them, working hard to perfect themselves the while. They would add three or four new players of talent to the company; he would write three or four fresh scenarios, and these should be tested and perfected until the troupe was in possession of at least half a dozen plays upon which they could depend; they would lay out a portion of their profits on better dresses and better scenery, and finally in a couple of months' time, if all went well, they should be ready to make their real bid for fortune at Nantes. It was quite true that distinction was usually demanded of the com-

175

panies appearing at the Feydau, but on the other hand Nantes had not seen a troupe of improvisers for a generation and longer. They would be supplying a novelty to which all Nantes should flock provided that the work were really well done, and Scaramouche undertook—pledged himself—that if matters were left in his own hands, his projected revival of the Commedia dell' Arte in all its glories would exceed whatever expectations the public of Nantes might bring to the theatre.

"We'll talk of Paris after Nantes," he finished, supremely matter-of-fact, "just as we will definitely decide on Nantes after Rédon."

The persuasiveness that could sway a mob ended by sweeping M. Binet off his feet. The prospect which Scaramouche unfolded, if terrifying, was also intoxicating, and as Scaramouche delivered a crushing answer to each weakening objection in a measure as it was advanced, Binet ended by promising to think the matter over.

"Rédon will point the way," said André-Louis, "and I don't doubt which way Rédon will point."

Thus the great adventure of Rédon dwindled to insignificance. Instead of a terrifying undertaking in itself, it became merely a rehearsal for something greater. In his momentary exaltation Binet proposed another bottle of Volnay. Scaramouche waited until the cork was drawn before he continued.

"The thing remains possible," said he then, holding his glass to the light, and speaking casually, "as long as I am with you."

"Agreed, my dear Scaramouche, agreed. Our chance meeting was a fortunate thing for both of us."

"For both of us," said Scaramouche, with stress. "That is as I would have it. So that I do not think you will surrender me just yet to the police."

"As if I could think of such a thing. My dear Scaramouche, you amuse yourself. I beg that you will never, never allude to that little joke of mine again."

"It is forgotten," said André-Louis. "And now for the remainder of my proposal. If I am to become the architect of your fortunes, if I am to build them as I have planned them, I must also and in the same degree become the architect of my own."

"In the same degree?" M. Binet frowned.

"In the same degree. From today, if you please, we will conduct the affairs of this company in a proper manner, and we will keep account-books."

"I am an artist," said M. Binet, with pride. "I am not a merchant."

"There is a business side to your art, and that shall be conducted in the business manner. I have thought it all out for you. You shall not be troubled with details that might hinder the due exercise of your art. All that you have to do is to say yes or no to my proposal."

"Ah? And the proposal?"

"Is that you constitute me your partner, with an equal share in the profits of your company."

Pantaloon's great countenance grew pale, his little eyes widened to their fullest extent as he conned the face of his companion. Then he exploded.

"You are mad, of course, to make me a proposal so monstrous."

"It has its injustices, I admit. But I have provided for them. It would not, for instance, be fair that in addition to all that I am proposing to do for you, I should also play Scaramouche and write your scenarios without any reward outside of the half-profit which would come to me as a partner. Thus before the profits come to be divided, there is a salary to be paid me as actor, and a small sum for each scenario with which I provide the company; that is a matter for mutual agreement. Similarly, you shall be paid a salary as Pantaloon. After those expenses are cleared up, as well as all the other salaries and disbursements, the residue is the profit to be divided equally between us."

It was not, as you can imagine, a proposal that M. Binet would swallow at a draught. He began with a point-blank refusal to consider it.

"In that case, my friend," said Scaramouche, "we part company at once. Tomorrow I shall bid you a reluctant farewell."

Binet fell to raging. He spoke of ingratitude in feeling terms; he even permitted himself another sly allusion to that little jest of his concerning the police, which he had promised never again to mention.

"As to that, you may do as you please. Play the informer, by all means. But consider that you will just as definitely be deprived of my services, and that without me you are nothing—as you were before I joined your company."

M. Binet did not care what the consequences might be. A fig for the consequences! He would teach this impudent young country attorney that M. Binet was not the man to be imposed upon.

Scaramouche rose. "Very well," said he, between indifference and resignation. "As you wish. But before you act, sleep on the matter. In the cold light of morning you may see our two proposals in their proper proportions. Mine spells fortune for both of us. Yours spells ruin for both of us. Goodnight, M. Binet. Heaven help you to a wise decision."

The decision to which M. Binet finally came was, naturally, the only one possible in the face of so firm a resolve as that of André-Louis, who held the trumps. Of course there were further discussions, before all was settled, and M. Binet was brought to an agreement only after an infinity of haggling surprising in one who was an artist and not a man of business. One or two concessions were made by André-Louis; he consented, for instance, to waive his claim to be paid for scenarios, and he also consented that M. Binet should appoint himself a salary that was out of all proportion to his deserts.

Thus in the end the matter was settled, and the announcement duly made to the assembled company. There were, of course, jealousies and resentments. But these were not deep-seated, and they were readily swallowed when it was discovered that under the new arrangement the lot of the entire company was to be materially improved from the point of view of salaries. This was a matter that had met with considerable opposition from M. Binet. But the irresistible Scaramouche swept away all objections.

"If we are to play at the Feydau, you want a company of self-respecting comedians, and not a pack of cringing starvelings. The better we pay them in reason, the more they will earn for us."

Thus was conquered the company's resentment of this too swift promotion of its latest recruit. Cheerfully now—with one exception—they accepted the dominance of Scaramouche, a dominance soon to be so firmly established that M. Binet himself came under it.

The one exception was Climène. Her failure to bring to heel this interesting young stranger, who had almost literally dropped into their midst that morning outside Guichen, had begotten in her a malice which his persistent ignoring of her had been steadily inflaming. She had remonstrated with her father when the new partnership was first formed. She had lost her temper with him, and called him a fool, whereupon M. Binet—in Pantaloon's best manner—had lost his temper in his turn and boxed her ears. She piled it up to the account of Scaramouche, and spied her opportunity to pay off some of that ever-increasing score. But opportunities were few. Scaramouche was too occupied just then. During the week of preparation at Fougeray, he was hardly seen save at the performances, whilst when once they were at Rédon, he came and went like the wind between the theatre and the inn.

The Rédon experiment had justified itself from the first. Stimulated and encouraged by this, André-Louis worked day and night during the month that they spent in that busy little town. The moment had been well chosen, for the trade in chestnuts of which Rédon is the centre was just then at its height. And every afternoon the little theatre was packed with spectators. The fame of the troupe had gone forth, borne by the chestnut-growers of the district, who were bringing their wares to Rédon market, and the audiences were made up of people from the surrounding country, and from neighbouring villages as far out as Allaire, Saint-Perrieux and Saint-Nicholas. To keep the business from slackening, André-Louis prepared a new scenario every week. He wrote three in addition to those two with which he had already supplied the company; these were *The Marriage of Pantaloon*, *The Shy Lover*, and *The Terrible Captain*. Of these the last was the greatest success. It was based upon the *Miles Gloriosus* of Plautus, with great opportunities for Rhodomont, and a good part for Scaramouche as the roaring captain's sly lieutenant. Its success was largely due to the fact that André-Louis amplified the scenario to the extent of indicating very fully in places the lines which the dialogue should follow, whilst here and there he had gone so far as to supply some of the actual dialogue to be spoken, without, however, making it obligatory upon the actors to keep to the letter of it.

And meanwhile as the business prospered, he became busy with tailors, improving the wardrobe of the company, which was sorely in need of improvement. He ran to earth a couple of needy artists, lured them into the company to play small parts—apothecaries and notaries—and set them to beguile their leisure in painting new scenery, so as to be ready for what he called the conquest of Nantes, which was to come in the new year. Never in his life had he worked so hard; never in his life had he worked at all by comparison with his activities now. His fund of energy and enthusiasm was inexhaustible, like that of his good humour. He came and went, acted, wrote, conceived, directed, planned, and executed, what time M. Binet took his ease at last in comparative affluence, drank Burgundy every night, ate white bread and other delicacies, and began to congratulate himself upon his astuteness in having made this industrious, tireless fellow his partner. Having discovered how idle had been his fears of performing at Rédon, he now began to dismiss the terrors with which the notion of Nantes had haunted him.

And his happiness was reflected throughout the ranks of his company, with the single exception always of Climène. She had ceased to sneer at Scaramouche, having realized at last that her sneers left him untouched and recoiled upon herself. Thus her almost indefinable resentment of him was increased by being stifled, until, at all costs, an outlet for it must be found.

One day she threw herself in his way as he was leaving the theatre after the performance. The others had already gone, and she had returned upon pretence of having forgotten something.

"Will you tell me what I have done to you?" she asked him, point-blank.

"Done to me, mademoiselle?" He did not understand.

She made a gesture of impatience. "Why do you hate me?"

"Hate you, mademoiselle? I do not hate anybody. It is the most stupid of all the emotions. I have never hated—not even my enemies."

"What Christian resignation!"

"As for hating you, of all people! Why . . . I consider you adorable. I envy Léandre every day of my life. I have seriously thought of setting him to play Scaramouche, and playing lovers myself."

"I don't think you would be a success," said she.

"That is the only consideration that restrains me. And yet, given the inspiration that is given Léandre, it is possible that I might be convincing."

"Why, what inspiration do you mean?"

"The inspiration of playing to so adorable a Climène."

Her lazy eyes were now alert to search that lean face of his.

"You are laughing at me," said she, and swept past him into the theatre on her pretended quest. There was nothing to be done with such a fellow. He was utterly without feeling. He was not a man at all.

Yet when she came forth again at the end of some five minutes, she found him still lingering at the door.

"Not gone yet?" she asked him, superciliously.

"I was waiting for you, mademoiselle. You will be walking to the inn. If I might escort you . . ."

"But what gallantry! What condescension!"

"Perhaps you would prefer that I did not?"

"How could I prefer that, M. Scaramouche? Besides, we are both going the same way, and the streets are common to all. It is that I am overwhelmed by the unusual honour."

He looked into her piquant little face, and noted how obscured it was by its cloud of dignity. He laughed.

"Perhaps I feared that the honour was not sought."

"Ah, now I understand," she cried. "It is for me to seek these honours. I am to woo a man before he will pay me the homage of civility. It must be so, since you, who clearly know everything, have said so. It remains for me to beg your pardon for my ignorance."

"It amuses you to be cruel," said Scaramouche. "No matter. Shall we walk?"

They set out together, stepping briskly to warm their blood against the wintry evening air. Awhile they went in silence, yet each furtively observing the other.

"And so, you find me cruel?" she challenged him at length, thereby betraying the fact that the accusation had struck home.

He looked at her with a half smile. "Will you deny it?"

"You are the first man that ever accused me of that."

"I dare not suppose myself the first man to whom you have

been cruel. That were an assumption too flattering to myself. I must prefer to think that the others suffered in silence."

"Mon Dieu! Have you suffered?" She was between serious-ness and raillery.

"I place the confession as an offering on the altar of your vanity."

"I should never have suspected it."

"How could you? Am I not what your father calls a natural actor? I was an actor long before I became Scaramouche. There-fore I have laughed. I often do when I am hurt. When you were pleased to be disdainful, I acted disdain in my turn."

"You acted very well," said she, without reflecting.

"Of course. I am an excellent actor."

"And why this sudden change?"

"In response to the change in you. You have grown weary of your part of cruel madam—a dull part, believe me, and unwor-thy of your talents. Were I a woman and had I your loveliness and your grace, Climène, I should disdain to use them as weap-ons of offence."

"Loveliness and grace!" she echoed, feigning amused surprise. But the vain baggage was mollified. "When was it that you dis-covered this beauty and this grace, M. Scaramouche?"

He looked at her a moment, considering the sprightly beauty of her, the adorable femininity that from the first had so irresist-ibly attracted him.

"One morning when I beheld you rehearsing a love-scene with Léandre."

He caught the surprise that leapt to her eyes, before she veiled them under drooping lids from his too-questing gaze.

"Why, that was the first time you saw me."

"I had no earlier occasion to remark your charms."

"You ask me to believe too much," said she, but her tone was softer than he had ever known it yet.

"Then you'll refuse to believe me if I confess that it was this grace and beauty that determined my destiny that day by urging me to join your father's troupe."

At that she became a little out of breath. There was no longer any question of finding an outlet for resentment. Resentment was all forgotten.

"But why? With what object?"

"With the object of asking you one day to be my wife."

She halted under the shock of that, and swung round to face him. Her glance met his own without shyness now; there was a hardening glitter in her eyes, a faint stir of colour in her cheeks. She suspected him of an unpardonable mockery.

"You go very fast, don't you?" she asked him, with heat.

"I do. Haven't you observed it? I am a man of sudden impulses. See what I have made of the Binet troupe in less than a couple of months. Another might have laboured for a year and not achieved the half of it. Shall I be slower in love than in work? Would it be reasonable to expect it? I have curbed and repressed myself not to scare you by precipitancy. In that I have done violence to my feelings, and more than all in using the same cold aloofness with which you chose to treat me. I have waited—oh! so patiently—until you should tire of that mood of cruelty."

"You are an amazing man," said she, quite colourlessly.

"I am," he agreed with her. "It is only the conviction that I am not commonplace that has permitted me to hope as I have hoped."

Mechanically, and as if by tacit consent, they resumed their walk.

"And I ask you to observe," he said, "when you complain that I go very fast, that, after all, I have so far asked you for nothing."

"How?" quoth she, frowning.

"I have merely told you of my hopes. I am not so rash as to ask at once whether I may realize them."

"My faith, but that is prudent," said she, tartly.

"Of course."

It was his self-possession that exasperated her; for after that she walked the short remainder of the way in silence, and so, for the moment, the matter was left just there.

But that night, after they had supped, it chanced that when Climène was about to retire, he and she were alone together in the room abovestairs that her father kept exclusively for his company. The Binet Troupe, you see, was rising in the world.

As Climène now rose to withdraw for the night, Scaramouche rose with her to light her candle. Holding it in her left hand, she offered him her right, a long, tapering, white hand at the end of a softly rounded arm that was bare to the elbow.

"Goodnight, Scaramouche," she said, but so softly, so tenderly, that he caught his breath, and stood conning her, his dark eyes aglow.

Thus a moment, then he took the tips of her fingers in his grasp, and bowing over the hand, pressed his lips upon it. Then he looked at her again. The intense femininity of her lured him on, invited him, surrendered to him. Her face was pale, there was a glitter in her eyes, a curious smile upon her parted lips, and under its *fichu-menteur* her bosom rose and fell to complete the betrayal of her.

By the hand he continued to hold, he drew her towards him. She came unresisting. He took the candle from her, and set it down on the sideboard by which she stood. The next moment her slight, lithe body was in his arms, and he was kissing her, murmuring her name as if it were a prayer.

"Am I cruel now?" she asked him, panting. He kissed her again for only answer. "You made me cruel because you would not see," she told him next in a whisper.

And then the door opened, and M. Binet came in to have his paternal eyes regaled by this highly indecorous behaviour of his daughter.

He stood at gaze, whilst they quite leisurely, and in a self-possession too complete to be natural, detached each from the other.

"And what may be the meaning of this?" demanded M. Binet, bewildered and profoundly shocked.

"Does it require explaining?" asked Scaramouche. "Doesn't it speak for itself—eloquently? It means that Climène and I have taken it into our heads to be married."

"And doesn't it matter what I may take into my head?"

"Of course. But you could have neither the bad taste nor the bad heart to offer any obstacle."

"You take that for granted? Aye, that is your way, to be sure—to take things for granted. But my daughter is not to be taken for granted. I have very definite views for my daughter. You have done an unworthy thing, Scaramouche. You have betrayed my trust in you. I am very angry with you."

He rolled forward with his ponderous yet curiously noiseless gait. Scaramouche turned to her, smiling, and handed her the candle.

"If you will leave us, Climène, I will ask your hand of your father in proper form."

She vanished, a little fluttered, lovelier than ever in her mixture of confusion and timidity. Scaramouche closed the door and faced the enraged M. Binet, who had flung himself into an armchair at the head of the short table, faced him with the avowed purpose of asking for Climène's hand in proper form. And this was how he did it:

"Father-in-law," said he, "I congratulate you. This will certainly mean the Comédie Française for Climéne, and that before long, and you shall shine in the glory she will reflect. As the father of Madame Scaramouche you may yet be famous."

Binet, his face slowly empurpling, glared at him in speechless stupefaction. His rage was the more utter from his humiliating conviction that whatever he might say or do, this irresistible fellow would bend him to his will. At last speech came to him.

"You're a damned corsair," he cried, thickly, banging his ham-like fist upon the table. "A corsair! First you sail in and plunder me of half my legitimate gains; and now you want to carry off my daughter. But I'll be damned if I'll give her to a graceless, name-less scoundrel like you, for whom the gallows are waiting already."

Scaramouche pulled the bell-rope, not at all discomposed. He smiled. There was a flush on his cheeks and a gleam in his eyes. He was very pleased with the world that night. He really owed a great debt to M. de Lesdiguières.

"Binet," said he, "forget for once that you are Pantaloon, and behave as a nice, amiable father-in-law should behave when he has secured a son-in-law of exceptional merits. We are going to have a bottle of Burgundy at my expense, and it shall be the best bottle of Burgundy to be found in Rédon. Compose yourself to do fitting honour to it. Excitations of the bile invariably impair the fine sensitiveness of the palate."

CHAPTER VII

The Conquest of Nantes

The Binet Troupe opened in Nantes—as you may discover in surviving copies of the *Courrier Nantais*—on the Feast of the Purification with *Les Fourberies de Scaramouche*. But they did not come to Nantes as hitherto they had gone to little country villages and townships, unheralded and depending entirely upon the parade of their entrance to attract attention to themselves. André-Louis had borrowed from the business methods of the Comédie Française. Carrying matters with a high hand entirely in his own fashion, he had ordered at Rédon the printing of play-bills, and four days before the company's descent upon Nantes, these bills were pasted outside the Théâtre Feydau and elsewhere about the town, and had attracted—being still sufficiently un-usual announcements at the time—considerable attention. He had entrusted the matter to one of the company's latest recruits, an intelligent young man named Basque, sending him on ahead

190

of the company for the purpose.

You may see for yourself one of these playbills in the Carnavalet Museum. It details the players by their stage names only, with the exception of M. Binet and his daughter, and leaving out of account that he who plays Trivelin in one piece appears as Tabarin in another, it makes the company appear to be at least half as numerous again as it really was. It announces that they will open with *Les Fourberies de Scaramouche,* to be followed by five other plays of which it gives the titles, and by others not named, which shall also be added should the patronage to be received in the distinguished and enlightened city of Nantes encourage the Binet Troupe to prolong its sojourn at the Théâtre Feydau. It lays great stress upon the fact that this is a company of improvisers in the old Italian manner, the like of which has not been seen in France for half a century, and it exhorts the public of Nantes not to miss this opportunity of witnessing these distinguished mimes who are reviving for them the glories of the Comédie de l'Art. Their visit to Nantes—the announcement proceeds—is preliminary to their visit to Paris, where they intend to throw down the glove to the actors of the Comédie Française, and to show the world how superior is the art of the improviser to that of the actor who depends upon an author for what he shall say, and who consequently says always the same thing every time that he plays in the same piece.

It is an audacious bill, and its audacity had scared M. Binet out of the little sense left him by the Burgundy which in these days he could afford to abuse. He had offered the most vehement opposition. Part of this André-Louis had swept aside; part he had disregarded.

"I admit that it is audacious," said Scaramouche. "But at your time of life you should have learnt that in this world nothing succeeds like audacity."

"I forbid it; I absolutely forbid it," M. Binet insisted.

"I knew you would. Just as I know that you'll be very grateful to me presently for not obeying you."

"You are inviting a catastrophe."

"I am inviting fortune. The worst catastrophe that can overtake you is to be back in the market-halls of the country villages from which I rescued you. I'll have you in Paris yet in spite of yourself. Leave this to me."

And he went out to attend to the printing. Nor did his preparations end there. He wrote a piquant article on the glories of the Comédie de l'Art, and its resurrection by the improvising troupe of the great mime Florimond Binet. Binet's name was not Florimond; it was just Pierre. But André-Louis had a great sense of the theatre. That article was an amplification of the stimulating matter contained in the playbills; and he persuaded Basque, who had relations in Nantes, to use all the influence he could command, and all the bribery they could afford, to get that article printed in the *Courrier Nantais* a couple of days before the arrival of the Binet Troupe.

Basque had succeeded, and, considering the undoubted literary merits and intrinsic interest of the article, this is not at all surprising.

And so it was upon an already expectant city that Binet and his company descended in that first week of February.

M. Binet would have made his entrance in the usual manner—a full-dress parade with banging drums and crashing cymbals. But to this André-Louis offered the most relentless opposition.

"We should but discover our poverty," said he. "Instead, we will creep into the city unobserved, and leave ourselves to the imagination of the public."

He had his way, of course. M. Binet, worn already with battling against the strong waters of this young man's will, was altogether unequal to the contest now that he found Climène in alliance with Scaramouche, adding her insistence to his, and joining with him in reprobation of her father's sluggish and reactionary wits. Metaphorically, M. Binet threw up his arms, and cursing the day on which he had taken this young man into his troupe, he allowed the current to carry him whither it would. He was persuaded that he would be drowned in the end. Meanwhile he would drown his vexation in Burgundy. At least there was abundance of Burgundy. Never in his life had he found Burgundy so plentiful. Perhaps things were not as bad as he imagined, after all. He reflected that, when all was said, he had to thank Scaramouche for the Burgundy. Whilst fearing the worst, he would hope for the best.

And it was very much the worst that he feared as he waited in the wings when the curtain rose on that first performance of theirs at the Théâtre Feydau to a house that was tolerably filled by a public whose curiosity the preliminary announcements had thoroughly stimulated.

Although the scenario of *Les Fourberies de Scaramouche* has not apparently survived, yet we know from André-Louis' *Confessions* that it is opened by Polichinelle in the character of an arrogant and fiercely jealous lover shown in the act of beguiling the waiting-maid, Columbine, to play the spy upon her mistress, Climène. Beginning with cajolery, but failing in this with the saucy Columbine, who likes cajolers to be at least attractive and to pay a due deference to her own very piquant charms, the fierce humpbacked scoundrel passes on to threats of the terrible vengeance he will wreak upon her if she betrays him or neglects to obey him implicitly; failing here, likewise, he finally has recourse to bribery, and after he has bled himself freely to the very expectant Columbine, he succeeds by these means in obtaining her consent to spy upon Climène, and to report to him upon her lady's conduct.

The pair played the scene well together, stimulated, perhaps, by their very nervousness at finding themselves before so imposing an audience. Polichinelle was everything that is fierce, contemptuous, and insistent. Columbine was the essence of pert indifference under his cajolery, saucily mocking under his threats, and finely sly in extorting the very maximum when it came to accepting a bribe. Laughter rippled through the audience and promised well. But M. Binet, standing trembling in the wings, missed the great guffaws of the rustic spectators to whom they had played hitherto, and his fears steadily mounted.

Then, scarcely has Polichinelle departed by the door than Scaramouche bounds in through the window. It was an effective entrance, usually performed with a broad comic effect that set the people in a roar. Not so on this occasion. Meditating in bed that morning, Scaramouche had decided to present himself in a totally different aspect. He would cut out all the broad play, all the usual clowning which had delighted their past rude audiences, and he would obtain his effects by subtlety instead. He would present a slyly humorous rogue, restrained, and of a certain dignity, wearing a countenance of complete solemnity, speaking his lines drily, as if unconscious of the humour with which he intended to invest them. Thus, though it might take the audience longer to understand and discover him, they would like him all the better in the end.

True to that resolve, he now played his part as the friend and hired ally of the lovesick Léandre, on whose behalf he came for news of Climène, seizing the opportunity to further his own *amour* with Columbine and his designs upon the money-bags of Pantaloon. Also he had taken certain liberties with the traditional costume of Scaramouche; he had caused the black doublet and breeches to be slashed with red, and the doublet to be cut more to a peak, *à la* Henri III. The conventional black velvet cap he had replaced by a conical hat with a turned-up brim, and a tuft of feathers on the left, and he had discarded the guitar.

M. Binet listened desperately for the roar of laughter that usually greeted the entrance of Scaramouche, and his dismay increased when it did not come. And then he became conscious of something alarmingly unusual in Scaramouche's manner. The sibilant foreign accent was there, but none of the broad boisterousness their audiences had loved.

He wrung his hands in despair. "It is all over!" he said. "The fellow has ruined us! It serves me right for being a fool, and allowing him to take control of everything!"

But he was profoundly mistaken. He began to have an inkling of this when presently himself he took the stage, and found the public attentive, remarked a grin of quiet appreciation on every upturned face. It was not, however, until the thunders of applause greeted the fall of the curtain on the first act that he felt quite sure they would be allowed to escape with their lives.

Had the part of Pantaloon in *Les Fourberies* been other than that of a blundering, timid old idiot, Binet would have ruined it by his apprehensions. As it was, those very apprehensions, magnifying as they did the hesitancy and bewilderment that were the essence of his part, contributed to the success. And a success it proved that more than justified all the heralding of which Scaramouche had been guilty.

For Scaramouche himself this success was not confined to the public. At the end of the play a great reception awaited him from his companions assembled in the green-room of the theatre. His talent, resource, and energy had raised them in a few weeks from a pack of vagrant mountebanks to a self-respecting company of first-rate players. They acknowledged it generously in a speech entrusted to Polichinelle, adding the tribute to his genius that, as they had conquered Nantes, so would they conquer the world under his guidance.

In their enthusiasm they were a little neglectful of the feelings of M. Binet. Irritated enough had he been already by the overriding of his every wish, by the consciousness of his weakness when opposed to Scaramouche. And although he had suffered the gradual process of usurpation of authority because its every step had been attended by his own greater profit, deep down in him the resentment abode to stifle every spark of that gratitude due from him to his partner. Tonight his nerves had been on the rack, and he had suffered agonies of apprehension, for all of which he blamed Scaramouche so bitterly that not even the ultimate success—almost miraculous when all the elements are considered—could justify his partner in his eyes.

And now, to find himself, in addition, ignored by this company—his own company, which he had so laboriously and slowly assembled and selected among the men of ability whom he had found here and there in the dregs of cities—was something that stirred his bile, and aroused the malevolence that never did more than slumber in him. But deeply though his rage was moved, it did not blind him to the folly of betraying it. Yet that he should assert himself in this hour was imperative unless he were for ever to become a thing of no account in this troupe over which he had lorded it for long months before this interloper came amongst them to fill his purse and destroy his authority.

So he stepped forward now when Polichinelle had done. His make-up assisting him to mask his bitter feelings, he professed to add his own to Polichinelle's acclamations of his dear partner. But he did it in such a manner as to make it clear that what Scaramouche had done, he had done by M. Binet's favour, and that in all M. Binet's had been the guiding hand. In associating himself with Polichinelle, he desired to thank Scaramouche, much in the manner of a lord rendering thanks to his steward for services diligently rendered and orders scrupulously carried out.

It neither deceived the troupe nor mollified himself. Indeed, his consciousness of the mockery of it but increased his bitterness. But at least it saved his face and rescued him from nullity— he who was their chief.

To say, as I have said, that it did not deceive them, is perhaps to say too much, for it deceived them at least on the score of his feelings. They believed, after discounting the insinuations in which he took all credit to himself, that at heart he was filled with gratitude, as they were. That belief was shared by André-Louis himself, who in his brief, grateful answer was very generous to M. Binet, more than endorsing the claims that M. Binet had made.

And then followed from him the announcement that their success in Nantes was the sweeter to him because it rendered almost immediately attainable the dearest wish of his heart, which was to make Climène his wife. It was a felicity of which he was the first to acknowledge his utter unworthiness. It was to bring him into still closer relations with his good friend M. Binet, to whom he owed all that he had achieved for himself and for them. The announcement was joyously received, for the world of the theatre loves a lover as dearly as does the greater world. So they acclaimed the happy pair, with the exception of poor Léandre, whose eyes were more melancholy than ever.

They were a happy family that night in the upstairs room of their inn on the Quai La Fosse—the same inn from which André-Louis had set out some weeks ago to play a vastly different rôle before an audience of Nantes. Yet was it so different, he wondered? Had he not then been a sort of Scaramouche—an intriguer, glib and specious, deceiving folk, cynically misleading them with opinions that were not really his own? Was it at all surprising that he should have made so rapid and signal a success as a mime? Was not this really all that he had ever been, the thing for which Nature had designed him?

On the following night they played *The Shy Lover* to a full house, the fame of their debut having gone abroad, and the success of Monday was confirmed. On Wednesday they gave *Figaro-Scaramouche,* and on Thursday morning the *Courrier Nantais* came out with an article of more than a column of praise of these brilliant improvisers, for whom it claimed that they utterly put to shame the mere reciters of memorized parts.

André-Louis, reading the sheet at breakfast, and having no delusions on the score of the falseness of that statement, laughed inwardly. The novelty of the thing, and the pretentiousness in which he had swaddled it, had deceived them finely. He turned to greet Binet and Climène, who entered at that moment. He waved the sheet above his head.

"It is settled," he announced, "we stay in Nantes until Easter."

"Do we?" said Binet, sourly. "You settle everything, my friend."

"Read for yourself." And he handed him the paper.

Moodily M. Binet read. He set the sheet down in silence, and turned his attention to his breakfast.

"Was I justified or not?" quoth André-Louis, who found M. Binet's behaviour a thought intriguing.

"In what?"

"In coming to Nantes?"

"If I had not thought so, we should not have come," said Binet, and he began to eat.

Andrè-Louis dropped the subject, wondering.

After breakfast he and Climène sallied forth to take the air upon the quays. It was a day of brilliant sunshine and less cold than it had lately been. Columbine tactlessly joined them as they were setting out, though in this respect matters were improved a little when Harlequin came running after them, and attached himself to Columbine.

André-Louis, stepping out ahead with Climène, spoke of the thing that was uppermost in his mind at the moment.

"Your father is behaving very oddly towards me," said he. "It is almost as if he had suddenly become hostile."

"You imagine it," said she. "My father is very grateful to you, as we all are."

"He is anything but grateful. He is infuriated against me; and I think I know the reason. Don't you? Can't you guess?"

"I can't, indeed."

"If you were my daughter, Climène, which God be thanked you are not, I should feel aggrieved against the man who carried you away from me. Poor old Pantaloon! He called me a corsair when I told him that I intend to marry you."

"He was right. You are a bold robber, Scaramouche."

"It is in the character," said he. "Your father believes in having his mimes play upon the stage the parts that suit their natural temperaments."

"Yes, you take everything you want, don't you?" She looked up at him, half adoringly, half shyly.

"If it is possible," said he. "I took his consent to our marriage by main force from him. I never waited for him to give it. When, in fact, he refused it, I just snatched it from him, and I'll defy him now to win it back from me. I think that is what he most resents."

She laughed, and launched upon an animated answer. But he did not hear a word of it. Through the bustle of traffic on the quay a cabriolet, the upper half of which was almost entirely made of glass, had approached them. It was drawn by two magnificent bay horses and driven by a superbly liveried coachman.

In the cabriolet alone sat a slight young girl wrapped in a lynx-fur pelisse, her face of a delicate loveliness. She was leaning

200

forward, her lips parted, her eyes devouring Scaramouche until they drew his gaze. When that happened, the shock of it brought him abruptly to a dumfounded halt.

Climène, checking in the middle of a sentence, arrested by his own sudden stopping, plucked at his sleeve.

"What is it, Scaramouche?"

But he made no attempt to answer her, and at that moment the coachman, to whom the little lady had already signalled, brought the carriage to a standstill beside them. Seen in the gorgeous setting of that coach with its escutcheoned panels, its portly coachman and its white-stockinged footman—who swung instantly to earth as the vehicle stopped—its dainty occupant seemed to Climène a princess out of a fairy-tale. And this princess leaned forward, with eyes aglow and cheeks aflush, stretching out a choicely gloved hand to Scaramouche.

"André-Louis!" she called him.

And Scaramouche took the hand of that exalted being, just as he might have taken the hand of Climéne herself, and with eyes that reflected the gladness of her own, in a voice that echoed the joyous surprise of hers, he addressed her familiarly by name, just as she had addressed him.

"Aline!"

CHAPTER VIII

The Dream

"The door," Aline commanded her footman, and "Mount here beside me," she commanded André-Louis, in the same breath.

"A moment, Aline."

He turned to his companion, who was all amazement, and to Harlequin and Columbine, who had that moment come up to share it. "You permit me, Climène?" said he, breathlessly. But it was more a statement than a question. "Fortunately you are not alone. Harlequin will take care of you. *Au revoir*, at dinner."

With that he sprang into the cabriolet without waiting for a reply. The footman closed the door, the coachman cracked his whip, and the regal equipage rolled away along the quay, leaving the three comedians staring after it, open-mouthed. Then Harlequin laughed.

"A prince in disguise, our Scaramouche!" said he.

Columbine clapped her hands and flashed her strong teeth.

"But what a romance for you, Climène! How wonderful!"

The frown melted from Climène's brow. Resentment changed to bewilderment.

"But who is she?"

"His sister, of course," said Harlequin, quite definitely.

"His sister? How do you know?"

"I know what he will tell you on his return."

"But why?"

"Because you wouldn't believe him if he said she was his mother."

Following the carriage with their glance, they wandered on in the direction it had taken. And in the carriage Aline was considering André-Louis with grave eyes, lips slightly compressed, and a tiny frown between her finely drawn eyebrows.

"You have taken to queer company, André," was the first thing she said to him. "Or else I am mistaken in thinking that your companion was Mlle. Binet of the Théâtre Feydau."

"You are not mistaken. But I had not imagined Mlle. Binet so famous already."

"Oh, as to that—" mademoiselle shrugged, her tone quietly scornful. And she explained. "It is simply that I was at the play last night. I thought I recognized her."

"You were at the Feydau last night? And I never saw you!"

"Were you there, too?"

"Was I there!" he cried. Then he checked, and abruptly changed his tone. "Oh, yes, I was there," he said, as commonplace as he could, beset by a sudden reluctance to avow that he had so willingly descended to depths that she must account unworthy, and grateful that his disguise of face and voice should

203

have proved impenetrable even to one who knew him so very well.

"I understand," said she, and compressed her lips a little more tightly.

"But what do you understand?"

"The rare attractions of Mlle. Binet. Naturally you would be at the theatre. Your tone conveyed it very clearly. Do you know that you disappoint me, André? It is stupid of me, perhaps; it betrays, I suppose, my imperfect knowledge of your sex. I am aware that most young men of fashion find an irresistible attraction for creatures who parade themselves upon the stage. But I did not expect you to ape the ways of a man of fashion. I was foolish enough to imagine you to be different; rather above such trivial pursuits. I conceived you something of an idealist."

"Sheer flattery."

"So I perceive. But you misled me. You talked so much morality of a kind, you made philosophy so readily, that I came to be deceived. In fact, your hypocrisy was so consummate that I never suspected it. With your gift of acting I wonder that you haven't joined Mlle. Binet's troupe."

"I have," said he.

It had really become necessary to tell her, making choice of the lesser of the two evils with which she confronted him.

He saw first incredulity, then consternation, and lastly disgust overspread her face.

"Of course," said she, after a long pause, "that would have the advantage of bringing you closer to your charmer."

"That was only one of the inducements. There was another. Finding myself forced to choose between the stage and the gallows, I had the incredible weakness to prefer the former. It was utterly unworthy of a man of my lofty ideals, but—what would you? Like other ideologists, I find it easier to preach than to practise. Shall I stop the carriage and remove the contamination of my disgusting person? Or shall I tell you how it happened?"

"Tell me how it happened first. Then we will decide."

He told her how he met the Binet Troupe, and how the men of the *maréchaussée* forced upon him the discovery that in its bosom he could lie safely lost until the hue and cry had died down. The explanation dissolved her iciness.

"My poor André, why didn't you tell me this at first?"

"For one thing, you didn't give me time; for another, I feared to shock you with the spectacle of my degradation."

She took him seriously. "But where was the need of it? And why did you not send us word as I required you of your whereabouts?"

"I was thinking of it only yesterday. I have hesitated for several reasons."

"You thought it would offend us to know what you were doing?"

"I think that I preferred to surprise you by the magnitude of my ultimate achievements."

"Oh, you are to become a great actor?" She was frankly scornful.

"That is not impossible. But I am more concerned to become a great author. There is no reason why you should sniff. The calling is an honourable one. All the world is proud to know such men as Beaumarchais and Chénier."

"And you hope to equal them?"

"I hope to surpass them, whilst acknowledging that it was they who taught me how to walk. What did you think of the play last night?"

"It was amusing and well conceived."

"Let me present you to the author."

"You? But the company is one of improvisers."

"Even improvisers require an author to write their scenarios. That is all I write at present. Soon I shall be writing plays in the modern manner."

"You deceive yourself, my poor André. The piece last night would have been nothing without the players. You are fortunate in your Scaramouche."

"In confidence—I present you to him."

"You—Scaramouche? You?" She turned to regard him fully. He smiled his close-lipped smile that made wrinkles like gashes in his cheeks. He nodded.

"And I didn't recognize you!"

"I thank you for the tribute. You imagined, of course, that I was a scene-shifter. And now that you know all about me, what of Gavrillac? What of my godfather?"

He was well, she told him, and still profoundly indignant with André-Louis for his defection, whilst secretly concerned on his behalf.

"I shall write to him today that I have seen you."

"Do so. Tell him that I am well and prospering. But say no more. Do not tell him what I am doing. He has his prejudices too. Besides, it might not be prudent. And now the question I have been burning to ask ever since I entered your carriage. Why are you in Nantes, Aline?"

"I am on a visit to my aunt, Mme. de Sautron. It was with her that I came to the play yesterday. We have been dull at the château; but it will be different now. Madame my aunt is receiving several guests today. M. de La Tour d'Azyr is to be one of them."

André-Louis frowned and sighed. "Did you ever hear, Aline, how poor Philippe de Vilmorin came by his end?"

"Yes; I was told, first by my uncle; then by M. de La Tour d'Azyr, himself."

"Did not that help you to decide this marriage question?"

"How could it? You forget that I am but a woman. You don't expect me to judge between men in matters such as these?"

"Why not? You are well able to do so. The more since you have heard two sides. For my godfather would tell you the truth. If you cannot judge, it is that you do not wish to judge." His tone became harsh. "Wilfully you close your eyes to justice that might check the course of your unhealthy, unnatural ambition."

"Excellent!" she exclaimed, and considered him with amusement and something else. "Do you know that you are almost droll? You rise unblushing from the dregs of life in which I find you, and shake off the arm of that theatre girl, to come and preach to me."

"If these were the dregs of life I might still speak from them to counsel you out of my respect and devotion, Aline." He was very stiff and stern. "But they are not the dregs of life. Honour and virtue are possible to a theatre girl; they are impossible to a lady who sells herself to gratify ambition; who for position, riches, and a great title barters herself in marriage."

She looked at him breathlessly. Anger turned her pale. She

reached for the cord.

"I think I had better let you alight so that you may go back to practise virtue and honour with your theatre wench."

"You shall not speak so of her, Aline."

"Faith, now we are to have heat on her behalf. You think I am too delicate? You think I should speak of her as a . . ."

"If you must speak of her at all," he interrupted, hotly, "you'll speak of her as my wife."

Amazement smothered her anger. Her pallor deepened. "My God!" she said, and looked at him in horror. And in horror she asked him presently: "You are married—married to that—?"

"Not yet. But I shall be, soon. And let me tell you that this girl whom you visit with your ignorant contempt is as good and pure as you are, Aline. She has wit and talent which have placed her where she is and shall carry her a deal farther. And she has the womanliness to be guided by natural instincts in the selection of her mate."

She was trembling with passion. She tugged the cord.

"You will descend this instant!" she told him fiercely. "That you should dare to make a comparison between me and . . ."

"And my wife-to-be," he interrupted, before she could speak the infamous word. He opened the door for himself without waiting for the footman, and leapt down. "My compliments," said he, furiously, "to the assassin you are to marry." He slammed the door. "Drive on," he bade the coachman.

The carriage rolled away up the Faubourg Gigan, leaving him standing where he had alighted, quivering with rage. Gradually, as he walked back to the inn, his anger cooled. Gradually, as he cooled, he perceived her point of view, and in the end forgave her. It was not her fault that she thought as she thought. Her rearing had been such as to make her look upon every actress as a trull, just as it had qualified her calmly to consider the monstrous marriage of convenience into which she was invited.

He got back to the inn to find the company at table. Silence fell when he entered, so suddenly that of necessity it must be supposed he was himself the subject of the conversation. Harlequin and Columbine had spread the tale of this prince in disguise caught up into the chariot of a princess and carried off by her; and it was a tale that had lost nothing in the telling.

Climène had been silent and thoughtful, pondering what Columbine had called this romance of hers. Clearly her Scaramouche must be vastly other than he had hitherto appeared, or else that great lady and he would never have used such familiarity with each other. Imagining him no better than he was, Climène had made him her own. And now she was to receive the reward of disinterested affection.

Even old Binet's secret hostility towards André-Louis melted before this astounding revelation. He had pinched his daughter's ear quite playfully. "Ah, ah, trust you to have penetrated his disguise, my child!"

She shrank resentfully from that implication.

"But I did not. I took him for what he seemed."

Her father winked at her very solemnly and laughed. "To be sure, you did. But like your father, who was once a gentleman, and knows the ways of gentlemen, you detected in him a subtle something different from those with whom misfortune has compelled you hitherto to herd. You knew as well as I did that he never caught that trick of haughtiness, that grand air of command, in a lawyer's musty office, and that his speech had hardly the ring or his thoughts the complexion of the bourgeois that he pretended to be. And it was shrewd of you to have made him yours. Do you know that I shall be very proud of you yet, Climène?"

She moved away without answering. Her father's oiliness offended her. Scaramouche was clearly a great gentleman, an eccentric if you please, but a man born. And she was to be his lady. Her father must learn to treat her differently.

She looked shyly—with a new shyness—at her lover when he came into the room where they were dining. She observed for the first time that proud carriage of the head, with the chin thrust forward, that was a trick of his, and she noticed with what a grace he moved—the grace of one who in youth has had his dancing-masters and fencing-masters.

It almost hurt her when he flung himself into a chair and exchanged a quip with Harlequin in the usual manner as with an equal, and it offended her still more that Harlequin, knowing what he now knew, should use him with the same unbecoming familiarity.

Chapter IX

The Awakening

Do you know," said Climène, "that I am waiting for the explanation which I think you owe me?"

They were alone together, lingering still at the table to which André-Louis had come belatedly, and André-Louis was loading himself a pipe. Of late—since joining the Binet Troupe—he had acquired the habit of smoking. The others had gone, some to take the air and others, like Binet and Madame, because they felt that it were discreet to leave those two to the explanations that must pass. It was a feeling that André-Louis did not share. He kindled a light and leisurely applied it to his pipe. A frown came to settle on his brow.

"Explanation?" he questioned presently, and looked at her. "But on what score?"

"On the score of the deception you have practised on us—on me."

"I have practised none," he assured her.

"You mean that you have simply kept your own counsel, and that in silence there is no deception. But it is deceitful to withhold facts concerning yourself and your true station from your future wife. You should not have pretended to be a simple country lawyer, which, of course, any one could see that you are not. It may have been very romantic, but . . . Enfin, will you explain?"

"I see," he said, and pulled at his pipe. "But you are wrong, Climène. I have practised no deception. If there are things about me that I have not told you, it is that I did not account them of much importance. But I have never deceived you by pretending to be other than I am. I am neither more nor less than I have represented myself."

This persistence began to annoy her, and the annoyance showed on her winsome face, coloured her voice.

"Ha! And that fine lady of the nobility with whom you are so intimate, who carried you off in her cabriolet with so little ceremony towards myself? What is she to you?"

"A sort of sister," said he.

"A sort of sister!" She was indignant. "Harlequin foretold that you would say so; but he was amusing himself. It was not very funny. It is less funny still from you. She has a name, I suppose, this sort of sister?"

"Certainly she has a name. She is Mlle. Aline de Kercadiou, the niece of Quintin de Kercadiou, Lord of Gavrillac."

"Oho! That's a sufficiently fine name for your sort of sister. What sort of sister, my friend?"

For the first time in their relationship he observed and deplored the taint of vulgarity, of shrewishness, in her manner.

"It would have been more accurate in me to have said a sort of reputed left-handed cousin."

"A reputed left-handed cousin! And what sort of relationship may that be? Faith, you dazzle me with your lucidity."

"It requires to be explained."

"That is what I have been telling you. But you seem very reluctant with your explanations."

"Oh, no. It is only that they are so unimportant. But be you the judge. Her uncle, M. de Kercadiou, is my godfather, and she and I have been playmates from infancy as a consequence. It is popularly believed in Gavrillac that M. de Kercadiou is my father. He has certainly cared for my rearing from my tenderest years, and it is entirely owing to him that I was educated at Louis le Grand. I owe to him everything that I have—or, rather, everything that I had; for of my own free will I have cut myself adrift, and today I possess nothing save what I can earn for myself in the theatre or elsewhere."

She sat stunned and pale under that cruel blow to her swelling pride. Had he told her this but yesterday, it would have made no impression upon her, it would have mattered not at all; the event of today coming as a sequel would but have enhanced him in her eyes. But coming now, after her imagination had woven for him so magnificent a background, after the rashly assumed discovery of his splendid identity had made her the envied of all the company, after having been in her own eyes and theirs enshrined by marriage with him as a great lady, this disclosure crushed and humiliated her. Her prince in disguise was merely the outcast bastard of a country gentleman! She would be the laughing-stock of every member of her father's troupe, of all those who had so lately envied her this romantic good fortune.

"You should have told me this before," she said, in a dull voice that she strove to render steady.

"Perhaps I should. But does it really matter?"

"Matter?" She suppressed her fury to ask another question. "You say that this M. de Kercadiou is popularly believed to be your father. What precisely do you mean?"

"Just that. It is a belief that I do not share. It is a matter of instinct, perhaps, with me. Moreover, once I asked M. de Kercadiou point-blank, and I received from him a denial. It is not, perhaps, a denial to which one would attach too much importance in all the circumstances. Yet I have never known M. de Kercadiou for other than a man of strictest honour, and I should hesitate to disbelieve him—particularly when his statement leaps with my own instincts. He assured me that he did not know who my father was."

"And your mother, was he equally ignorant?" She was sneering, but he did not remark it. Her back was to the light.

"He would not disclose her name to me. He confessed her to be a dear friend of his."

She startled him by laughing, and her laugh was not pleasant.

"A very dear friend, you may be sure, you simpleton. What name do you bear?"

He restrained his own rising indignation to answer her question calmly: "Moreau. It was given me, so I am told, from the Brittany village in which I was born. But I have no claim to it. In fact I have no name, unless it be Scaramouche, to which I have earned a title. So that you see, my dear," he ended with a smile, "I have practised no deception whatever."

214

"No, no. I see that now." She laughed without mirth, then drew a deep breath and rose. "I am very tired," she said.

He was on his feet in an instant, all solicitude. But she waved him wearily back.

"I think I will rest until it is time to go to the theatre."

She moved towards the door, dragging her feet a little. He sprang to open it, and she passed out without looking at him.

Her so brief romantic dream was ended. The glorious world of fancy which in the last hour she had built with such elaborate detail, over which it should be her exalted destiny to rule, lay shattered about her feet, its débris so many stumbling-blocks that prevented her from winning back to her erstwhile content in Scaramouche as he really was.

André-Louis sat in the window embrasure, smoking and looking idly out across the river. He was intrigued and meditative. He had shocked her. The fact was clear; not so the reason. That he should confess himself nameless should not particularly injure him in the eyes of a girl reared amid the surroundings that had been Climène's. And yet that his confession had so injured him was fully apparent.

There, still at his brooding, the returning Columbine discovered him a half-hour later.

"All alone, my prince!" was her laughing greeting, which suddenly threw light upon his mental darkness. Climène had been disappointed of hopes that the wild imagination of these players had suddenly erected upon the incident of his meeting with Aline. Poor child! He smiled whimsically at Columbine.

"I am likely to be so for some little time," said he, "until it becomes a commonplace that I am not, after all, a prince."

"Not a prince? Oh, but a duke, then—at least a marquis."

"Not even a chevalier, unless it be of the order of fortune. I am just Scaramouche. My castles are all in Spain."

Disappointment clouded the lively, good-natured face.

"And I had imagined you . . ."

"I know," he interrupted. "That is the mischief."

He might have gauged the extent of that mischief by Climène's conduct that evening towards the gentlemen of fashion who clustered now in the green-room between the acts to pay their homage to the incomparable *amoureuse*. Hitherto she had received them with a circumspection compelling respect. Tonight she was recklessly gay, impudent, almost wanton.

He spoke of it gently to her as they walked home together, counselling more prudence in the future.

"We are not married yet," she told him, tartly. "Wait until then before you criticize my conduct."

"I trust that there will be no occasion then," said he.

"You trust? Ah, yes. You are very trusting."

"Climène, I have offended you. I am sorry."

"It is nothing," said she. "You are what you are." Still was he not concerned. He perceived the source of her ill-humour; understood, whilst deploring it; and, because he understood, forgave. He perceived also that her ill-humour was shared by her father, and by this he was frankly amused. Towards M. Binet a tolerant contempt was the only feeling that complete acquaintance could beget. As for the rest of the company, they were disposed to be very kindly towards Scaramouche. It was almost as if in reality he had fallen from the high estate to which their own imaginations had raised him; or possibly it was because they saw

the effect which that fall from his temporary and fictitious eleva-
tion had produced upon Climène.

Léandre alone made himself an exception. His habitual melancholy seemed to be dispelled at last, and his eyes gleamed now
with malicious satisfaction when they rested upon Scaramouche,
whom occasionally he continued to address with sly mockery as
"*mon prince.*"

On the morrow André-Louis saw but little of Climène. This
was not in itself extraordinary, for he was very hard at work again,
with preparations now for *Figaro-Scaramouche* which was to be
played on Saturday. Also, in addition to his manifold theatrical
occupations, he now devoted an hour every morning to the study
of fencing in an academy of arms. This was done not only to
repair an omission in his education, but also, and chiefly, to give
him added grace and poise upon the stage. He found his mind
that morning distracted by thoughts of both Climène and Aline.
And oddly enough it was Aline who provided the deeper pertur-
bation. Climène's attitude he regarded as a passing phase which
need not seriously engage him. But the thought of Aline's conduct towards him kept rankling, and still more deeply rankled
the thought of her possible betrothal to M. de La Tour d'Azyr.

This it was that brought forcibly to his mind the self-imposed
but by now half-forgotten mission that he had made his own. He
had boasted that he would make the voice which M. de La Tour
d'Azyr had sought to silence ring through the length and breadth
of the land. And what had he done of all this that he had boasted?
He had incited the mob of Rennes and the mob of Nantes in
such terms as poor Philippe might have employed, and then because of a hue and cry he had fled like a cur and taken shelter in

the first kennel that offered, there to lie quiet and devote himself to other things—self-seeking things. What a fine contrast between the promise and the fulfilment!

Thus André-Louis to himself in his self-contempt. And whilst he trifled away his time and played Scaramouche, and centred all his hopes in presently becoming the rival of such men as Chénier and Mercier, M. de La Tour d'Azyr went his proud ways unchallenged and wrought his will. It was idle to tell himself that the seed he had sown was bearing fruit. That the demands he had voiced in Nantes for the Third Estate had been granted by M. Necker, thanks largely to the commotion which his anonymous speech had made. That was not his concern or his mission. It was no part of his concern to set about the regeneration of mankind, or even the regeneration of the social structure of France. His concern was to see that M. de La Tour d'Azyr paid to the uttermost *liard* for the brutal wrong he had done Philippe de Vilmorin. And it did not increase his self-respect to find that the danger in which Aline stood of being married to the Marquis was the real spur to his rancour and to remembrance of his vow. He was—too unjustly, perhaps—disposed to dismiss as mere sophistries his own arguments that there was nothing he could do; that, in fact, he had but to show his head to find himself going to Rennes under arrest and making his final exit from the world's stage by way of the gallows.

It is impossible to read that part of his *Confessions* without feeling a certain pity for him. You realize what must have been his state of mind. You realize what a prey he was to emotions so conflicting, and if you have the imagination that will enable you to put yourself in his place, you will also realize how impossible was any decision save the one to which he says he came, that he would move at the first moment that he perceived in what direction it would serve his real aims to move.

It happened that the first person he saw when he took the stage on that Thursday evening was Aline; the second was the Marquis de La Tour d'Azyr. They occupied a box on the right of, and immediately above, the stage. There were others with them—notably a thin, elderly, resplendent lady whom André-Louis supposed to be Madame la Comtesse de Sautron. But at the time he had no eyes for any but those two, who of late had so haunted his thoughts. The sight of either of them would have been sufficiently disconcerting. The sight of both together very nearly made him forget the purpose for which he had come upon the stage. Then he pulled himself together, and played. He played, he says, with an unusual nerve, and never in all that brief but eventful career of his was he more applauded.

That was the evening's first shock. The next came after the second act. Entering the green-room he found it more thronged than usual, and at the far end with Climène, over whom he was bending from his fine height, his eyes intent upon her face, what time his smiling lips moved in talk, M. de La Tour d'Azyr. He had her entirely to himself, a privilege none of the men of fashion who were in the habit of visiting the coulisses had yet enjoyed. Those lesser gentlemen had all withdrawn before the Marquis, as jackals withdraw before the lion.

André-Louis stared a moment, stricken. Then recovering from his surprise he became critical in his study of the Marquis. He considered the beauty and grace and splendour of him, his courtly air, his complete and unshakable self-possession. But more than all he considered the expression of the dark eyes that were devouring Climéne's lovely face, and his own lips tightened.

M. de La Tour d'Azyr never heeded him or his stare; nor, had he done so, would he have known who it was that looked at him from behind the make-up of Scaramouche; nor, again, had he known, would he have been in the least troubled or concerned.

André-Louis sat down apart, his mind in turmoil. Presently he found a mincing young gentleman addressing him, and made shift to answer as was expected. Climène having been thus sequestered, and Columbine being already thickly besieged by gallants, the lesser visitors had to content themselves with Madame and the male members of the troupe. M. Binet, indeed, was the centre of a gay cluster that shook with laughter at his sallies. He seemed of a sudden to have emerged from the gloom of the last two days into high good-humour, and Scaramouche observed how persistently his eyes kept flickering upon his daughter and her splendid courtier.

That night there were high words between André-Louis and Climène, the high words proceeding from Climène. When André-Louis again, and more insistently, enjoined prudence upon his betrothed, and begged her to beware how far she encouraged the advances of such a man as M. de La Tour d'Azyr, she became roundly abusive. She shocked and stunned him by her virulently shrewish tone, and her still more unexpected force of invective.

He sought to reason with her, and finally she came to certain terms with him.

"If you have become betrothed to me simply to stand as an obstacle in my path, the sooner we make an end the better."

"You do not love me then, Climène?"

"Love has nothing to do with it. I'll not tolerate your insensate jealousy. A girl in the theatre must make it her business to accept homage from all."

"Agreed; and there is no harm, provided she gives nothing in exchange."

White-faced, with flaming eyes she turned on him at that.

"Now, what exactly do you mean?"

"My meaning is clear. A girl in your position may receive all the homage that is offered, provided she receives it with a dignified aloofness implying clearly that she has no favours to bestow in return beyond the favour of her smile. If she is wise she will see to it that the homage is always offered collectively by her admirers, and that no single one amongst them shall ever have the privilege of approaching her alone. If she is wise she will give no encouragement, nourish no hopes that it may afterwards be beyond her power to deny realization."

"How? You dare?"

"I know my world. And I know M. de La Tour d'Azyr," he answered her. "He is a man without charity, without humanity almost; a man who takes what he wants wherever he finds it and whether it is given willingly or not; a man who reckons nothing of the misery he scatters on his self-indulgent way; a man whose only law is force. Ponder it, Climène, and ask yourself if I do you less than honour in warning you."

He went out on that, feeling a degradation in continuing the subject.

The days that followed were unhappy days for him, and for at least one other. That other was Léandre, who was cast into the profoundest dejection by M. de La Tour d'Azyr's assiduous attendance upon Climène. The Marquis was to be seen at every performance; a box was perpetually reserved for him, and invariably he came either alone or else with his cousin M. de Chabrillane.

On Tuesday of the following week, André-Louis went out alone early in the morning. He was out of temper, fretted by an overwhelming sense of humiliation, and he hoped to clear his mind by walking. In turning the corner of the Place du Bouffay he ran into a slightly built, sallow-complexioned gentleman very neatly dressed in black, wearing a tie-wig under a round hat. The man fell back at sight of him, levelling a spy-glass, then hailed him in a voice that rang with amazement.

"Moreau! Where the devil have you been hiding yourself these months?"

It was Le Chapelier, the lawyer, the leader of the Literary Chamber of Rennes.

"Behind the skirts of Thespis," said Scaramouche.

"I don't understand."

"I didn't intend that you should. What of yourself, Isaac? And what of the world which seems to have been standing still of late?"

"Standing still!" Le Chapelier laughed. "But where have you been, then? Standing still!" He pointed across the square to a café under the shadow of the gloomy prison. "Let us go and drink a *bavaroise*. You are of all men the man we want, the man we have been seeking everywhere, and—behold!—you drop from the skies into my path."

They crossed the square and entered the café.

"So you think the world has been standing still! Dieu de Dieu! I suppose you haven't heard of the royal order for the convocation of the States General, or the terms of them—that we are to have what we demanded, what you demanded for us here in Nantes! You haven't heard that the order has gone forth for the primary elections—the elections of the electors. You haven't heard of the fresh uproar in Rennes, last month. The order was that the three estates should sit together at the States General of the *bailliages*, but in the *bailliage* of Rennes the nobles must ever be recalcitrant. They took up arms actually—six hundred of them with their *valetaille*, headed by your old friend M. de La Tour d'Azyr, and they were for slashing us—the members of the Third Estate—into ribbons so as to put an end to our insolence." He laughed delicately. "But, by God, we showed them that we, too, could take up arms. It was what you yourself advocated here in Nantes, last November. We fought them a pitched battle in the streets, under the leadership of your namesake Moreau, the provost, and we so peppered them that they were glad to take shelter in the Cordelier Convent. That is the end of their resistance to the royal authority and the people's will."

He ran on at great speed detailing the events that had taken place, and finally came to the matter which had, he announced, been causing him to hunt for André-Louis until he had all but despaired of finding him.

Nantes was sending fifty delegates to the assembly of Rennes which was to select the deputies to the Third Estate and edit their *cahier* of grievances. Rennes itself was being as fully represented, whilst such villages as Gavrillac were sending two delegates for every two hundred hearths or less. Each of these three had clamoured that André-Louis Moreau should be one of its delegates. Gavrillac wanted him because he belonged to the village, and it was known there what sacrifices he had made in the popular cause; Rennes wanted him because it had heard his spirited address on the day of the shooting of the students; and Nantes—to whom his identity was unknown—asked for him as the speaker who had addressed them under the name of Omnes Omnibus and who had framed for them the memorial that was believed so largely to have influenced M. Necker in formulating the terms of the convocation.

Since he could not be found, the delegations had been made up without him. But now it happened that one or two vacancies had occurred in the Nantes representation; and it was the business of filling these vacancies that had brought Le Chapelier to Nantes.

André-Louis firmly shook his head in answer to Le Chapelier's proposal.

"You refuse?" the other cried. "Are you mad? Refuse, when you are demanded from so many sides? Do you realize that it is more than probable you will be elected one of the deputies, that you will be sent to the States General at Versailles to represent us in this work of saving France?"

But André-Louis, we know, was not concerned to save France. At the moment he was concerned to save two women, both of whom he loved, though in vastly different ways, from a man he had vowed to ruin. He stood firm in his refusal until Le Chapelier dejectedly abandoned the attempt to persuade him.

"It is odd," said André-Louis, "that I should have been so deeply immersed in trifles as never to have perceived that Nantes is being politically active."

"Active! My friend, it is a seething cauldron of political emotions. It is kept quiet on the surface only by the persuasion that all goes well. At a hint to the contrary it would boil over."

"Would it so?" said Scaramouche, thoughtfully. "The knowledge may be useful." And then he changed the subject. "You know that La Tour d'Azyr is here?"

"In Nantes? He has courage if he shows himself. They are not a docile people, these Nantais, and they know his record and the part he played in the rising at Rennes. I marvel they haven't stoned him. But they will, sooner or later. It only needs that some one should suggest it."

"That is very likely," said André-Louis, and smiled. "He doesn't show himself much; not in the streets, at least. So that he has not the courage you suppose; nor any kind of courage, as I told him once. He has only insolence."

At parting Le Chapelier again exhorted him to give thought to what he proposed. "Send me word if you change your mind. I am lodged at the Cerf, and I shall be here until the day after tomorrow. If you have ambition, this is your moment."

"I have no ambition, I suppose," said André-Louis, and went his way.

That night at the theatre he had a mischievous impulse to test what Le Chapelier had told him of the state of public feeling in the city. They were playing *The Terrible Captain,* in the last act of which the empty cowardice of the bullying braggart Rhodomont is revealed by Scaramouche.

After the laughter which the exposure of the roaring captain invariably produced, it remained for Scaramouche contemptuously to dismiss him in a phrase that varied nightly, according to the inspiration of the moment. This time he chose to give his phrase a political complexion:

"Thus, O thrasonical coward, is your emptiness exposed. Because of your long length and the great sword you carry and the angle at which you cock your hat, people have gone in fear of you, have believed in you, have imagined you to be as terrible and as formidable as you insolently make yourself appear. But at the first touch of true spirit you crumple up, you tremble, you whine pitifully, and the great sword remains in your scabbard. You remind me of the Privileged Orders when confronted by the Third Estate."

It was audacious of him, and he was prepared for anything—a laugh, applause, indignation, or all together. But he was not prepared for what came. And it came so suddenly and spontaneously from the groundlings and the body of those in the amphitheatre that he was almost scared by it—as a boy may be scared who has held a match to a sun-scorched hayrick. It was a hurricane of furious applause. Men leapt to their feet, sprang up on to the benches, waving their hats in the air, deafening him with the terrific uproar of their acclamations. And it rolled on and on, nor ceased until the curtain fell.

Scaramouche stood meditatively smiling with tight lips. At the last moment he had caught a glimpse of M. de La Tour d'Azyr's face thrust farther forward than usual from the shadows of his box, and it was a face set in anger, with eyes on fire.

"Mon Dieu!" laughed Rhodomont, recovering from the real scare that had succeeded his histrionic terror, "but you have a great trick of tickling them in the right place, Scaramouche."

Scaramouche looked up at him and smiled. "It can be useful upon occasion," said he, and went off to his dressing-room to change.

But a reprimand awaited him. He was delayed at the theatre by matters concerned with the scenery of the new piece they were to mount upon the morrow. By the time he was rid of the business the rest of the company had long since left. He called a chair and had himself carried back to the inn in solitary state. It was one of many minor luxuries his comparatively affluent present circumstances permitted.

Coming into that upstairs room that was common to all the troupe, he found M. Binet talking loudly and vehemently. He had caught sounds of his voice whilst yet upon the stairs. As he entered Binet broke off short, and wheeled to face him.

"You are here at last!" It was so odd a greeting that André-Louis did no more than look his mild surprise. "I await your explanations of the disgraceful scene you provoked tonight."

"Disgraceful? Is it disgraceful that the public should applaud me?"

"The public? The rabble, you mean. Do you want to deprive us of the patronage of all gentlefolk by vulgar appeals to the low passions of the mob?"

André-Louis stepped past M. Binet and forward to the table. He shrugged contemptuously. The man offended him, after all.

"You exaggerate grossly—as usual."

"I do not exaggerate. And I am the master in my own theatre. This is the Binet Troupe, and it shall be conducted in the Binet way."

"Who are the gentlefolk the loss of whose patronage to the Feydau will be so poignantly felt?" asked André-Louis.

"You imply that there are none? See how wrong you are. Af-

227

ter the play tonight M. le Marquis de La Tour d'Azyr came to
me, and spoke to me in the severest terms about your scandalous
outburst. I was forced to apologize, and . . ."

"The more fool you," said André-Louis. "A man who respected
himself would have shown that gentleman the door." M. Binet's
face began to empurple. "You call yourself the head of the Binet
Troupe, you boast that you will be master in your own theatre,
and you stand like a lackey to take the orders of the first insolent
fellow who comes to your green-room to tell you that he does
not like a line spoken by one of your company! I say again that
had you really respected yourself you would have turned him
out."

There was a murmur of approval from several members of
the company, who, having heard the arrogant tone assumed by
the Marquis, were filled with resentment against the slur cast
upon them all.

"And I say further," André-Louis went on, "that a man who
respects himself, on quite other grounds, would have been only
too glad to have seized this pretext to show M. de La Tour d'Azyr
the door."

"What do you mean by that?" There was a rumble of thunder in the question.

André-Louis' eyes swept round the company assembled at
the supper-table. "Where is Climène?" he asked, sharply.

Léandre leapt up to answer him, white in the face, tense and
quivering with excitement.

"She left the theatre in the Marquis de La Tour d'Azyr's carriage immediately after the performance. We heard him offer to
drive her to this inn."

André-Louis glanced at the timepiece on the overmantel. He seemed unnaturally calm.

"That would be an hour ago—rather more. And she has not yet arrived?"

His eyes sought M. Binet's. M. Binet's eyes eluded his glance. Again it was Léandre who answered him.

"Not yet."

"Ah!" André-Louis sat down, and poured himself wine. There was an oppressive silence in the room. Léandre watched him expectantly, Columbine commiseratingly. Even M. Binet appeared to be waiting for a cue from Scaramouche. But Scaramouche disappointed him. "Have you left me anything to eat?" he asked.

Platters were pushed towards him. He helped himself calmly to food, and ate in silence, apparently with a good appetite. M. Binet sat down, poured himself wine, and drank. Presently he attempted to make conversation with one and another. He was answered curtly, in monosyllables. M. Binet did not appear to be in favour with his troupe that night.

At long length came a rumble of wheels below and a rattle of halting hooves. Then voices, the high, trilling laugh of Climène floating upwards. André-Louis went on eating unconcernedly.

"What an actor!" said Harlequin under his breath to Polichinelle, and Polichinelle nodded gloomily.

She came in, a leading lady taking the stage, head high, chin thrust forward, eyes dancing with laughter; she expressed triumph and arrogance. Her cheeks were flushed, and there was some disorder in the mass of nut-brown hair that crowned her head. In her left hand she carried an enormous bouquet of white camellias. On its middle finger a diamond of great price drew almost at once by its effulgence the eyes of all.

Her father sprang to meet her with an unusual display of paternal tenderness. "At last, my child!"

He conducted her to the table. She sank into a chair, a little wearily, a little nervelessly, but the smile did not leave her face, not even when she glanced across at Scaramouche. It was only Léandre, observing her closely, with hungry, scowling stare, who detected something as of fear in the hazel eyes momentarily seen between the fluttering of her lids.

André-Louis, however, still went on eating stolidly, without so much as a look in her direction. Gradually the company came to realize that just as surely as a scene was brooding, just so surely would there be no scene as long as they remained. It was Polichinelle, at last, who gave the signal by rising and withdrawing, and within two minutes none remained in the room but M. Binet, his daughter, and André-Louis. And then, at last, André-Louis set down knife and fork, washed his throat with a draught of Burgundy, and sat back in his chair to consider Climène.

"I trust," said he, "that you had a pleasant ride, mademoiselle."

"Most pleasant, monsieur." Impudently she strove to emulate his coolness, but did not completely succeed.

"And not unprofitable, if I may judge that jewel at this distance. It should be worth at least a couple of hundred *louis,* and that is a formidable sum even to so wealthy a nobleman as M. de La Tour d'Azyr. Would it be impertinent in one who has had some notion of becoming your husband, to ask you, mademoiselle, what you have given him in return?"

M. Binet uttered a gross laugh, a queer mixture of cynicism

and contempt.

"I have given nothing," said Climène, indignantly.

"Ah! Then the jewel is in the nature of a payment in advance."

"My God, man, you're not decent!" M. Binet protested.

"Decent?" André-Louis' smouldering eyes turned to discharge upon M. Binet such a fulmination of contempt that the old scoundrel shifted uncomfortably in his chair. "Did you mention decency, Binet? Almost you make me lose my temper, which is a thing that I detest above all others!" Slowly his glance returned to Climène, who sat with elbows on the table, her chin cupped in her palms, regarding him with something between scorn and defiance. "Mademoiselle," he said, slowly, "I desire you purely in your own interests to consider whither you are going."

"I am well able to consider it for myself, and to decide without advice from you, monsieur."

"And now you've got your answer," chuckled Binet. "I hope you like it."

André-Louis had paled a little; there was incredulity in his great sombre eyes as they continued steadily to regard her. Of M. Binet he took no notice.

"Surely, mademoiselle, you cannot mean that willingly, with open eyes and a full understanding of what you do, you would exchange an honourable wifehood for . . . for the thing that such men as M. de La Tour d'Azyr may have in store for you?"

M. Binet made a wide gesture, and swung to his daughter. "You hear him, the mealy-mouthed prude! Perhaps you'll believe at last that marriage with him would be the ruin of you. He would always be there—the inconvenient husband—to mar your every chance, my girl."

She tossed her lovely head in agreement with her father. "I begin to find him tiresome with his silly jealousies," she confessed. "As a husband I am afraid he would be impossible."

André-Louis felt a constriction of the heart. But—always the actor—he showed nothing of it. He laughed a little, not very pleasantly, and rose.

"I bow to your choice, mademoiselle. I pray that you may not regret it."

"Regret it?" cried M. Binet. He was laughing, relieved to see his daughter at last rid of this suitor of whom he had never approved, if we except those few hours when he really believed him to be an eccentric of distinction. "And what shall she regret? That she accepted the protection of a nobleman so powerful and wealthy that as a mere trinket he gives her a jewel worth as much as an actress earns in a year at the Comédie Française?" He got up, and advanced towards André-Louis. His mood became conciliatory. "Come, come, my friend, no rancour now. What the devil! You wouldn't stand in the girl's way? You can't really blame her for making this choice? Have you thought what it means to her? Have you thought that under the protection of such a gentleman there are no heights which she may not reach? Don't you see the wonderful luck of it? Surely, if you're fond of her, particularly being of a jealous temperament, you wouldn't wish it otherwise?"

André-Louis looked at him in silence for a long moment. Then he laughed again. "Oh, you are fantastic," he said. "You are not real." He turned on his heel and strode to the door.

The action, and more the contempt of his look, laugh, and words stung M. Binet to passion, drove out the conciliatoriness of his mood.

"Fantastic, are we?" he cried, turning to follow the departing Scaramouche with his little eyes that now were inexpressibly evil. "Fantastic that we should prefer the powerful protection of this great nobleman to marriage with a beggarly, nameless bastard. Oh, we are fantastic!"

André-Louis turned, his hand upon the door-handle. "No," he said, "I was mistaken. You are not fantastic. You are just vile—both of you." And he went out.

CHAPTER X

Contrition

Mlle. de Kercadiou walked with her aunt in the bright morning sunshine of a Sunday in March on the broad terrace of the Château de Sautron.

For one of her natural sweetness of disposition she had been oddly irritable of late, manifesting signs of a cynical worldliness, which convinced Mme. de Sautron more than ever that her brother Quintin had scandalously conducted the child's education. She appeared to be instructed in all the things of which a girl is better ignorant, and ignorant of all the things that a girl should know. That at least was the point of view of Mme. de Sautron.

"Tell me, madame," quoth Aline, "are all men beasts?" Unlike her brother, Madame la Comtesse was tall and majestically built. In the days before her marriage with M. de Sautron, ill-natured folk described her as the only man in the family. She looked down now from her noble height upon her little niece with startled eyes.

"Really, Aline, you have a trick of asking the most disconcerting and improper questions."

"Perhaps it is because I find life disconcerting and improper."

"Life? A young girl should not discuss life."

"Why not, since I am alive? You do not suggest that it is an impropriety to be alive?"

"It is an impropriety for a young unmarried girl to seek to know too much about life. As for your absurd question about men, when I remind you that man is the noblest work of God, perhaps you will consider yourself answered."

Mme. de Sautron did not invite a pursuance of the subject. But Mlle. de Kercadiou's outrageous rearing had made her headstrong.

"That being so," said she, "will you tell me why they find such an overwhelming attraction in the immodest of our sex?"

Madame stood still and raised shocked hands. Then she looked down her handsome, high-bridged nose.

"Sometimes—often, in fact, my dear Aline—you pass all understanding. I shall write to Quintin that the sooner you are married the better it will be for all."

"Uncle Quintin has left that matter to my own deciding," Aline reminded her.

"That," said madame with complete conviction, "is the last and most outrageous of his errors. Whoever heard of a girl being left to decide the matter of her own marriage? It is . . . indelicate almost to expose her to thoughts of such things." Mme. de Sautron shuddered. "Quintin is a boor. His conduct is unheard-of. That

M. de La Tour d'Azyr should parade himself before you so that
you may make up your mind whether he is the proper man for
you!" Again she shuddered. "It is of a grossness, of . . . of a pruri-
ence almost . . . Mon Dieu! When I married your uncle, all this
was arranged between our parents. I first saw him when he came
to sign the contract. I should have died of shame had it been
otherwise. And that is how these affairs should be conducted."

"You are no doubt right, madame. But since that is not how
my own case is being conducted, you will forgive me if I deal
with it apart from others. M. de La Tour d'Azyr desires to marry
me. He has been permitted to pay his court. I should be glad to
have him informed that he may cease to do so."

Mme. de Sautron stood still, petrified by amazement. Her
long face turned white; she seemed to breathe with difficulty.

"But . . . but . . . what are you saying?" she gasped.

Quietly Aline repeated her statement.

"But this is outrageous! You cannot be permitted to play fast-
and-loose with a gentleman of M. le Marquis' quality! Why, it is
little more than a week since you permitted him to be informed
that you would become his wife!"

"I did so in a moment of . . . rashness. Since then M. le Marquis' own conduct has convinced me of my error."

"But—mon Dieu!" cried the Countess. "Are you blind to the
great honour that is being paid you? M. le Marquis will make
you the first lady in Brittany. Yet, little fool that you are, and
greater fool that Quintin is, you trifle with this extraordinary
good fortune! Let me warn you." She raised an admonitory fore-
finger. "If you continue in this stupid humour M. de La Tour
d'Azyr may definitely withdraw his offer and depart in justified

mortification."

"That, madame, as I am endeavouring to convey to you, is what I most desire."

"Oh, you are mad."

"It may be, madame, that I am sane in preferring to be guided by my instincts. It may be even that I am justified in resenting that the man who aspires to become my husband should at the same time be paying such assiduous homage to a wretched theatre girl at the Feydau."

"Aline!"

"Is it not true? Or perhaps you do not find it strange that M. de La Tour d'Azyr should so conduct himself at such a time?"

"Aline, you are so extraordinary a mixture. At moments you shock me by the indecency of your expressions; at others you amaze me by the excess of your prudery. You have been brought up like a little bourgeoise, I think. Yes, that is it—a little bourgeoise. Quintin was always something of a shopkeeper at heart."

"I was asking your opinion on the conduct of M. de La Tour d'Azyr, madame. Not on my own."

"But it is an indelicacy in you to observe such things. You should be ignorant of them, and I can't think who is so . . . so unfeeling as to inform you. But since you are informed, at least you should be modestly blind to things that take place outside the . . . orbit of a properly conducted demoiselle."

"Will they still be outside my orbit when I am married?"

"If you are wise. You should remain without knowledge of them. It . . . it deflowers your innocence. I would not for the world that M. de La Tour d'Azyr should know you so extraordinarily instructed. Had you been properly reared in a convent this would never have happened to you."

"But you do not answer me, madame!" cried Aline in despair. "It is not my chastity that is in question; but that of M. de La Tour d'Azyr."

"Chastity!" Madame's lips trembled with horror. Horror overspread her face. "Wherever did you learn that dreadful, that so improper word?"

And then Mme. de Sautron did violence to her feelings. She realized that here great calm and prudence were required. "My child, since you know so much that you ought not to know, there can be no harm in my adding that a gentleman must have these little distractions."

"But why, madame? Why is it so?"

"Ah, mon Dieu, you are asking me riddles of nature. It is so because it is so. Because men are like that."

"Because men are beasts, you mean—which is what I began by asking you."

"You are incorrigibly stupid, Aline."

"You mean that I do not see things as you do, madame. I am not over-expectant as you appear to think; yet surely I have the right to expect that whilst M. de La Tour d'Azyr is wooing me, he shall not be wooing at the same time a drab of the theatre. I feel that in this there is a subtle association of myself with that unspeakable creature which soils and insults me. The Marquis is a dullard whose wooing takes the form at best of stilted compliments, stupid and unoriginal. They gain nothing when they fall from lips still warm from the contamination of that woman's kisses."

So utterly scandalized was madame that for a moment she

remained speechless. Then—"Mon Dieu!" she exclaimed. "I should never have suspected you of so indelicate an imagination."

"I cannot help it, madame. Each time his lips touch my fingers I find myself thinking of the last object that they touched. I at once retire to wash my hands. Next time, madame, unless you are good enough to convey my message to him, I shall call for water and wash them in his presence."

"But what am I to tell him? How . . . in what words can I convey such a message?" Madame was aghast.

"Be frank with him, madame. It is easiest in the end. Tell him that however impure may have been his life in the past, however impure he intend that it shall be in the future, he must at least study purity whilst approaching with a view to marriage a virgin who is herself pure and without stain."

Madame recoiled, and put her hands to her ears, horror stamped on her handsome face. Her massive bosom heaved.

"Oh, how can you?" she panted. "How can you make use of such terrible expressions? Wherever have you learnt them?"

"In church," said Aline.

"Ah, but in church many things are said that . . . that one would not dream of saying in the world. My dear child, how could I possibly say such a thing to M. le Marquis? How could I possibly?"

"Shall I say it?"

"Aline!"

"Well, there it is," said Aline. "Something must be done to shelter me from insult. I am utterly disgusted with M. le Marquis—a disgusting man. And however fine a thing it may be to become Marquise de La Tour d'Azyr, why, frankly, I'd sooner marry a cobbler who practised decency."

Such was her vehemence and obvious determination that Mme. de Sautron fetched herself out of her despair to attempt persuasion. Aline was her niece, and such a marriage in the family would be to the credit of the whole of it. At all costs nothing must frustrate it.

"Listen, my dear," she said. "Let us reason. M. le Marquis is away and will not be back until tomorrow."

"True. And I know where he has gone—or at least whom he has gone with. Mon Dieu, and the drab has a father and a lout of a fellow who intends to make her his wife, and neither of them chooses to do anything. I suppose they agree with you, madame, that a great gentleman must have his little distractions." Her contempt was as scorching as a thing of fire. "However, madame, you were about to say?"

"That on the day after tomorrow you are returning to Gavrillac. M. de La Tour d'Azyr will most likely follow at his leisure."

"You mean when this dirty candle is burnt out?"

"Call it what you will." Madame, you see, despaired by now of controlling the impropriety of her niece's expressions. "At Gavrillac there will be no Mlle. Binet. This thing will be in the past. It is unfortunate that he should have met her at such a moment. The chit is very attractive, after all. You cannot deny that. And you must make allowances."

"M. le Marquis formally proposed to me a week ago. Partly to satisfy the wishes of the family, and partly—" She broke off, hesitating a moment, to resume on a note of dull pain, "Partly because it does not seem greatly to matter whom I marry, I gave him my consent. That consent, for the reasons I have given you, madame, I desire now definitely to withdraw."

Madame fell into agitation of the wildest. "Aline, I should never forgive you! Your uncle Quintin would be in despair. You do not know what you are saying, what a wonderful thing you are refusing. Have you no sense of your position, of the station into which you were born?"

"If I had not, madame, I should have made an end long since. If I have tolerated this suit for a single moment, it is because I realize the importance of a suitable marriage in the worldly sense. But I ask of marriage something more; and Uncle Quintin has placed the decision in my hands."

"God forgive him!" said madame. And then she hurried on: "Leave this to me now, Aline. Be guided by me—oh, be guided by me!" Her tone was beseeching. "I will take counsel with your uncle Charles. But do not definitely decide until this unfortunate affair has blown over. Charles will know how to arrange it. M. le Marquis shall do penance, child, since your tyranny demands it; but not in sackcloth and ashes. You'll not ask so much?"

Aline shrugged. "I ask nothing at all," she said, which was neither assent nor dissent.

So Mme. de Sautron interviewed her husband, a slight, middle-aged man, very aristocratic in appearance and gifted with a certain shrewd sense. She took with him precisely the tone that Aline had taken with herself and which in Aline she had found so disconcertingly indelicate. She even borrowed several of Aline's phrases.

The result was that on the Monday afternoon when at last
M. de La Tour d'Azyr's returning berline drove up to the château,
he was met by M. le Comte de Sautron who desired a word with
him even before he changed.

"Gervais, you're a fool," was the excellent opening made by
M. le Comte.

"Charles, you give me no news," answered M. le Marquis.
"Of what particular folly do you take the trouble to complain?"

He flung himself wearily upon a sofa, and his long graceful
body sprawling there he looked up at his friend with a tired smile
on that nobly handsome pale face that seemed to defy the on-
slaught of age.

"Of your last. This Binet girl."

"That! Pooh! An incident; hardly a folly."

"A folly—at such a time," Sautron insisted. The Marquis
looked a question. The Count answered it. "Aline," said he, preg-
nantly. "She knows. How she knows I can't tell you, but she
knows, and she is deeply offended."

The smile perished on the Marquis' face. He gathered himself up.

"Offended?" said he, and his voice was anxious.

"But yes. You know what she is. You know the ideals she has
formed. It wounds her that at such a time—whilst you are here
for the purpose of wooing her—you should at the same time be
pursuing this affair with that chit of a Binet girl."

"How do you know?" asked La Tour d'Azyr.

"She has confided in her aunt. And the poor child seems to
have some reason. She says she will not tolerate that you should

242

come to kiss her hand with lips that are still contaminated from . . . Oh, you understand. You appreciate the impression of such a thing upon a pure, sensitive girl such as Aline. She said— I had better tell you—that the next time you kiss her hand, she will call for water and wash it in your presence."

The Marquis' face flamed scarlet. He rose. Knowing his violent, intolerant spirit, M. de Sautron was prepared for an outburst. But no outburst came. The Marquis turned away from him, and paced slowly to the window, his head bowed, his hands behind his back. Halted there he spoke, without turning, his voice was at once scornful and wistful.

"You are right, Charles, I am a fool—a wicked fool! I have just enough sense left to perceive it. It is the way I have lived, I suppose. I have never known the need to deny myself anything I wanted." Then suddenly he swung round, and the outburst came. "But, my God, I want Aline as I have never wanted anything yet! I think I should kill myself in rage if through my folly I should have lost her." He struck his brow with his hand. "I am a beast!" he said. "I should have known that if that sweet saint got word of these petty devilries of mine she would despise me; and I tell you, Charles, I'd go through fire to regain her respect."

"I hope it is to be regained on easier terms," said Charles; and then to ease the situation which began to irk him by its solemnity, he made a feeble joke. "It is merely asked of you that you refrain from going through certain fires that are not accounted by mademoiselle of too purifying a nature."

"As to that Binet girl, it is finished—finished," said the Marquis.

"I congratulate you. When did you make that decision?"

"This moment. I would to God I had made it twenty-four hours ago. As it is—" he shrugged—"why, twenty-four hours of her have been enough for me as they would have been for any man—a mercenary, self-seeking little baggage with the soul of a trull. Bah!" He shuddered in disgust of himself and her.

"Ah! That makes it easier for you," said M. de Sautron, cynically.

"Don't say it, Charles. It is not so. Had you been less of a fool, you would have warned me sooner."

"I may prove to have warned you soon enough if you'll profit by the warning."

"There is no penance I will not do. I will prostrate myself at her feet. I will abase myself before her. I will make confession in the proper spirit of contrition, and Heaven helping me, I'll keep to my purpose of amendment for her sweet sake." He was tragically in earnest.

To M. de Sautron, who had never seen him other than self-contained, supercilious, and mocking, this was an amazing revelation. He shrank from it almost; it gave him the feeling of prying, of peeping through a keyhole. He slapped his friend's shoulder.

"My dear Gervais, here is a magnificently romantic mood. Enough said. Keep to it, and I promise you that all will presently be well. I will be your ambassador, and you shall have no cause to complain."

"But may I not go to her myself?"

"If you are wise you will at once efface yourself. Write to her if you will—make your act of contrition by letter. I will explain why you have gone without seeing her. I will tell her that you did so upon my advice, and I will do it tactfully. I am a good diplomat, Gervais. Trust me."

M. le Marquis raised his head, and showed a face that pain was searing. He held out his hand. "Very well, Charles. Serve me in this, and count me your friend in all things."

CHAPTER XI

The Fracas at
the Théâtre Feydau

Leaving his host to act as his plenipotentiary with Mademoiselle de Kercadiou, and to explain to her that it was his profound contrition that compelled him to depart without taking
formal leave of her, the Marquis rolled away from Sautron in a
cloud of gloom. Twenty-four hours with La Binet had been more
than enough for a man of his fastidious and discerning taste. He
looked back upon the episode with nausea—the inevitable psy-
chological reaction—marvelling at himself that until yesterday
he should have found her so desirable, and cursing himself that
for the sake of that ephemeral and worthless gratification he should
seriously have imperilled his chances of winning Mademoiselle
de Kercadiou to wife. There is, after all, nothing very extraordinary in his frame of mind, so that I need not elaborate it further.
It resulted from the conflict between the beast and the angel that
go to make up the composition of every man.

The Chevalier de Chabrillane—who in reality occupied towards the Marquis a position akin to that of gentleman-in-waiting—sat opposite to him in the enormous travelling berline. A small folding table had been erected between them, and the Chevalier suggested piquet. But M. le Marquis was in no humour for cards. His thoughts absorbed him. As they were rattling over the cobbles of Nantes' streets, he remembered a promise to La Binet to witness her performance that night in *The Faithless Lover*. And now he was running away from her. The thought was repugnant to him on two scores. He was breaking his pledged word, and he was acting like a coward. And there was more than that. He had led the mercenary little strumpet—it was thus he thought of her at present, and with some justice—to expect favours from him in addition to the lavish awards which already he had made her. The baggage had almost sought to drive a bargain with him as to her future. He was to take her to Paris, put her into her own furniture—as the expression ran, and still runs—and under the shadow of his powerful protection see that the doors of the great theatres of the capital should be opened to her talents. He had not—he was thankful to reflect—exactly committed himself. But neither had he definitely refused her. It became necessary now to come to an understanding, since he was compelled to choose between his trivial passion for her—a passion quenched already—and his deep, almost spiritual devotion to Mademoiselle de Kercadiou.

His honour, he considered, demanded of him that he should at once deliver himself from a false position. La Binet would make a scene, of course; but he knew the proper specific to apply to hysteria of that nature. Money, after all, has its uses.

He pulled the cord. The carriage rolled to a standstill; a foot-man appeared at the door.

"To the Théâtre Feydau," said he.

The footman vanished and the berline rolled on. M. de Chabrillane laughed cynically.

"I'll trouble you not to be amused," snapped the Marquis. "You don't understand." Thereafter he explained himself. It was a rare condescension in him. But, then, he could not bear to be misunderstood in such a matter. Chabrillane grew serious in re-flection of the Marquis' extreme seriousness.

"Why not write?" he suggested. "Myself, I confess that I should find it easier."

Nothing could better have revealed M. le Marquis' state of mind than his answer.

"Letters are liable both to miscarriage and to misconstruc-tion. Two risks I will not run. If she did not answer, I should never know which had been incurred. And I shall have no peace of mind until I know that I have set a term to this affair. The berline can wait while we are at the theatre. We will go on after-wards. We will travel all night if necessary."

"*Peste!*" said M. de Chabrillane with a grimace. But that was all.

The great travelling carriage drew up at the lighted portals of the Feydau, and M. le Marquis stepped out. He entered the the-atre with Chabrillane, all unconsciously to deliver himself into the hands of André-Louis.

André-Louis was in a state of exasperation produced by Climène's long absence from Nantes in the company of M. le Marquis, and fed by the unspeakable complacency with which

M. Binet regarded that event of quite unmistakable import.

However much he might affect the frame of mind of the stoics, and seek to judge with a complete detachment, in the heart and soul of him André-Louis was tormented and revolted. It was not Climène he blamed. He had been mistaken in her. She was just a poor weak vessel driven helplessly by the first breath, however foul, that promised her advancement. She suffered from the plague of greed; and he congratulated himself upon having discovered it before making her his wife. He felt for her now nothing but a deal of pity and some contempt. The pity was begotten of the love she had lately inspired in him. It might be likened to the dregs of love, all that remained after the potent wine of it had been drained off. His anger he reserved for her father and her seducer.

The thoughts that were stirring in him on that Monday morning, when it was discovered that Climène had not yet returned from her excursion of the previous day in the coach of M. le Marquis, were already wicked enough without the spurring they received from the distraught Léandre.

Hitherto the attitude of each of these men towards the other had been one of mutual contempt. The phenomenon has frequently been observed in like cases. Now, what appeared to be a common misfortune brought them into a sort of alliance. So, at least, it seemed to Léandre when he went in quest of André-Louis, who with apparent unconcern was smoking a pipe upon the quay immediately facing the inn.

"Name of a pig!" said Léandre. "How can you take your ease and smoke at such a time?"

Scaramouche surveyed the sky. "I do not find it too cold,"

said he. "The sun is shining. I am very well here."

"Do I talk of the weather?" Léandre was very excited.

"Of what, then?"

"Of Climène, of course."

"Oh! The lady has ceased to interest me," he lied.

Léandre stood squarely in front of him, a handsome figure handsomely dressed in these days, his hair well powdered, his stockings of silk. His face was pale, his large eyes looked larger than usual.

"Ceased to interest you? Are you not to marry her?"

André-Louis expelled a cloud of smoke. "You cannot wish to be offensive. Yet you almost suggest that I live on other men's leavings."

"My God!" said Léandre, overcome, and he stared awhile. Then he burst out afresh. "Are you quite heartless? Are you always Scaramouche?"

"What do you expect me to do?" asked André-Louis, evincing surprise in his own turn, but faintly.

"I do not expect you to let her go without a struggle."

"But she has gone already." André-Louis pulled at his pipe a moment, what time Léandre clenched and unclenched his hands in impotent rage. "And to what purpose struggle against the inevitable? Did you struggle when I took her from you?"

"She was not mine to be taken from me. I but aspired, and you won the race. But even had it been otherwise where is the comparison? That was a thing in honour; this—this is hell."

His emotion moved André-Louis. He took Léandre's arm.

"You're a good fellow, Léandre. I am glad I intervened to save you from your fate."

"Oh, you don't love her!" cried the other, passionately. "You never did. You don't know what it means to love, or you'd not talk like this. My God! if she had been my affianced wife and this had happened, I should have killed the man—killed him! Do you hear me? But you . . . Oh, you, you come out here and smoke, and take the air, and talk of her as another man's leavings. I wonder I didn't strike you for the word."

He tore his arm from the other's grip, and looked almost as if he would strike him now.

"You should have done it," said André-Louis. "It's in your part."

With an imprecation Léandre turned on his heel to go. André-Louis arrested his departure.

"A moment, my friend. Test me by yourself. Would you marry her now?"

"Would I?" The young man's eyes blazed with passion. "Would I? Let her say that she will marry me, and I am her slave."

"Slave is the right word—a slave in hell."

"It would never be hell to me where she was, whatever she had done. I love her, man, I am not like you. I love her, do you hear me?"

"I have known it for some time," said André-Louis. "Though I didn't suspect your attack of the disease to be quite so violent. Well, God knows I loved her, too, quite enough to share your thirst for killing. For myself, the blue blood of La Tour d'Azyr would hardly quench this thirst. I should like to add to it the dirty fluid that flows in the veins of the unspeakable Binet."

For a second his emotion had been out of hand, and he revealed to Léandre in the mordant tone of those last words some-

251

thing of the fires that burned under his icy exterior. The young man caught him by the hand.

"I knew you were acting," said he. "You feel—you feel as I do."

"Behold us, fellows in viciousness. I have betrayed myself, it seems. Well, and what now? Do you want to see this pretty Marquis torn limb from limb? I might afford you the spectacle."

"What?" Léandre stared, wondering was this another of Scaramouche's cynicisms.

"It isn't really difficult provided I have aid. I require only a little. Will you lend it me?"

"Anything you ask," Léandre exploded. "My life if you require it."

André-Louis took his arm again. "Let us walk," he said. "I will instruct you."

When they came back the company was already at dinner. Mademoiselle had not yet returned. Sullenness presided at the table. Columbine and Madame wore anxious expressions. The fact was that relations between Binet and his troupe were daily growing more strained.

André-Louis and Léandre went each to his accustomed place. Binet's little eyes followed them with a malicious gleam, his thick lips pouted into a crooked smile.

"You two are grown very friendly of a sudden," he mocked.

"You are a man of discernment, Binet," said Scaramouche, the cold loathing of his voice itself an insult. "Perhaps you discern the reason?"

"It is readily discerned."

"Regale the company with it!" he begged; and waited.

"What? You hesitate? Is it possible that there are limits to your shamelessness?"

Binet reared his great head. "Do you want to quarrel with me, Scaramouche?" Thunder was rumbling in his deep voice.

"Quarrel? You want to laugh. A man doesn't quarrel with creatures like you. We all know the place held in the public esteem by complacent husbands. But, in God's name, what place is there at all for complacent fathers?"

Binet heaved himself up, a great towering mass of manhood. Violently he shook off the restraining hand of Pierrot who sat on his left.

"A thousand devils!" he roared; "if you take that tone with me, I'll break every bone in your filthy body."

"If you were to lay a finger on me, Binet, you would give me the only provocation I still need to kill you." André-Louis was as calm as ever, and therefore the more menacing. Alarm stirred the company. He protruded from his pocket the butt of a pistol— newly purchased. "I go armed, Binet. It is only fair to give you warning. Provoke me as you have suggested, and I'll kill you with no more compunction than I should kill a slug, which after all is the thing you most resemble—a slug, Binet; a fat, slimy body; foulness without soul and without intelligence. When I come to think of it I can't suffer to sit at table with you. It turns my stomach."

He pushed away his platter and got up. "I'll go and eat at the ordinary below stairs."

Thereupon up jumped Columbine.

"And I'll come with you, Scaramouche!" cried she.

It acted like a signal. Had the thing been concerted it couldn't have fallen out more uniformly. Binet, in fact, was persuaded of a conspiracy. For in the wake of Columbine went Léandre, in the wake of Léandre, Polichinelle; and then all the rest together, until Binet found himself sitting alone at the head of an empty table in an empty room—a badly shaken man whose rage could afford him no support against the dread by which he was suddenly invaded.

He sat down to think things out, and he was still at that melancholy occupation when perhaps a half-hour later his daughter entered the room, returned at last from her excursion.

She looked pale, even a little scared—in reality excessively self-conscious now that the ordeal of facing all the company awaited her.

Seeing no one but her father in the room, she checked on the threshold.

"Where is everybody?" she asked, in a voice rendered natural by effort.

M. Binet reared his great head and turned upon her eyes that were blood-injected. He scowled, blew out his thick lips and made harsh noises in his throat. Yet he took stock of her, so graceful and comely and looking so completely the lady of fashion in her long fur-trimmed travelling coat of bottle green, her muff and her broad hat adorned by a sparkling Rhinestone buckle above her adorably coiffed brown hair. No need to fear the future whilst he owned such a daughter, let Scaramouche play what tricks he would.

He expressed, however, none of these comforting reflections.

"So you're back at last, little fool," he growled in greeting. "I was beginning to ask myself if we should perform this evening. It wouldn't greatly have surprised me if you had not returned in time. Indeed, since you have chosen to play the fine hand you held in your own way and scorning my advice, nothing can surprise me."

She crossed the room to the table, and leaning against it, looked down upon him almost disdainfully.

"I have nothing to regret," she said.

"So every fool says at first. Nor would you admit it if you had. You are like that. You go your own way in spite of advice from older heads. Death of my life, girl, what do you know of men?"

"I am not complaining," she reminded him.

"No, but you may be presently, when you discover that you would have done better to have been guided by your old father. So long as your Marquis languished for you, there was nothing you could not have done with the fool. So long as you let him have no more than your fingertips to kiss ... ah, name of a name! that was the time to build your future. If you live to be a thousand you'll never have such a chance again, and you've squandered it, for what?"

Mademoiselle sat down. "You're sordid," she said, with disgust.

"Sordid, am I?" His thick lips curled again. "I have had enough of the dregs of life, and so I should have thought have you. You held a hand on which to have won a fortune if you had played it as I bade you. Well, you've played it, and where's the fortune? We can whistle for that as a sailor whistles for wind. And, by Heaven, we'll need to whistle presently if the weather in the troupe continues as it's set in. That scoundrel Scaramouche has been at his ape's tricks with them. They've suddenly turned moral. They won't sit at table with me any more." He was spluttering between anger and sardonic mirth. "It was your friend Scaramouche set them the example of that. He threatened my life actually. Threatened my life! Called me . . . Oh, but what does that matter? What matters is that the next thing to happen to us will be that the Binet Troupe will discover it can manage without M. Binet and his daughter. This scoundrelly bastard I've befriended has little by little robbed me of everything. It's in his power today to rob me of my troupe, and the knave's ungrateful enough and vile enough to make use of his power."

"Let him," said mademoiselle contemptuously.

"Let him?" He was aghast. "And what's to become of us?"

"In no case will the Binet Troupe interest me much longer," said she. "I shall be going to Paris soon. There are better theatres there than the Feydau. There's Mlle. Montansier's theatre in the Palais Royal; there's the Ambigu Comique; there's the Comédie Française; there's even a possibility I may have a theatre of my own."

His eyes grew big for once. He stretched out a fat hand, and placed it on one of hers. She noticed that it trembled.

"Has he promised that? Has he promised?"

She looked at him with her head on one side, eyes sly and a queer little smile on her perfect lips.

"He did not refuse me when I asked it," she answered, with conviction that all was as she desired it.

"Bah!" He withdrew his hand, and heaved himself up. There was disgust on his face. "He did not refuse!" he mocked her; and then with passion: "Had you acted as I advised you, he would have consented to anything that you asked, and what is more he would have provided anything that you asked—anything that lay within his means, and they are inexhaustible. You have changed a certainty into a possibility, and I hate possibilities—God of God! I have lived on possibilities, and infernally near starved on them."

Had she known of the interview taking place at that moment at the Château de Sautron she would have laughed less confidently at her father's gloomy forebodings. But she was destined never to know, which indeed was the cruellest punishment of all. She was to attribute all the evil that of a sudden overwhelmed her, the shattering of all the future hopes she had founded upon the Marquis and the sudden disintegration of the Binet Troupe, to the wicked interference of that villain Scaramouche.

She had this much justification that possibly, without the warning from M. de Sautron, the Marquis would have found in the events of that evening at the Théâtre Feydau a sufficient reason for ending an entanglement that was fraught with too much unpleasant excitement, whilst the breaking-up of the Binet Troupe was most certainly the result of André-Louis' work. But it was not a result that he intended or even foresaw.

So much was this the case that in the interval after the second act, he sought the dressing-room shared by Polichinelle and Rhodomont. Polichinelle was in the act of changing.

"I shouldn't trouble to change," he said. "The piece isn't likely to go beyond my opening scene of the next act with Léandre."

"What do you mean?"

"You'll see." He put a paper on Polichinelle's table amid the grease-paints. "Cast your eye over that. It's a sort of last will and testament in favour of the troupe. I was a lawyer once; the document is in order. I relinquish to all of you the share produced by my partnership in the Company."

"But you don't mean that you are leaving us?" cried Polichinelle in alarm, whilst Rhodomont's sudden stare asked the same question.

Scaramouche's shrug was eloquent. Polichinelle ran on gloomily: "Of course it was to have been foreseen. But why should you be the one to go? It is you who have made us; and it is you who are the real head and brains of the troupe; it is you who have raised it into a real theatrical company. If any one must go, let it be Binet—Binet and his infernal daughter. Or if you go, name of a name! we all go with you!"

"Aye," added Rhodomont, "we've had enough of that fat scoundrel."

"I had thought of it, of course," said André-Louis. "It was not vanity, for once; it was trust in your friendship. After tonight we may consider it again, if I survive."

"If you survive?" both cried.

Polichinelle got up. "Now, what madness have you in mind?" he asked.

"For one thing I think I am indulging Léandre; for another I am pursuing an old quarrel."

The three knocks sounded as he spoke.

"There, I must go. Keep that paper, Polichinelle. After all, it may not be necessary."

He was gone. Rhodomont stared at Polichinelle. Polichinelle stared at Rhodomont.

"What the devil is he thinking of?" quoth the latter.

"That is most readily ascertained by going to see," replied Polichinelle. He completed changing in haste, and despite what Scaramouche had said; and then followed with Rhodomont.

As they approached the wings a roar of applause met them coming from the audience. It was applause and something else; applause on an unusual note. As it faded away they heard the voice of Scaramouche ringing clear as a bell:

"And so you see, my dear M. Léandre, that when you speak of the Third Estate, it is necessary to be more explicit. What precisely is the Third Estate?"

"Nothing," said Léandre.

There was a gasp from the audience, audible in the wings, and then swiftly followed Scaramouche's next question:

"True. Alas! But what should it be?"

"Everything," said Léandre.

The audience roared its acclamations, the more violent because of the unexpectedness of that reply.

"True again," said Scaramouche. "And what is more, that is what it will be; that is what it already is. Do you doubt it?"

"I hope it," said the schooled Léandre.

"You may believe it," said Scaramouche, and again the acclamations rolled into thunder.

Polichinelle and Rhodomont exchanged glances: indeed, the former winked, not without mirth.

"Sacred name!" growled a voice behind them. "Is the scoundrel at his political tricks again?"

They turned to confront M. Binet. Moving with that noiseless tread of his, he had come up unheard behind them, and there he stood now in his scarlet suit of Pantaloon under a trailing

259

bedgown, his little eyes glaring from either side of his false nose. But their attention was held by the voice of Scaramouche. He had stepped to the front of the stage.

"He doubts it," he was telling the audience. "But then this M. Léandre is himself akin to those who worship the worm-eaten idol of Privilege, and so he is a little afraid to believe a truth that is becoming apparent to all the world. Shall I convince him? Shall I tell him how a company of noblemen backed by their servants under arms—six hundred men in all—sought to dictate to the Third Estate of Rennes a few short weeks ago? Must I remind him of the martial front shown on that occasion by the Third Estate, and how they swept the streets clean of that rabble of nobles—*cette canaille noble . . .*"

Applause interrupted him. The phrase had struck home and caught. Those who had writhed under that infamous designation from their betters leapt at this turning of it against the nobles themselves.

"But let me tell you of their leader—*le plus noble de cette canaille, ou bien le plus canaille de ces nobles!* You know him— that one. He fears many things, but the voice of truth he fears most. With such as him the eloquent truth eloquently spoken is a thing instantly to be silenced. So he marshalled his peers and their *valetailles*, and led them out to slaughter these miserable bourgeois who dared to raise a voice. But these same miserable bourgeois did not choose to be slaughtered in the streets of Rennes. It occurred to them that since the nobles decreed that blood should flow, it might as well be the blood of the nobles. They marshalled themselves too—this noble rabble against the rabble of nobles—and they marshalled themselves so well that they drove M. de La Tour d'Azyr and his warlike following from the field with broken heads and shattered delusions. They sought shelter at the hands of the Cordeliers; and the shavelings gave them sanctuary in their convent—those who survived, among whom was their proud leader, M. de La Tour d'Azyr. You have heard of this valiant Marquis, this great lord of life and death?"

The pit was in an uproar a moment. It quieted again as Scaramouche continued:

"Oh, it was a fine spectacle to see this mighty hunter scuttling to cover like a hare, going to earth in the Cordelier Convent. Rennes has not seen him since. Rennes would like to see him again. But if he is valorous, he is also discreet. And where do you think he has taken refuge, this great nobleman who wanted to see the streets of Rennes washed in the blood of its citizens, this man who would have butchered old and young of the contemptible *canaille* to silence the voice of reason and of liberty that presumes to ring through France today? Where do you think he hides himself? Why, here in Nantes."

Again there was uproar.

"What do you say? Impossible? Why, my friends, at this moment he is here in this theatre—skulking up there in that box. He is too shy to show himself—oh, a very modest gentleman. But there he is behind the curtains. Will you not show yourself to your friends, M. de La Tour d'Azyr, Monsieur le Marquis who considers eloquence so very dangerous a gift? See, they would like a word with you; they do not believe me when I tell them that you are here."

Now, whatever he may have been, and whatever the views held on the subject by André-Louis, M. de La Tour d'Azyr was

261

certainly not a coward. To say that he was hiding in Nantes was not true. He came and went there openly and unabashed. It happened, however, that the Nantais were ignorant until this moment of his presence among them. But then he would have disdained to have informed them of it just as he would have disdained to have concealed it from them.

Challenged thus, however, and despite the ominous manner in which the bourgeois element in the audience had responded to Scaramouche's appeal to its passions, despite the attempts made by Chabrillane to restrain him, the Marquis swept aside the curtain at the side of the box, and suddenly showed himself, pale but self-contained and scornful as he surveyed first the daring Scaramouche and then those others who at sight of him had given tongue to their hostility.

Hoots and yells assailed him, fists were shaken at him, canes were brandished menacingly.

"Assassin! Scoundrel! Coward! Traitor!"

But he braved the storm, smiling upon them his ineffable contempt. He was waiting for the noise to cease; waiting to address them in his turn. But he waited in vain, as he very soon perceived.

The contempt he did not trouble to dissemble served but to goad them on.

In the pit pandemonium was already raging. Blows were being freely exchanged; there were scuffling groups, and here and there swords were being drawn, but fortunately the press was too dense to permit of their being used effectively. Those who had women with them and the timid by nature were making haste to leave a house that looked like becoming a cockpit, where chairs were being smashed to provide weapons, and parts of chandeliers were already being used as missiles.

One of these hurled by the hand of a gentleman in one of the boxes narrowly missed Scaramouche where he stood, looking down in a sort of grim triumph upon the havoc which his words had wrought. Knowing of what inflammable material the audience was composed, he had deliberately flung down amongst them the lighted torch of discord, to produce this conflagration.

He saw men falling quickly into groups representative of one side or the other of this great quarrel that already was beginning to agitate the whole of France. Their rallying cries were ringing through the theatre.

"Down with the *canaille*!" from some.

"Down with the privileged!" from others.

And then above the general din one cry rang out sharply and insistently:

"To the box! Death to the butcher of Rennes! Death to La Tour d'Azyr who makes war upon the people!"

There was a rush for one of the doors of the pit that opened upon the staircase leading to the boxes.

And now, whilst battle and confusion spread with the speed of fire, overflowing from the theatre into the street itself, La Tour d'Azyr's box, which had become the main object of the attack of the bourgeoisie, had also become the rallying ground for such gentlemen as were present in the theatre and for those who, without being men of birth themselves, were nevertheless attached to the party of the nobles.

La Tour d'Azyr had quitted the front of the box to meet those who came to join him. And now in the pit one group of infuriated gentlemen, in attempting to reach the stage across the empty orchestra, so that they might deal with the audacious comedian who was responsible for this explosion, found themselves opposed and held back by another group composed of men to whose feelings André-Louis had given expression.

Perceiving this, and remembering the chandelier, he turned to Léandre, who had remained beside him.

"I think it is time to be going," said he.

Léandre, looking ghastly under his paint, appalled by the storm which exceeded by far anything that his unimaginative brain could have conjectured, gurgled an inarticulate agreement. But it looked as if already they were too late, for in that moment they were assailed from behind.

M. Binet had succeeded at last in breaking past Polichinelle and Rhodomont, who in view of his murderous rage had been endeavouring to restrain him. Half a dozen gentlemen, habitués of the green-room, had come round to the stage to disembowel the knave who had created this riot, and it was they who had flung aside those two comedians who hung upon Binet. After him they came now, their swords out; but after them again came Polichinelle, Rhodomont, Harlequin, Pierrot, Pasquariel, and Basque the artist, armed with such implements as they could hastily snatch up, and intent upon saving the man with whom they sympathized in spite of all, and in whom now all their hopes were centred.

Well ahead rolled Binet, moving faster than any had ever seen him move, and swinging the long cane from which Pantaloon is inseparable.

"Infamous scoundrel!" he roared. "You have ruined me! But,

name of a name, you shall pay!"

André-Louis turned to face him. "You confuse cause with effect," said he. But he got no farther. Binet's cane, viciously driven, descended and broke upon his shoulder.

Had he not moved swiftly aside as the blow fell it must have taken him across the head, and possibly stunned him. As he moved, he dropped his hand to his pocket, and swift upon the cracking of Binet's breaking cane came the crack of the pistol with which André-Louis replied.

"You had your warning, you filthy pander!" he cried. And on the word he shot him through the body.

Binet went down screaming, whilst the fierce Polichinelle, fiercer than ever in that moment of fierce reality, spoke quickly into André-Louis' ear:

"Fool! So much was not necessary! Away with you now, or you'll leave your skin here! Away with you!"

André-Louis thought it good advice, and took it. The gentlemen who had followed Binet in that punitive rush upon the stage, partly held in check by the improvised weapons of the players, partly intimidated by the second pistol that Scaramouche presented, let him go. He gained the wings, and here found himself faced by a couple of sergeants of the watch, part of the police that was already invading the theatre with a view to restoring order. The sight of them reminded him unpleasantly of how he must stand towards the law for this night's work, and more particularly for that bullet lodged somewhere in Binet's obese body. He flourished his pistol.

"Make way, or I'll burn your brains!" he threatened them, and intimidated, themselves without firearms, they fell back and let him pass. He slipped by the door of the green-room, where the ladies of the company had shut themselves in until the storm should be over, and so gained the street behind the theatre. It was deserted. Down this he went at a run, intent on reaching the inn for clothes and money, since it was impossible that he should take the road in the garb of Scaramouche.

BOOK III

THE SWORD

CHAPTER I

Transition

"You may agree," wrote André-Louis from Paris to Le Chapelier, in a letter which survives, "that it is to be regretted I should definitely have discarded the livery of Scaramouche, since clearly there could be no livery fitter for my wear. It seems to be my part always to stir up strife and then to slip away before I am caught in the crash of the warring elements I have aroused. It is a humiliating reflection. I seek consolation in the reminder of Epictetus (do you ever read Epictetus?) that we are but actors in a play of such a part as it may please the Director to assign us. It does not, however, console me to have been cast for a part so contemptible, to find myself excelling ever in the art of running away. But if I am not brave, at least I am prudent; so that where I lack one virtue I may lay claim to possessing another almost to excess. On a previous occasion they wanted to hang me for sedition. Should I have stayed to be hanged? This time they may want to hang me for several things, including murder; for I do not know whether that scoundrel Binet be alive or dead from the dose of lead I pumped into his fat paunch. Nor can I say that I very greatly care. If I have a hope at all in the matter it is that he is dead—and damned. But I am really indifferent. My own concerns are troubling me enough. I have all but spent the little money that I contrived to conceal about me before I fled from Nantes on that dreadful night; and both of the only two professions of which I can claim to know anything—the law and the stage—are closed to me, since I cannot find employment in either without revealing myself as a fellow who is urgently wanted by the hangman. As things are it is very possible that I may die of hunger, especially considering the present price of victuals in this ravenous city. Again I have recourse to Epictetus for comfort. 'It is better,' he says, 'to die of hunger having lived without grief and fear, than to live with a troubled spirit amid abundance.' I seem likely to perish in the estate that he accounts so enviable. That it does not seem exactly enviable to me merely proves that as a Stoic I am not a success."

There is also another letter of his written at about the same time to the Marquis de La Tour d'Azyr—a letter since published by M. Emile Quersac in his *Undercurrents of the Revolution in Brittany*, unearthed by him from the archives of Rennes, to which it had been consigned by M. de Lesdiguières, who had received it for justiciary purposes from the Marquis.

"The Paris newspapers," he writes in this, "which have reported in considerable detail the fracas at the Théâtre Feydau and disclosed the true identity of the Scaramouche who provoked it, inform me also that you have escaped the fate I had intended for you when I raised that storm of public opinion and public indignation. I would not have you take satisfaction in the thought that I regret your escape. I do not. I rejoice in it. To deal justice by death has this disadvantage: that the victim has no knowledge that justice has overtaken him. Had you died, had you been torn limb from limb that night, I should now repine in the thought of your eternal and untroubled slumber. Not in euthanasia, but in torment of mind should the guilty atone. You see, I am not sure that hell hereafter is a certainty, whilst I am quite sure that it can be a certainty in this life; and I desire you to continue to live yet awhile that you may taste something of its bitterness.

"You murdered Philippe de Vilmorin because you feared what you described as his very dangerous gift of eloquence. I took an oath that day that your evil deed should be fruitless; that I would render it so; that the voice you had done murder to stifle should in spite of that ring like a trumpet through the land. That was my conception of revenge. Do you realize how I have been fulfilling it, how I shall continue to fulfil it as occasion offers? In the speech with which I fired the people of Rennes on the very morrow of that deed, did you not hear the voice of Philippe de Vilmorin uttering the ideas that were his with a fire and a passion greater than he could have commanded because Nemesis lent me her inflaming aid? In the voice of Omnes Omnibus at Nantes— my voice again—demanding the petition that sounded the knell of your hopes of coercing the Third Estate, did you not hear again the voice of Philippe de Vilmorin? Did you not reflect that it was the mind of the man you had murdered, resurrected in me his surviving friend, which made necessary your futile attempt under arms last January, wherein your order, finally beaten, was driven to seek sanctuary in the Cordelier Convent? And that night when from the stage of the Feydau you were denounced to the people, did you not hear yet again, in the voice of Scaramouche, the voice of Philippe de Vilmorin, using that dangerous gift of eloquence which you so foolishly imagined you could silence with a sword-thrust? It is becoming a persecution—is it not?—this voice from the grave that insists upon making itself heard, that will not rest until you have been cast into the pit. You will be regretting by now that you did not kill me too, as I invited you on that occasion. I can picture to myself the bitterness of this regret, and I contemplate it with satisfaction. Regret of neglected opportunity is the worst hell that a living soul can inhabit, particularly such a soul as yours. It is because of this that I am glad to know that you survived the riot at the Feydau, although at the time it was no part of my intention that you should. Because of this I am content that you should live to enrage and suffer in the shadow of your evil deed, knowing at last—since you had not hitherto the wit to discern it for yourself—that the voice of Philippe de Vilmorin will follow you to denounce you ever more loudly, ever more insistently, until having lived in dread you shall go down in blood under the just rage which your victim's dangerous gift of eloquence is kindling against you."

I find it odd that he should have omitted from this letter all mention of Mlle. Binet, and I am disposed to account it at least a partial insincerity that he should have assigned entirely to his self-imposed mission, and not at all to his lacerated feelings in the matter of Climène, the action which he had taken at the Feydau.

Those two letters, both written in April of that year 1789,

had for only immediate effect to increase the activity with which André-Louis Moreau was being sought.

Le Chapelier would have found him so as to lend him assistance, to urge upon him once again that he should take up a political career. The electors of Nantes would have found him—at least, they would have found Omnes Omnibus, of whose identity with himself they were still in ignorance—on each of the several occasions when a vacancy occurred in their body. And the Marquis de La Tour d'Azyr and M. de Lesdiguières would have found him that they might send him to the gallows.

With a purpose no less vindictive was he being sought by M. Binet, now unhappily recovered from his wound to face completest ruin. His troupe had deserted him during his illness, and reconstituted under the direction of Polichinelle it was now striving with tolerable success to continue upon the lines which André-Louis had laid down. M. le Marquis, prevented by the riot from expressing in person to Mlle. Binet his purpose of making an end of their relations, had been constrained to write to her to that effect from Azyr a few days later. He tempered the blow by enclosing in discharge of all liabilities a bill on the Caisse d'Escompte for a hundred *louis*. Nevertheless it almost crushed the unfortunate Climène, and it enabled her father when he recovered to enrage her by pointing out that she owed this turn of events to the premature surrender she had made in defiance of his sound worldly advice. Father and daughter alike were left to assign the Marquis' desertion, naturally enough, to the riot at the Feydau. They laid that with the rest to the account of Scaramouche, and were forced in bitterness to admit that the scoundrel had taken a superlative revenge. Climène may even have come to consider that it would have paid her better to have run a straight course with Scaramouche and by marrying him to have trusted to his undoubted talents to place her on the summit to which her ambition urged her, and to which it was now futile for her to aspire. If so, that reflection must have been her sufficient punishment. For, as André-Louis so truly says, there is no worse hell than that provided by the regrets for wasted opportunities.

Meanwhile the fiercely-sought André-Louis Moreau had gone to earth completely for the present. And the brisk police of Paris, urged on by the King's Lieutenant from Rennes, hunted for him in vain. Yet he might have been found in a house in the Rue du Hasard within a stone's throw of the Palais Royal, whither purest chance had conducted him.

That which in his letter to Le Chapelier he represents as a contingency of the near future was, in fact, the case in which already he found himself. He was destitute. His money was exhausted, including that procured by the sale of such articles of adornment as were not of absolute necessity.

So desperate was his case that strolling one gusty April morning down the Rue du Hasard with his nose in the wind looking for what might be picked up, he stopped to read a notice outside the door of a house on the left side of the street as you approach the Rue de Richelieu. There was no reason why he should have gone down the Rue du Hasard. Perhaps its name attracted him, as appropriate to his case.

The notice written in a big round hand announced that a young man of good address with some knowledge of swordsmanship was required by M. Bertrand des Amis on the second floor. Above this notice was a black oblong board, and on this a shield, which in vulgar terms may be described as red charged with two swords crossed and four *fleurs de lys*, one in each angle of the saltire. Under the shield, in letters of gold, ran the legend:

BERTRAND DES AMIS
Maître en fait d'Armes des Académies du Roi

Andre-Louis stood considering. He could claim, he thought, to possess the qualifications demanded. He was certainly young and he believed of tolerable address, whilst the fencing-lessons he had received in Nantes had given him at least an elementary knowledge of swordsmanship. The notice looked as if it had been pinned there some days ago, suggesting that applicants for the post were not very numerous. In that case perhaps M. Bertrand des Amis would not be too exigent. And anyway, André-Louis had not eaten for four-and-twenty hours, and whilst the employment here offered—the precise nature of which he was yet to ascertain—did not appear to be such as André-Louis would deliberately have chosen, he was in no case now to be fastidious.

Then, too, he liked the name of Bertrand des Amis. It felicitously combined suggestions of chivalry and friendliness. Also the man's profession being of a kind that is flavoured with romance it was possible that M. Bertrand des Amis would not ask too many questions.

In the end he climbed to the second floor. On the landing he paused outside a door, on which was written "Academy of M. Bertrand des Amis." He pushed this open, and found himself in a sparsely furnished, untenanted antechamber. From a room beyond, the door of which was closed, came the stamping of feet, the click and slither of steel upon steel, and dominating these sounds a vibrant, sonorous voice speaking a language that was certainly French; but such French as is never heard outside a fencing-school.

"*Coulez! Mais, coulez donc!* . . . So! Now the *flanconnade—en carte* . . . And here is the riposte . . . Let us begin again. Come! The ward of *tierce* . . . Make the *coupé*, and then the *quinte par dessus les armes* . . . O, *mais allongez! Allongez! Allez au fond!*" the voice cried in expostulation. "Come, that was better." The blades ceased.

"Remember: the hand in pronation, the elbow not too far out. That will do for today. On Wednesday we shall see you *tirer au mur*. It is more deliberate. Speed will follow when the mechanism of the movements is more assured."

Another voice murmured in answer. The steps moved aside. The lesson was at an end. André-Louis tapped on the door.

It was opened by a tall, slender, gracefully proportioned man of perhaps forty. Black silk breeches and stockings ending in light shoes clothed him from the waist down. Above he was encased to the chin in a closely fitting plastron of leather. His face was aquiline and swarthy, his eyes full and dark, his mouth firm and his clubbed hair was of a lustrous black with here and there a thread of silver showing.

In the crook of his left arm he carried a fencing-mask, a thing of leather with a wire grating to protect the eyes. His keen glance played over André-Louis from head to foot.

"Monsieur?" he inquired, politely.

It was clear that he mistook André-Louis' quality, which is not surprising, for despite his sadly reduced fortunes, his exterior was irreproachable, and M. des Amis was not to guess that he carried upon his back the whole of his possessions.

"You have a notice below, monsieur," he said, and from the swift lighting of the fencing-master's eyes he saw that he had been correct in his assumption that applicants for the position had not been jostling one another on his threshold. And then that flash of satisfaction was followed by a look of surprise.

"You are come in regard to that?"

André-Louis shrugged and half smiled. "One must live," said he.

"But come in. Sit down there. I shall be at your . . . I shall be free to attend to you in a moment."

André-Louis took a seat on the bench ranged against one of the whitewashed walls. The room was long and low, its floor entirely bare. Plain wooden forms such as that which he occupied were placed here and there against the wall. These last were plastered with fencing trophies, masks, crossed foils, stuffed plastrons, and a variety of swords, daggers, and targets, belonging to a variety of ages and countries. There was also a portrait of an obese, big-nosed gentleman in an elaborately curled wig, wearing the blue ribbon of the Saint Esprit, in whom André-Louis recognized the King. And there was a framed parchment—M. des Amis' certificate from the King's Academy. A bookcase occupied one corner, and near this, facing the last of the four windows that abundantly lighted the long room, there was a small writing-table and an armchair. A plump and beautifully dressed young gentleman stood by this table in the act of resuming coat and wig. M. des Amis sauntered over to him—moving, thought André-Louis, with extraordinary grace and elasticity—and stood in talk with him whilst also assisting him to complete his toilet.

At last the young gentleman took his departure, mopping himself with a fine kerchief that left a trail of perfume on the air. M. des Amis closed the door, and turned to the applicant, who rose at once.

"Where have you studied?" quoth the fencing-master abruptly.

"Studied?" André-Louis was taken aback by the question. "Oh, at Louis le Grand."

M. des Amis frowned, looking up sharply as if to see whether his applicant was taking the liberty of amusing himself.

"In Heaven's name! I am not asking you where you did your humanities, but in what academy you studied fencing."

"Oh—fencing!" It had hardly ever occurred to André-Louis that the sword ranked seriously as a study. "I never studied it very much. I had some lessons in . . . in the country once."

The master's eyebrows went up. "But then?" he cried. "Why trouble to come up two flights of stairs?" He was impatient.

"The notice does not demand a high degree of proficiency. If I am not proficient enough, yet knowing the rudiments I can easily improve. I learn most things readily," André-Louis commended himself. "For the rest: I possess the other qualifications. I am young, as you observe: and I leave you to judge whether I am wrong in assuming that my address is good. I am by profession a man of the robe, though I realize that the motto here is *cedat toga armis.*"

M. des Amis smiled approvingly. Undoubtedly the young man had a good address, and a certain readiness of wit, it would appear. He ran a critical eye over his physical points.

"What is your name?" he asked.

André-Louis hesitated a moment. "André-Louis," he said.
The dark, keen eyes conned him more searchingly.

"Well? André-Louis what?"

"Just André Louis. Louis is my surname."

"Oh! An odd surname. You come from Brittany by your accent. Why did you leave it?"

"To save my skin," he answered, without reflecting. And then
made haste to cover the blunder. "I have an enemy," he explained.

M. des Amis frowned, stroking his square chin. "You ran
away?"

"You may say so."

"A coward, eh?"

"I don't think so." And then he lied romantically. Surely a
man who lived by the sword should have a weakness for the romantic. "You see, my enemy is a swordsman of great strength—
the best blade in the province, if not the best blade in France.
That is his repute. I thought I would come to Paris to learn something of the art, and then go back and kill him. That, to be frank,
is why your notice attracted me. You see, I have not the means to
take lessons otherwise. I thought to find work here in the law.
But I have failed. There are too many lawyers in Paris as it is, and
whilst waiting I have consumed the little money that I had, so
that . . . so that, *enfin*, your notice seemed to me something to
which a special providence had directed me."

M. des Amis gripped him by the shoulders, and looked into
his face.

"Is this true, my friend?" he asked.

"Not a word of it," said André-Louis, wrecking his chances
on an irresistible impulse to say the unexpected. But he didn't

wreck them. M. des Amis burst into laughter; and having laughed his fill, confessed himself charmed by his applicant's fundamental honesty.

"Take off your coat," he said, "and let us see what you can do. Nature, at least, designed you for a swordsman. You are light, active, and supple, with a good length of arm, and you seem intelligent. I may make something of you, teach you enough for my purpose, which is that you should give the elements of the art to new pupils before I take them in hand to finish them. Let us try. Take that mask and foil, and come over here."

He led him to the end of the room, where the bare floor was scored with lines of chalk to guide the beginner in the management of his feet.

At the end of a ten-minutes' bout, M. des Amis offered him the situation, and explained it. In addition to imparting the rudiments of the art to beginners, he was to brush out the fencing-room every morning, keep the foils furbished, assist the gentlemen who came for lessons to dress and undress, and make himself generally useful. His wages for the present were to be forty *livres* a month, and he might sleep in an alcove behind the fencing-room if he had no other lodging.

The position, you see, had its humiliations. But, if André-Louis would hope to dine, he must begin by eating his pride as an hors d'oeuvre.

"And so," he said, controlling a grimace, "the robe yields not only to the sword, but to the broom as well. Be it so. I stay."

It is characteristic of him that, having made that choice, he should have thrown himself into the work with enthusiasm. It was ever his way to do whatever he did with all the resources of his mind and energies of his body. When he was not instructing very young gentlemen in the elements of the art, showing them the elaborate and intricate salute—which with a few days' hard practice he had mastered to perfection—and the eight guards, he was himself hard at work on those same guards, exercising eye, wrist, and knees.

Perceiving his enthusiasm, and seeing the obvious possibilities it opened out of turning him into a really effective assistant, M. des Amis presently took him more seriously in hand.

"Your application and zeal, my friend, are deserving of more than forty *livres* a month," the master informed him at the end of a week. "For the present, however, I will make up what else I consider due to you by imparting to you secrets of this noble art. Your future depends upon how you profit by your exceptional good fortune in receiving instruction from me."

Thereafter every morning before the opening of the academy, the master would fence for half an hour with his new assistant. Under this really excellent tuition André-Louis improved at a rate that both astounded and flattered M. des Amis. He would have been less flattered and more astounded had he known that at least half the secret of André-Louis' amazing progress lay in the fact that he was devouring the contents of the master's library, which was made up of a dozen or so treatises on fencing by such great masters as La Bessière, Danet, and the syndic of the King's Academy, Augustin Rousseau. To M. des Amis, whose swordsmanship was all based on practice and not at all on theory, who was indeed no theorist or student in any sense, that little library was merely a suitable adjunct to a fencing-academy, a proper piece of decorative furniture. The books themselves meant nothing to him in any other sense. He had not the type of mind that could have read them with profit nor could he understand that another should do so. André-Louis, on the contrary, a man with the habit of study, with the acquired faculty of learning from books, read those works with enormous profit, kept their precepts in mind, critically set off those of one master against those of another, and made for himself a choice which he proceeded to put into practice.

At the end of a month it suddenly dawned upon M. des Amis that his assistant had developed into a fencer of very considerable force, a man in a bout with whom it became necessary to exert himself if he were to escape defeat.

"I said from the first," he told him one day, "that Nature designed you for a swordsman. See how justified I was, and see also how well I have known how to mould the material with which Nature has equipped you."

"To the master be the glory," said André-Louis.

His relations with M. des Amis had meanwhile become of the friendliest, and he was now beginning to receive from him other pupils than mere beginners. In fact André-Louis was becoming an assistant in a much fuller sense of the word. M. des Amis, a chivalrous, open-handed fellow, far from taking advantage of what he had guessed to be the young man's difficulties, rewarded his zeal by increasing his wages to four *louis* a month.

From the earnest and thoughtful study of the theories of others, it followed now—as not uncommonly happens—that André-Louis came to develop theories of his own. He lay one June morning on his little truckle bed in the alcove behind the academy, considering a passage that he had read last night in Danet on double and triple feints. It had seemed to him when reading it that Danet had stopped short on the threshold of a great discovery in the art of fencing. Essentially a theorist, André-Louis perceived the theory suggested, which Danet himself in suggesting it had not perceived. He lay now on his back, surveying the cracks in the ceiling and considering this matter further with the lucidity that early morning often brings to an acute intelligence. You are to remember that for close upon two months now the sword had been André-Louis' daily exercise and almost hourly thought. Protracted concentration upon the subject was giving him an extraordinary penetration of vision. Swordsmanship as he learnt and taught and saw it daily practised consisted of a series of attacks and parries, a series of disengages from one line into another. But always a limited series. A half-dozen disengages on either side was, strictly speaking, usually as far as any engagement went. Then one recommenced. But even so, these disengages were fortuitous. What if from first to last they should be calculated?

That was part of the thought—one of the two legs on which his theory was to stand; the other was: what would happen if one so elaborated Danet's ideas on the triple feint as to merge them into a series of actual calculated disengages to culminate at the fourth or fifth or even sixth disengage? That is to say, if one were to make a series of attacks inviting ripostes again to be countered, each of which was not intended to go home, but simply to play the opponent's blade into a line that must open him ultimately, and as predetermined, for an irresistible lunge. Each counter of the opponent's would have to be preconsidered in this widening of his guard, a widening so gradual that he should himself be unconscious of it, and throughout intent upon getting home his own point on one of those counters.

André-Louis had been in his time a chess-player of some force, and at chess he had excelled by virtue of his capacity for thinking ahead. That virtue applied to fencing should all but revolutionize the art. It was so applied already, of course, but only in an elementary and very limited fashion, in mere feints, single, double, or triple. But even the triple feint should be a clumsy device compared with this method upon which he theorized.

He considered further, and the conviction grew that he held the key of a discovery. He was impatient to put his theory to the test.

That morning he was given a pupil of some force, against whom usually he was hard put to it to defend himself. Coming on guard, he made up his mind to hit him on the fourth disengage, predetermining the four passes that should lead up to it. They engaged in *tierce*, and Andre-Louis led the attack by a beat and a straightening of the arm. Came the *demi-contre* he expected, which he promptly countered by a thrust in *quinte*; this being countered again, he reëntered still lower, and being again correctly parried, as he had calculated, he lunged swirling his point into *carte*, and got home full upon his opponent's breast. The ease of it surprised him.

They began again. This time he resolved to go in on the fifth disengage, and in on that he went with the same ease. Then, complicating the matter further, he decided to try the sixth, and worked out in his mind the combination of the five preliminary engages. Yet again he succeeded as easily as before.

The young gentleman opposed to him laughed with just a

tinge of mortification in his voice.

"I am all to pieces this morning," he said.

"You are not of your usual force," André-Louis politely agreed. And then greatly daring, always to test that theory of his to the uttermost: "So much so," he added, "that I could almost be sure of hitting you as and when I declare."

The capable pupil looked at him with a half-sneer. "Ah, that, no," said he.

"Let us try. On the fourth disengage I shall touch you. *Allons! En garde!*"

And as he promised, so it happened.

The young gentleman who, hitherto, had held no great opinion of André-Louis' swordsmanship, accounting him well enough for purposes of practice when the master was otherwise engaged, opened wide his eyes. In a burst of mingled generosity and intoxication, André-Louis was almost for disclosing his method—a method which a little later was to become a commonplace of the fencing-rooms. Betimes he checked himself. To reveal his secret would be to destroy the prestige that must accrue to him from exercising it.

At noon, the academy being empty, M. des Amis called André-Louis to one of the occasional lessons which he still received. And for the first time in all his experience with André-Louis, M. des Amis received from him a full hit in the course of the first bout. He laughed, well pleased, like the generous fellow he was.

"Aha! You are improving very fast, my friend."

He still laughed, though not so well pleased, when he was hit in the second bout. After that he settled down to fight in earnest with the result that André-Louis was hit three times in succession. The speed and accuracy of the fencing-master when fully exerting himself disconcerted André-Louis' theory, which for want of being exercised in practice still demanded too much consideration.

But that his theory was sound he accounted fully established, and with that, for the moment, he was content. It remained only to perfect by practice the application of it. To this he now devoted himself with the passionate enthusiasm of the discoverer. He confined himself to a half-dozen combinations, which he practised assiduously until each had become almost automatic. And he proved their infallibility upon the best among M. des Amis' pupils.

Finally, a week or so after that last bout of his with des Amis, the master called him once more to practice.

Hit again in the first bout, the master set himself to exert all his skill against his assistant. But today it availed him nothing before André-Louis' impetuous attacks.

After the third hit, M. des Amis stepped back and pulled off his mask.

"What's this?" he asked. He was pale, and his dark brows were contracted in a frown. Not in years had he been so wounded in his self-love. "Have you been taught a secret *botte*?"

He had always boasted that he knew too much about the sword to believe any nonsense about secret *bottes*; but this performance of André-Louis had shaken his convictions on that score.

"No," said André-Louis. "I have been working hard; and it happens that I fence with my brains."

"So I perceive. Well, well, I think I have taught you enough, my friend. I have no intention of having an assistant who is superior to myself."

"Little danger of that," said André-Louis, smiling pleasantly. "You have been fencing hard all morning, and you are tired, whilst I, having done little, am entirely fresh. That is the only secret of my momentary success."

His tact and the fundamental good-nature of M. des Amis prevented the matter from going farther along the road it was almost threatening to take. And thereafter, when they fenced together, André-Louis, who continued daily to perfect his theory into an almost infallible system, saw to it that M. des Amis always scored against him at least two hits for every one of his own. So much he would grant to discretion, but no more. He desired that M. des Amis should be conscious of his strength, without, however, discovering so much of its real extent as would have excited in him an unnecessary degree of jealousy.

And so well did he contrive that whilst he became ever of greater assistance to the master—for his style and general fencing, too, had materially improved—he was also a source of pride to him as the most brilliant of all the pupils that had ever passed through his academy. Never did André-Louis disillusion him by revealing the fact that his skill was due far more to M. des Amis' library and his own mother wit than to any lessons received.

CHAPTER II

Quos Deus Vult Perdere

O nce again, precisely as he had done when he joined the
Binet troupe, did André-Louis now settle down whole-
heartedly to the new profession into which necessity had driven
him, and in which he found effective concealment from those
who might seek him to his hurt. This profession might—although
in fact it did not—have brought him to consider himself at last as
a man of action. He had not, however, on that account ceased to
be a man of thought, and the events of the spring and summer
months of that year 1789 in Paris provided him with abundant
matter for reflection. He read there in the raw what is perhaps
the most amazing page in the history of human development,
and in the end he was forced to the conclusion that all his early
preconceptions had been at fault, and that it was such exalted,
passionate enthusiasts as Vilmorin who had been right.

I suspect him of actually taking pride in the fact that he had

288

been mistaken, complacently attributing his error to the circumstance that he had been, himself, of too sane and logical a mind to gauge the depths of human insanity now revealed.

He watched the growth of hunger, the increasing poverty and distress of Paris during that spring, and assigned it to its proper cause, together with the patience with which the people bore it. The world of France was in a state of hushed, of paralyzed expectancy, waiting for the States General to assemble and for centuries of tyranny to end. And because of this expectancy, industry had come to a standstill, the stream of trade had dwindled to a trickle. Men would not buy or sell until they clearly saw the means by which the genius of the Swiss banker, M. Necker, was to deliver them from this morass. And because of this paralysis of affairs the men of the people were thrown out of work and left to starve with their wives and children.

Looking on, André-Louis smiled grimly. So far he was right. The sufferers were ever the proletariat. The men who sought to make this revolution, the electors—here in Paris as elsewhere—were men of substance, notable bourgeois, wealthy traders. And whilst these, despising the *canaille*, and envying the privileged, talked largely of equality—by which they meant an ascending equality that should confuse themselves with the gentry—the proletariat perished of want in its kennels.

At last with the month of May the deputies arrived, André-Louis' friend Le Chapelier prominent amongst them, and the States General were inaugurated at Versailles. It was then that affairs began to become interesting, then that André-Louis began seriously to doubt the soundness of the views he had held hitherto.

When the royal proclamation had gone forth decreeing that the deputies of the Third Estate should number twice as many as those of the other two orders together, André-Louis had believed that the preponderance of votes thus assured to the Third Estate rendered inevitable the reforms to which they had pledged themselves.

But he had reckoned without the power of the privileged orders over the proud Austrian queen, and her power over the obese, phlegmatic, irresolute monarch. That the privileged orders should deliver battle in defence of their privileges, André-Louis could understand. Man being what he is, and labouring under his curse of acquisitiveness, will never willingly surrender possessions, whether they be justly or unjustly held. But what surprised André-Louis was the unutterable crassness of the methods by which the Privileged ranged themselves for battle. They opposed brute force to reason and philosophy, and battalions of foreign mercenaries to ideas. As if ideas were to be impaled on bayonets!

The war between the Privileged and the Court on one side, and the Assembly and the People on the other had begun.

The Third Estate contained itself, and waited; waited with the patience of nature; waited a month whilst, with the paralysis of business now complete, the skeleton hand of famine took a firmer grip of Paris; waited a month whilst Privilege gradually assembled an army in Versailles to intimidate it—an army of fifteen regiments, nine of which were Swiss and German—and mounted a park of artillery before the building in which the deputies sat. But the deputies refused to be intimidated; they refused to see the guns and foreign uniforms; they refused to see anything but the purpose for which they had been brought together by royal proclamation.

Thus until the 10th of June, when that great thinker and metaphysician, the Abbé Siéyès, gave the signal: "It is time," said he, "to cut the cable."

And the opportunity came soon, at the very beginning of July. M. du Châtelet, a harsh, haughty disciplinarian, proposed to transfer the eleven French Guards placed under arrest from the military gaol of the Abbaye to the filthy prison of Bicêtre reserved for thieves and felons of the lowest order. Word of that intention going forth, the people at last met violence with violence. A mob four thousand strong broke into the Abbaye, and delivered thence not only the eleven guardsmen, but all the other prisoners, with the exception of one whom they discovered to be a thief, and whom they put back again.

That was open revolt at last, and with revolt Privilege knew how to deal. It would strangle this mutinous Paris in the iron grip of the foreign regiments. Measures were quickly concerted. Old Maréchal de Broglie, a veteran of the Seven Years' War, imbued with a soldier's contempt for civilians, conceiving that the sight of a uniform would be enough to restore peace and order, took control with Besenval as his second-in-command. The foreign regiments were stationed in the environs of Paris, regiments whose very names were an irritation to the Parisians, regiments of Reisbach, of Diesbach, of Nassau, Esterhazy, and Roehmer. Reënforcements of Swiss were sent to the Bastille between whose crenels already since the 30th of June were to be seen the menacing mouths of loaded cannon.

On the 10th of July the electors once more addressed the King to request the withdrawal of the troops. They were answered next day that the troops served the purpose of defending the liberties of the Assembly! And on the next day to that, which was a Sunday, the philanthropist Dr. Guillotin—whose philanthropic engine of painless death was before very long to find a deal of work—came from the Assembly, of which he was a member, to assure the electors of Paris that all was well, appearances notwithstanding, since Necker was more firmly in the saddle than ever. He did not know that at the very moment in which he was speaking so confidently, the oft-dismissed and oft-recalled M. Necker had just been dismissed yet again by the hostile cabal about the Queen. Privilege wanted conclusive measures, and conclusive measures it would have—conclusive to itself.

And at the same time yet another philanthropist, also a doctor, one Jean-Paul Mara, of Italian extraction—better known as Marat, the gallicized form of name he adopted—a man of letters, too, who had spent some years in England, and there published several works on sociology, was writing:

"Have a care! Consider what would be the fatal effect of a seditious movement. If you should have the misfortune to give way to that, you will be treated as people in revolt, and blood will flow."

André-Louis was in the gardens of the Palais Royal, that place of shops and puppet-shows, of circus and cafés, of gaming houses and brothels, that universal rendezvous, on that Sunday morning when the news of Necker's dismissal spread, carrying with it dismay and fury. Into Necker's dismissal the people read the triumph of the party hostile to themselves. It sounded the knell of all hope of redress of their wrongs.

He beheld a slight young man with a pock-marked face, redeemed from utter ugliness by a pair of magnificent eyes, leap to a table outside the Café de Foy, a drawn sword in his hand, crying, "To arms!" And then upon the silence of astonishment that cry imposed, this young man poured a flood of inflammatory eloquence, delivered in a voice marred at moments by a stutter. He told the people that the Germans on the Champ de Mars would enter Paris that night to butcher the inhabitants. "Let us mount a cockade!" he cried, and tore a leaf from a tree to serve his purpose—the green cockade of hope.

Enthusiasm swept the crowd, a motley crowd made up of men and women of every class, from vagabond to nobleman, from harlot to lady of fashion. Trees were despoiled of their leaves, and the green cockade was flaunted from almost every head.

"You are caught between two fires," the incendiary's stuttering voice raved on. "Between the Germans on the Champ de Mars and the Swiss in the Bastille. To arms, then! To arms!"

Excitement boiled up and over. From a neighbouring waxworks show came the bust of Necker, and presently a bust of that comedian the Duke of Orléans, who had a party and who was as ready as any other of the budding opportunists of those days to take advantage of the moment for his own aggrandizement. The bust of Necker was draped with crepe.

André-Louis looked on, and grew afraid. Marat's pamphlet had impressed him. It had expressed what he himself had expressed more than half a year ago to the mob at Rennes. This crowd, he felt, must be restrained. That hot-headed, irresponsible stutterer would have the town in a blaze by night unless something were done. The young man, a causeless advocate of the Palais named Camille Desmoulins, later to become famous, leapt down from his table still waving his sword, still shouting, "To arms! Follow me!" André-Louis advanced to occupy the improvised rostrum, which the stutterer had just vacated, to make an effort at counteracting that inflammatory performance. He thrust through the crowd, and came suddenly face to face with a tall man beautifully dressed, whose handsome countenance was sternly set, whose great sombre eyes smouldered as if with suppressed anger.

Thus face to face, each looking into the eyes of the other, they stood for a long moment, the jostling crowd streaming past them, unheeded. Then André-Louis laughed.

"That fellow, too, has a very dangerous gift of eloquence, M. le Marquis," he said. "In fact there are a number of such in France today. They grow from the soil, which you and yours have irrigated with the blood of the martyrs of liberty. Soon it may be your blood instead. The soil is parched, and thirsty for it."

"Gallows-bird!" he was answered. "The police will do your affair for you. I shall tell the Lieutenant-General that you are to be found in Paris."

"My God, man!" cried André-Louis, "will you never get sense? Will you talk like that of Lieutenant-Generals when Paris itself is likely to tumble about your ears or take fire under your feet? Raise your voice, M. le Marquis. Denounce me here, to these. You will make a hero of me in such an hour as this. Or shall I denounce you? I think I will. I think it is high time you received your wages. Hi! You others, listen to me! Let me present you to . . ."

A rush of men hurtled against him, swept him along with

them, do what he would, separating him from M. de La Tour d'Azyr, so oddly met. He sought to breast that human torrent; the Marquis, caught in an eddy of it, remained where he had been, and André-Louis' last glimpse of him was of a man smiling with tight lips, an ugly smile.

Meanwhile the gardens were emptying in the wake of that stuttering firebrand who had mounted the green cockade. The human torrent poured out into the Rue de Richelieu, and André-Louis perforce must suffer himself to be borne along by it, at least as far as the Rue du Hasard. There he sidled out of it, and having no wish to be crushed to death or to take further part in the madness that was afoot, he slipped down the street, and so got home to the deserted academy. For there were no pupils to-day, and even M. des Amis, like André-Louis, had gone out to seek for news of what was happening at Versailles.

This was no normal state of things at the Academy of Bertrand des Amis. Whatever else in Paris might have been at a standstill lately, the fencing academy had flourished as never hitherto. Usually both the master and his assistant were busy from morning until dusk, and already André-Louis was being paid now by the lessons that he gave, the master allowing him one half of the fee in each case for himself, an arrangement which the assistant found profitable. On Sundays the academy made half-holiday; but on this Sunday such had been the state of suspense and ferment in the city that no one having appeared by eleven o'clock both des Amis and André-Louis had gone out. Little they thought as they lightly took leave of each other—they were very good friends by now—that they were never to meet again in this world.

295

Bloodshed there was that day in Paris. On the Place Vendôme a detachment of dragoons awaited the crowd out of which André-Louis had slipped. The horsemen swept down upon the mob, dispersed it, smashed the waxen effigy of M. Necker, and killed one man on the spot—an unfortunate French Guard who stood his ground. That was a beginning. As a consequence Besenval brought up his Swiss from the Champ de Mars and marshalled them in battle order on the Champs Élysées with four pieces of artillery. His dragoons he stationed in the Place Louis XV. That evening an enormous crowd, streaming along the Champs Élysées and the Tuileries Gardens, considered with eyes of alarm that warlike preparation. Some insults were cast upon those foreign mercenaries and some stones were flung. Besenval, losing his head, or acting under orders, sent for his dragoons and ordered them to disperse the crowd. But that crowd was too dense to be dispersed in this fashion; so dense that it was impossible for the horsemen to move without crushing someone. There were several crushed, and as a consequence when the dragoons, led by the Prince de Lambesc, advanced into the Tuileries Gardens, the outraged crowd met them with a fusillade of stones and bottles. Lambesc gave the order to fire. There was a stampede. Pouring forth from the Tuileries through the city went those indignant people with their story of German cavalry trampling upon women and children, and uttering now in grimmest earnest the call to arms, raised at noon by Desmoulins in the Palais Royal.

The victims were taken up and borne thence, and amongst them was Bertrand des Amis, himself—like all who lived by the sword—an ardent upholder of the noblesse, trampled to death under hooves of foreign horsemen launched by the noblesse and led by a nobleman.

To André-Louis, waiting that evening on the second floor of No. 13 Rue du Hasard for the return of his friend and master, four men of the people brought that broken body of one of the earliest victims of the Revolution that was now launched in earnest.

CHAPTER III

Président Le Chapelier

The ferment of Paris which, during the two following days, resembled an armed camp rather than a city, delayed the burial of Bertrand des Amis until the Wednesday of that eventful week. Amid events that were shaking a nation to its foundations the death of a fencing-master passed almost unnoticed even among his pupils, most of whom did not come to the academy during the two days that his body lay there. Some few, however, did come, and these conveyed the news to others, with the result that the master was followed to Père Lachaise by a score of young men at the head of whom as chief mourner walked André-Louis.

There were no relatives to be advised so far as André-Louis was aware, although within a week of M. des Amis' death a sister turned up from Passy to claim his heritage. This was considerable, for the master had prospered and saved money, most of which was invested in the Compagnie des Eaux and the National Debt. André-Louis consigned her to the lawyers, and saw her no more.

The death of des Amis left him with so profound a sense of loneliness and desolation that he had no thought or care for the sudden access of fortune which it automatically procured him. To the master's sister might fall such wealth as he had amassed, but André-Louis succeeded to the mine itself from which that wealth had been extracted, the fencing-school in which by now he was himself so well established as an instructor that its numerous pupils looked to him to carry it forward successfully as its chief. And never was there a season in which fencing-academies knew such prosperity as in these troubled days, when every man was sharpening his sword and schooling himself in the uses of it.

It was not until a couple of weeks later that André-Louis realized what had really happened to him, and he found himself at the same time an exhausted man, for during that fortnight he had been doing the work of two. If he had not hit upon the happy expedient of pairing-off his more advanced pupils to fence with each other, himself standing by to criticize, correct and otherwise instruct, he must have found the task utterly beyond his strength. Even so, it was necessary for him to fence some six hours daily, and every day he brought arrears of lassitude from yesterday until he was in danger of succumbing under the increasing burden of fatigue. In the end he took an assistant to deal with beginners, who gave the hardest work. He found him readily enough by good fortune in one of his own pupils named Le Duc. As the summer advanced, and the concourse of pupils steadily increased, it became necessary for him to take yet another assistant—an able young instructor named Galoche—and another room on the floor above.

They were strenuous days for André-Louis, more strenuous than he had ever known, even when he had been at work to build up the Binet Company; but it follows that they were days of extraordinary prosperity. He comments regretfully upon the fact that Bertrand des Amis should have died by ill-chance on the very eve of so profitable a vogue of sword-play.

The arms of the Académie du Roi, to which André-Louis had no title, still continued to be displayed outside his door. He had overcome the difficulty in a manner worthy of Scaramouche. He left the escutcheon and the legend "Académie de Bertrand des Amis, Maitre en fait d'Armes des Académies du Roi," appending to it the further legend:

"Conducted by André Louis."

With little time now in which to go abroad it was from his pupils and the newspapers—of which a flood had risen in Paris with the establishment of the freedom of the Press—that he learnt of the revolutionary processes around him, following upon, as a measure of anticlimax, the fall of the Bastille. That had happened whilst M. des Amis lay dead, on the day before they buried him, and was indeed the chief reason of the delay in his burial. It was an event that had its inspiration in that ill-considered charge of Prince Lambesc in which the fencing-master had been killed.

The outraged people had besieged the electors in the Hôtel de Ville, demanding arms with which to defend their lives from these foreign murderers hired by despotism. And in the end the electors had consented to give them arms, or, rather—for arms it had none to give—to permit them to arm themselves. Also it had given them a cockade, of red and blue, the colours of Paris. Because these colours were also those of the liveries of the Duke of Orléans, white was added to them—the white of the ancient standard of France—and thus was the tricolour born. Further, a permanent committee of electors was appointed to watch over public order.

Thus empowered the people went to work with such good effect that within thirty-six hours sixty thousand pikes had been forged. At nine o'clock on Tuesday morning thirty thousand men were before the Invalides. By eleven o'clock they had ravished it of its store of arms amounting to some thirty thousand muskets, whilst others had seized the Arsenal and possessed themselves of powder.

Thus they prepared to resist the attack that from seven points was to be launched that evening upon the city. But Paris did not wait for the attack. It took the initiative. Mad with enthusiasm it conceived the insane project of taking that terrible menacing fortress, the Bastille, and, what is more, it succeeded, as you know, before five o'clock that night, aided in the enterprise by the French Guards with cannon.

The news of it, borne to Versailles by Lambesc in flight with his dragoons before the vast armed force that had sprouted from the paving-stones of Paris, gave the Court pause. The people were in possession of the guns captured from the Bastille. They were erecting barricades in the streets, and mounting these guns upon them. The attack had been too long delayed. It must be abandoned since now it could lead only to fruitless slaughter that must further shake the already sorely shaken prestige of Royalty.

And so the Court, growing momentarily wise again under

the spur of fear, preferred to temporize. Necker should be brought back yet once again, the three orders should sit united as the National Assembly demanded. It was the completest surrender of force to force, the only argument. The King went alone to inform the National Assembly of that eleventh-hour resolve, to the great comfort of its members, who viewed with pain and alarm the dreadful state of things in Paris. "No force but the force of reason and argument" was their watchword, and it was so to continue for two years yet, with a patience and fortitude in the face of ceaseless provocation to which insufficient justice has been done.

As the King was leaving the Assembly, a woman, embracing his knees, gave tongue to what might well be the question of all France:

"Ah, sire, are you really sincere? Are you sure they will not make you change your mind?"

Yet no such question was asked when a couple of days later the King, alone and unguarded save by the representatives of the Nation, came to Paris to complete the peacemaking, the surrender of Privilege. The Court was filled with terror by the adventure. Were they not the "enemy," these mutinous Parisians? And should a King go thus among his enemies? If he shared some of that fear, as the gloom of him might lead us to suppose, he must have found it idle. What if two hundred thousand men under arms—men without uniforms and with the most extraordinary motley of weapons ever seen—awaited him? They awaited him as a guard of honour.

Mayor Bailly at the barrier presented him with the keys of the city. "These are the same keys that were presented to Henri

IV. He had reconquered his people. Now the people have reconquered their King."

At the Hôtel de Ville Mayor Bailly offered him the new cockade, the tricoloured symbol of constitutional France, and when he had given his royal confirmation to the formation of the Garde Bourgeoise and to the appointments of Bailly and Lafayette, he departed again for Versailles amid the shouts of "Vive le Roi!" from his loyal people.

And now you see Privilege—before the cannon's mouth, as it were—submitting at last, where had they submitted sooner they might have saved oceans of blood—chiefly their own. They come, nobles and clergy, to join the National Assembly, to labour with it upon this constitution that is to regenerate France. But the reunion is a mockery—as much a mockery as that of the Archbishop of Paris singing the Te Deum for the fall of the Bastille— most grotesque and incredible of all these grotesque and incredible events. All that has happened to the National Assembly is that it has introduced five or six hundred enemies to hamper and hinder its deliberations.

But all this is an oft-told tale, to be read in detail elsewhere. I give you here just so much of it as I have found in André-Louis' own writings, almost in his own words, reflecting the changes that were operated in his mind. Silent now, he came fully to believe in those things in which he had not believed when earlier he had preached them.

Meanwhile together with the change in his fortune had come a change in his position towards the law, a change brought about by the other changes wrought around him. No longer need he hide himself. Who in these days would prefer against him the grotesque charge of sedition for what he had done in Brittany? What court would dare to send him to the gallows for having said in advance what all France was saying now? As for that other possible charge of murder, who should concern himself with the death of the miserable Binet killed by him—if, indeed, he had killed him, as he hoped—in self-defence.

And so one fine day in early August, André-Louis gave himself a holiday from the academy, which was now working smoothly under his assistants, hired a chaise and drove out to Versailles to the Café d'Amaury, which he knew for the meeting-place of the Club Breton, the seed from which was to spring that Society of the Friends of the Constitution better known as the Jacobins. He went to seek Le Chapelier, who had been one of the founders of the club, a man of great prominence now, president of the Assembly in this important season when it was deliberating upon the Declaration of the Rights of Man.

Le Chapelier's importance was reflected in the sudden servility of the shirt-sleeved, white-aproned waiter of whom André-Louis inquired for the representative.

M. Le Chapelier was above-stairs with friends. The waiter desired to serve the gentleman, but hesitated to break in upon the assembly in which M. le Député found himself.

André-Louis gave him a piece of silver to encourage him to make the attempt. Then he sat down at a marble-topped table by the window looking out over the wide tree-encircled square. There, in that common-room of the café, deserted at this hour of mid-afternoon, the great man came to him. Less than a year ago he had yielded precedence to André-Louis in a matter of delicate leadership; today he stood on the heights, one of the great leaders of the Nation in travail, and André-Louis was deep down in the shadows of the general mass.

The thought was in the minds of both as they scanned each other, each noting in the other the marked change that a few months had wrought. In Le Chapelier, André-Louis observed certain heightened refinements of dress that went with certain subtler refinements of countenance. He was thinner than of old, his face was pale and there was a weariness in the eyes that considered his visitor through a gold-rimmed spy-glass. In André-Louis those jaded but quick-moving eyes of the Breton deputy noted changes even more marked. The almost constant swordmanship of these last months had given Andre-Louis a grace of movement, a poise, and a curious, indefinable air of dignity, of command. He seemed taller by virtue of this, and he was dressed with an elegance which if quiet was none the less rich. He wore a small silver-hilted sword, and wore it as if used to it, and his black hair that Le Chapelier had never seen other than fluttering lank about his bony cheeks was glossy now and gathered into a club. Almost he had the air of a *petit-maître*.

In both, however, the changes were purely superficial, as each was soon to reveal to the other. Le Chapelier was ever the same direct and downright Breton, abrupt of manner and of speech. He stood smiling a moment in mingled surprise and pleasure; then opened wide his arms. They embraced under the awe-stricken gaze of the waiter, who at once effaced himself.

"André-Louis, my friend! Whence do you drop?"

"We drop from above. I come from below to survey at close quarters one who is on the heights."

"On the heights! But that you willed it so, it is yourself might now be standing in my place."

"I have a poor head for heights, and I find the atmosphere too rarefied. Indeed, you look none too well on it yourself, Isaac. You are pale."

"The Assembly was in session all last night. That is all. These damned Privileged multiply our difficulties. They will do so until we decree their abolition."

They sat down. "Abolition! You contemplate so much? Not that you surprise me. You have always been an extremist."

"I contemplate it that I may save them. I seek to abolish them officially, so as to save them from abolition of another kind at the hands of a people they exasperate."

"I see. And the King?"

"The King is the incarnation of the Nation. We shall deliver him together with the Nation from the bondage of Privilege. Our constitution will accomplish it. You agree?"

André-Louis shrugged. "Does it matter? I am a dreamer in politics, not a man of action. Until lately I have been very moderate; more moderate than you think. But now almost I am a republican. I have been watching, and I have perceived that this King is—just nothing, a puppet who dances according to the hand that pulls the string."

"This King, you say? What other king is possible? You are surely not of those who weave dreams about Orléans? He has a sort of party, a following largely recruited by the popular hatred of the Queen and the known fact that she hates him. There are some who have thought of making him regent, some even more; Robespierre is of the number."

"Who?" asked André-Louis, to whom the name was unknown.

"Robespierre—a preposterous little lawyer who represents Arras, a shabby, clumsy, timid dullard, who will make speeches through his nose to which nobody listens—an ultra-royalist whom the royalists and the Orléanists are using for their own ends. He has pertinacity, and he insists upon being heard. He may be listened to someday. But that he, or the others, will ever make anything of Orléans . . . pish! Orléans himself may desire it, but . . . the man is a eunuch in crime; he would, but he can't. The phrase is Mirabeau's."

He broke off to demand André-Louis' news of himself.

"You did not treat me as a friend when you wrote to me," he complained. "You gave me no clue to your whereabouts; you represented yourself as on the verge of destitution and withheld from me the means to come to your assistance. I have been troubled in mind about you, André. Yet to judge by your appearance I might have spared myself that. You seem prosperous, assured. Tell me of it."

André-Louis told him frankly all that there was to tell.

"Do you know that you are an amazement to me?" said the deputy. "From the robe to the buskin, and now from the buskin to the sword! What will be the end of you, I wonder?"

"The gallows, probably."

"Pish! Be serious. Why not the toga of the senator in senatorial France? It might be yours now if you had willed it so."

"The surest way to the gallows of all," laughed André-Louis.

At the moment Le Chapelier manifested impatience. I wonder did the phrase cross his mind that day four years later when he himself rode in the death-cart to the Grève.

"We are sixty-six Breton deputies in the Assembly. Should a

307

vacancy occur, will you act as *suppléant?* A word from me together with the influence of your name in Rennes and Nantes, and the thing is done."

André-Louis laughed outright. "Do you know, Isaac, that I never meet you but you seek to thrust me into politics?"

"Because you have a gift for politics. You were born for politics."

"Ah, yes—Scaramouche in real life. I've played it on the stage. Let that suffice. Tell me, Isaac, what news of my old friend, La Tour d'Azyr?"

"He is here in Versailles, damn him—a thorn in the flesh of the Assembly. They've burnt his château at La Tour d'Azyr. Unfortunately he wasn't in it at the time. The flames haven't even singed his insolence. He dreams that when this philosophic aberration is at an end, there will be serfs to rebuild it for him."

"So there has been trouble in Brittany?" André-Louis had become suddenly grave, his thoughts swinging to Gavrillac.

"An abundance of it, and elsewhere too. Can you wonder? These delays at such a time, with famine in the land? Châteaux have been going up in smoke during the last fortnight. The peasants took their cue from the Parisians, and treated every castle as a Bastille. Order is being restored, there as here, and they are quieter now."

"What of Gavrillac? Do you know?"

"I believe all to be well. M. de Kercadiou was not a Marquis de La Tour d'Azyr. He was in sympathy with his people. It is not likely that they would injure Gavrillac. But don't you correspond with your godfather?"

"In the circumstances—no. What you tell me would make it

now more difficult than ever, for he must account me one of those who helped to light the torch that has set fire to so much belonging to his class. Ascertain for me that all is well, and let me know."

"I will, at once."

At parting, when André-Louis was on the point of stepping into his cabriolet to return to Paris, he sought information on another matter.

"Do you happen to know if M. de La Tour d'Azyr has married?" he asked.

"I don't; which really means that he hasn't. One would have heard of it in the case of that exalted Privileged."

"To be sure." André-Louis spoke indifferently. "*Au revoir,* Isaac! You'll come and see me—13 Rue du Hasard. Come soon."

"As soon and as often as my duties will allow. They keep me chained here at present."

"Poor slave of duty with your gospel of liberty!"

"True! And because of that I will come. I have a duty to Brittany: to make Omnes Omnibus one of her representatives in the National Assembly."

"That is a duty you will oblige me by neglecting," laughed André-Louis, and drove away.

CHAPTER IV

At Meudon

Later in the week he received a visit from Le Chapelier just before noon.

"I have news for you, André. Your godfather is at Meudon. He arrived there two days ago. Had you heard?"

"But no. How should I hear? Why is he at Meudon?" He was conscious of a faint excitement, which he could hardly have explained.

"I don't know. There have been fresh disturbances in Brittany. It may be due to that."

"And so he has come for shelter to his brother?" asked André-Louis.

"To his brother's house, yes; but not to his brother. Where do you live at all, André? Do you never hear any of the news? Étienne de Gavrillac emigrated years ago. He was of the household of M. d'Artois, and he crossed the frontier with him. By now, no doubt, he is in Germany with him, conspiring against France. For that is what the émigrés are doing. That Austrian woman at the Tuileries will end by destroying the monarchy."

"Yes, yes," said André-Louis impatiently. Politics interested him not at all this morning. "But about Gavrillac?"

"Why, haven't I told you that Gavrillac is at Meudon, installed in the house his brother has left? *Dieu de Dieu!* Don't I speak French or don't you understand the language? I believe that Rabouillet, his intendant, is in charge of Gavrillac. I have brought you the news the moment I received it. I thought you would probably wish to go out to Meudon."

"Of course. I will go at once—that is, as soon as I can. I can't today, nor yet tomorrow. I am too busy here."

He waved a hand towards the inner room, whence proceeded the click-click of blades, the quick moving of feet, and the voice of the instructor, Le Duc.

"Well, well, that is your own affair. You are busy. I leave you now. Let us dine this evening at the Café de Foy. Kersain will be of the party."

"A moment!" André-Louis' voice arrested him on the threshold. "Is Mlle. de Kercadiou with her uncle?"

"How the devil should I know? Go and find out."

He was gone, and André-Louis stood there a moment deep in thought. Then he turned and went back to resume with his pupil, the Vicomte de Villeniort, the interrupted exposition of the *demi-contre* of Danet, illustrating with a small-sword the advantages to be derived from its adoption.

Thereafter he fenced with the Vicomte, who was perhaps the ablest of his pupils at the time, and all the while his thoughts were on the heights of Meudon, his mind casting up the lessons he had to give that afternoon and on the morrow, and wondering which of these he might postpone without deranging the academy. When having touched the Vicomte three times in succession, he paused and wrenched himself back to the present, it was to marvel at the precision to be gained by purely mechanical action. Without bestowing a thought upon what he was doing, his wrist and arm and knees had automatically performed their work, like the accurate fighting engine into which constant practice for a year and more had combined them.

Not until Sunday was André-Louis able to satisfy a wish which the impatience of the intervening days had converted into a yearning. Dressed with more than ordinary care, his head elegantly coiffed—by one of those hairdressers to the nobility of whom so many were being thrown out of employment by the stream of emigration which was now flowing freely—André-Louis mounted his hired carriage, and drove out to Meudon.

The house of the younger Kercadiou no more resembled that of the head of the family than did his person. A man of the Court, where his brother was essentially a man of the soil, an officer of the household of M. le Comte d'Artois, he had built for himself and his family an imposing villa on the heights of Meudon in a miniature park, conveniently situated for him midway between Versailles and Paris, and easily accessible from either. M. d'Artois—the royal tennis-player—had been amongst the very first to emigrate. Together with the Condés, the Contis, the Polignacs, and others of the Queen's intimate council, old Marshal de Broglie and the Prince de Lambesc, who realized that their very names had become odious to the people, he had quitted France immediately after the fall of the Bastille. He had gone to play tennis beyond the frontier—and there consummate the work of ruining the French monarchy upon which he and those others had been engaged in France. With him, amongst several members of his household went Étienne de Kercadiou, and with Étienne de Kercadiou went his family, a wife and four children. Thus it was that the Seigneur de Gavrillac, glad to escape from a province so peculiarly disturbed as that of Brittany—where the nobles had shown themselves the most intransigent of all France— had come to occupy in his brother's absence the courtier's hand- some villa at Meudon.

That he was quite happy there is not to be supposed. A man of his almost Spartan habits, accustomed to plain fare and self- help, was a little uneasy in this sybaritic abode, with its soft car- pets, profusion of gilding, and battalion of sleek, silent-footed servants—for Kercadiou the younger had left his entire house- hold behind. Time, which at Gavrillac he had kept so fully em- ployed in agrarian concerns, here hung heavily upon his hands. In self-defence he slept a great deal, and but for Aline, who made no attempt to conceal her delight at this proximity to Paris and the heart of things, it is possible that he would have beat a retreat almost at once from surroundings that sorted so ill with his hab- its. Later on, perhaps, he would accustom himself and grow re- signed to this luxurious inactivity. In the meantime the novelty of it fretted him, and it was into the presence of a peevish and rather somnolent M. de Kercadiou that André-Louis was ush- ered in the early hours of the afternoon of that Sunday in June. He was unannounced, as had ever been the custom at Gavrillac. This because Bénoît, M. de Kercadiou's old seneschal, had accompanied his seigneur upon this soft adventure, and was installed—to the ceaseless and but half-concealed hilarity of the impertinent *valetaille* that M. Étienne had left—as his maître d'hôtel here at Meudon.

Bénoît had welcomed M. André with incoherencies of delight; almost had he gambolled about him like some faithful dog, whilst conducting him to the salon and the presence of the Lord of Gavrillac, who would—in the words of Bénoît—be ravished to see M. André again.

"Monseigneur! Monseigneur!" he cried in a quavering voice, entering a pace or two in advance of the visitor. "It is M. André . . . M. André, your godson, who comes to kiss your hand. He is here . . . and so fine that you would hardly know him. Here he is, monseigneur! Is he not beautiful?"

And the old servant rubbed his hands in conviction of the delight that he believed he was conveying to his master.

André-Louis crossed the threshold of that great room, soft-carpeted to the foot, dazzling to the eye. It was immensely lofty, and its festooned ceiling was carried on fluted pillars with gilded capitals. The door by which he entered, and the windows that opened upon the garden, were of an enormous height—almost, indeed, the full height of the room itself. It was a room overwhelmingly gilded, with an abundance of ormolu encrustations on the furniture, in which it nowise differed from what was customary in the dwellings of people of birth and wealth. Never, indeed, was there a time in which so much gold was employed decoratively as in this age when coined gold was almost unprocurable, and paper money had been put into circulation to supply the lack. It was a saying of André-Louis' that if these people could only have been induced to put the paper on their walls and the gold into their pockets, the finances of the kingdom might soon have been in better case.

The Seigneur—furbished and beruffled to harmonize with his surroundings—had risen, startled by this exuberant invasion on the part of Bénoît, who had been almost as forlorn as himself since their coming to Meudon.

"What is it? Eh?" His pale, short-sighted eyes peered at the visitor. "André!" said he, between surprise and sternness, and the colour deepened in his great pink face.

Bénoît, with his back to his master, deliberately winked and grinned at André-Louis to encourage him not to be put off by any apparent hostility on the part of his godfather. That done, the intelligent old fellow discreetly effaced himself.

"What do you want here?" growled M. de Kercadiou.

"No more than to kiss your hand, as Bénoît has told you, monsieur my godfather," said André-Louis submissively, bowing his sleek black head.

"You have contrived without kissing it for two years."

"Do not, monsieur, reproach me with my misfortune." The little man stood very stiffly erect, his disproportionately large head thrown back, his pale prominent eyes very stern.

"Did you think to make your outrageous offence any better by vanishing in that heartless manner, by leaving us without knowledge of whether you were alive or dead?"

"At first it was dangerous—dangerous to my life—to disclose my whereabouts. Then for a time I was in need, almost destitute, and my pride forbade me, after what I had done and the view you must take of it, to appeal to you for help. Later . . ."

315

"Destitute?" The Seigneur interrupted. For a moment his lip trembled. Then he steadied himself, and the frown deepened as he surveyed this very changed and elegant godson of his, noted the quiet richness of his apparel, the paste buckles and red heels to his shoes, the sword hilted in mother-o'-pearl and silver, and the carefully dressed hair that he had always seen hanging in wisps about his face. "At least you do not look destitute now," he sneered.

"I am not. I have prospered since. In that, monsieur, I differ from the ordinary prodigal, who returns only when he needs assistance. I return solely because I love you, monsieur—to tell you so. I have come at the very first moment after hearing of your presence here." He advanced. "Monsieur my godfather!" he said, and held out his hand.

But M. de Kercadiou remained unbending, wrapped in his cold dignity and resentment.

"Whatever tribulations you may have suffered or consider that you may have suffered, they are far less than your disgraceful conduct deserved, and I observe that they have nothing abated your impudence. You think that you have but to come here and say, 'Monsieur my godfather!' and everything is to be forgiven and forgotten. That is your error. You have committed too great a wrong; you have offended against everything by which I hold, and against myself personally, by your betrayal of my trust in you. You are one of those unspeakable scoundrels who are responsible for this revolution."

"Alas, monsieur, I see that you share the common delusion. These unspeakable scoundrels but demanded a constitution, as was promised them from the throne. They were not to know that the promise was insincere, or that its fulfilment would be baulked by the privileged orders. The men who have precipitated this revolution, monsieur, are the nobles and the prelates."

"You dare—and at such a time as this—stand there and tell me such abominable lies! You dare to say that the nobles have made the revolution, when scores of them, following the example of M. le Duc d'Aiguillon, have flung their privileges, even their title-deeds, into the lap of the people! Or perhaps you deny it?"

"Oh, no. Having wantonly set fire to their house, they now try to put it out by throwing water on it; and where they fail they put the entire blame on the flames."

"I see that you have come here to talk politics."

"Far from it. I have come, if possible, to explain myself. To understand is always to forgive. That is a great saying of Montaigne's. If I could make you understand . . ."

"You can't. You'll never make me understand how you came to render yourself so odiously notorious in Brittany."

"Ah, not odiously, monsieur!"

"Certainly, odiously—among those that matter. It is said even that you were Omnes Omnibus, though that I cannot, will not believe."

"Yet it is true."

M. de Kercadiou choked. "And you confess it? You dare to confess it?"

"What a man dares to do, he should dare to confess—unless he is a coward."

"Oh, and to be sure you were very brave, running away each time after you had done the mischief, turning comedian to hide yourself, doing more mischief as a comedian, provoking a riot in

317

Nantes, and then running away again, to become God knows what—something dishonest by the affluent look of you. My God, man, I tell you that in these past two years I have hoped that you were dead, and you profoundly disappoint me that you are not!" He beat his hands together, and raised his shrill voice to call— "Bénoît!" He strode away towards the fireplace, scarlet in the face, shaking with the passion into which he had worked himself. "Dead, I might have forgiven you, as one who had paid for his evil, and his folly. Living, I never can forgive you. You have gone too far. God alone knows where it will end.

"Bénoît, the door. M. André-Louis Moreau to the door!" The tone argued an irrevocable determination. Pale and self-contained, but with a queer pain at his heart, André-Louis heard that dismissal, saw Bénoît's white, scared face and shaking hands half-raised as if he were about to expostulate with his master. And then another voice, a crisp, boyish voice, cut in.

"Uncle!" it cried, a world of indignation and surprise in its pitch, and then: "André!" And this time a note almost of gladness, certainly of welcome, was blended with the surprise that still remained.

Both turned, half the room between them at the moment, and beheld Aline in one of the long, open windows, arrested there in the act of entering from the garden, Aline in a milk-maid bonnet of the latest mode, though without any of the tricolour embellishments that were so commonly to be seen upon them.

The thin lips of André's long mouth twisted into a queer smile. Into his mind had flashed the memory of their last parting. He saw himself again, standing burning with indignation upon the pavement of Nantes, looking after her carriage as it receded down the Avenue de Gigan.

She was coming towards him now with outstretched hands, a heightened colour in her cheeks, a smile of welcome on her lips. He bowed low and kissed her hand in silence.

Then with a glance and a gesture she dismissed Bénoît, and in her imperious fashion constituted herself André's advocate against that harsh dismissal which she had overheard.

"Uncle," she said, leaving André and crossing to M. de Kercadiou, "you make me ashamed of you! To allow a feeling of peevishness to overwhelm all your affection for André!"

"I have no affection for him. I had once. He chose to extinguish it. He can go to the devil; and please observe that I don't permit you to interfere."

"But if he confesses that he has done wrong . . ."

"He confesses nothing of the kind. He comes here to argue with me about these infernal Rights of Man. He proclaims himself unrepentant. He announces himself with pride to have been, as all Brittany says, the scoundrel who hid himself under the sobriquet of Omnes Omnibus. Is that to be condoned?"

She turned to look at André across the wide space that now separated them.

"But is this really so? Don't you repent, André—now that you see all the harm that has come?"

It was a clear invitation to him, a pleading to him to say that he repented, to make his peace with his godfather. For a moment it almost moved him. Then, considering the subterfuge unworthy, he answered truthfully, though the pain he was suffering rang in his voice.

"To confess repentance," he said slowly, "would be to confess to a monstrous crime. Don't you see that? Oh, monsieur, have patience with me; let me explain myself a little. You say that I am in part responsible for something of all this that has happened. My exhortations of the people at Rennes and twice afterwards at Nantes are said to have had their share in what followed there. It may be so. It would be beyond my power positively to deny it. Revolution followed and bloodshed. More may yet come. To repent implies a recognition that I have done wrong. How shall I say that I have done wrong, and thus take a share of the responsibility for all that blood upon my soul? I will be quite frank with you to show you how far, indeed, I am from repentance. What I did, I actually did against all my convictions at the time. Because there was no justice in France to move against the murderer of Philippe de Vilmorin, I moved in the only way that I imagined could make the evil done recoil upon the hand that did it, and those other hands that had the power but not the spirit to punish. Since then I have come to see that I was wrong, and that Philippe de Vilmorin and those who thought with him were in the right.

"You must realize, monsieur, that it is with sincerest thankfulness that I find I have done nothing calling for repentance; that, on the contrary, when France is given the inestimable boon of a constitution, as will shortly happen, I may take pride in having played my part in bringing about the conditions that have made this possible."

There was a pause. M. de Kercadiou's face turned from pink to purple.

"You have quite finished?" he said harshly.

"If you have understood me, monsieur."

"Oh, I have understood you, and . . . and I beg that you will go."

André-Louis shrugged his shoulders and hung his head. He had come there so joyously, in such yearning, merely to receive a final dismissal. He looked at Aline. Her face was pale and troubled; but her wit failed to show her how she could come to his assistance. His excessive honesty had burnt all his boats.

"Very well, monsieur. Yet this I would ask you to remember after I am gone. I have not come to you as one seeking assistance, as one driven to you by need. I am no returning prodigal, as I have said. I am one who, needing nothing, asking nothing, master of his own destinies, has come to you driven by affection only, urged by the love and gratitude he bears you and will continue to bear you."

"Ah, yes!" cried Aline, turning now to her uncle. Here at least was an argument in André's favour, thought she. "That is true. Surely that . . ."

Inarticulately he hissed her into silence, exasperated.

"Hereafter perhaps that will help you to think of me more kindly, monsieur."

"I see no occasion, sir, to think of you at all. Again, I beg that you will go."

André-Louis looked at Aline an instant, as if still hesitating.

She answered him by a glance at her furious uncle, a faint shrug, and a lift of the eyebrows, dejection the while in her countenance.

It was as if she said: "You see his mood. There is nothing to be done."

He bowed with that singular grace the fencing-room had given him and went out by the door.

"Oh, it is cruel!" cried Aline, in a stifled voice, her hands clenched, and she sprang to the window.

"Aline!" her uncle's voice arrested her. "Where are you going?"

"But we do not know where he is to be found."

"Who wants to find the scoundrel?"

"We may never see him again."

"That is most fervently to be desired."

Aline said "Ouf!" and went out by the window.

He called after her, imperiously commanding her return. But Aline—dutiful child—closed her ears lest she must disobey him, and sped light-footed across the lawn to the avenue there to intercept the departing André-Louis.

As he came forth wrapped in gloom, she stepped from the bordering trees into his path.

"Aline!" he cried, joyously almost.

"I did not want you to go like this. I couldn't let you," she explained herself. "I know him better than you do, and I know that his great soft heart will presently melt. He will be filled with regret. He will want to send for you, and he will not know where to send."

"You think that?"

"Oh, I know it! You arrive in a bad moment. He is peevish and cross-grained, poor man, since he came here. These soft surroundings are all so strange to him. He wearies himself away from his beloved Gavrillac, his hunting and tillage, and the truth is that in his mind he very largely blames you for what has happened—for the necessity, or at least, the wisdom, of this change. Brittany, you must know, was becoming too unsafe. The château of La Tour d'Azyr, amongst others, was burnt to the ground some months ago. At any moment, given a fresh excitement, it may be the turn of Gavrillac. And for this and his present discomfort he blames you and your friends. But he will come round presently. He will be sorry that he sent you away like this—for I know that he loves you, André, in spite of all. I shall reason with him when the time comes. And then we shall want to know where to find you."

"At number 13, Rue du Hasard. The number is unlucky, the name of the street appropriate. Therefore both are easy to remember."

She nodded. "I will walk with you to the gates." And side by side now they proceeded at a leisurely pace down the long avenue in the June sunshine dappled by the shadows of the bordering trees. "You are looking well, André; and do you know that you have changed a deal? I am glad that you have prospered." And then, abruptly changing the subject before he had time to answer her, she came to the matter uppermost in her mind.

"I have so wanted to see you in all these months, André. You were the only one who could help me; the only one who could tell me the truth, and I was angry with you for never having written to say where you were to be found."

"Of course you encouraged me to do so when last we met in Nantes."

"What? Still resentful?"

"I am never resentful. You should know that." He expressed one of his vanities. He loved to think himself a Stoic. "But I still bear the scar of a wound that would be the better for the balm of your retraction."

"Why, then, I retract, André. And now tell me . . ."

"Yes, a self-seeking retraction," said he. "You give me something that you may obtain something." He laughed quite pleasantly. "Well, well; command me."

"Tell me, André." She paused, as if in some difficulty, and then went on, her eyes upon the ground: "Tell me—the truth of that event at the Feydau."

The request fetched a frown to his brow. He suspected at once the thought that prompted it. Quite simply and briefly he gave her his version of the affair.

She listened very attentively. When he had done she sighed; her face was very thoughtful.

"That is much what I was told," she said. "But it was added that M. de La Tour d'Azyr had gone to the theatre expressly for the purpose of breaking finally with La Binet. Do you know if that was so?"

"I don't; nor of any reason why it should be so. La Binet provided him the sort of amusement that he and his kind are forever craving . . ."

"Oh, there was a reason," she interrupted him. "I was the reason. I spoke to Mme. de Sautron. I told her that I would not continue to receive one who came to me contaminated in that fashion." She spoke of it with obvious difficulty, her colour rising as he watched her half-averted face.

"Had you listened to me . . ." he was beginning, when again she interrupted him.

"M. de Sautron conveyed my decision to him, and afterwards represented him to me as a man in despair, repentant, ready to give proofs—any proofs—of his sincerity and devotion to me.

He told me that M. de La Tour d'Azyr had sworn to him that he would cut short that affair, that he would see La Binet no more. And then, on the very next day I heard of his having all but lost his life in that riot at the theatre. He had gone straight from that interview with M. de Sautron, straight from those protestations of future wisdom, to La Binet. I was indignant. I pronounced myself finally. I stated definitely that I would not in any circumstances receive M. de La Tour d'Azyr again. And then they pressed this explanation upon me. For a long time I would not believe it."

"So that you believe it now," said André quickly. "Why?"

"I have not said that I believe it now. But . . . but . . . neither can I disbelieve. Since we came to Meudon M. de La Tour d'Azyr has been here, and he himself has sworn to me that it was so."

"Oh, if M. de La Tour d'Azyr has sworn . . ." André-Louis was laughing on a bitter note of sarcasm.

"Have you ever known him lie?" she cut in sharply. That checked him. "M. de La Tour d'Azyr is, after all, a man of honour, and men of honour never deal in falsehood. Have you ever known him do so, that you should sneer as you have done?"

"No," he confessed. Common justice demanded that he should admit that virtue at least in his enemy. "I have not known him lie, it is true. His kind is too arrogant, too self-confident to have recourse to untruth. But I have known him do things as vile . . ."

"Nothing is as vile," she interrupted, speaking from the code by which she had been reared. "It is for liars only—who are first cousin to thieves—that there is no hope. It is in falsehood only that there is real loss of honour."

"You are defending that satyr, I think," he said frostily.

"I desire to be just."

"Justice may seem to you a different matter when at last you shall have resolved yourself to become Marquise de La Tour d'Azyr." He spoke bitterly.

"I don't think that I shall ever take that resolve."

"But you are still not sure—in spite of everything."

"Can one ever be sure of anything in this world?"

"Yes. One can be sure of being foolish."

Either she did not hear or did not heed him.

"You do not of your own knowledge know that it was not as M. de La Tour d'Azyr asserts—that he went to the Feydau that night?"

"I don't," he admitted. "It is of course possible. But does it matter?"

"It might matter. Tell me; what became of La Binet after all?"

"I don't know."

"You don't know?" She turned to consider him. "And you can say it with that indifference! I thought . . . I thought you loved her, André."

"So did I, for a little while. I was mistaken. It required a La Tour d'Azyr to disclose the truth to me. They have their uses, these gentlemen. They help stupid fellows like myself to perceive important truths. I was fortunate that revelation in my case preceded marriage. I can now look back upon the episode with equanimity and thankfulness for my near escape from the consequences of what was no more than an aberration of the senses. It is a thing commonly confused with love. The experience, as you see, was very instructive."

She looked at him in frank surprise.

"Do you know, André, I sometimes think that you have no heart."

"Presumably because I sometimes betray intelligence. And what of yourself, Aline? What of your own attitude from the outset where M. de La Tour d'Azyr is concerned? Does that show heart? If I were to tell you what it really shows, we should end by quarrelling again, and God knows I can't afford to quarrel with you now. I . . . I shall take another way."

"What do you mean?"

"Why, nothing at the moment, for you are not in any danger of marrying that animal."

"And if I were?"

"Ah! In that case affection for you would discover to me some means of preventing it—unless . . ." He paused.

"Unless?" she demanded, challengingly, drawn to the full of her short height, her eyes imperious.

"Unless you could also tell me that you loved him," said he simply, whereat she was as suddenly and most oddly softened. And then he added, shaking his head: "But that of course is impossible."

"Why?" she asked him, quite gently now.

"Because you are what you are, Aline—utterly good and pure and adorable. Angels do not mate with devils. His wife you might become, but never his mate, Aline—never."

They had reached the wrought-iron gates at the end of the avenue. Through these they beheld the waiting yellow chaise which had brought André-Louis. From near at hand came the creak of other wheels, the beat of other hooves, and now another vehicle came in sight, and drew to a standstill beside the yellow chaise—a handsome equipage with polished mahogany panels on which the gold and azure of armorial bearings flashed brilliantly in the sunlight. A footman swung to earth to throw wide the gates; but in that moment the lady who occupied the carriage, perceiving Aline, waved to her and issued a command.

CHAPTER V

Madame de Plougastel

The postilion drew rein, and the footman opened the door, letting down the steps and proffering his arm to his mistress to assist her to alight, since that was the wish she had expressed. Then he opened one wing of the iron gates, and held it for her. She was a woman of something more than forty, who once must have been very lovely, who was very lovely still with the refining quality that age brings to some women. Her dress and carriage alike advertised great rank.

"I take my leave here, since you have a visitor," said André-Louis.

But it is an old acquaintance of your own, André. You remember Mme. la Comtesse de Plougastel?"

He looked at the approaching lady, whom Aline was now hastening forward to meet, and because she was named to him he recognized her. He must, he thought, had he but looked, have recognized her without prompting anywhere at any time, and this although it was some sixteen years since last he had seen her. The sight of her now brought it all back to him—a treasured memory that had never permitted itself to be entirely overlaid by subsequent events.

When he was a boy of ten, on the eve of being sent to school at Rennes, she had come on a visit to his godfather, who was her cousin. It happened that at the time he was taken by Rabouillet to the Manor of Gavrillac, and there he had been presented to Mme. de Plougastel. The great lady, in all the glory then of her youthful beauty, with her gentle, cultured voice—so cultured that she had seemed to speak a language almost unknown to the little Breton lad—and her majestic air of the great world, had scared him a little at first. Very gently had she allayed those fears of his, and by some mysterious enchantment she had completely enslaved his regard. He recalled now the terror in which he had gone to the embrace to which he was bidden, and the subsequent reluctance with which he had left those soft round arms. He remembered, too, how sweetly she had smelled and the very perfume she had used, a perfume as of lilac—for memory is singularly tenacious in these matters.

For three days whilst she had been at Gavrillac, he had gone daily to the manor, and so had spent hours in her company. A childless woman with the maternal instinct strong within her, she had taken this precociously intelligent, wide-eyed lad to her heart.

"Give him to me, Cousin Quintin," he remembered her saying on the last of those days to his godfather. "Let me take him back with me to Versailles as my adopted child."

But the Seigneur had gravely shaken his head in silent refusal, and there had been no further question of such a thing. And then, when she said goodbye to him—the thing came flooding back to him now—there had been tears in her eyes.

"Think of me sometimes, André-Louis," had been her last words.

He remembered how flattered he had been to have won within so short a time the affection of this great lady. The thing had given him a sense of importance that had endured for months thereafter, finally to fade into oblivion.

But all was vividly remembered now upon beholding her again, after sixteen years, profoundly changed and matured, the girl—for she had been no more in those old days—sunk in this worldly woman with the air of calm dignity and complete self-possession. Yet, he insisted, he must have known her anywhere again.

Aline embraced her affectionately, and then answering the questioning glance with faintly raised eyebrows that madame was directing towards Aline's companion— "This is André-Louis," she said. "You remember André-Louis, madame?"

Madame checked. André-Louis saw the surprise ripple over her face, taking with it some of her colour, leaving her for a moment breathless.

And then the voice—the well-remembered rich, musical voice—richer and deeper now than of yore, repeated his name:

"André-Louis!"

Her manner of uttering it suggested that it awakened memories, memories perhaps of the departed youth with which it was associated. And she paused a long moment, considering him, a little wide-eyed, what time he bowed before her.

"But of course I remember him," she said at last, and came towards him, putting out her hand. He kissed it dutifully, submissively, instinctively. "And this is what you have grown into?" She appraised him, and he flushed with pride at the satisfaction in her tone. He seemed to have gone back sixteen years, and to be again the little Breton lad at Gavrillac. She turned to Aline. "How mistaken Quintin was in his assumptions. He was pleased to see him again, was he not?"

"So pleased, madame, that he has shown me the door," said André-Louis.

"Ah!" She frowned, conning him still with those dark, wistful eyes of hers. "We must change that, Aline. He is of course very angry with you. But it is not the way to make converts. I will plead for you, André-Louis. I am a good advocate."

He thanked her and took his leave.

"I leave my case in your hands with gratitude. My homage, madame."

And so it happened that in spite of his godfather's forbidding reception of him, the fragment of a song was on his lips as his yellow chaise whirled him back to Paris and the Rue du Hasard. That meeting with Mme. de Plougastel had enheartened him; her promise to plead his case in alliance with Aline gave him assurance that all would be well.

That he was justified of this was proved when on the following Thursday towards noon his academy was invaded by M. de Kercadiou. Gilles, the boy, brought him word of it, and breaking off at once the lesson upon which he was engaged, he pulled off his mask, and went as he was—in a chamois waistcoat buttoned to the chin and with his foil under his arm to the modest salon below, where his godfather awaited him.

The florid little Lord of Gavrillac stood almost defiantly to receive him.

"I have been over-persuaded to forgive you," he announced aggressively, seeming thereby to imply that he consented to this merely so as to put an end to tiresome importunities.

André-Louis was not misled. He detected a pretence adopted by the Seigneur so as to enable him to retreat in good order.

"My blessings on the persuaders, whoever they may have been. You restore me my happiness, monsieur my godfather."

He took the hand that was proffered and kissed it, yielding to the impulse of the unfailing habit of his boyish days. It was an act symbolical of his complete submission, reëstablishing between himself and his godfather the bond of protected and protector, with all the mutual claims and duties that it carries. No mere words could more completely have made his peace with this man who loved him.

M. de Kercadiou's face flushed a deeper pink, his lip trembled, and there was a huskiness in the voice that murmured "My dear boy!" Then he recollected himself, threw back his great head and frowned. His voice resumed its habitual shrillness. "You realize, I hope, that you have behaved damnably . . . damnably, and with the utmost ingratitude?"

"Does not that depend upon the point of view?" quoth André-Louis, but his tone was studiously conciliatory.

"It depends upon a fact, and not upon any point of view. Since I have been persuaded to overlook it, I trust that at least you have some intention of reforming."

"I . . . I will abstain from politics," said André-Louis, that being the utmost he could say with truth.

"That is something, at least." His godfather permitted himself to be mollified, now that a concession—or a seeming concession—had been made to his just resentment.

"A chair, monsieur."

"No, no. I have come to carry you off to pay a visit with me. You owe it entirely to Mme. de Plougastel that I consent to receive you again. I desire that you come with me to thank her."

"I have my engagements here . . ." began André-Louis, and then broke off. "No matter! I will arrange it. A moment." And he was turning away to reënter the academy.

"What are your engagements? You are not by chance a fencing-instructor?" M. de Kercadiou had observed the leather waistcoat and the foil tucked under André-Louis' arm.

"I am the master of this academy—the academy of the late Bertrand des Amis, the most flourishing school of arms in Paris today."

M. de Kercadiou's brows went up.

"And you are master of it?"

"*Maître en fait d'armes.* I succeeded to the academy upon the death of des Amis."

He left M. Kercadiou to think it over, and went to make his arrangements and effect the necessary changes in his toilet.

"So that is why you have taken to wearing a sword," said M. de Kercadiou, as they climbed into his waiting carriage.

"That and the need to guard one's self in these times."

"And do you mean to tell me that a man who lives by what is after all an honourable profession, a profession mainly supported by the nobility, can at the same time associate himself with these peddling attorneys and low pamphleteers who are spreading dissension and insubordination?"

"You forget that I am a peddling attorney myself, made so by your own wishes, monsieur."

M. de Kercadiou grunted, and took snuff. "You say the academy flourishes?" he asked presently.

"It does. I have two assistant instructors. I could employ a third. It is hard work."

"That should mean that your circumstances are affluent."

"I have reason to be satisfied. I have far more than I need."

"Then you'll be able to do your share in paying off this national debt," growled the nobleman, well content that—as he conceived it—some of the evil André-Louis had helped to sow should recoil upon him.

Then the talk veered to Mme. de Plougastel. M. de Kercadiou, André-Louis gathered, but not the reason for it, disapproved most strongly of this visit. But then Madame la Comtesse was a headstrong woman whom there was no denying, whom all the world obeyed. M. de Plougastel was at present absent in Germany, but would shortly be returning. It was an indiscreet admission from which it was easy to infer that M. de Plougastel was one of those intriguing emissaries who came and went between the Queen of France and her brother, the Emperor of Austria.

The carriage drew up before a handsome hotel in the Faubourg Saint-Denis, at the corner of the Rue Paradis, and they were ushered by a sleek servant into a little boudoir, all gilt and brocade, that opened upon a terrace above a garden that was a park in miniature. Here madame awaited them. She rose, dismissing the

335

young person who had been reading to her, and came forward with both hands outheld to greet her cousin Kercadiou.

"I almost feared you would not keep your word," she said. "It was unjust. But then I hardly hoped that you would succeed in bringing him." And her glance, gentle, and smiling welcome upon him, indicated André-Louis.

The young man made answer with formal gallantry.

"The memory of you, madame, is too deeply imprinted on my heart for any persuasions to have been necessary."

"Ah, the courtier!" said madame, and abandoned him her hand. "We are to have a little talk, André-Louis," she informed him, with a gravity that left him vaguely ill at ease.

They sat down, and for a while the conversation was of general matters, chiefly concerned, however, with André-Louis, his occupations and his views. And all the while madame was studying him attentively with those gentle, wistful eyes, until again that sense of uneasiness began to pervade him. He realized instinctively that he had been brought here for some purpose deeper than that which had been avowed.

At last, as if the thing were concerted—and the clumsy Lord of Gavrillac was the last man in the world to cover his tracks—his godfather rose and, upon a pretext of desiring to survey the garden, sauntered through the windows on to the terrace, over whose white stone balustrade the geraniums trailed in a scarlet riot. Thence he vanished among the foliage below.

"Now we can talk more intimately," said madame. "Come here, and sit beside me." She indicated the empty half of the settee she occupied.

André-Louis went obediently, but a little uncomfortably. "You know," she said gently, placing a hand upon his arm, "that you have behaved very ill, that your godfather's resentment is very justly founded?"

"Madame, if I knew that, I should be the most unhappy, the most despairing of men." And he explained himself, as he had explained himself on Sunday to his godfather. "What I did, I did because it was the only means to my hand in a country in which justice was paralyzed by Privilege to make war upon an infamous scoundrel who had killed my best friend—a wanton, brutal act of murder, which there was no law to punish. And as if that were not enough—forgive me if I speak with the utmost frankness, madame—he afterwards debauched the woman I was to have married."

"Ah, *mon Dieu!*" she cried out.

"Forgive me. I know that it is horrible. You perceive, perhaps, what I suffered, how I came to be driven. That last affair of which I am guilty—the riot that began in the Feydau Theatre and afterwards enveloped the whole city of Nantes—was provoked by this."

"Who was she, this girl?"

It was like a woman, he thought, to fasten upon the unessential.

"Oh, a theatre girl, a poor fool of whom I have no regrets. La Binet was her name. I was a player at the time in her father's troupe. That was after the Rennes business, when it was necessary to hide from such justice as exists in France—the gallows' justice for unfortunates who are not 'born.' This added wrong led me to provoke a riot in the theatre."

"Poor boy," she said tenderly. "Only a woman's heart can

realize what you must have suffered; and because of that I can so readily forgive you. But now . . ."

"Ah, but you don't understand, madame. If today I thought that I had none but personal grounds for having lent a hand in the holy work of abolishing Privilege, I think I should cut my throat. My true justification lies in the insincerity of those who intended that the convocation of the States General should be a sham, mere dust in the eyes of the nation."

"Was it not, perhaps, wise to have been insincere in such a matter?"

He looked at her blankly.

"Can it ever be wise, madame, to be insincere?"

"Oh, indeed it can; believe me, who am twice your age, and know my world."

"I should say, madame, that nothing is wise that complicates existence; and I know of nothing that so complicates it as insincerity. Consider a moment the complications that have arisen out of this."

"But surely, André-Louis, your views have not been so perverted that you do not see that a governing class is a necessity in any country?"

"Why, of course. But not necessarily a hereditary one."

"What else?"

He answered her with an epigram. "Man, madame, is the child of his own work. Let there be no inheriting of rights but from such a parent. Thus a nation's best will always predominate, and such a nation will achieve greatly."

"But do you account birth of no importance?"

"Of none, madame—or else my own might trouble me."

From the deep flush that stained her face, he feared that he had offended by what was almost an indelicacy. But the reproof that he was expecting did not come. Instead— "And does it not?" she asked. "Never, André?"

"Never, madame. I am content."

"You have never . . . never regretted your lack of parents' care?"

He laughed, sweeping aside her sweet charitable concern that was so superfluous. "On the contrary, madame, I tremble to think what they might have made of me, and I am grateful to have had the fashioning of myself."

She looked at him for a moment very sadly, and then, smiling, gently shook her head.

"You do not want self-satisfaction. Yet I could wish that you saw things differently, André. It is a moment of great opportunities for a young man of talent and spirit. I could help you; I could help you, perhaps, to go very far if you would permit yourself to be helped after my fashion."

"Yes," he thought, "help me to a halter by sending me on treasonable missions to Austria on the Queen's behalf, like M. de Plougastel. That would certainly end in a high position for me."

Aloud he answered more as politeness prompted.

"I am grateful, madame. But you will see that, holding the ideals I have expressed, I could not serve any cause that is opposed to their realization."

"You are misled by prejudice, André-Louis, by personal grievances. Will you allow them to stand in the way of your advancement?"

"If what I call ideals were really prejudices, would it be honest of me to run counter to them whilst holding them?"

"If I could convince you that you are mistaken! I could help you so much to find a worthy employment for the talents you possess. In the service of the King you would prosper quickly. Will you think of it, André-Louis, and let us talk of this again?"

He answered her with formal, chill politeness.

"I fear that it would be idle, madame. Yet your interest in me is very flattering, and I thank you. It is unfortunate for me that I am so headstrong."

"And now who deals in insincerity?" she asked him.

"Ah, but you see, madame, it is an insincerity that does not mislead."

And then M. de Kercadiou came in through the window again, and announced fussily that he must be getting back to Meudon, and that he would take his godson with him and set him down at the Rue du Hasard.

"You must bring him again, Quintin," the Countess said, as they took their leave of her.

"Some day, perhaps," said M. de Kercadiou vaguely, and swept his godson out.

In the carriage he asked him bluntly of what madame had talked.

"She was very kind—a sweet woman," said André-Louis pensively.

"Devil take you, I didn't ask you the opinion that you presume to have formed of her. I asked you what she said to you."

"She strove to point out to me the error of my ways. She spoke of great things that I might do—to which she would very kindly help me—if I were to come to my senses. But as miracles do not happen, I gave her little encouragement to hope."

"I see. I see. Did she say anything else?"

He was so peremptory that André-Louis turned to look at him.

"What else did you expect her to say, monsieur my god-father?"

"Oh, nothing."

"Then she fulfilled your expectations."

"Eh? Oh, a thousand devils, why can't you express yourself in a sensible manner that a plain man can understand without having to think about it?"

He sulked after that most of the way to the Rue du Hasard, or so it seemed to André-Louis. At least he sat silent, gloomily thoughtful to judge by his expression.

"You may come and see us soon again at Meudon," he told André-Louis at parting. "But please remember—no revolutionary politics in future, if we are to remain friends."

CHAPTER VI

Politicians

O ne morning in August the academy in the Rue du Hasard
was invaded by Le Chapelier accompanied by a man of
remarkable appearance, whose herculean stature and disfigured
countenance seemed vaguely familiar to André-Louis. He was a
man of little, if anything, over thirty, with small bright eyes buried in an enormous face. His cheekbones were prominent, his
nose awry, as if it had been broken by a blow, and his mouth was
rendered almost shapeless by the scars of another injury. (A bull
had horned him in the face when he was but a lad.) As if that
were not enough to render his appearance terrible, his cheeks
were deeply pock-marked. He was dressed untidily in a long scarlet
coat that descended almost to his ankles, soiled buckskin breeches
and boots with reversed tops. His shirt, none too clean, was open
at the throat, the collar hanging limply over an unknotted cravat,
displaying fully the muscular neck that rose like a pillar from his

massive shoulders. He swung a cane that was almost a club in his left hand, and there was a cockade in his biscuit-coloured, conical hat. He carried himself with an aggressive, masterful air, that great head of his thrown back as if he were eternally at defiance.

Le Chapelier, whose manner was very grave, named him to André-Louis.

"This is M. Danton, a brother-lawyer, President of the Cordeliers, of whom you will have heard."

Of course André-Louis had heard of him. Who had not, by then?

Looking at him now with interest, André-Louis wondered how it came that all, or nearly all the leading innovators, were pock-marked. Mirabeau, the journalist Desmoulins, the philanthropist Marat, Robespierre the little lawyer from Arras, this formidable fellow Danton, and several others he could call to mind all bore upon them the scars of smallpox. Almost he began to wonder was there any connection between the two. Did an attack of smallpox produce certain moral results which found expression in this way?

He dismissed the idle speculation, or rather it was shattered by the startling thunder of Danton's voice.

"This —— Chapelier has told me of you. He says that you are a patriotic ——."

More than by the tone was André-Louis startled by the obscenities with which the Colossus did not hesitate to interlard his first speech to a total stranger. He laughed outright. There was nothing else to do.

"If he has told you that, he has told you more than the truth! I am a patriot. The rest my modesty compels me to disavow."

"You're a joker too, it seems," roared the other, but he laughed nevertheless, and the volume of it shook the windows. "There's no offence in me. I am like that."

"What a pity," said André-Louis.

It disconcerted the king of the markets. "Eh? what's this, Chapelier? Does he give himself airs, your friend here?"

The spruce Breton, a very *petit-maître* in appearance by contrast with his companion, but nevertheless of a downright manner quite equal to Danton's in brutality, though dispensing with the emphasis of foulness, shrugged as he answered him:

"It is merely that he doesn't like your manners, which is not at all surprising. They are execrable."

"Ah, bah! You are all like that, you —— Bretons. Let's come to business. You'll have heard what took place in the Assembly yesterday? You haven't? My God, where do you live? Have you heard that this scoundrel who calls himself King of France gave passage across French soil the other day to Austrian troops going to crush those who fight for liberty in Belgium? Have you heard that, by any chance?"

"Yes," said André-Louis coldly, masking his irritation before the other's hectoring manner. "I have heard that."

"Oh! And what do you think of it?" Arms akimbo, the Colossus towered above him.

André-Louis turned aside to Le Chapelier.

"I don't think I understand. Have you brought this gentleman here to examine my conscience?"

"Name of a name! He's prickly as a —— porcupine!" Danton protested.

"No, no." Le Chapelier was conciliatory, seeking to provide

344

an antidote to the irritant administered by his companion. "We require your help, André. Danton here thinks that you are the very man for us. Listen now . . ."

"That's it. You tell him," Danton agreed. "You both talk the same mincing —— sort of French. He'll probably understand you."

Le Chapelier went on without heeding the interruption.

"This violation by the King of the obvious rights of a country engaged in framing a constitution that shall make it free has shattered every philanthropic illusion we still cherished. There are those who go so far as to proclaim the King the vowed enemy of France. But that, of course, is excessive."

"Who says so?" blazed Danton, and swore horribly by way of conveying his total disagreement.

Le Chapelier waved him into silence, and proceeded.

"Anyhow, the matter has been more than enough, added to all the rest, to set us by the ears again in the Assembly. It is open war between the Third Estate and the Privileged."

"Was it ever anything else?"

"Perhaps not; but it has assumed a new character. You'll have heard of the duel between Lameth and the Duc de Castries?"

"A trifling affair."

"In its results. But it might have been far other. Mirabeau is challenged and insulted now at every sitting. But he goes his way, cold-bloodedly wise. Others are not so circumspect; they meet insult with insult, blow with blow, and blood is being shed in private duels. The thing is reduced by these swordsmen of the nobility to a system."

André-Louis nodded. He was thinking of Philippe de

Vilmorin. "Yes," he said, "it is an old trick of theirs. It is so simple and direct—like themselves. I wonder only that they didn't hit upon this system sooner. In the early days of the States General, at Versailles, it might have had a better effect. Now, it comes a little late."

"But they mean to make up for lost time—sacred name!" cried Danton. "Challenges are flying right and left between these bully-swordsmen, these *spadassinicides*, and poor devils of the robe who have never learnt to fence with anything but a quill. It's just—murder. Yet if I were to go amongst *messieurs les nobles* and crunch an addled head or two with this stick of mine, snap a few aristocratic necks between these fingers which the good God has given me for the purpose, the law would send me to atone upon the gallows. This in a land that is striving after liberty. Why, *Dieu me damne!* I am not even allowed to keep my hat on in the theatre. But they—these ——s!"

"He is right," said Le Chapelier. "The thing has become un-endurable, insufferable. Two days ago M. d'Ambly threatened Mirabeau with his cane before the whole Assembly. Yesterday M. de Faussigny leapt up and harangued his order by inviting murder. 'Why don't we fall on these scoundrels, sword in hand?' he asked. Those were his very words: 'Why don't we fall on these scoundrels, sword in hand.'"

"It is so much simpler than lawmaking," said André-Louis.

"Lagron, the deputy from Ancenis in the Loire, said something that we did not hear in answer. As he was leaving the Manège one of these bullies grossly insulted him. Lagron no more than used his elbow to push past when the fellow cried out that he had been struck, and issued his challenge. They fought this morning early in the Champs Èlysées, and Lagron was killed, run through the stomach deliberately by a man who fought like a fencing-master, and poor Lagron did not even own a sword. He had to borrow one to go to the assignation."

André-Louis—his mind ever on Vilmorin, whose case was here repeated, even to the details—was swept by a gust of passion. He clenched his hands, and his jaws set. Danton's little eyes observed him keenly.

"Well? And what do you think of that? *Noblesse oblige*, eh? The thing is we must oblige them too, these ——s. We must pay them back in the same coin; meet them with the same weapons. Abolish them; tumble these *assassinateurs* into the abyss of nothingness by the same means."

"But how?"

"How? Name of God! Haven't I said it?"

"That is where we require your help," Le Chapelier put in. "There must be men of patriotic feeling among the more advanced of your pupils. M. Danton's idea is that a little band of these—say a half-dozen, with yourself at their head—might read these bullies a sharp lesson."

André-Louis frowned.

"And how, precisely, had M. Danton thought that this might be done?"

M. Danton spoke for himself, vehemently.

"Why, thus: We post you in the Manège, at the hour when the Assembly is rising. We point out the six leading phlebotomists, and let you loose to insult them before they have time to insult any of the representatives. Then tomorrow morning, six —— phlebotomists themselves phlebotomized *secundum artem*.

347

That will give the others something to think about. It will give them a great deal to think about, by ——! If necessary the dose may be repeated to ensure a cure. If you kill the ——s, so much the better."

He paused, his sallow face flushed with the enthusiasm of his idea. André-Louis stared at him inscrutably.

"Well, what do you say to that?"

"That it is most ingenious." And André-Louis turned aside to look out of the window.

"And is that all you think of it?"

"I will not tell you what else I think of it because you probably would not understand. For you, M. Danton, there is at least this excuse that you did not know me. But you, Isaac—to bring this gentleman here with such a proposal!"

Le Chapelier was overwhelmed in confusion. "I confess I hesitated," he apologized. "But M. Danton would not take my word for it that the proposal might not be to your taste."

"I would not!" Danton broke in, bellowing. He swung upon Le Chapelier, brandishing his great arms. "You told me monsieur was a patriot. Patriotism knows no scruples. You call this mincing dancing-master a patriot?"

"Would you, monsieur, out of patriotism consent to become an assassin?"

"Of course I would. Haven't I told you so? Haven't I told you that I would gladly go among them with my club, and crack them like so many —— fleas?"

"Why not, then?"

"Why not? Because I should get myself hanged. Haven't I said so?"

"But what of that—being a patriot? Why not, like another Curtius, jump into the gulf, since you believe that your country would benefit by your death?"

M. Danton showed signs of exasperation. "Because my country will benefit more by my life."

"Permit me, monsieur, to suffer from a similar vanity."

"You? But where would be the danger to you? You would do your work under the cloak of duelling—as they do."

"Have you reflected, monsieur, that the law will hardly regard a fencing-master who kills his opponent as an ordinary combatant, particularly if it can be shown that the fencing-master himself provoked the attack?"

"So! Name of a name!" M. Danton blew out his cheeks and delivered himself with withering scorn. "It comes to this, then: you are afraid!"

"You may think so if you choose—that I am afraid to do slyly and treacherously that which a thrasonical patriot like yourself is afraid of doing frankly and openly. I have other reasons. But that one should suffice you."

Danton gasped. Then he swore more amazingly and variedly than ever.

"By ——! you are right," he admitted, to André-Louis' amazement. "You are right, and I am wrong. I am as bad a patriot as you are, and I am a coward as well." And he invoked the whole Panthéon to witness his self-denunciation. "Only, you see, I count for something: and if they take me and hang me, why, there it is! Monsieur, we must find some other way. Forgive the intrusion. Adieu!" He held out his enormous hand.

Le Chapelier stood hesitating, crestfallen.

"You understand, André? I am sorry that . . ."

"Say no more, please. Come and see me soon again. I would press you to remain, but it is striking nine, and the first of my pupils is about to arrive."

"Nor would I permit it," said Danton. "Between us we must resolve the riddle of how to extinguish M. de La Tour d'Azyr and his friends."

"Who?"

Sharp as a pistol-shot came that question, as Danton was turning away. The tone of it brought him up short. He turned again, Le Chapelier with him.

"I said M. de La Tour d'Azyr."

"What has he to do with the proposal you were making me?"

"He? Why, he is the phlebotomist in chief."

And Le Chapelier added. "It is he who killed Legron."

"Not a friend of yours, is he?" wondered Danton.

"And it is La Tour d'Azyr you desire me to kill?" asked André-Louis very slowly, after the manner of one whose thoughts are meanwhile pondering the subject.

"That's it," said Danton. "And not a job for a prentice hand, I can assure you."

"Ah, but this alters things," said André-Louis, thinking aloud. "It offers a great temptation."

"Why, then . . . ?" The Colossus took a step towards him again.

"Wait!" He put up his hand. Then with chin sunk on his breast, he paced away to the window, musing.

Le Chapelier and Danton exchanged glances, then watched him, waiting, what time he considered.

At first he almost wondered why he should not of his own accord have decided upon some such course as this to settle that long-standing account of M. de La Tour d'Azyr. What was the use of this great skill in fencing that he had come to acquire, unless he could turn it to account to avenge Vilmorin, and to make Aline safe from the lure of her own ambition? It would be an easy thing to seek out La Tour d'Azyr, put a mortal affront upon him, and thus bring him to the point. Today this would be murder, murder as treacherous as that which La Tour d'Azyr had done upon Philippe de Vilmorin; for today the old positions were reversed, and it was André-Louis who might go to such an assignation without a doubt of the issue. It was a moral obstacle of which he made short work. But there remained the legal obstacle he had expounded to Danton. There was still a law in France; the same law which he had found it impossible to move against La Tour d'Azyr, but which would move briskly enough against himself in like case. And then, suddenly, as if by inspiration, he saw the way—a way which if adopted would probably bring La Tour d'Azyr to a poetic justice, bring him, insolent, confident, to thrust himself upon André-Louis' sword, with all the odium of provocation on his own side.

He turned to them again, and they saw that he was very pale, that his great dark eyes glowed oddly.

"There will probably be some difficulty in finding a *suppléant* for this poor Lagron," he said. "Our fellow-countrymen will be none so eager to offer themselves to the swords of Privilege."

"True enough," said Le Chapelier gloomily; and then, as if suddenly leaping to the thing in André-Louis' mind: "André!" he cried. "Would you . . ."

"It is what I was considering. It would give me a legitimate place in the Assembly. If your Tour d'Azyrs choose to seek me out then, why, their blood be upon their own heads. I shall certainly do nothing to discourage them." He smiled curiously. "I am just a rascal who tries to be honest—Scaramouche always, in fact; a creature of sophistries. Do you think that Ancenis would have me for its representative?"

"Will it have Omnes Omnibus for its representative?" La Chapelier was laughing, his countenance eager. "Ancenis will be convulsed with pride. It is not Rennes or Nantes, as it might have been had you wished it. But it gives you a voice for Brittany."

"I should have to go to Ancenis . . . ?"

"No need at all. A letter from me to the Municipality, and the Municipality will confirm you at once. No need to move from here. In a fortnight at most the thing can be accomplished. It is settled, then?"

André-Louis considered yet a moment. There was his academy. But he could make arrangements with La Duc and Galoche to carry it on for him whilst himself directing and advising. Le Duc, after all, was become a thoroughly efficient master, and he was a trustworthy fellow. At need a third assistant could be engaged.

"Be it so," he said at last.

Le Chapelier clasped hands with him and became congratulatorily voluble, until interrupted by the red-coated giant at the door.

"What exactly does it mean to our business, anyway?" he asked. "Does it mean that when you are a representative you will not scruple to skewer M. le Marquis?"

"If M. le Marquis should offer himself to be skewered, as he no doubt will."

"I perceive the distinction," said M. Danton, and sneered. "You've an ingenious mind." He turned to La Chapelier. "What did you say he was to begin with—a lawyer, wasn't it?"

"Yes, I was a lawyer, and afterwards a mountebank."

"And this is the result!"

"As you say. And do you know that we are after all not so dissimilar, you and I?"

"What?"

"Once like you I went about inciting other people to go and kill the man I wanted dead. You'll say I was a coward, of course."

Le Chapelier prepared to slip between them as the clouds gathered on the giant's brow. Then these were dispelled again, and the great laugh vibrated through the long room.

"You've touched me for the second time, and in the same place. Oh, you can fence, my lad. We should be friends. Rue des Cordeliers is my address. Any —— scoundrel will tell you where Danton lodges. Desmoulins lives underneath. Come and visit us one evening. There's always a bottle for a friend."

CHAPTER VII

The Spadassinicides

After an absence of rather more than a week, M. le Marquis de La Tour d'Azyr was back in his place on the Côté Droit of the National Assembly. Properly speaking, we should already at this date allude to him as the *ci-devant* Marquis de La Tour d'Azyr, for the time was September of 1790, two months after the passing—on the motion of that downright Breton leveller, Le Chapelier—of the decree that nobility should no more be hereditary than infamy; that just as the brand of the gallows must not defile the possibly worthy descendants of one who had been convicted of evil, neither should the blazon advertising achievement glorify the possibly unworthy descendants of one who had proved himself good. And so the decree had been passed abolishing hereditary nobility and consigning family escutcheons to the rubbish-heap of things no longer to be tolerated by an enlightened generation of philosophers. M. le Comte de Lafayette, who had supported the motion, left the Assembly as plain M. Motier, the great tribune Count Mirabeau became plain M. Riquetti, and M. le Marquis de La Tour d'Azyr just simple M. Lesarques. The thing was done in one of those exaltations produced by the approach of the great National Festival of the Champ de Mars, and no doubt it was thoroughly repented on the morrow by those who had lent themselves to it. Thus, although law by now, it was a law that no one troubled just yet to enforce.

That, however, is by the way. The time, as I have said, was September, the day dull and showery, and some of the damp and gloom of it seemed to have penetrated the long Hall of the Manège, where on their eight rows of green benches elliptically arranged in ascending tiers about the space known as La Piste, sat some eight or nine hundred of the representatives of the three orders that composed the nation.

The matter under debate by the constitution-builders was whether the deliberating body to succeed the Constituent Assembly should work in conjunction with the King, whether it should be periodic or permanent, whether it should govern by two chambers or by one.

The Abbé Maury, son of a cobbler, and therefore in these days of antitheses orator-in-chief of the party of the Right—the Blacks, as those who fought Privilege's losing battles were known—was in the tribune. He appeared to be urging the adoption of a two-chambers system framed on the English model. He was, if anything, more long-winded and prosy even than his habit; his arguments assumed more and more the form of a sermon; the tribune of the National Assembly became more and more like a pulpit; but the members, conversely, less and less like a congregation. They grew restive under that steady flow of pompous verbiage, and it was in vain that the four ushers in black satin breeches and carefully powdered heads, chain of office on their breasts, gilded sword at their sides, circulated in the Piste, clapping their hands, and hissing—

"*Silence! En place!*"

Equally vain was the intermittent ringing of the bell by the president at his green-covered table facing the tribune. The Abbé Maury had talked too long, and for some time had failed to interest the members. Realizing it at last, he ceased, whereupon the hum of conversation became general. And then it fell abruptly. There was a silence of expectancy, and a turning of heads, a craning of necks. Even the group of secretaries at the round table below the president's daïs roused themselves from their usual apathy to consider this young man who was mounting the tribune of the Assembly for the first time.

"M. André-Louis Moreau, deputy *suppléant*, vice Emmanuel Lagron, deceased, for Ancenis in the Department of the Loire."

M. de La Tour d'Azyr shook himself out of the gloomy abstraction in which he had sat. The successor of the deputy he had slain must, in any event, be an object of grim interest to him. You conceive how that interest was heightened when he heard him named, when, looking across, he recognized indeed in this André-Louis Moreau the young scoundrel who was continually crossing his path, continually exerting against him a deep-moving, sinister influence to make him regret that he should have spared his life that day at Gavrillac two years ago. That he should thus have stepped into the shoes of Lagron seemed to M. de La Tour d'Azyr too apt for mere coincidence, a direct challenge in itself.

He looked at the young man in wonder rather than in anger, and looking at him he was filled by a vague, almost a premonitory, uneasiness.

At the very outset, the presence which in itself he conceived to be a challenge was to demonstrate itself for this in no equivocal terms.

"I come before you," André-Louis began, "as a *deputysuppléant* to fill the place of one who was murdered some three weeks ago."

It was a challenging opening that instantly provoked an indignant outcry from the Blacks. André-Louis paused, and looked at them, smiling a little, a singularly self-confident young man.

"The gentlemen of the Right, M. le Président, do not appear to like my words. But that is not surprising. The gentlemen of the Right notoriously do not like the truth."

This time there was uproar. The members of the Left roared with laughter, those of the Right thundered menacingly. The ushers circulated at a pace beyond their usual, agitated themselves, clapped their hands, and called in vain for silence.

The President rang his bell.

Above the general din came the voice of La Tour d'Azyr, who had half-risen from his seat: "Mountebank! This is not the theatre!"

"No, monsieur, it is becoming a hunting-ground for bully-swordsmen," was the answer, and the uproar grew.

The deputy-*suppléant* looked round and waited. Near at hand he met the encouraging grin of Le Chapelier, and the quiet, approving smile of Kersain, another Breton deputy of his acquaintance. A little farther off he saw the great head of Mirabeau thrown back, the great eyes regarding him from under a frown in a sort of wonder, and yonder, among all that moving sea of faces, the sallow countenance of the Arras' lawyer Robespierre—or *de* Robespierre, as the little snob now called himself, having assumed the aristocratic particle as the prerogative of a man of his distinction in the councils of his country. With his tip-tilted nose in the air, his carefully curled head on one side, the deputy for Arras was observing André-Louis attentively. The horn-rimmed spectacles he used for reading were thrust up on to his pale forehead, and it was through a levelled spy-glass that he considered the speaker, his thin-lipped mouth stretched a little in that tiger-cat smile that was afterwards to become so famous and so feared.

Gradually the uproar wore itself out, and diminished so that at last the President could make himself heard. Leaning forward, he gravely addressed the young man in the tribune:

"Monsieur, if you wish to be heard, let me beg of you not to be provocative in your language." And then to the others: "Messieurs, if we are to proceed, I beg that you will restrain your feelings until the deputy-*suppléant* has concluded his discourse."

"I shall endeavour to obey, M. le Président, leaving provocation to the gentlemen of the Right. If the few words I have used so far have been provocative, I regret it. But it was necessary that I should refer to the distinguished deputy whose place I come so unworthily to fill, and it was unavoidable that I should refer to the event which has procured us this sad necessity. The deputy Lagron was a man of singular nobility of mind, a selfless, dutiful, zealous man, inflamed by the high purpose of doing his duty by his electors and by this Assembly. He possessed what his opponents would call a dangerous gift of eloquence."

La Tour d'Azyr writhed at the well-known phrase—his own

phrase—the phrase that he had used to explain his action in the matter of Philippe de Vilmorin, the phrase that from time to time had been cast in his teeth with such vindictive menace.

And then the crisp voice of the witty Cazalés, that very rapier of the Privileged party, cut sharply into the speaker's momentary pause.

"M. le Président," he asked with great solemnity, "has the deputy-*suppléant* mounted the tribune for the purpose of taking part in the debate on the constitution of the legislative assemblies, or for the purpose of pronouncing a funeral oration upon the departed deputy Lagron?"

This time it was the Blacks who gave way to mirth, until checked by the deputy-*suppléant*.

"That laughter is obscene!" In this truly Gallic fashion he flung his glove into the face of Privilege, determined, you see, upon no half measures; and the rippling laughter perished on the instant quenched in speechless fury.

Solemnly he proceeded.

"You all know how Lagron died. To refer to his death at all requires courage, to laugh in referring to it requires something that I will not attempt to qualify. If I have alluded to his decease, it is because my own appearance among you seemed to render some such allusion necessary. It is mine to take up the burden which he set down. I do not pretend that I have the strength, the courage, or the wisdom of Lagron; but with every ounce of such strength and courage and wisdom as I possess that burden will I bear. And I trust, for the sake of those who might attempt it, that the means taken to impose silence upon that eloquent voice will not be taken to impose silence upon mine."

There was a faint murmur of applause from the Left, a splutter of contemptuous laughter from the Right.

"Rhodomont!" a voice called to him.

He looked in the direction of that voice, proceeding from the group of *spadassins* amid the Blacks across the Piste, and he smiled. Inaudibly his lips answered:

"No, my friend—Scaramouche; Scaramouche, the subtle, dangerous fellow who goes tortuously to his ends." Aloud, he resumed: "M. le Président, there are those who will not understand that the purpose for which we are assembled here is the making of laws by which France may be equitably governed, by which France may be lifted out of the morass of bankruptcy into which she is in danger of sinking. For there are some who want, it seems, not laws, but blood; I solemnly warn them that this blood will end by choking them, if they do not learn in time to discard force and allow reason to prevail."

Again in that phrase there was something that stirred a memory in La Tour d'Azyr. He turned in the fresh uproar to speak to his cousin Chabrillane who sat beside him.

"A daring rogue, this bastard of Gavrillac's," said he.

Chabrillane looked at him with gleaming eyes, his face white with anger.

"Let him talk himself out. I don't think he will be heard again after today. Leave this to me."

Hardly could La Tour have told you why, but he sank back in his seat with a sense of relief. He had been telling himself that here was matter demanding action, a challenge that he must take up. But despite his rage he felt a singular unwillingness. This fellow had a trick of reminding him, he supposed, too unpleasantly of that young abbé done to death in the garden behind the Bréton Armé at Gavrillac. Not that the death of Philippe de Vilmorin lay heavily upon M. de La Tour d'Azyr's conscience. He had accounted himself fully justified of his action. It was that the whole thing as his memory revived it for him made an unpleasant picture: that distraught boy kneeling over the bleeding body of the friend he had loved, and almost begging to be slain with him, dubbing the Marquis murderer and coward to incite him.

Meanwhile, leaving now the subject of the death of Lagron, the deputy-*suppléant* had at last brought himself into order, and was speaking upon the question under debate. He contributed nothing of value to it; he urged nothing definite. His speech on the subject was very brief—that being the pretext and not the purpose for which he had ascended the tribune.

When later he was leaving the hall at the end of the sitting, with Le Chapelier at his side, he found himself densely surrounded by deputies as by a body-guard. Most of them were Bretons, who aimed at screening him from the provocations which his own provocative words in the Assembly could not fail to bring down upon his head. For a moment the massive form of Mirabeau brought up alongside of him.

"Felicitations, M. Moreau," said the great man. "You acquitted yourself very well. They will want your blood, no doubt. But be discreet, monsieur, if I may presume to advise you, and do not allow yourself to be misled by any false sense of quixotry. Ignore their challenges. I do so myself. I place each challenger upon my list. There are some fifty there already, and there they will remain. Refuse them what they are pleased to call satisfaction, and all will be well." André-Louis smiled and sighed. "It requires courage," said the hypocrite.

"Of course it does. But you would appear to have plenty."

"Hardly enough, perhaps. But I shall do my best."

They had come through the vestibule, and although this was lined with eager Blacks waiting for the young man who had insulted them so flagrantly from the rostrum, André-Louis' bodyguard had prevented any of them from reaching him.

Emerging now into the open, under the great awning at the head of the Carrière, erected to enable carriages to reach the door under cover, those in front of him dispersed a little, and there was a moment as he reached the limit of the awning when his front was entirely uncovered. Outside the rain was falling heavily, churning the ground into thick mud, and for a moment André-Louis, with Le Chapelier ever at his side, stood hesitating to step out into the deluge.

The watchful Chabrillane had seen his chance, and by a détour that took him momentarily out into the rain, he came face to face with the too-daring young Breton. Rudely, violently, he thrust André-Louis back, as if to make room for himself under the shelter.

Not for a second was André-Louis under any delusion as to the man's deliberate purpose, nor were those who stood near him, who made a belated and ineffectual attempt to close about him. He was grievously disappointed. It was not Chabrillane he had been expecting. His disappointment was reflected on his countenance, to be mistaken for something very different by the arrogant Chevalier.

But if Chabrillane was the man appointed to deal with him,

he would make the best of it.

"I think you are pushing against me, monsieur," he said, very civilly, and with elbow and shoulder he thrust M. de Chabrillane back into the rain.

"I desire to take shelter, monsieur," the Chevalier hectored.

"You may do so without standing on my feet. I have a prejudice against anyone standing on my feet. My feet are very tender. Perhaps you did not know it, monsieur. Please say no more."

"Why, I wasn't speaking, you lout!" exclaimed the Chevalier, slightly discomposed.

"Were you not? I thought perhaps you were about to apologize."

"Apologize?" Chabrillane laughed. "To you! Do you know that you are amusing?" He stepped under the awning for the second time, and again in view of all thrust André-Louis rudely back.

"Ahi!" cried André-Louis, with a grimace. "You hurt me, monsieur. I have told you not to push against me." He raised his voice that all might hear him, and once more impelled M. de Chabrillane back into the rain.

Now, for all his slenderness, his assiduous daily sword-practice had given André-Louis an arm of iron. Also he threw his weight into the thrust. His assailant reeled backwards a few steps, and then his heel struck a baulk of timber left on the ground by some workmen that morning, and he sat down suddenly in the mud.

A roar of laughter rose from all who witnessed the fine gentleman's downfall. He rose, mud-bespattered, in a fury, and in that fury sprang at André-Louis.

André-Louis had made him ridiculous, which was altogether unforgivable.

"You shall meet me for this!" he spluttered. "I shall kill you for it."

His inflamed face was within a foot of André-Louis'. Andre-Louis laughed. In the silence everybody heard the laugh and the words that followed.

"Oh, is that what you wanted? But why didn't you say so before? You would have spared me the trouble of knocking you down. I thought gentlemen of your profession invariably conducted these affairs with decency, decorum, and a certain grace. Had you done so, you might have saved your breeches."

"How soon shall we settle this?" snapped Chabrillane, livid with very real fury.

"Whenever you please, monsieur. It is for you to say when it will suit your convenience to kill me. I think that was the intention you announced, was it not?" André-Louis was suavity itself.

"Tomorrow morning, in the Bois. Perhaps you will bring a friend."

"Certainly, monsieur. Tomorrow morning, then. I hope we shall have fine weather. I detest the rain."

Chabrillane looked at him almost with amazement. André-Louis smiled pleasantly.

"Don't let me detain you now, monsieur. We quite understand each other. I shall be in the Bois at nine o'clock tomorrow morning."

"That is too late for me, monsieur."

"Any other hour would be too early for me. I do not like to

have my habits disturbed. Nine o'clock or not at all, as you please."

"But I must be at the Assembly at nine, for the morning session."

"I am afraid, monsieur, you will have to kill me first, and I have a prejudice against being killed before nine o'clock."

Now this was too complete a subversion of the usual procedure for M. de Chabrillane's stomach. Here was a rustic deputy assuming with him precisely the tone of sinister mockery which his class usually dealt out to their victims of the Third Estate. And to heighten the irritation, André-Louis—the actor, Scaramouche always—produced his snuffbox, and proffered it with a steady hand to Le Chapelier before helping himself.

Chabrillane, it seemed, after all that he had suffered, was not even to be allowed to make a good exit.

"Very well, monsieur," he said. "Nine o'clock, then; and we'll see if you'll talk as pertly afterwards."

On that he flung away, before the jeers of the provincial deputies. Nor did it soothe his rage to be laughed at by urchins all the way down the Rue Dauphine because of the mud and filth that dripped from his satin breeches and the tails of his elegant, striped coat.

But though the members of the Third had jeered on the surface, they trembled underneath with fear and indignation. It was too much. Lagron killed by one of these bullies, and now his successor challenged, and about to be killed by another of them on the very first day of his appearance to take the dead man's place. Several came now to implore André-Louis not to go to the Bois, to ignore the challenge and the whole affair, which was but a deliberate attempt to put him out of the way. He listened seriously, shook his head gloomily, and promised at last to think it over.

He was in his seat again for the afternoon session as if nothing disturbed him.

But in the morning, when the Assembly met, his place was vacant, and so was M. de Chabrillane's. Gloom and resentment sat upon the members of the Third, and brought a more than usually acrid note into their debates. They disapproved of the rashness of the new recruit to their body. Some openly condemned his lack of circumspection. Very few—and those only the little group in Le Chapelier's confidence—ever expected to see him again.

It was, therefore, as much in amazement as in relief that at a few minutes after ten they saw him enter, calm, composed, and bland, and thread his way to his seat. The speaker occupying the rostrum at that moment—a member of the Privileged—stopped short to stare in incredulous dismay. Here was something that he could not understand at all. Then from somewhere, to satisfy the amazement on both sides of the assembly, a voice explained the phenomenon contemptuously.

"They haven't met. He has shirked it at the last moment."

It must be so, thought all; the mystification ceased, and men were settling back into their seats. But now, having reached his place, having heard the voice that explained the matter to the universal satisfaction, André-Louis paused before taking his seat. He felt it incumbent upon him to reveal the true fact.

"M. le Président, my excuses for my late arrival." There was no necessity for this. It was a mere piece of theatricality, such as it was not in Scaramouche's nature to forgo. "I have been detained by an engagement of a pressing nature. I bring you also the excuses of M. de Chabrillane. He, unfortunately, will be permanently absent from this Assembly in future."

The silence was complete. André-Louis sat down.

CHAPTER VIII

The Paladin
of the Third

M le Chevalier de Chabrillane had been closely connected, you will remember, with the iniquitous affair in which Philippe de Vilmorin had lost his life. We know enough to justify a surmise that he had not merely been La Tour d'Azyr's second in the encounter, but actually an instigator of the business. André-Louis may therefore have felt a justifiable satisfaction in offering up the Chevalier's life to the Manes of his murdered friend. He may have viewed it as an act of common justice not to be procured by any other means. Also it is to be remembered that Chabrillane had gone confidently to the meeting, conceiving that he, a practised *ferrailleur*, had to deal with a bourgeois utterly unskilled in swordsmanship. Morally, then, he was little better than a murderer, and that he should have tumbled into the pit he conceived that he dug for André-Louis was a poetic retribution. Yet, notwithstanding all this, I should find the cynical note on which André-Louis announced the issue to the Assembly utterly detestable did I believe it sincere. It would justify Aline of the expressed opinion, which she held in common with so many others who had come into close contact with him, that André-Louis was quite heartless.

You have seen something of the same heartlessness in his conduct when he discovered the faithlessness of La Binet, although that is belied by the measures he took to avenge himself. His subsequent contempt of the woman I account to be born of the affection in which for a time he held her. That this affection was as deep as he first imagined, I do not believe; but that it was as shallow as he would almost be at pains to make it appear by the completeness with which he affects to have put her from his mind when he discovered her worthlessness, I do not believe; nor, as I have said, do his actions encourage that belief. Then, again, his callous cynicism in hoping that he had killed Binet is also an affectation. Knowing that such things as Binet are better out of the world, he can have suffered no compunction; he had, you must remember, that rarely-level vision which sees things in their just proportions, and never either magnifies or reduces them by sentimental considerations. At the same time, that he should contemplate the taking of life with such complete and cynical equanimity, whatever the justification, is quite incredible.

Similarly now, it is not to be believed that in coming straight from the Bois de Boulogne, straight from the killing of a man, he should be sincerely expressing his nature in alluding to the fact in terms of such outrageous flippancy. Not quite to such an extent was he the incarnation of Scaramouche. But sufficiently was he so ever to mask his true feelings by an arresting gesture, his true thoughts by an effective phrase. He was the actor always, a man ever calculating the effect he would produce, ever avoiding self-revelation, ever concerned to overlay his real character by an assumed and quite fictitious one. There was in this something of impishness, and something of other things.

Nobody laughed now at his flippancy. He did not intend that anybody should. He intended to be terrible; and he knew that the more flippant and casual his tone, the more terrible would be its effect. He produced exactly the effect he desired.

What followed in a place where feelings and practices had become what they had become is not difficult to surmise. When the session rose, there were a dozen *spadassins* awaiting him in the vestibule, and this time the men of his own party were less concerned to guard him. He seemed so entirely capable of guarding himself; he appeared, for all his circumspection, to have so completely carried the war into the enemy's camp, so completely to have adopted their own methods, that his fellows scarcely felt the need to protect him as yesterday.

As he emerged, he scanned that hostile file, whose air and garments marked them so clearly for what they were. He paused, seeking the man he expected, the man he was most anxious to oblige. But M. de La Tour d'Azyr was absent from those eager ranks. This seemed to him odd. La Tour d'Azyr was Chabrillane's cousin and closest friend. Surely he should have been among the first today. The fact was that La Tour d'Azyr was too deeply overcome by amazement and grief at the utterly unexpected event. Also his vindictiveness was held curiously in leash. Perhaps he, too, remembered the part played by Chabrillane in the affair at Gavrillac, and saw in this obscure André-Louis Moreau, who had so persistently persecuted him ever since, an ordained avenger. The repugnance he felt to come to the point with him, particularly after this culminating provocation, was puzzling even to himself. But it existed, and it curbed him now.

To André-Louis, since La Tour was not one of that waiting pack, it mattered little on that Tuesday morning who should be the next. The next, as it happened, was the young Vicomte de La Motte-Royau, one of the deadliest blades in the group.

On the Wednesday morning, coming again an hour or so late to the Assembly, Andre-Louis announced—in much the same terms as he had announced the death of Chabrillane—that M. de La Motte-Royau would probably not disturb the harmony of the Assembly for some weeks to come, assuming that he were so fortunate as to recover ultimately from the effects of an unpleasant accident with which he had quite unexpectedly had the misfortune to meet that morning.

On Thursday he made an identical announcement with regard to the Vidame de Blavon. On Friday he told them that he had been delayed by M. de Troiscantins, and then turning to the members of the Côté Droit, and lengthening his face to a sympathetic gravity:

"I am glad to inform you, messieurs, that M. des Troiscantins is in the hands of a very competent surgeon who hopes with care to restore him to your councils in a few weeks' time."

It was paralyzing, fantastic, unreal; and friend and foe in that assembly sat alike stupefied under those bland daily announcements. Four of the most redoubtable *spadassinicides* put away for a time, one of them dead—and all this performed with such an air of indifference and announced in such casual terms by a wretched little provincial lawyer!

He began to assume in their eyes a romantic aspect. Even that group of philosophers of the Côté Gauche, who refused to worship any force but the force of reason, began to look upon him with a respect and consideration which no oratorical triumphs could ever have procured him.

And from the Assembly the fame of him oozed out gradually over Paris. Desmoulins wrote a panegyric upon him in his paper *Les Revolutions,* wherein he dubbed him the "Paladin of the Third Estate," a name that caught the fancy of the people, and clung to him for some time. Disdainfully was he mentioned in the *Actes des Apôtres,* the mocking organ of the Privileged party, so lightheartedly and provocatively edited by a group of gentlemen afflicted by a singular mental myopy.

The Friday of that very busy week in the life of this young man who even thereafter is to persist in reminding us that he is not in any sense a man of action, found the vestibule of the Manège empty of swordsmen when he made his leisurely and expectant egress between Le Chapelier and Kersain.

So surprised was he that he checked in his stride.

"Have they had enough?" he wondered, addressing the question to Le Chapelier.

"They have had enough of you, I should think," was the answer. "They will prefer to turn their attention to someone less able to take care of himself."

Now this was disappointing. André-Louis had lent himself to this business with a very definite object in view. The slaying of Chabrillane had, as far as it went, been satisfactory. He had regarded that as a sort of acceptable hors d'oeuvre. But the three who had followed were no affair of his at all. He had met them with a certain amount of repugnance, and dealt with each as lightly as consideration of his own safety permitted. Was the baiting of him now to cease whilst the man at whom he aimed had not presented himself? In that case it would be necessary to force the pace!

Out there under the awning a group of gentlemen stood in earnest talk. Scanning the group in a rapid glance, André-Louis perceived M. de La Tour d'Azyr amongst them. He tightened his lips. He must afford no provocation. It must be for them to fasten their quarrels upon him. Already the *Actes des Apôtres* that morning had torn the mask from his face, and proclaimed him the fencing-master of the Rue du Hasard, successor to Bertrand des Amis. Hazardous as it had been hitherto for a man of his condition to engage in single combat it was rendered doubly so by this exposure, offered to the public as an aristocratic apologia.

Still, matters could not be left where they were, or he should have had all his pains for nothing. Carefully looking away from that group of gentlemen, he raised his voice so that his words must carry to their ears.

"It begins to look as if my fears of having to spend the remainder of my days in the Bois were idle."

Out of the corner of his eye he caught the stir his words created in that group. Its members had turned to look at him; but for the moment that was all. A little more was necessary. Pacing slowly along between his friends he resumed:

"But is it not remarkable that the assassin of Lagron should make no move against Lagron's successor? Or perhaps it is not remarkable. Perhaps there are good reasons. Perhaps the gentleman is prudent."

He had passed the group by now, and he left that last sentence of his to trail behind him, and after it sent laughter, insolent and provoking.

He had not long to wait. Came a quick step behind him, and a hand falling upon his shoulder, spun him violently round. He was brought face to face with M. de La Tour d'Azyr, whose handsome countenance was calm and composed, but whose eyes reflected something of the sudden blaze of passion stirring in him. Behind him several members of the group were approaching more slowly. The others—like André-Louis' two companions—remained at gaze.

"You spoke of me, I think," said the Marquis quietly.

"I spoke of an assassin—yes. But to these my friends." André-Louis' manner was no less quiet, indeed the quieter of the two, for he was the more experienced actor.

"You spoke loudly enough to be overheard," said the Marquis, answering the insinuation that he had been eavesdropping.

"Those who wish to overhear frequently contrive to do so."

"I perceive that it is your aim to be offensive."

"Oh, but you are mistaken, M. le Marquis. I have no wish to be offensive. But I resent having hands violently laid upon me, especially when they are hands that I cannot consider clean. In the circumstances I can hardly be expected to be polite."

The elder man's eyelids flickered. Almost he caught himself admiring André-Louis' bearing. Rather, he feared that his own must suffer by comparison. Because of this, he enraged altogether, and lost control of himself.

"You spoke of me as the assassin of Lagron. I do not affect to

374

misunderstand you. You expounded your views to me once before, and I remember."

"But what flattery, monsieur."

"You called me an assassin then, because I used my skill to dispose of a turbulent hot-head who made the world unsafe for me. But how much better are you, M. the fencing-master, when you oppose yourself to men whose skill is as naturally inferior to your own!"

M. de La Tour d'Azyr's friends looked grave, perturbed. It was really incredible to find this great gentleman so far forgetting himself as to descend to argument with a *canaille* of a lawyer-swordsman. And what was worse, it was an argument in which he was being made ridiculous.

"I oppose myself to them!" said André-Louis on a tone of amused protest. "Ah, pardon, M. le Marquis; it is they who chose to oppose themselves to me—and so stupidly. They push me, they slap my face, they tread on my toes, they call me by unpleasant names. What if I am a fencing-master? Must I on that account submit to every manner of ill-treatment from your bad-mannered friends? Perhaps had they found out sooner that I am a fencing-master their manners would have been better. But to blame me for that! What injustice!"

"Comedian!" the Marquis contemptuously apostrophized him. "Does it alter the case? Are these men who have opposed you men who live by the sword like yourself?"

"On the contrary, M. le Marquis, I have found them men who died by the sword with astonishing ease. I cannot suppose that you desire to add yourself to their number."

"And why, if you please?" La Tour d'Azyr's face had flamed

scarlet before that sneer.

"Oh," André-Louis raised his eyebrows and pursed his lips, a man considering. He delivered himself slowly. "Because, monsieur, you prefer the easy victim—the Lagrons and Vilmorins of this world, mere sheep for your butchering. That is why."

And then the Marquis struck him.

André-Louis stepped back. His eyes gleamed a moment; the next they were smiling up into the face of his tall enemy.

"No better than the others, after all! Well, well! Remark, I beg you, how history repeats itself—with certain differences. Because poor Vilmorin could not bear a vile lie with which you goaded him, he struck you. Because you cannot bear an equally vile truth which I have uttered, you strike me. But always is the vileness yours. And now as then for the striker there is . . ." He broke off. "But why name it? You will remember what there is. Yourself you wrote it that day with the point of your too-ready sword. But there. I will meet you if you desire it, monsieur."

"What else do you suppose that I desire? To talk?"

André-Louis turned to his friends and sighed. "So that I am to go another jaunt to the Bois. Isaac, perhaps you will kindly have a word with one of these friends of M. le Marquis', and arrange for nine o'clock tomorrow, as usual."

"Not tomorrow," said the Marquis shortly to Le Chapelier. "I have an engagement in the country, which I cannot postpone."

Le Chapelier looked at André-Louis.

"Then for M. le Marquis' convenience, we will say Sunday at the same hour."

"I do not fight on Sunday. I am not a pagan to break the holy day."

"But surely the good God would not have the presumption to damn a gentleman of M. le Marquis' quality on that account? Ah, well, Isaac, please arrange for Monday, if it is not a feast-day or monsieur has not some other pressing engagement. I leave it in your hands."

He bowed with the air of a man wearied by these details, and threading his arm through Kersain's withdrew.

"Ah, *Dieu de Dieu!* But what a trick of it you have," said the Breton deputy, entirely unsophisticated in these matters.

"To be sure I have. I have taken lessons at their hands." He laughed. He was in excellent good-humour. And Kersain was enrolled in the ranks of those who accounted André-Louis a man without heart or conscience.

But in his *Confessions* he tells us—and this is one of the glimpses that reveal the true man under all that make-believe—that on that night he went down on his knees to commune with his dead friend Philippe, and to call his spirit to witness that he was about to take the last step in the fulfilment of the oath sworn upon his body at Gavrillac two years ago.

CHAPTER IX

Torn Pride

M de la Tour d'Azyr's engagement in the country on that Sunday was with M. de Kercadiou. To fulfil it he drove out early in the day to Meudon, taking with him in his pocket a copy of the last issue of *Les Actes des Apôtres*, a journal whose merry sallies at the expense of the innovators greatly diverted the Seigneur de Gavrillac. The venomous scorn it poured upon those worthless rapscallions afforded him a certain solatium against the discomforts of expatriation by which he was afflicted as a result of their detestable energies.

Twice in the last month had M. de La Tour d'Azyr gone to visit the Lord of Gavrillac at Meudon, and the sight of Aline, so sweet and fresh, so bright and of so lively a mind, had caused those embers smouldering under the ashes of the past, embers which until now he had believed utterly extinct, to kindle into flame once more. He desired her as we desire Heaven. I believe that it was the purest passion of his life; that had it come to him earlier he might have been a vastly different man. The cruellest wound that in all his selfish life he had taken was when she sent him word, quite definitely after the affair at the Feydau, that she could not again in any circumstances receive him. At one blow— through that disgraceful riot—he had been robbed of a mistress he prized and of a wife who had become a necessity to the very soul of him. The sordid love of La Binet might have consoled him for the compulsory renunciation of his exalted love of Aline, just as to his exalted love of Aline he had been ready to sacrifice his attachment to La Binet. But that ill-timed riot had robbed him at once of both. Faithful to his word to Sautron he had definitely broken with La Binet, only to find that Aline had definitely broken with him. And by the time that he had sufficiently recovered from his grief to think again of La Binet, the comédienne had vanished beyond discovery.

For all this he blamed, and most bitterly blamed, André-Louis. That low-born provincial lout pursued him like a Nemesis, was become indeed the evil genius of his life. That was it—the evil genius of his life! And it was odds that on Monday . . . He did not like to think of Monday. He was not particularly afraid of death. He was as brave as his kind in that respect, too brave in the ordinary way, and too confident of his skill, to have considered even remotely such a possibility as that of dying in a duel. It was only that it would seem like a proper consummation of all the evil that he had suffered directly or indirectly through this André-Louis Moreau that he should perish ignobly by his hand. Almost he could hear that insolent, pleasant voice making the flippant announcement to the Assembly on Monday morning.

He shook off the mood, angry with himself for entertaining it. It was maudlin. After all Chabrillane and La Motte-Royau were quite exceptional swordsmen, but neither of them really approached his own formidable calibre. Reaction began to flow, as he drove out through country lanes flooded with pleasant September sunshine. His spirits rose. A premonition of victory stirred within him. Far from fearing Monday's meeting, as he had so unreasonably been doing, he began to look forward to it. It should afford him the means of setting a definite term to this persecution of which he had been the victim. He would crush this insolent and persistent flea that had been stinging him at every opportunity. Borne upward on that wave of optimism, he took presently a more hopeful view of his case with Aline.

At their first meeting a month ago he had used the utmost frankness with her. He had told her the whole truth of his motives in going that night to the Feydau; he had made her realize that she had acted unjustly towards him. True he had gone no farther.

But that was very far to have gone as a beginning. And in their last meeting, now a fortnight old, she had received him with frank friendliness. True, she had been a little aloof. But that was to be expected until he quite explicitly avowed that he had revived the hope of winning her. He had been a fool not to have returned before today.

Thus in that mood of new-born confidence—a confidence risen from the very ashes of despondency—came he on that Sunday morning to Meudon. He was gay and jovial with M. de Kercadiou what time he waited in the salon for mademoiselle to show herself. He pronounced with confidence on the country's future. There were signs already—he wore the rosiest spectacles that morning—of a change of opinion, of a more moderate note. The Nation began to perceive whither this lawyer rabble was leading it. He pulled out *The Acts of the Apostles* and read a stinging paragraph. Then, when mademoiselle at last made her appearance, he resigned the journal into the hands of M. de Kercadiou.

M. de Kercadiou, with his niece's future to consider, went to read the paper in the garden, taking up there a position whence he could keep the couple within sight—as his obligations seemed to demand of him—whilst being discreetly out of earshot.

The Marquis made the most of an opportunity that might be brief. He quite frankly declared himself, and begged, implored to be taken back into Aline's good graces, to be admitted at least to the hope that one day before very long she would bring herself to consider him in a nearer relationship.

"Mademoiselle," he told her, his voice vibrating with a feeling that admitted of no doubt, "you cannot lack conviction of my utter sincerity. The very constancy of my devotion should afford you this. It is just that I should have been banished from you, since I showed myself so utterly unworthy of the great honour to which I aspired. But this banishment has nowise diminished my devotion. If you could conceive what I have suffered, you would agree that I have fully expiated my abject fault."

She looked at him with a curious, gentle wistfulness on her lovely face.

"Monsieur, it is not you whom I doubt. It is myself."

"You mean your feelings towards me?"

"Yes."

"But that I can understand. After what has happened . . ."

"It was always so, monsieur," she interrupted quietly. "You speak of me as if lost to you by your own action. That is to say too much. Let me be frank with you. Monsieur, I was never yours to lose. I am conscious of the honour that you do me. I esteem you very deeply . . ."

"But, then," he cried, on a high note of confidence, "from such a beginning . . ."

"Who shall assure me that it is a beginning? May it not be the whole? Had I held you in affection, monsieur, I should have sent for you after the affair of which you have spoken. I should at least not have condemned you without hearing your explanation. As it was . . ." She shrugged, smiling gently, sadly. "You see."

But his optimism far from being crushed was stimulated. "But it is to give me hope, mademoiselle. If already I possess so much, I may look with confidence to win more. I shall prove myself worthy. I swear to do that. Who that is permitted the privilege of being near you could do other than seek to render himself worthy?"

And then before she could add a word, M. de Kercadiou came blustering through the window, his spectacles on his forehead, his face inflamed, waving in his hand *The Acts of the Apostles*, and apparently reduced to speechlessness.

Had the Marquis expressed himself aloud he would have been profane. As it was he bit his lip in vexation at this most inopportune interruption.

Aline sprang up, alarmed by her uncle's agitation.

"What has happened?"

"Happened?" He found speech at last. "The scoundrel! The

faithless dog! I consented to overlook the past on the clear condition that he should avoid revolutionary politics in future. That condition he accepted, and now"—he smacked the news-sheet furiously—"he has played me false again. Not only has he gone into politics, once more, but he is actually a member of the Assembly, and what is worse he has been using his assassin's skill as a fencing-master, turning himself into a bully-swordsman. My God! Is there any law at all left in France?"

One doubt M. de La Tour d'Azyr had entertained, though only faintly, to mar the perfect serenity of his growing optimism. That doubt concerned this man Moreau and his relations with M. de Kercadiou. He knew what once they had been, and how changed they subsequently were by the ingratitude of Moreau's own behavior in turning against the class to which his benefactor belonged. What he did not know was that a reconciliation had been effected. For in the past month—ever since circumstances had driven André-Louis to depart from his undertaking to steer clear of politics—the young man had not ventured to approach Meudon, and as it happened his name had not been mentioned in La Tour d'Azyr's hearing on the occasion of either of his own previous visits. He learnt of that reconciliation now; but he learnt at the same time that the breach was now renewed, and rendered wider and more impassable than ever. Therefore he did not hesitate to avow his own position.

"There is a law," he answered. "The law that this rash young man himself evokes. The law of the sword." He spoke very gravely, almost sadly. For he realized that after all the ground was tender. "You are not to suppose that he is to continue indefinitely his career of evil and of murder. Sooner or later he will meet a sword that will avenge the others. You have observed that my cousin Chabrillane is among the number of this assassin's victims; that he was killed on Tuesday last."

"If I have not expressed my condolence, Azyr, it is because my indignation stifles at the moment every other feeling. The scoundrel! You say that sooner or later he will meet a sword that will avenge the others. I pray that it may be soon."

The Marquis answered him quietly, without anything but sorrow in his voice. "I think your prayer is likely to be heard. This wretched young man has an engagement for tomorrow, when his account may be definitely settled."

He spoke with such calm conviction that his words had all the sound of a sentence of death. They suddenly stemmed the flow of M. de Kercadiou's anger. The colour receded from his inflamed face; dread looked out of his pale eyes, to inform M. de La Tour d'Azyr, more clearly than any words, that M. de Kercadiou's hot speech had been the expression of unreflecting anger, that his prayer that retribution might soon overtake his godson had been unconsciously insincere. Confronted now by the fact that this retribution was about to be visited upon that scoundrel, the fundamental gentleness and kindliness of his nature asserted itself; his anger was suddenly whelmed in apprehension; his affection for the lad beat up to the surface, making André-Louis' sin, however hideous, a thing of no account by comparison with the threatened punishment.

M. de Kercadiou moistened his lips.

"With whom is this engagement?" he asked in a voice that by an effort he contrived to render steady.

M. de La Tour d'Azyr bowed his handsome head, his eyes

upon the gleaming parquetry of the floor. "With myself," he answered quietly, conscious already with a tightening of the heart that his answer must sow dismay. He caught the sound of a faint outcry from Aline; he saw the sudden recoil of M. de Kercadiou. And then he plunged headlong into the explanation that he deemed necessary.

"In view of his relations with you, M. de Kercadiou, and because of my deep regard for you, I did my best to avoid this, even though as you will understand the death of my dear friend and cousin Chabrillane seemed to summon me to action, even though I knew that my circumspection was becoming matter for criticism among my friends. But yesterday this unbridled young man made further restraint impossible to me. He provoked me deliberately and publicly. He put upon me the very grossest affront, and . . . tomorrow morning in the Bois . . . we meet."

He faltered a little at the end, fully conscious of the hostile atmosphere in which he suddenly found himself. Hostility from M. de Kercadiou, the latter's earlier change of manner had already led him to expect; the hostility of mademoiselle came more in the nature of a surprise.

He began to understand what difficulties the course to which he was committed must raise up for him. A fresh obstacle was to be flung across the path which he had just cleared, as he imagined. Yet his pride and his sense of the justice due to be done admitted of no weakening.

In bitterness he realized now, as he looked from uncle to niece—his glance, usually so direct and bold, now oddly furtive—that though tomorrow he might kill André-Louis, yet even by his death André-Louis would take vengeance upon him. He had exaggerated nothing in reaching the conclusion that this André-Louis Moreau was the evil genius of his life. He saw now that do what he would, kill him even though he might, he could never conquer him. The last word would always be with André-Louis Moreau. In bitterness, in rage, and in humiliation—a thing almost unknown to him—did he realize it, and the realization steeled his purpose for all that he perceived its futility.

Outwardly he showed himself calm and self-contained, properly suggesting a man regretfully accepting the inevitable. It would have been as impossible to find fault with his bearing as to attempt to turn him from the matter to which he was committed. And so M. de Kercadiou perceived.

"My God!" was all that he said, scarcely above his breath, yet almost in a groan.

M. de La Tour d'Azyr did, as always, the thing that sensibility demanded of him. He took his leave. He understood that to linger where his news had produced such an effect would be impossible, indecent. So he departed, in a bitterness comparable only with his erstwhile optimism, the sweet fruit of hope turned to a thing of gall even as it touched his lips. Oh, yes; the last word, indeed, was with André-Louis Moreau—always!

Uncle and niece looked at each other as he passed out, and there was horror in the eyes of both. Aline's pallor was deathly almost, and standing there now she wrung her hands as if in pain.

"Why did you not ask him—beg him . . ." She broke off.

"To what end? He was in the right, and . . . and . . . there are things one cannot ask; things it would be a useless humiliation to ask." He sat down, groaning. "Oh, the poor boy—the poor, misguided boy."

In the mind of neither, you see, was there any doubt of what must be the issue. The calm confidence in which La Tour d'Azyr had spoken compelled itself to be shared. He was no vainglorious boaster, and they knew of what a force as a swordsman he was generally accounted.

"What does humiliation matter? A life is at issue—André's life."

"I know. My God, don't I know? And I would humiliate myself if by humiliating myself I could hope to prevail. But Azyr is a hard, relentless man, and . . ."

Abruptly she left him.

She overtook the Marquis as he was in the act of stepping into his carriage. He turned as she called, and bowed.

"Mademoiselle?"

At once he guessed her errand, tasted in anticipation the unparalleled bitterness of being compelled to refuse her. Yet at her invitation he stepped back into the cool of the hall.

In the middle of the floor of chequered marbles, black and white, stood a carved table of black oak. By this he halted, leaning lightly against it whilst she sat enthroned in the great crimson chair beside it.

"Monsieur, I cannot allow you so to depart," she said. "You cannot realize, monsieur, what a blow would be dealt my uncle if . . . if evil, irrevocable evil were to overtake his godson tomorrow. The expressions that he used at first . . ."

"Mademoiselle, I perceived their true value. Spare yourself. Believe me I am profoundly desolated by circumstances which I had not expected to find. You must believe me when I say that. It is all that I can say."

"Must it really be all? André is very dear to his godfather."

The pleading tone cut him like a knife; and then suddenly it aroused another emotion—an emotion which he realized to be utterly unworthy, an emotion which, in his overwhelming pride of race, seemed almost sullying, yet not to be repressed. He hesitated to give it utterance; hesitated even remotely to suggest so horrible a thing as that in a man of such lowly origin he might conceivably discover a rival. Yet that sudden pang of jealousy was stronger than his monstrous pride.

"And to you, mademoiselle? What is this André-Louis Moreau to you? You will pardon the question. But I desire clearly to understand."

Watching her he beheld the scarlet stain that overspread her face. He read in it at first confusion, until the gleam of her blue eyes announced its source to lie in anger. That comforted him; since he had affronted her, he was reassured. It did not occur to him that the anger might have another source.

"André and I have been playmates from infancy. He is very dear to me, too; almost I regard him as a brother. Were I in need of help, and were my uncle not available, André would be the first man to whom I should turn. Are you sufficiently answered, monsieur? Or is there more of me you would desire revealed?"

He bit his lip. He was unnerved, he thought, this morning; otherwise the silly suspicion with which he had offended could never have occurred to him.

He bowed very low. "Mademoiselle, forgive that I should have troubled you with such a question. You have answered more fully than I could have hoped or wished."

He said no more than that. He waited for her to resume. At a loss, she sat in silence awhile, a pucker on her white brow, her fingers nervously drumming on the table. At last she flung herself headlong against the impassive, polished front that he presented.

"I have come, monsieur, to beg you to put off this meeting."

She saw the faint raising of his dark eyebrows, the faintly regretful smile that scarcely did more than tinge his fine lips, and she hurried on. "What honour can await you in such an engagement, monsieur?"

It was a shrewd thrust at the pride of race that she accounted his paramount sentiment, that had as often lured him into error as it had urged him into good.

"I do not seek honour in it, mademoiselle, but—I must say it—justice. The engagement, as I have explained, is not of my seeking. It has been thrust upon me, and in honour I cannot draw back."

"Why, what dishonour would there be in sparing him? Surely, monsieur, none would call your courage in question? None could misapprehend your motives."

"You are mistaken, mademoiselle. My motives would most certainly be misapprehended. You forget that this young man has acquired in the past week a certain reputation that might well make a man hesitate to meet him."

She brushed that aside almost contemptuously, conceiving it the merest quibble.

"Some men, yes. But not you, M. le Marquis."

Her confidence in him on every count was most sweetly flattering. But there was a bitterness behind the sweet.

"Even I, mademoiselle, let me assure you. And there is more than that. This quarrel which M. Moreau has forced upon me is no new thing. It is merely the culmination of a long-drawn persecution . . ."

"Which you invited," she cut in. "Be just, monsieur."

"I hope that it is not in my nature to be otherwise, mademoiselle."

"Consider, then, that you killed his friend."

"I find in that nothing with which to reproach myself. My justification lay in the circumstances—the subsequent events in this distracted country surely confirm it."

"And . . ." She faltered a little, and looked away from him for the first time. "And that you . . . that you . . . And what of Mademoiselle Binet, whom he was to have married?"

He stared at her for a moment in sheer surprise. "Was to have married?" he repeated incredulously, dismayed almost.

"You did not know that?"

"But how do you?"

"Did I not tell you that we are as brother and sister almost? I have his confidence. He told me, before . . . before you made it impossible."

He looked away, chin in hand, his glance thoughtful, disturbed, almost wistful.

"There is," he said slowly, musingly, "a singular fatality at work between that man and me, bringing us ever each by turns athwart the other's path . . ."

He sighed; then swung to face her again, speaking more briskly: "Mademoiselle, until this moment I had no knowledge— no suspicion of this thing. But . . ." He broke off, considered, and then shrugged. "If I wronged him, I did so unconsciously. It would be unjust to blame me, surely. In all our actions it must be the intention alone that counts."

"But does it make no difference?"

"None that I can discern, mademoiselle. It gives me no justification to withdraw from that to which I am irrevocably committed. No justification, indeed, could ever be greater than my concern for the pain it must occasion my good friend, your uncle, and perhaps yourself, mademoiselle."

She rose suddenly, squarely confronting him, desperate now, driven to play the only card upon which she thought she might count.

"Monsieur," she said, "you did me the honour today to speak in certain terms; to . . . to allude to certain hopes with which you honour me."

He looked at her almost in fear. In silence, not daring to speak, he waited for her to continue.

"I . . . I . . . Will you please to understand, monsieur, that if you persist in this matter, if . . . unless you can break this engagement of yours tomorrow morning in the Bois, you are not to presume to mention this subject to me again, or, indeed, ever again to approach me."

To put the matter in this negative way was as far as she could possibly go. It was for him to make the positive proposal to which she had thus thrown wide the door.

"Mademoiselle, you cannot mean . . ."

"I do, monsieur . . . irrevocably, please to understand."

He looked at her with eyes of misery, his handsome, manly face as pale as she had ever seen it. The hand he had been holding out in protest began to shake. He lowered it to his side again, lest she should perceive its tremor. Thus a brief second, while the battle was fought within him, the bitter engagement between his desires and what he conceived to be the demands of his honour, never perceiving how far his honour was buttressed by implacable vindictiveness. Retreat, he conceived, was impossible without shame; and shame was to him an agony unthinkable. She asked too much. She could not understand what she was asking, else she would never be so unreasonable, so unjust. But also he saw that it would be futile to attempt to make her understand.

It was the end. Though he kill André-Louis Moreau in the morning as he fiercely hoped he would, yet the victory even in death must lie with André-Louis Moreau.

He bowed profoundly, grave and sorrowful of face as he was grave and sorrowful of heart.

"Mademoiselle, my homage," he murmured, and turned to go.

Startled, appalled, she stepped back, her hand pressed to her tortured breast.

"But you have not answered me!" she called after him in terror.

He checked on the threshold, and turned; and there from the cool gloom of the hall she saw him a black, graceful silhouette against the brilliant sunshine beyond—a memory of him that was to cling as something sinister and menacing in the dread hours that were to follow

"What would you, mademoiselle? I but spared myself and you the pain of a refusal."

He was gone leaving her crushed and raging. She sank down

again into the great red chair, and sat there crumpled, her elbows on the table, her face in her hands—a face that was on fire with shame and passion. She had offered herself, and she had been refused! The inconceivable had befallen her. The humiliation of it seemed to her something that could never be effaced.

CHAPTER X

The Returning Carriage

M de Kercadiou wrote a letter.

"Godson," he began, without any softening adjective, "I have learnt with pain and indignation that you have dishonoured yourself again by breaking the pledge you gave me to abstain from politics. With still greater pain and indignation do I learn that your name has become in a few short days a byword, that you have discarded the weapon of false, insidious arguments against my class—the class to which you owe everything—for the sword of the assassin. It has come to my knowledge that you have an assignation tomorrow with my good friend M. de La Tour d'Azyr. A gentleman of his station is under certain obligations imposed upon him by his birth, which do not permit him to draw back from an engagement. But you labour under no such disadvantages. For a man of your class to refuse an engagement of honour, or to neglect it when made, entails no sacrifice.

Your peers will probably be of the opinion that you display a commendable prudence. Therefore I beg you, indeed, did I think that I still exercise over you any such authority as the favours you have received from me should entitle me to exercise, I would command you, to allow this matter to go no farther, and to refrain from rendering yourself to your assignation tomorrow morning. Having no such authority, as your past conduct now makes clear, having no reason to hope that a proper sentiment of gratitude to me will induce to give heed to this my most earnest request, I am compelled to add that should you survive tomorrow's encounter, I can in no circumstances ever again permit myself to be conscious of your existence. If any spark survives of the affection that once you expressed for me, or if you set any value upon the affection, which, in spite of all that you have done to forfeit it, is the chief prompter of this letter, you will not refuse to do as I am asking."

It was not a tactful letter. M. de Kercadiou was not a tactful man. Read it as he would, André-Louis—when it was delivered to him on that Sunday afternoon by the groom dispatched with it into Paris—could read into it only concern for M. La Tour d'Azyr, M. de Kercadiou's good friend, as he called him, and prospective nephew-in-law.

He kept the groom waiting a full hour while composing his answer. Brief though it was, it cost him very considerable effort and several unsuccessful attempts. In the end this is what he wrote:

Monsieur my godfather—You make refusal singularly hard for me when you appeal to me upon the ground of affection. It is a thing of which all my life I shall hail the opportunity to give you proofs, and I am therefore desolated beyond anything I could hope to express that I cannot give you the proof you ask today. There is too much between M. de La Tour d'Azyr and me. Also you do me and my class—whatever it may be—less than justice when you say that obligations of honour are not binding upon us. So binding do I count them, that, if I would, I could not now draw back.

If hereafter you should persist in the harsh intention you express, I must suffer it. That I shall suffer be assured.

Your affectionate and grateful godson
André-Louis

He dispatched that letter by M. de Kercadiou's groom, and conceived this to be the end of the matter. It cut him keenly; but he bore the wound with that outward stoicism he affected.

Next morning, at a quarter past eight, as with Le Chapelier—who had come to break his fast with him—he was rising from table to set out for the Bois, his housekeeper startled him by announcing Mademoiselle de Kercadiou.

He looked at his watch. Although his cabriolet was already at the door, he had a few minutes to spare. He excused himself from Le Chapelier, and went briskly out to the anteroom.

She advanced to meet him, her manner eager, almost feverish.

"I will not affect ignorance of why you have come," he said quickly, to make short work. "But time presses, and I warn you that only the most solid of reasons can be worth stating."

It surprised her. It amounted to a rebuff at the very outset, before she had uttered a word; and that was the last thing she had expected from André-Louis. Moreover, there was about him an air of aloofness that was unusual where she was concerned, and his voice had been singularly cold and formal.

It wounded her. She was not to guess the conclusion to which he had leapt. He made with regard to her—as was but natural, after all—the same mistake that he had made with regard to yesterday's letter from his godfather. He conceived that the mainspring of action here was solely concern for M. de La Tour d'Azyr. That it might be concern for himself never entered his mind. So absolute was his own conviction of what must be the inevitable issue of that meeting that he could not conceive of any one entertaining a fear on his behalf.

What he assumed to be anxiety on the score of the predestined victim had irritated him in M. de Kercadiou; in Aline it filled him with a cold anger; he argued from it that she had hardly been frank with him; that ambition was urging her to consider with favour the suit of M. de La Tour d'Azyr. And than this there was no spur that could have driven more relentlessly in his purpose, since to save her was in his eyes almost as momentous as to avenge the past.

She conned him searchingly, and the complete calm of him at such a time amazed her. She could not repress the mention of it.

"How calm you are, André!"

"I am not easily disturbed. It is a vanity of mine."

"But . . . Oh, André, this meeting must not take place!" She came close up to him, to set her hands upon his shoulders, and stood so, her face within a foot of his own.

"You know, of course, of some good reason why it should not?" said he.

"You may be killed," she answered him, and her eyes dilated as she spoke.

It was so far from anything that he had expected that for a moment he could only stare at her. Then he thought he had understood. He laughed as he removed her hands from his shoulders, and stepped back. This was a shallow device, childish and unworthy in her.

"Can you really think to prevail by attempting to frighten me?" he asked, and almost sneered.

"Oh, you are surely mad! M. de La Tour d'Azyr is reputed the most dangerous sword in France."

"Have you never noticed that most reputations are undeserved? Chabrillane was a dangerous swordsman, and Chabrillane is underground. La Motte-Royau was an even more dangerous swordsman, and he is in a surgeon's hands. So are the other *spadassinicides* who dreamt of skewering a poor sheep of a provincial lawyer. And here today comes the chief, the fine flower of these bully-swordsmen. He comes, for wages long overdue. Be sure of that. So if you have no other reason to urge . . ."

It was the sarcasm of him that mystified her. Could he possibly be sincere in his assurance that he must prevail against M. de La Tour d'Azyr? To her in her limited knowledge, her mind filled with her uncle's contrary conviction, it seemed that André-Louis was only acting; he would act a part to the very end.

Be that as it might, she shifted her ground to answer him.

"You had my uncle's letter?"

"And I answered it."

"I know. But what he said, he will fulfil. Do not dream that he will relent if you carry out this horrible purpose."

"Come, now, that is a better reason than the other," said he. "If there is a reason in the world that could move me it would be

398

that. But there is too much between La Tour d'Azyr and me. There is an oath I swore on the dead hand of Philippe de Vilmorin. I could never have hoped that God would afford me so great an opportunity of keeping it."

"You have not kept it yet," she warned him.

He smiled at her. "True!" he said. "But nine o'clock will soon be here. Tell me," he asked her suddenly, "why did you not carry this request of yours to M. de La Tour d'Azyr?"

"I did," she answered him, and flushed as she remembered her yesterday's rejection. He interpreted the flush quite otherwise.

"And he?" he asked.

"M. de La Tour d'Azyr's obligations . . ." she was beginning: then she broke off to answer shortly: "Oh, he refused."

"So, so. He must, of course, whatever it may have cost him. Yet in his place I should have counted the cost as nothing. But men are different, you see." He sighed. "Also in your place, had that been so, I think I should have left the matter there. But then . . ."

"I don't understand you, André."

"I am not so very obscure. Not nearly so obscure as I can be. Turn it over in your mind. It may help to comfort you presently." He consulted his watch again. "Pray use this house as your own. I must be going."

Le Chapelier put his head in at the door.

"Forgive the intrusion. But we shall be late, André, unless you . . ."

"Coming," André answered him. "If you will await my return, Aline, you will oblige me deeply. Particularly in view of your uncle's resolve."

She did not answer him. She was numbed. He took her silence for assent, and, bowing, left her. Standing there she heard his steps going down the stairs together with Le Chapelier's. He was speaking to his friend, and his voice was calm and normal.

Oh, he was mad—blinded by self-confidence and vanity. As his carriage rattled away, she sat down limply, with a sense of exhaustion and nausea. She was sick and faint with horror. André-Louis was going to his death. Conviction of it—an unreasoning conviction, the result, perhaps, of all M. de Kercadiou's rantings—entered her soul. Awhile she sat thus, paralyzed by hopelessness. Then she sprang up again, wringing her hands. She must do something to avert this horror. But what could she do? To follow him to the Bois and intervene there would be to make a scandal for no purpose. The conventions of conduct were all against her, offering a barrier that was not to be overstepped. Was there no one could help her?

Standing there, half-frenzied by her helplessness, she caught again a sound of vehicles and hooves on the cobbles of the street below. A carriage was approaching. It drew up with a clatter before the fencing-academy. Could it be André-Louis returning? Passionately she snatched at that straw of hope. Knocking, loud and urgent, fell upon the door. She heard André-Louis' housekeeper, her wooden shoes clanking upon the stairs, hurrying down to open.

She sped to the door of the anteroom, and pulling it wide stood breathlessly to listen. But the voice that floated up to her was not the voice she so desperately hoped to hear. It was a woman's voice asking in urgent tones for M. André-Louis—a voice at first vaguely familiar, then clearly recognized, the voice of Mme. de Plougastel.

Excited, she ran to the head of the narrow staircase in time to hear Mme. de Plougastel exclaim in agitation:

"He has gone already! Oh, but how long since? Which way did he take?"

It was enough to inform Aline that Mme. de Plougastel's errand must be akin to her own. At the moment, in the general distress and confusion of her mind, her mental vision focussed entirely on the one vital point, she found in this no matter for astonishment. The singular regard conceived by Mme. de Plougastel for André-Louis seemed to her then a sufficient explanation.

Without pausing to consider, she ran down that steep staircase, calling:

"Madame! Madame!"

The portly, comely housekeeper drew aside, and the two ladies faced each other on that threshold. Mme. de Plougastel looked white and haggard, a nameless dread staring from her eyes.

"Aline! You here!" she exclaimed. And then in the urgency sweeping aside all minor considerations, "Were you also too late?" she asked.

"No, madame. I saw him. I implored him. But he would not listen."

"Oh, this is horrible!" Mme. de Plougastel shuddered as she spoke. "I heard of it only half an hour ago, and I came at once, to prevent it at all costs."

The two women looked blankly, despairingly, at each other. In the sunshine-flooded street one or two shabby idlers were pausing to eye the handsome equipage with its magnificent bay horses,

401

and the two great ladies on the doorstep of the fencing-academy. From across the way came the raucous voice of an itinerant bellows-mender raised in the cry of his trade:

"*À raccommoder les vieux soufflets!*"

Madame swung to the housekeeper.

"How long is it since monsieur left?"

"Ten minutes, maybe; hardly more." Conceiving these great ladies to be friends of her invincible master's latest victim, the good woman preserved a decently stolid exterior.

Madame wrung her hands. "Ten minutes! Oh!" It was almost a moan. "Which way did he go?"

"The assignation is for nine o'clock in the Bois de Boulogne," Aline informed her. "Could we follow? Could we prevail if we did?"

"Ah, my God! The question is should we come in time? At nine o'clock! And it wants but little more than a quarter of an hour. *Mon Dieu! Mon Dieu!*" Madame clasped and unclasped her hands in anguish. "Do you know, at least, where in the Bois they are to meet?"

"No—only that it is in the Bois."

"In the Bois!" Madame was flung into a frenzy. "The Bois is nearly half as large as Paris." But she swept breathlessly on. "Come, Aline: get in, get in!"

Then to her coachman: "To the Bois de Boulogne by way of the Cours la Reine," she commanded, "as fast as you can drive. There are ten pistoles for you if we are in time. Whip up, man!"

She thrust Aline into the carriage, and sprang after her with the energy of a girl. The heavy vehicle—too heavy by far for this race with time—was moving before she had taken her seat. Rocking and lurching it went, earning the maledictions of more than one pedestrian whom it narrowly avoided crushing against a wall or trampling underfoot.

Madame sat back with closed eyes and trembling lips. Her face showed very white and drawn. Aline watched her in silence. Almost it seemed to her that Mme. de Plougastel was suffering as deeply as herself, enduring an anguish of apprehension as great as her own.

Later Aline was to wonder at this. But at the moment all the thought of which her half-numbed mind was capable was bestowed upon their desperate errand.

The carriage rolled across the Place Louis XV and out on to the Cours la Reine at last. Along that beautiful, tree-bordered avenue between the Champs Élysées and the Seine, almost empty at this hour of the day, they made better speed, leaving now a cloud of dust behind them.

But fast to danger-point as was the speed, to the women in that carriage it was too slow. As they reached the barrier at the end of the Cours, nine o'clock was striking in the city behind them, and every stroke of it seemed to sound a note of doom.

Yet here at the barrier the regulations compelled a momentary halt. Aline enquired of the sergeant-in-charge how long it was since a cabriolet such as she described had gone that way. She was answered that some twenty minutes ago a vehicle had passed the barrier containing the deputy M. le Chapelier and the Paladin of the Third Estate, M. Moreau. The sergeant was very well informed. He could make a shrewd guess, he said, with a grin, of the business that took M. Moreau that way so early in the day.

They left him, to speed on now through the open country, following the road that continued to hug the river. They sat back mutely despairing, staring hopelessly ahead, Aline's hand clasped tight in madame's. In the distance, across the meadows on their right, they could see already the long, dusky line of trees of the Bois, and presently the carriage swung aside following a branch of the road that turned to the right, away from the river and heading straight for the forest.

Mademoiselle broke at last the silence of hopelessness that had reigned between them since they had passed the barrier.

"Oh, it is impossible that we should come in time! Impossible!"

"Don't say it! Don't say it!" madame cried out.

"But it is long past nine, madame! André would be punctual, and these . . . affairs do not take long. It . . . it will be all over by now."

Madame shivered, and closed her eyes. Presently, however, she opened them again, and stirred. Then she put her head from the window. "A carriage is approaching," she announced, and her tone conveyed the thing she feared.

"Not already! Oh, not already!" Thus Aline expressed the silently communicated thought. She experienced a difficulty in breathing, felt the sudden need of air. Something in her throat was throbbing as if it would suffocate her; a mist came and went before her eyes.

In a cloud of dust an open calèche was speeding towards them, coming from the Bois. They watched it, both pale, neither venturing to speak, Aline, indeed, without breath to do so.

As it approached, it slowed down, perforce, as they did, to effect a safe passage in that narrow road. Aline was at the window with Mme. de Plougastel, and with fearful eyes both looked into this open carriage that was drawing abreast of them.

"Which of them is it, madame? Oh, which of them?" gasped Aline, scarce daring to look, her senses swimming.

On the near side sat a swarthy young gentleman unknown to either of the ladies. He was smiling as he spoke to his companion. A moment later and the man sitting beyond came into view. He was not smiling. His face was white and set, and it was the face of the Marquis de La Tour d'Azyr.

For a long moment, in speechless horror, both women stared at him, until, perceiving them, blankest surprise invaded his stern face.

In that moment, with a long shuddering sigh Aline sank swooning to the carriage floor behind Mme. de Plougastel.

Chapter XI

Inferences

By fast driving André-Louis had reached the ground some minutes ahead of time, notwithstanding the slight delay in setting out. There he had found M. de La Tour d'Azyr already awaiting him, supported by a M. d'Ormesson, a swarthy young gentleman in the blue uniform of a captain in the Gardes du Corps.

André-Louis had been silent and preoccupied throughout that drive. He was perturbed by his last interview with Mademoiselle de Kercadiou and the rash inferences which he had drawn as to her motives.

"Decidedly," he had said, "this man must be killed."

Le Chapelier had not answered him. Almost, indeed, had the Breton shuddered at his compatriot's cold-bloodedness. He had often of late thought that this fellow Moreau was hardly human. Also he had found him incomprehensibly inconsistent. When first this *spadassinicide* business had been proposed to him, he had been so very lofty and disdainful. Yet, having embraced it, he went about it at times with a ghoulish flippancy that was revolting, at times with a detachment that was more revolting still.

Their preparations were made quickly and in silence, yet without undue haste or other sign of nervousness on either side. In both men the same grim determination prevailed. The opponent must be killed; there could be no half-measures here. Stripped each of coat and waistcoat, shoeless and with shirt-sleeves rolled to the elbow, they faced each other at last, with the common resolve of paying in full the long score that stood between them. I doubt if either of them entertained a misgiving as to what must be the issue.

Beside them, and opposite each other, stood Le Chapelier and the young captain, alert and watchful.

"*Allez, messieurs!*"

The slender, wickedly delicate blades clashed together, and after a momentary *glizade*, were whirling, swift and bright as lightnings, and almost as impossible to follow with the eye. The Marquis led the attack, impetuously and vigorously, and almost at once André-Louis realized that he had to deal with an opponent of a very different mettle from those successive duellists of last week, not excluding La Motte-Royau, of terrible reputation.

Here was a man whom much and constant practice had given extraordinary speed and a technique that was almost perfect. In addition, he enjoyed over André-Louis physical advantages of strength and length of reach, which rendered him altogether formidable. And he was cool, too; cool and self-contained; fearless and purposeful. Would anything shake that calm, wondered André-Louis?

He desired the punishment to be as full as he could make it. Not content to kill the Marquis as the Marquis had killed Philippe, he desired that he should first know himself as powerless to avert that death as Philippe had been. Nothing less would content André-Louis. M. le Marquis must begin by tasting of that cup of despair. It was in the account; part of the quittance due.

As with a breaking sweep André-Louis parried the heavy lunge in which that first series of passes culminated, he actually laughed—gleefully, after the fashion of a boy at a sport he loves.

That extraordinary, ill-timed laugh made M. de La Tour d'Azyr's recovery hastier and less correctly dignified than it would otherwise have been. It startled and discomposed him, who had already been discomposed by the failure to get home with a lunge so beautifully timed and so truly delivered.

He, too, had realized that his opponent's force was above anything that he could have expected, fencing-master though he might be, and on that account he had put forth his utmost energy to make an end at once.

More than the actual parry, the laugh by which it was accompanied seemed to make of that end no more than a beginning. And yet it was the end of something. It was the end of that absolute confidence that had hitherto inspired M. de La Tour d'Azyr. He no longer looked upon the issue as a thing forgone. He realized that if he was to prevail in this encounter, he must go warily and fence as he had never fenced yet in all his life.

They settled down again; and again—on the principle this time that the soundest defence is in attack—it was the Marquis who made the game. André-Louis allowed him to do so, desired him to do so; desired him to spend himself and that magnificent speed of his against the greater speed that whole days of fencing in succession for nearly two years had given the master. With a beautiful, easy pressure of forte on foible André-Louis kept himself completely covered in that second bout, which once more culminated in a lunge.

Expecting it now, André-Louis parried it by no more than a deflecting touch. At the same moment he stepped suddenly forward, right within the other's guard, thus placing his man so completely at his mercy that, as if fascinated, the Marquis did not even attempt to recover himself.

This time André-Louis did not laugh. He just smiled into the dilating eyes of M. de La Tour d'Azyr, and made no shift to use his advantage.

"Come, come, monsieur!" he bade him sharply. "Am I to run my blade through an uncovered man?" Deliberately he fell back, whilst his shaken opponent recovered himself at last.

M. d'Ormesson released the breath which horror had for a moment caught. Le Chapelier swore softly, muttering:

"Name of a name. It is tempting Providence to play the fool in this fashion!"

André-Louis observed the ashen pallor that now overspread the face of his opponent.

"I think you begin to realize, monsieur, what Philippe de Vilmorin must have felt that day at Gavrillac. I desired that you should first do so. Since that is accomplished, why, here's to make an end."

He went in with lightning rapidity. For a moment his point seemed to La Tour d'Azyr to be everywhere at once, and then from a low engagement in *sixte*, André-Louis stretched forward with swift and vigorous ease to lunge in *tierce*. He drove his point to transfix his opponent whom a series of calculated disengages uncovered in that line. But to his amazement and chagrin, La Tour d'Azyr parried the stroke; infinitely more to his chagrin La Tour d'Azyr parried it just too late. Had he completely parried it, all would yet have been well. But striking the blade in the last fraction of a second, the Marquis deflected the point from the line of his body, yet not so completely but that a couple of feet of that hard-driven steel tore through the muscles of his sword-arm.

To the seconds none of these details had been visible. All that they had seen had been a swift whirl of flashing blades, and then André-Louis stretched almost to the ground in an upward lunge that had pierced the Marquis' right arm just below the shoulder.

The sword fell from the suddenly relaxed grip of La Tour d'Azyr's fingers, which had been rendered powerless, and he stood now disarmed, his lip in his teeth, his face white, his chest heaving, before his opponent, who had at once recovered. With the blood-tinged tip of his sword resting on the ground, André-Louis surveyed him grimly, as we survey the prey that through our own clumsiness has escaped us at the last moment.

In the Assembly and in the newspapers this might be hailed as another victory for the Paladin of the Third Estate; only himself could know the extent and the bitterness of the failure.

M. d'Ormesson had sprung to the side of his principal.

"You are hurt!" he had cried stupidly.

"It is nothing," said La Tour d'Azyr. "A scratch." But his lip writhed, and the torn sleeve of his fine cambric shirt was full of blood.

D'Ormesson, a practical man in such matters, produced a linen kerchief, which he tore quickly into strips to improvise a bandage.

Still André-Louis continued to stand there, looking on as if bemused. He continued so until Le Chapelier touched him on the arm. Then at last he roused himself, sighed, and turned away to resume his garments, nor did he address or look again at his late opponent, but left the ground at once.

As, with Le Chapelier, he was walking slowly and in silent dejection towards the entrance of the Bois, where they had left their carriage, they were passed by the calèche conveying La Tour d'Azyr and his second—which had originally driven almost right up to the spot of the encounter. The Marquis' wounded arm was carried in a sling improvised from his companion's sword-belt. His sky-blue coat with three collars had been buttoned over this, so that the right sleeve hung empty. Otherwise, saving a certain pallor, he looked much his usual self.

And now you understand how it was that he was the first to return, and that seeing him thus returning, apparently safe and sound, the two ladies, intent upon preventing the encounter, should have assumed that their worst fears were realized.

Mme. de Plougastel attempted to call out, but her voice refused its office. She attempted to throw open the door of her own carriage; but her fingers fumbled clumsily and ineffectively with the handle. And meanwhile the calèche was slowly passing, La Tour d'Azyr's fine eyes sombrely yet intently meeting her own anguished gaze. And then she saw something else. M. d'Ormesson, leaning back again from the forward inclination of his body to

411

join his own to his companion's salutation of the Countess, disclosed the empty right sleeve of M. de La Tour d'Azyr's blue coat. More, the near side of the coat itself turned back from the point near the throat where it was caught together by a single button, revealed the slung arm beneath in its blood-sodden cambric sleeve.

Even now she feared to jump to the obvious conclusion—feared lest perhaps the Marquis, though himself wounded, might have dealt his adversary a deadlier wound.

She found her voice at last, and at the same moment signalled to the driver of the calèche to stop.

As it was pulled to a standstill, M. d'Ormesson alighted, and so met madame in the little space between the two carriages.

"Where is M. Moreau?" was the question with which she surprised him.

"Following at his leisure, no doubt, madame," he answered, recovering.

"He is not hurt?"

"Unfortunately it is we who . . ." M. d'Ormesson was beginning, when from behind him M. de La Tour d'Azyr's voice cut in crisply:

"This interest on your part in M. Moreau, dear Countess . . ."

He broke off, observing a vague challenge in the air with which she confronted him. But indeed his sentence did not need completing.

There was a vaguely awkward pause. And then she looked at M. d'Ormesson. Her manner changed. She offered what appeared to be an explanation of her concern for M. Moreau.

"Mademoiselle de Kercadiou is with me. The poor child has fainted."

There was more, a deal more, she would have said just then, but for M. d'Ormesson's presence.

Moved by a deep solicitude for Mademoiselle de Kercadiou, de La Tour d'Azyr sprang up despite his wound.

"I am in poor case to render assistance, madame," he said, an apologetic smile on his pale face. "But . . ."

With the aid of d'Ormesson, and in spite of the latter's pro-testations, he got down from the calèche, which then moved on a little way, so as to leave the road clear—for another carriage that was approaching from the direction of the Bois.

And thus it happened that when a few moments later that approaching cabriolet overtook and passed the halted vehicles, André-Louis beheld a very touching scene. Standing up to ob-tain a better view, he saw Aline in a half-swooning condition— she was beginning to revive by now—seated in the doorway of the carriage, supported by Mme. de Plougastel. In an attitude of deepest concern, M. de La Tour d'Azyr, his wound notwithstand-ing, was bending over the girl, whilst behind him stood M. d'Ormesson and madame's footman.

The Countess looked up and saw him as he was driven past. Her face lighted; almost it seemed to him she was about to greet him or to call him, wherefore, to avoid a difficulty, arising out of the presence there of his late antagonist, he anticipated her by bowing frigidly—for his mood was frigid, the more frigid by vir-tue of what he saw—and then resumed his seat with eyes that looked deliberately ahead.

Could anything more completely have confirmed him in his conviction that it was on M. de La Tour d'Azyr's account that Aline had come to plead with him that morning? For what his eyes had seen, of course, was a lady overcome with emotion at the sight of blood of her dear friend, and that same dear friend restoring her with assurances that his hurt was very far from mortal. Later, much later, he was to blame his own perverse stupidity. Almost is he too severe in his self-condemnation. For how else could he have interpreted the scene he beheld, his preconceptions being what they were?

That which he had already been suspecting, he now accounted proven to him. Aline had been wanting in candour on the subject of her feelings towards M. de La Tour d'Azyr. It was, he supposed, a woman's way to be secretive in such matters, and he must not blame her. Nor could he blame her in his heart for having succumbed to the singular charm of such a man as the Marquis—for not even his hostility could blind him to M. de La Tour d'Azyr's attractions. That she had succumbed was betrayed, he thought, by the weakness that had overtaken her upon seeing him wounded.

"My God!" he cried aloud. "What must she have suffered, then, if I had killed him as I intended!"

If only she had used candour with him, she could so easily have won his consent to the thing she asked. If only she had told him what now he saw, that she loved M. de La Tour d'Azyr, instead of leaving him to assume her only regard for the Marquis to be based on unworthy worldly ambition, he would at once have yielded.

He fetched a sigh, and breathed a prayer for forgiveness to the shade of Vilmorin.

"It is perhaps as well that my lunge went wide," he said.

"What do you mean?" wondered Le Chapelier.

"That in this business I must relinquish all hope of recommencing."

CHAPTER XII

The
Overwhelming Reason

M de la Tour d'Azyr was seen no more in the Manège—or indeed in Paris at all—throughout all the months that the National Assembly remained in session to complete its work of providing France with a constitution. After all, though the wound to his body had been comparatively slight, the wound to such a pride as his had been all but mortal.

The rumour ran that he had emigrated. But that was only half the truth. The whole of it was that he had joined that group of noble travellers who came and went between the Tuileries and the headquarters of the émigrés at Coblenz. He became, in short, a member of the royalist secret service that in the end was to bring down the monarchy in ruins.

As for André-Louis, his godfather's house saw him no more, as a result of his conviction that M. de Kercadiou would not relent from his written resolve never to receive him again if the duel were fought.

He threw himself into his duties at the Assembly with such zeal and effect that when—its purpose accomplished—the Constituent was dissolved in September of the following year, membership of the Legislative, whose election followed immediately, was thrust upon him.

He considered then, like many others, that the Revolution was a thing accomplished, that France had only to govern herself by the Constitution which had been given her, and that all would now be well. And so it might have been but that the Court could not bring itself to accept the altered state of things. As a result of its intrigues half Europe was arming to hurl herself upon France, and her quarrel was the quarrel of the French King with his people. That was the horror at the root of all the horrors that were to come.

Of the counter-revolutionary troubles that were everywhere being stirred up by the clergy, none were more acute than those of Brittany, and, in view of the influence it was hoped he would wield in his native province, it was proposed to André-Louis by the Commission of Twelve, in the early days of the Girondin ministry, that he should go thither to combat the unrest. He was desired to proceed peacefully, but his powers were almost absolute, as is shown by the orders he carried—orders enjoining all to render him assistance and warning those who might hinder him that they would do so at their peril.

He accepted the task, and he was one of the five plenipotentiaries despatched on the same errand in that spring of 1792. It kept him absent from Paris for four months and might have kept him longer but that at the beginning of August he was recalled.

More imminent than any trouble in Brittany was the trouble brewing in Paris itself; when the political sky was blacker than it had been since '89. Paris realized that the hour was rapidly approaching which would see the climax of the long struggle between Equality and Privilege. And it was towards a city so disposed that André-Louis came speeding from the West, to find there also the climax of his own disturbed career.

Mlle. de Kercadiou, too, was in Paris in those days of early August, on a visit to her uncle's cousin and dearest friend, Mme. de Plougastel. And although nothing could now be plainer than the seething unrest that heralded the explosion to come, yet the air of gaiety, indeed of jocularity, prevailing at Court—whither madame and mademoiselle went almost daily—reassured them. M. de Plougastel had come and gone again, back to Coblenz on that secret business that kept him now almost constantly absent from his wife. But whilst with her he had positively assured her that all measures were taken, and that an insurrection was a thing to be welcomed, because it could have only one conclusion, the final crushing of the Revolution in the courtyard of the Tuileries. That, he added, was why the King remained in Paris. But for his confidence in that he would put himself in the centre of his Swiss and his knights of the dagger, and quit the capital. They would hack a way out for him easily if his departure were opposed. But not even that would be necessary.

Yet in those early days of August, after her husband's departure the effect of his inspiring words was gradually dissipated by the march of events under madame's own eyes. And finally on the afternoon of the ninth, there arrived at the Hôtel Plougastel a messenger from Meudon bearing a note from M. de Kercadiou in which he urgently bade mademoiselle join him there at once, and advised her hostess to accompany her.

You may have realized that M. de Kercadiou was of those who make friends with men of all classes. His ancient lineage placed him on terms of equality with members of the *noblesse*; his simple manners—something between the rustic and the bourgeois—and his natural affability placed him on equally good terms with those who by birth were his inferiors. In Meudon he was known and esteemed of all the simple folk, and it was Rougane, the friendly mayor, who, informed on the 9th of August of the storm that was brewing for the morrow, and knowing of mademoiselle's absence in Paris, had warningly advised him to withdraw her from what in the next four-and-twenty hours might be a zone of danger for all persons of quality, particularly those suspected of connections with the Court party.

Now there was no doubt whatever of Mme. de Plougastel's connection with the Court. It was not even to be doubted—indeed, measure of proof of it was to be forthcoming—that those vigilant and ubiquitous secret societies that watched over the cradle of the young revolution were fully informed of the frequent journeyings of M. de Plougastel to Coblenz, and entertained no illusions on the score of the reason for them. Given, then, a defeat of the Court party in the struggle that was preparing, the position in Paris of Mme. de Plougastel could not be other than fraught with danger, and that danger would be shared by any guest of birth at her hôtel.

M. de Kercadiou's affection for both those women quickened the fears aroused in him by Rougane's warning. Hence that hastily dispatched note, desiring his niece and imploring his friend to come at once to Meudon.

The friendly mayor carried his complaisance a step farther, and dispatched the letter to Paris by the hands of his own son, an intelligent lad of nineteen. It was late in the afternoon of that perfect August day when young Rougane presented himself at the Hôtel Plougastel.

He was graciously received by Mme. de Plougastel in the salon, whose splendours, when combined with the great air of the lady herself, overwhelmed the lad's simple, unsophisticated soul. Madame made up her mind at once. M. de Kercadiou's urgent message no more than confirmed her own fears and inclinations. She decided upon instant departure.

"*Bien*, madame," said the youth. "Then I have the honour to take my leave."

But she would not let him go. First to the kitchen to refresh himself, whilst she and mademoiselle made ready, and then a seat for him in her carriage as far as Meudon. She could not suffer him to return on foot as he had come.

Though in all the circumstances it was no more than his due, yet the kindliness that in such a moment of agitation could take thought for another was presently to be rewarded. Had she done less than this, she would have known—if nothing worse—at least some hours of anguish even greater than those that were already in store for her.

It wanted, perhaps, a half-hour to sunset when they set out in her carriage with intent to leave Paris by the Porte Saint-Martin. They travelled with a single footman behind. Rougane—terrifying condescension—was given a seat inside the carriage with the ladies, and proceeded to fall in love with Mlle. de Kercadiou,

420

whom he accounted the most beautiful being he had ever seen, yet who talked to him simply and unaffectedly as with an equal. The thing went to his head a little, and disturbed certain republican notions which he had hitherto conceived himself to have thoroughly digested.

The carriage drew up at the barrier, checked there by a picket of the National Guard posted before the iron gates.

The sergeant in command strode to the door of the vehicle. The Countess put her head from the window.

"The barrier is closed, madame," she was curtly informed.

"Closed!" she echoed. The thing was incredible. "But . . . but do you mean that we cannot pass?"

"Not unless you have a permit, madame." The sergeant leaned nonchalantly on his pike. "The orders are that no one is to leave or enter without proper papers."

"Whose orders?"

"Orders of the Commune of Paris."

"But I must go into the country this evening." Madame's voice was almost petulant. "I am expected."

"In that case let madame procure a permit."

"Where is it to be procured?"

"At the Hôtel de Ville or at the headquarters of madame's section."

She considered a moment. "To the section, then. Be so good as to tell my coachman to drive to the Bondy Section."

He saluted her and stepped back. "Section Bondy, Rue des Morts," he bade the driver.

Madame sank into her seat again, in a state of agitation fully shared by mademoiselle. Rougane set himself to pacify and reassure them. The section would put the matter in order. They would most certainly be accorded a permit. What possible reason could there be for refusing them? A mere formality, after all!

His assurance uplifted them merely to prepare them for a still more profound dejection when presently they met with a flat refusal from the president of the section who received the Countess.

"Your name, madame?" he had asked brusquely. A rude fellow of the most advanced republican type, he had not even risen out of deference to the ladies when they entered. He was there, he would have told you, to perform the duties of his office, not to give dancing-lessons.

"Plougastel," he repeated after her, without title, as if it had been the name of a butcher or baker. He took down a heavy volume from a shelf on his right, opened it and turned the pages. It was a sort of directory of his section. Presently he found what he sought. "Comte de Plougastel, Hôtel Plougastel, Rue du Paradis. Is that it?"

"That is correct, monsieur," she answered, with what civility she could muster before the fellow's affronting rudeness.

There was a long moment of silence, during which he studied certain pencilled entries against the name. The sections had been working in the last few weeks much more systematically than was generally suspected.

"Your husband is with you, madame?" he asked curtly, his eyes still conning that page.

"M. le Comte is not with me," she answered, stressing the title.

"Not with you?" He looked up suddenly, and directed upon

422

her a glance in which suspicion seemed to blend with derision. "Where is he?"

"He is not in Paris, monsieur."

"Ah! Is he at Coblenz, do you think?"

Madame felt herself turning cold. There was something ominous in all this. To what end had the sections informed themselves so thoroughly of the comings and goings of their inhabitants? What was preparing? She had a sense of being trapped, of being taken in a net that had been cast unseen.

"I do not know, monsieur," she said, her voice unsteady.

"Of course not." He seemed to sneer. "No matter. And you wish to leave Paris also? Where do you desire to go?"

"To Meudon."

"Your business there?"

The blood leapt to her face. His insolence was unbearable to a woman who in all her life had never known anything but the utmost deference from inferiors and equals alike. Nevertheless, realizing that she was face to face with forces entirely new, she controlled herself, stifled her resentment, and answered steadily.

"I wish to conduct this lady, Mlle. de Kercadiou, back to her uncle who resides there."

"Is that all? Another day will do for that, madame. The matter is not pressing."

"Pardon, monsieur, to us the matter is very pressing."

"You have not convinced me of it, and the barriers are closed to all who cannot prove the most urgent and satisfactory reasons for wishing to pass. You will wait, madame, until the restriction is removed. Good evening."

"But, monsieur . . ."

"Good evening, madame," he repeated significantly, a dismissal more contemptuous and despotic than any royal "You have leave to go."

Madame went out with Aline. Both were quivering with the anger that prudence had urged them to suppress. They climbed into the coach again, desiring to be driven home.

Rougane's astonishment turned into dismay when they told him what had taken place. "Why not try the Hôtel de Ville, madame?" he suggested.

"After that? It would be useless. We must resign ourselves to remaining in Paris until the barriers are opened again."

"Perhaps it will not matter to us either way by then, madame," said Aline.

"Aline!" she exclaimed in horror.

"Mademoiselle!" cried Rougane on the same note. And then, because he perceived that people detained in this fashion must be in some danger not yet discernible, but on that account more dreadful, he set his wits to work. As they were approaching the Hôtel Plougastel once more, he announced that he had solved the problem.

"A passport from without would do equally well," he announced. "Listen, now, and trust to me. I will go back to Meudon at once. My father shall give me two permits—one for myself alone, and another for three persons from Meudon to Paris and back to Meudon. I reënter Paris with my own permit, which I then proceed to destroy, and we leave together, we three, on the strength of the other one, representing ourselves as having come from Meudon in the course of the day. It is quite simple, after all. If I go at once, I shall be back tonight."

"But how will you leave?" asked Aline.

"I? Pooh! As to that, have no anxiety. My father is Mayor of Meudon. There are plenty who know him. I will go to the Hôtel de Ville, and tell them what is, after all, true—that I am caught in Paris by the closing of the barriers, and that my father is expecting me home this evening. They will pass me through. It is quite simple."

His confidence uplifted them again. The thing seemed as easy as he represented it.

"Then let your passport be for four, my friend," madame begged him. "There is Jacques," she explained, indicating the footman who had just assisted them to alight.

Rougane departed confident of soon returning, leaving them to await him with the same confidence. But the hours succeeded one another, the night closed in, bedtime came, and still there was no sign of his return.

They waited until midnight, each pretending for the other's sake to a confidence fully sustained, each invaded by vague premonitions of evil, yet beguiling the time by playing tric-trac in the great salon, as if they had not a single anxious thought between them.

At last on the stroke of midnight, madame sighed and rose.

"It will be for tomorrow morning," she said, not believing it.

"Of course," Aline agreed. "It would really have been impossible for him to have returned tonight. And it will be much better to travel tomorrow. The journey at so late an hour would tire you so much, dear madame."

Thus they made pretence.

Early in the morning they were awakened by a din of bells—

the tocsins of the sections ringing the alarm. To their startled ears came later the rolling of drums, and at one time they heard the sounds of a multitude on the march. Paris was rising. Later still came the rattle of small-arms in the distance and the deeper boom of cannon. Battle was joined between the men of the sections and the men of the Court. The people in arms had attacked the Tuileries. Wildest rumours flew in all directions, and some of them found their way through the servants to the Hôtel Plougastel, of that terrible fight for the palace which was to end in the purposeless massacre of all those whom the invertebrate monarch abandoned there, whilst placing himself and his family under the protection of the Assembly. Purposeless to the end, ever adopting the course pointed out to him by evil counsellors, he prepared for resistance only until the need for resistance really arose, whereupon he ordered a surrender which left those who had stood by him to the last at the mercy of a frenzied mob.

And while this was happening in the Tuileries, the two women at the Hôtel Plougastel still waited for the return of Rougane, though now with ever-lessening hope. And Rougane did not return. The affair did not appear so simple to the father as to the son. Rougane the elder was rightly afraid to lend himself to such a piece of deception.

He went with his son to inform M. de Kercadiou of what had happened, and told him frankly of the thing his son suggested, but which he dared not do.

M. de Kercadiou sought to move him by intercessions and even by the offer of bribes. But Rougane remained firm.

"Monsieur," he said, "if it were discovered against me, as it inevitably would be, I should hang for it. Apart from that, and in spite of my anxiety to do all in my power to serve you, it would be a breach of trust such as I could not contemplate. You must not ask me, monsieur."

"But what do you conceive is going to happen?" asked the half-demented gentleman.

"It is war," said Rougane, who was well informed, as we have seen. "War between the people and the Court. I am desolated that my warning should have come too late. But, when all is said, I do not think that you need really alarm yourself. War will not be made on women."

M. de Kercadiou clung for comfort to that assurance after the mayor and his son had departed. But at the back of his mind there remained the knowledge of the traffic in which M. de Plougastel was engaged. What if the revolutionaries were equally well informed? And most probably they were. The women-folk of political offenders had been known aforetime to suffer for the sins of their men. Anything was possible in a popular upheaval, and Aline would be exposed jointly with Mme. de Plougastel.

Late that night, as he sat gloomily in his brother's library, the pipe in which he had sought solace extinguished between his fingers, there came a sharp knocking at the door.

To the old seneschal of Gavrillac who went to open there stood revealed upon the threshold a slim young man in a dark olive surcoat, the skirts of which reached down to his calves. He wore boots, buckskins, and a small-sword, and round his waist there was a tricolour sash, in his hat a tricolour cockade, which gave him an official look extremely sinister to the eyes of that old retainer of feudalism, who shared to the full his master's present fears.

427

"Monsieur desires?" he asked, between respect and mistrust. And then a crisp voice startled him.

"Why, Bénoît! Name of a name! Have you completely forgotten me?"

With a shaking hand the old man raised the lantern he carried so as to throw its light more fully upon that lean, wide-mouthed countenance.

"M. André!" he cried. "M. André!" And then he looked at the sash and the cockade, and hesitated, apparently at a loss.

But André-Louis stepped past him into the wide vestibule, with its tessellated floor of black-and-white marble.

"If my godfather has not yet retired, take me to him. If he has retired, take me to him all the same."

"Oh, but certainly, M. André—and I am sure he will be ravished to see you. No, he has not yet retired. This way, M. André; this way, if you please."

The returning André-Louis, reaching Meudon a half-hour ago, had gone straight to the mayor for some definite news of what might be happening in Paris that should either confirm or dispel the ominous rumours that he had met in ever-increasing volume as he approached the capital. Rougane informed him that insurrection was imminent, that already the sections had possessed themselves of the barriers, and that it was impossible for any person not fully accredited to enter or leave the city.

André-Louis bowed his head, his thoughts of the gravest. He had for some time perceived the danger of this second revolution from within the first, which might destroy everything that had been done, and give the reins of power to a villainous faction that would plunge the country into anarchy. The thing he had feared

428

was more than ever on the point of taking place. He would go on at once, that very night, and see for himself what was happening.

And then, as he was leaving, he turned again to Rougane to ask if M. de Kercadiou was still at Meudon.

"You know him, monsieur?"

"He is my godfather."

"Your godfather! And you a representative! Why, then, you may be the very man he needs." And Rougane told him of his son's errand into Paris that afternoon and its result.

No more was required. That two years ago his godfather should upon certain terms have refused him his house weighed for nothing at the moment. He left his travelling carriage at the little inn and went straight to M. de Kercadiou.

And M. de Kercadiou, startled in such an hour by this sudden apparition, of one against whom he nursed a bitter grievance, greeted him in terms almost identical with those in which in that same room he had greeted him on a similar occasion once before.

"What do you want here, sir?"

"To serve you if possible, my godfather," was the disarming answer.

But it did not disarm M. de Kercadiou. "You have stayed away so long that I hoped you would not again disturb me."

"I should not have ventured to disobey you now were it not for the hope that I can be of service. I have seen Rougane, the mayor . . ."

"What's that you say about not venturing to disobey?"

"You forbade me your house, monsieur."

M. de Kercadiou stared at him helplessly.

"And is that why you have not come near me in all this time?"

"Of course. Why else?"

M. de Kercadiou continued to stare. Then he swore under his breath. It disconcerted him to have to deal with a man who insisted upon taking him so literally. He had expected that André-Louis would have come contritely to admit his fault and beg to be taken back into favour. He said so.

"But how could I hope that you meant less than you said, monsieur? You were so very definite in your declaration. What expressions of contrition could have served me without a purpose of amendment? And I had no notion of amending. We may yet be thankful for that."

"Thankful?"

"I am a representative. I have certain powers. I am very opportunely returning to Paris. Can I serve you where Rougane cannot? The need, monsieur, would appear to be very urgent if the half of what I suspect is true. Aline should be placed in safety at once."

M. de Kercadiou surrendered unconditionally. He came over and took André-Louis' hand.

"My boy," he said, and he was visibly moved, "there is in you a certain nobility that is not to be denied. If I seemed harsh with you, then, it was because I was fighting against your evil proclivities. I desired to keep you out of the evil path of politics that have brought this unfortunate country into so terrible a pass. The enemy on the frontier; civil war about to flame out at home. That is what you revolutionaries have done."

André-Louis did not argue. He passed on.

"About Aline?" he asked. And himself answered his own question: "She is in Paris, and she must be brought out of it at once, before the place becomes a shambles, as well it may once the passions that have been brewing all these months are let loose. Young Rougane's plan is good. At least, I cannot think of a better one."

"But Rougane the elder will not hear of it."

"You mean he will not do it on his own responsibility. But he has consented to do it on mine. I have left him a note over my signature to the effect that a safe-conduct for Mlle. de Kercadiou to go to Paris and return is issued by him in compliance with orders from me. The powers I carry and of which I have satisfied him are his sufficient justification for obeying me in this. I have left him that note on the understanding that he is to use it only in an extreme case, for his own protection. In exchange he has given me this safe-conduct."

"You already have it!"

M. de Kercadiou took the sheet of paper that André-Louis held out. His hand shook. He approached it to the cluster of candles burning on the console and screwed up his short-sighted eyes to read.

"If you send that to Paris by young Rougane in the morning," said André-Louis, "Aline should be here by noon. Nothing, of course, could be done tonight without provoking suspicion. The hour is too late. And now, monsieur my godfather, you know exactly why I intrude in violation of your commands. If there is any other way in which I can serve you, you have but to name it whilst I am here."

"But there is, André. Did not Rougane tell you that there were others . . . ?"

"He mentioned Mme. de Plougastel and her servant."

"Then why . . . ?" M. de Kercadiou broke off, looking his question.

Very solemnly André-Louis shook his head.

"That is impossible," he said.

M. de Kercadiou's mouth fell open in astonishment. "Impossible!" he repeated. "But why?"

"Monsieur, I can do what I am doing for Aline without offending my conscience. Besides, for Aline I would offend my conscience and do it. But Mme. de Plougastel is in very different case. Neither Aline nor any of hers have been concerned in counter-revolutionary work, which is the true source of the calamity that now threatens to overtake us. I can procure her removal from Paris without self-reproach, convinced that I am doing nothing that anyone could censure, or that might become the subject of enquiries. But Mme. de Plougastel is the wife of M. le Comte de Plougastel, whom all the world knows to be an agent between the Court and the émigrés."

"That is no fault of hers," cried M. de Kercadiou through his consternation.

"Agreed. But she may be called upon at any moment to establish the fact that she is not a party to these manoeuvres. It is known that she was in Paris today. Should she be sought tomorrow and should it be found that she has gone, enquiries will certainly be made, from which it must result that I have betrayed my trust, and abused my powers to serve personal ends. I hope, monsieur, that you will understand that the risk is too great to be run for the sake of a stranger."

"André, my reasons are overwhelming."

"Pray allow me to be the judge of that." André-Louis' manner was almost peremptory.

The demand seemed to reduce M. de Kercadiou to despair. He paced the room, his hands tight-clasped behind him, his brow wrinkled. At last he came to stand before his godson.

"Can't you take my word for it that these reasons exist?" he cried in anguish.

"In such a matter as this—a matter that may involve my neck? Oh, monsieur, is that reasonable?"

"I violate my word of honour, my oath, if I tell you." M. de Kercadiou turned away, wringing his hands, his condition visibly piteous; then turned again to André. "But in this extremity, in this desperate extremity, and since you so ungenerously insist, I shall have to tell you. God help me, I have no choice. She will realize that when she knows. André, my boy . . ." He paused again, a man afraid. He set a hand on his godson's shoulder, and to his increasing amazement André-Louis perceived that over those pale, short-sighted eyes there was a film of tears. "Mme. de Plougastel is your mother."

Followed, for a long moment, utter silence. This thing that he was told was not immediately understood. When understanding came at last André-Louis' first impulse was to cry out. But he possessed himself, and played the Stoic. He must ever be playing something. That was in his nature. And he was true to his nature even in this supreme moment. He continued silent until, obeying that queer histrionic instinct, he could trust himself to speak without emotion.

"I see," he said, at last, quite coolly.

His mind was sweeping back over the past. Swiftly he reviewed his memories of Mme. de Plougastel, her singular if sporadic interest in him, the curious blend of affection and wistfulness which her manner towards him had always presented, and at last he understood so much that hitherto had intrigued him.

"I see," he said again; and added now, "Of course, any but a fool would have guessed it long ago."

It was M. de Kercadiou who cried out, M. de Kercadiou who recoiled as from a blow.

"My God, André, of what are you made? You can take such an announcement in this fashion?"

"And how would you have me take it? Should it surprise me to discover that I had a mother? After all, a mother is an indispensable necessity to getting one's self born."

He sat down abruptly, to conceal the too-revealing fact that his limbs were shaking. He pulled a handkerchief from his pocket to mop his brow, which had grown damp. And then, quite suddenly, he found himself weeping.

At the sight of those tears streaming silently down that face that had turned so pale, M. de Kercadiou came quickly across to him. He sat down beside him and threw an arm affectionately over his shoulder.

"André, my poor lad," he murmured. "I . . . I was fool enough to think you had no heart. You deceived me with your infernal pretence, and now I see . . . I see . . ." He was not sure what it was that he saw, or else he hesitated to express it.

"It is nothing, monsieur. I am tired out, and . . . and I have a cold in the head." And then, finding the part beyond his power, he abruptly threw it up, utterly abandoned all pretence. "Why . . . why has there been all this mystery?" he asked. "Was it intended that I should never know?"

"It was, André. It . . . it had to be, for prudence' sake."

"But why? Complete your confidence, sir. Surely you cannot leave it there. Having told me so much, you must tell me all."

"The reason, my boy, is that you were born some three years after your mother's marriage with M. de Plougastel, some eighteen months after M. de Plougastel had been away with the army, and some four months before his return to his wife. It is a matter that M. de Plougastel has never suspected, and for gravest family reasons must never suspect. That is why the utmost secrecy has been preserved. That is why none was ever allowed to know. Your mother came betimes into Brittany, and under an assumed name spent some months in the village of Moreau. It was while she was there that you were born."

André-Louis turned it over in his mind. He had dried his tears. And sat now rigid and collected.

"When you say that none was ever allowed to know, you are telling me, of course, that you, monsieur . . ."

"Oh, mon Dieu, no!" The denial came in a violent outburst. M. de Kercadiou sprang to his feet propelled from André's side by the violence of his emotions. It was as if the very suggestion filled him with horror. "I was the only other one who knew. But it is not as you think, André. You cannot imagine that I should lie to you, that I should deny you if you were my son?"

"If you say that I am not, monsieur, that is sufficient."

"You are not. I was Thérèse's cousin and also, as she well knew, her truest friend. She knew that she could trust me; and it was to me she came for help in her extremity. Once, years before, I would have married her. But, of course, I am not the sort of man a woman could love. She trusted, however, to my love for her, and I have kept her trust."

"Then, who was my father?"

"I don't know. She never told me. It was her secret, and I did not pry. It is not in my nature, André."

André-Louis got up, and stood silently facing M. de Kercadiou.

"You believe me, André."

"Naturally, monsieur; and I am sorry, I am sorry that I am not your son."

M. de Kercadiou gripped his godson's hand convulsively, and held it a moment with no word spoken. Then as they fell away from each other again.

"And now, what will you do, André?" he asked. "Now that you know?"

André-Louis stood awhile considering, then broke into laughter. The situation had its humours. He explained them.

"What difference should the knowledge make? Is filial piety to be called into existence by the mere announcement of relationship? Am I to risk my neck through lack of circumspection on behalf of a mother so very circumspect that she had no intention of ever revealing herself? The discovery rests upon the merest chance, upon a fall of the dice of Fate. Is that to weigh with me?"

"The decision is with you, André."

"Nay, it is beyond me. Decide it who can, I cannot."

"You mean that you refuse even now?"

"I mean that I consent. Since I cannot decide what it is that I should do, it only remains for me to do what a son should. It is grotesque; but all life is grotesque."

"You will never, never regret it."

"I hope not," said André. "Yet I think it very likely that I shall. And now I had better see Rougane again at once, and obtain from him the other two permits required. Then perhaps it will be best that I take them to Paris myself, in the morning. If you will give me a bed, monsieur, I shall be grateful. I . . . I confess that I am hardly in case to do more tonight."

CHAPTER XIII

Sanctuary

Into the late afternoon of that endless day of horror with its perpetual alarms, its volleying musketry, rolling drums, and distant muttering of angry multitudes, Mme. de Plougastel and Aline sat waiting in that handsome house in the Rue du Paradis. It was no longer for Rougane they waited. They realized that, be the reason what it might—and by now many reasons must no doubt exist—this friendly messenger would not return. They waited without knowing for what. They waited for whatever might betide.

At one time early in the afternoon the roar of battle approached them, racing swiftly in their direction, swelling each moment in volume and in horror. It was the frenzied clamour of a multitude drunk with blood and bent on destruction. Near at hand that fierce wave of humanity checked in its turbulent progress. Followed blows of pikes upon a door and imperious calls to open, and thereafter came the rending of timbers, the shivering of glass, screams of terror blending with screams of rage, and, running through these shrill sounds, the deeper diapason of bestial laughter.

It was a hunt of two wretched Swiss guardsmen seeking blindly to escape. And they were run to earth in a house in the neighbourhood, and there cruelly done to death by that demoniac mob. The thing accomplished, the hunters, male and female, forming into a battalion, came swinging down the Rue du Paradis, chanting the song of Marseilles—a song new to Paris in those days:

> *Allons, enfants de la patrie!*
> *Le jour de gloire est arrivé.*
> *Contre nous de la tyrannie*
> *L'étendard sanglant est levé.*

Nearer it came, raucously bawled by some hundreds of voices, a dread sound that had come so suddenly to displace at least temporarily the merry, trivial air of the "*Ça ira!*" which hitherto had been the revolutionary carillon.

Instinctively Mme. de Plougastel and Aline clung to each other. They had heard the sound of the ravishing of that other house in the neighbourhood, without knowledge of the reason. What if now it should be the turn of the Hôtel Plougastel! There was no real cause to fear it, save that amid a turmoil imperfectly understood and therefore the more awe-inspiring, the worst must be feared always.

The dreadful song so dreadfully sung, and the thunder of

439

heavily shod feet upon the roughly paved street, passed on and receded. They breathed again, almost as if a miracle had saved them, to yield to fresh alarm an instant later, when madame's young footman, Jacques, the most trusted of her servants, burst into their presence unceremoniously with a scared face, bringing the announcement that a man who had just climbed over the garden wall professed himself a friend of madame's, and desired to be brought immediately to her presence.

"But he looks like a *sansculotte*, madame!" the staunch fellow warned her.

Her thoughts and hopes leapt at once to Rougane.

"Bring him in," she commanded breathlessly.

Jacques went out, to return presently accompanied by a tall man in a long, shabby, and very ample overcoat and a wide-brimmed hat that was turned down all round, and adorned by an enormous tricolour cockade. This hat he removed as he entered.

Jacques, standing behind him, perceived that his hair, although now in some disorder, bore signs of having been carefully dressed. It was clubbed, and it carried some lingering vestiges of powder. The young footman wondered what it was in the man's face, which was turned from him, that should cause his mistress to cry out and recoil. Then he found himself dismissed abruptly by a gesture.

The newcomer advanced to the middle of the salon, moving like a man exhausted and breathing hard. There he leaned against a table, across which he confronted Mme. de Plougastel. And she stood regarding him, a strange horror in her eyes.

In the background, on a settle at the salon's far end, sat Aline staring in bewilderment and some fear at a face which, if unrecognizable through the mask of blood and dust that smeared it, was yet familiar. And then the man spoke, and instantly she knew the voice for that of the Marquis de La Tour d'Azyr.

"My dear friend," he was saying, "forgive me if I startled you. Forgive me if I thrust myself in here without leave, at such a time, in such a manner. But . . . you see how it is with me. I am a fugitive. In the course of my distracted flight, not knowing which way to turn for safety, I thought of you. I told myself that if I could but safely reach your house, I might find sanctuary."

"You are in danger?"

"In danger?" Almost he seemed silently to laugh at the unnecessary question. "If I were to show myself openly in the streets just now, I might with luck contrive to live for five minutes! My friend, it has been a massacre. Some few of us escaped from the Tuileries at the end, to be hunted to death in the streets. I doubt if by this time a single Swiss survives. They had the worst of it, poor devils. And as for us—my God! they hate us more than they hate the Swiss. Hence this filthy disguise."

He peeled off the shaggy greatcoat, and casting it from him stepped forth in the black satin that had been the general livery of the hundred knights of the dagger who had rallied in the Tuileries that morning to the defence of their king.

His coat was rent across the back, his neckcloth and the ruffles at his wrists were torn and bloodstained; with his smeared face and disordered headdress he was terrible to behold. Yet he contrived to carry himself with his habitual easy assurance, remembered to kiss the trembling hand which Mme. de Plougastel extended to him in welcome.

"You did well to come to me, Gervais," she said. "Yes, here is sanctuary for the present. You will be quite safe, at least for as long as we are safe. My servants are entirely trustworthy. Sit down and tell me all."

He obeyed her, collapsing almost into the armchair which she thrust forward, a man exhausted, whether by physical exertion or by nerve-strain, or both. He drew a handkerchief from his pocket and wiped some of the blood and dirt from his face.

"It is soon told." His tone was bitter with the bitterness of despair. "This, my dear, is the end of us. Plougastel is lucky in being across the frontier at such a time. Had I not been fool enough to trust those who today have proved themselves utterly unworthy of trust, that is where I should be myself. My remaining in Paris is the crowning folly of a life full of follies and mistakes. That I should come to you in my hour of most urgent need adds point to it." He laughed in his bitterness.

Madame moistened her dry lips. "And . . . and now?" she asked him.

"It only remains to get away as soon as may be, if it is still possible. Here in France there is no longer any room for us—at least, not above ground. Today has proved it." And then he looked up at her, standing there beside him so pale and timid, and he smiled. He patted the fine hand that rested upon the arm of his chair. "My dear Thérèse, unless you carry charitableness to the length of giving me to drink, you will see me perish of thirst under your eyes before ever the *canaille* has a chance to finish me."

She started. "I should have thought of it!" she cried in self-reproach, and she turned quickly. "Aline," she begged, "tell Jacques to bring . . ."

"Aline!" he echoed, interrupting, and swinging round in his turn. Then, as Aline rose into view, detaching from her background, and he at last perceived her, he heaved himself abruptly to his weary legs again, and stood there stiffly bowing to her across the space of gleaming floor. "Mademoiselle, I had not suspected your presence," he said, and he seemed extraordinarily ill-at-ease, a man startled, as if caught in an illicit act.

"I perceived it, monsieur," she answered, as she advanced to do madame's commission. She paused before him. "From my heart, monsieur, I grieve that we should meet again in circumstances so very painful."

Not since the day of his duel with André-Louis—the day which had seen the death and burial of his last hope of winning her—had they stood face to face.

He checked as if on the point of answering her. His glance strayed to Mme. de Plougastel, and, oddly reticent for one who could be very glib, he bowed in silence.

"But sit, monsieur, I beg. You are fatigued."

"You are gracious to observe it. With your permission, then." And he resumed his seat. She continued on her way to the door and passed out upon her errand.

When presently she returned they had almost unaccountably changed places. It was Mme. de Plougastel who was seated in that armchair of brocade and gilt, and M. de La Tour d'Azyr who, despite his lassitude, was leaning over the back of it talking earnestly, seeming by his attitude to plead with her. On Aline's entrance he broke off instantly and moved away, so that she was left with a sense of having intruded. Further she observed that the Countess was in tears.

Following her came presently the diligent Jacques, bearing a tray laden with food and wine. Madame poured for her guest, and he drank a long draught of the Burgundy, then begged, holding forth his grimy hands, that he might mend his appearance before sitting down to eat.

He was led away and valeted by Jacques, and when he returned he had removed from his person the last vestige of the rough handling he had received. He looked almost his normal self, the disorder in his attire repaired, calm and dignified and courtly in his bearing, but very pale and haggard of face, seeming suddenly to have increased in years, to have reached in appearance the age that was in fact his own.

As he ate and drank—and this with appetite, for as he told them he had not tasted food since early morning—he entered into the details of the dreadful events of the day, and gave them the particulars of his own escape from the Tuileries when all was seen to be lost and when the Swiss, having burnt their last cartridge, were submitting to wholesale massacre at the hands of the indescribably furious mob.

"Oh, it was all most ill done," he ended critically. "We were timid when we should have been resolute, and resolute at last when it was too late. That is the history of our side from the beginning of this accursed struggle. We have lacked proper leadership throughout, and now—as I have said already—there is an end to us. It but remains to escape, as soon as we can discover how the thing is to be accomplished."

Madame told him of the hopes that she had centred upon Rougane.

It lifted him out of his gloom. He was disposed to be optimistic.

"You are wrong to have abandoned that hope," he assured her. "If this mayor is so well disposed, he certainly can do as his son promised. But last night it would have been too late for him to have reached you, and today, assuming that he had come to Paris, almost impossible for him to win across the streets from the other side. It is most likely that he will yet come. I pray that he may; for the knowledge that you and Mlle. de Kercadiou are out of this would comfort me above all."

"We should take you with us," said madame.

"Ah! But how?"

"Young Rougane was to bring me permits for three persons—Aline, myself, and my footman, Jacques. You would take the place of Jacques."

"Faith, to get out of Paris, madame, there is no man whose place I would not take." And he laughed.

Their spirits rose with his and their flagging hopes revived. But as dusk descended again upon the city, without any sign of the deliverer they awaited, those hopes began to ebb once more.

M. de La Tour d'Azyr at last pleaded weariness, and begged to be permitted to withdraw that he might endeavour to take some rest against whatever might have to be faced in the immediate future. When he had gone, madame persuaded Aline to go and lie down.

"I will call you, my dear, the moment he arrives," she said, bravely maintaining that pretence of a confidence that had by now entirely evaporated.

Aline kissed her affectionately, and departed, outwardly so calm and unperturbed as to leave the Countess wondering whether she realized the peril by which they were surrounded, a peril infinitely increased by the presence in that house of a man so widely known and detested as M. de La Tour d'Azyr, a man who was probably being sought for by his enemies at this moment.

Left alone, madame lay down on a couch in the salon itself, to be ready for any emergency. It was a hot summer night, and the glass doors opening upon the luxuriant garden stood wide to admit the air. On that air came intermittently from the distance sounds of the continuing horrible activities of the populace, the aftermath of that bloody day.

Mme. de Plougastel lay there, listening to those sounds for upwards of an hour, thanking Heaven that for the present at least the disturbances were distant, dreading lest at any moment they should occur nearer at hand, lest this Bondy section in which her hôtel was situated should become the scene of horrors similar to those whose echoes reached her ears from other sections away to the south and west.

The couch occupied by the Countess lay in shadow; for all the lights in that long salon had been extinguished with the exception of a cluster of candles in a massive silver candlebranch placed on a round marquetry table in the middle of the room—an island of light in the surrounding gloom.

The timepiece on the overmantel chimed melodiously the hour of ten, and then, startling in the suddenness with which it broke the immediate silence, another sound vibrated through the house, and brought madame to her feet, in a breathless mingling of hope and dread. Someone was knocking sharply on the door below. Followed moments of agonized suspense, culminating in the abrupt invasion of the room by the footman Jacques. He looked round, not seeing his mistress at first.

"Madame! Madame!" he panted, out of breath.

"What is it, Jacques!" Her voice was steady now that the need for self-control seemed thrust upon her. She advanced from the shadows into that island of light about the table.

"There is a man below. He is asking . . . he is demanding to see you at once."

"A man?" she questioned.

"He . . . he seems to be an official; at least he wears the sash of office. And he refuses to give any name; he says that his name would convey nothing to you. He insists that he must see you in person and at once."

"An official?" said madame.

"An official," Jacques repeated. "I would not have admitted him, but that he demanded it in the name of the Nation. Madame, it is for you to say what shall be done. Robert is with me. If you wish it . . . whatever it may be . . ."

"My good Jacques, no, no." She was perfectly composed. "If this man intended evil, surely he would not come alone. Conduct him to me, and then beg Mlle. de Kercadiou to join me if she is awake."

Jacques departed, himself partly reassured. Madame seated herself in the armchair by the table well within the light. She smoothed her dress with a mechanical hand. If, as it would seem, her hopes had been futile, so had her momentary fears. A man on any but an errand of peace would have brought some following with him, as she had said.

The door opened again, and Jacques reappeared; after him, stepping briskly past him, came a slight man in a wide-brimmed hat, adorned by a tricolour cockade. About the waist of an olive-green riding-coat he wore a broad tricolour sash; a sword hung at his side.

He swept off his hat, and the candlelight glinted on the steel buckle in front of it. Madame found herself silently regarded by a pair of large, dark eyes set in a lean, brown face, eyes that were most singularly intent and searching.

She leaned forward, incredulity swept across her countenance. Then her eyes kindled, and the colour came creeping back into her pale cheeks. She rose suddenly. She was trembling.

"André-Louis!" she exclaimed.

Chapter XIV

The Barrier

That gift of laughter of his seemed utterly extinguished. For once there was no gleam of humour in those dark eyes, as they continued to consider her with that queer stare of scrutiny. And yet, though his gaze was sombre, his thoughts were not. With his cruelly-true mental vision which pierced through shams, and his capacity for detached observation—which properly applied might have carried him very far, indeed—he perceived the grotesqueness, the artificiality of the emotion which in that moment he experienced, but by which he refused to be possessed. It sprang entirely from the consciousness that she was his mother; as if, all things considered, the more or less accidental fact that she had brought him into the world could establish between them any real bond at this time of day! The motherhood that bears and forsakes is less than animal. He had considered this; he had been given ample leisure in which to consider it during those long, turbulent hours in which he had been forced to wait, because it would have been almost impossible to have won across that seething city, and certainly unwise to have attempted so to do.

He had reached the conclusion that by consenting to go to her rescue at such a time he stood committed to a piece of purely sentimental quixotry. The quittances which the Mayor of Meudon had exacted from him before he would issue the necessary safe-conducts placed the whole of his future, perhaps his very life, in jeopardy. And he had consented to do this not for the sake of a reality, but out of regard for an idea—he who all his life had avoided the false lure of worthless and hollow sentimentality.

Thus thought André-Louis as he considered her now so searchingly, finding it, naturally enough, a matter of extraordinary interest to look consciously upon his mother for the first time at the age of eight-and-twenty.

From her he looked at last at Jacques, who remained at attention, waiting by the open door.

"Could we be alone, madame?" he asked her.

She waved the footman away, and the door closed. In agitated silence, unquestioning, she waited for him to account for his presence there at so extraordinary a time.

"Rougane could not return," he informed her shortly. "At M. de Kercadiou's request, I come instead."

"You! You are sent to rescue us!" The note of amazement in her voice was stronger than that of her relief.

"That, and to make your acquaintance, madame."

"To make my acquaintance? But what do you mean, André-Louis?"

"This letter from M. de Kercadiou will tell you."

Intrigued by his odd words and odder manner, she took the folded sheet. She broke the seal with shaking hands, and with shaking hands approached the written page to the light. Her eyes grew troubled as she read; the shaking of her hands increased, and midway through that reading a moan escaped her. One glance that was almost terror she darted at the slim, straight man standing so incredibly impassive upon the edge of the light, and then she endeavoured to read on. But the crabbed characters of M. de Kercadiou swam distortedly under her eyes. She could not read. Besides, what could it matter what else he said. She had read enough. The sheet fluttered from her hands to the table, and out of a face that was like a face of wax, she looked now with a wistfulness, a sadness indescribable, at André-Louis.

"And so you know, my child?" Her voice was stifled to a whisper.

"I know, madame my mother."

The grimness, the subtle blend of merciless derision and reproach in which it was uttered completely escaped her. She cried out at the new name. For her in that moment time and the world stood still. Her peril there in Paris as the wife of an intriguer at Coblenz was blotted out, together with every other consideration—thrust out of a consciousness that could find room for nothing else beside the fact that she stood acknowledged by her only son, this child begotten in adultery, borne furtively and in shame in a remote Brittany village eight-and-twenty years ago. Not even a thought for the betrayal of that inviolable secret, or the consequences that might follow, could she spare in this supreme moment.

She took one or two faltering steps towards him, hesitating.

451

Then she opened her arms. Sobs suffocated her voice.

"Won't you come to me, André-Louis?"

A moment yet he stood hesitating, startled by that appeal, angered almost by his heart's response to it, reason and sentiment at grips in his soul. This was not real, his reason postulated; this poignant emotion that she displayed and that he experienced was fantastic. Yet he went. Her arms enfolded him; her wet cheek was pressed hard against his own; her frame, which the years had not yet succeeded in robbing of its grace, was shaken by the passionate storm within her.

"Oh, André-Louis, my child, if you knew how I have hungered to hold you so! If you knew how in denying myself this I have atoned and suffered! Kercadiou should not have told you— not even now. It was wrong—most wrong, perhaps, to you. It would have been better that he should have left me here to my fate, whatever that may be. And yet—come what may of this— to be able to hold you so, to be able to acknowledge you, to hear you call me mother—oh André-Louis, I cannot now regret it. I cannot . . . I cannot wish it otherwise."

"Is there any need, madame?" he asked her, his stoicism deeply shaken. "There is no occasion to take others into our confidence. This is for tonight alone. Tonight we are mother and son. To-morrow we resume our former places, and, outwardly at least, forget."

"Forget? Have you no heart, André-Louis?"

The question recalled him curiously to his attitude towards life—that histrionic attitude of his that he accounted true philosophy. Also he remembered what lay before them; and he realized that he must master not only himself but her; that to yield too far to sentiment at such a time might be the ruin of them all.

"It is a question propounded to me so often that it must contain the truth," said he. "My rearing is to blame for that."

She tightened her clutch about his neck even as he would have attempted to disengage himself from her embrace.

"You do not blame me for your rearing? Knowing all, as you do, André-Louis, you cannot altogether blame. You must be merciful to me. You must forgive me. You must! I had no choice."

"When we know all of whatever it may be, we can never do anything but forgive, madame. That is the profoundest religious truth that was ever written. It contains, in fact, a whole religion— the noblest religion any man could have to guide him. I say this for your comfort, madame my mother."

She sprang away from him with a startled cry. Beyond him in the shadows by the door a pale figure shimmered ghostly. It advanced into the light, and resolved itself into Aline. She had come in answer to that forgotten summons madame had sent her by Jacques. Entering unperceived she had seen André-Louis in the embrace of the woman whom he addressed as "mother." She had recognized him instantly by his voice, and she could not have said what bewildered her more: his presence there or the thing she overheard.

"You heard, Aline?" madame exclaimed.

"I could not help it, madame. You sent for me. I am sorry if . . ." She broke off, and looked at André-Louis long and curiously. She was pale, but quite composed. She held out her hand to him. "And so you have come at last, André," said she. "You might have come before."

"I come when I am wanted," was his answer. "Which is the

only time in which one can be sure of being received." He said it without bitterness, and having said it stooped to kiss her hand.

"You can forgive me what is past, I hope, since I failed of my purpose," he said gently, half-pleading. "I could not have come to you pretending that the failure was intentional—a compromise between the necessities of the case and your own wishes. For it was not that. And yet, you do not seem to have profited by my failure. You are still a maid."

She turned her shoulder to him.

"There are things," she said, "that you will never understand."

"Life, for one," he acknowledged. "I confess that I am finding it bewildering. The very explanations calculated to simplify it seem but to complicate it further." And he looked at Mme. de Plougastel.

"You mean something, I suppose," said mademoiselle.

"Aline!" It was the Countess who spoke. She knew the danger of half-discoveries. "I can trust you, child, I know, and André-Louis, I am sure, will offer no objection." She had taken up the letter to show it to Aline. Yet first her eyes questioned him.

"Oh, none, madame," he assured her. "It is entirely a matter for yourself."

Aline looked from one to the other with troubled eyes, hesitating to take the letter that was now proffered. When she had read it through, she very thoughtfully replaced it on the table. A moment she stood there with bowed head, the other two watching her. Then impulsively she ran to madame and put her arms about her.

"Aline!" It was a cry of wonder, almost of joy. "You do not utterly abhor me!"

"My dear," said Aline, and kissed the tear-stained face that seemed to have grown years older in these last few hours.

In the background André-Louis, steeling himself against emotionalism, spoke with the voice of Scaramouche.

"It would be well, mesdames, to postpone all transports until they can be indulged at greater leisure and in more security. It is growing late. If we are to get out of this shambles we should be wise to take the road without more delay."

It was a tonic as effective as it was necessary. It startled them into remembrance of their circumstances, and under the spur of it they went at once to make their preparations.

They left him for perhaps a quarter of an hour, to pace that long room alone, saved only from impatience by the turmoil of his mind. When at length they returned, they were accompanied by a tall man in a full-skirted shaggy greatcoat and a broad hat the brim of which was turned down all around. He remained respectfully by the door in the shadows.

Between them the two women had concerted it thus, or rather the Countess had so concerted it when Aline had warned her that André-Louis' bitter hostility towards the Marquis made it unthinkable that he should move a finger consciously to save him.

Now despite the close friendship uniting M. de Kercadiou and his niece with Mme. de Plougastel, there were several matters concerning them of which the Countess was in ignorance. One of these was the project at one time existing of a marriage between Aline and M. de La Tour d'Azyr. It was a matter that Aline—naturally enough in the state of her feelings—had never mentioned, nor had M. de Kercadiou ever alluded to it since his coming to Meudon, by when he had perceived how unlikely it was ever to be realized.

M. de La Tour d'Azyr's concern for Aline on that morning of the duel when he had found her half-swooning in Mme. de Plougastel's carriage had been of a circumspection that betrayed nothing of his real interest in her, and therefore had appeared no more than natural in one who must account himself the cause of her distress. Similarly Mme. de Plougastel had never realized nor did she realize now—for Aline did not trouble fully to enlighten her—that the hostility between the two men was other than political, the quarrel other than that which already had taken André-Louis to the Bois on every day of the preceding week. But, at least, she realized that even if André-Louis' rancour should have no other source, yet that inconclusive duel was cause enough for Aline's fears.

And so she had proposed this obvious deception; and Aline had consented to be a passive party to it. They had made the mistake of not fully forewarning and persuading M. de La Tour d'Azyr. They had trusted entirely to his anxiety to escape from Paris to keep him rigidly within the part imposed upon him. They had reckoned without the queer sense of honour that moved such men as M. le Marquis, nurtured upon a code of shams.

André-Louis, turning to scan that muffled figure, advanced from the dark depths of the salon. As the light beat on his white, lean face the pseudo-footman started. The next moment he too stepped forward into the light, and swept his broad-brimmed hat from his brow. As he did so André-Louis observed that his hand was fine and white and that a jewel flashed from one of the fingers. Then he caught his breath, and stiffened in every line as he recognized the face revealed to him.

"Monsieur," that stern, proud man was saying, "I cannot take advantage of your ignorance. If these ladies can persuade you to save me, at least it is due to you that you shall know whom you are saving."

He stood there by the table very erect and dignified, ready to perish as he had lived—if perish he must—without fear and without deception.

André-Louis came slowly forward until he reached the table on the other side, and then at last the muscles of his set face relaxed, and he laughed.

"You laugh?" said M. de La Tour d'Azyr, frowning, offended.

"It is so damnably amusing," said André-Louis.

"You've an odd sense of humour, M. Moreau."

"Oh, admitted. The unexpected always moves me so. I have found you many things in the course of our acquaintance. To-night you are the one thing I never expected to find you: an honest man."

M. de La Tour d'Azyr quivered. But he attempted no reply.

"Because of that, monsieur, I am disposed to be clement. It is probably a foolishness. But you have surprised me into it. I give you three minutes, monsieur, in which to leave this house, and to take your own measures for your safety. What afterwards happens to you shall be no concern of mine."

"Ah, no, André! Listen . . ." Madame began in anguish.

"Pardon, madame. It is the utmost that I will do, and already I am violating what I conceive to be my duty. If M. de La Tour d'Azyr remains he not only ruins himself, but he imperils you. For unless he departs at once, he goes with me to the headquarters of the section, and the section will have his head on a pike inside the hour. He is a notorious counter-revolutionary, a knight of the dagger, one of those whom an exasperated populace is determined to exterminate. Now, monsieur, you know what awaits you. Resolve yourself and at once, for these ladies' sake."

"But you don't know, André-Louis!" Mme. de Plougastel's condition was one of anguish indescribable. She came to him and clutched his arm. "For the love of Heaven, André-Louis, be merciful with him! You must!"

"But that is what I am being, madame—merciful; more merciful than he deserves. And he knows it. Fate has meddled most oddly in our concerns to bring us together tonight. Almost it is as if Fate were forcing retribution at last upon him. Yet, for your sakes, I take no advantage of it, provided that he does at once as I have desired him."

And now from beyond the table the Marquis spoke icily, and as he spoke his right hand stirred under the ample folds of his greatcoat.

"I am glad, M. Moreau, that you take that tone with me. You relieve me of the last scruple. You spoke of Fate just now, and I must agree with you that Fate has meddled oddly, though perhaps not to the end that you discern. For years now you have chosen to stand in my path and thwart me at every turn, holding over me a perpetual menace. Persistently you have sought my life in various ways, first indirectly and at last directly. Your intervention in my affairs has ruined my highest hopes—more effectively, perhaps, than you suppose. Throughout you have been my evil genius. And you are even one of the agents of this climax of despair that has been reached by me tonight."

"Wait! Listen!" Madame was panting. She flung away from André-Louis, as if moved by some premonition of what was coming. "Gervais! This is horrible!"

"Horrible, perhaps, but inevitable. Himself he has invited it. I am a man in despair, the fugitive of a lost cause. That man holds the keys of escape. And, besides, between him and me there is a reckoning to be paid."

His hand came from beneath the coat at last, and it came armed with a pistol.

Mme. de Plougastel screamed, and flung herself upon him. On her knees now, she clung to his arm with all her strength and might.

Vainly he sought to shake himself free of that desperate clutch.

"Thérèse!" he cried. "Are you mad? Will you destroy me and yourself? This creature has the safe-conducts that mean our salvation. Himself, he is nothing."

From the background Aline, a breathless, horror-stricken spectator of that scene, spoke sharply, her quick mind pointing out the line of checkmate.

"Burn the safe-conducts, André-Louis. Burn them at once— in the candles there."

But André-Louis had taken advantage of that moment of M. de La Tour d'Azyr's impotence to draw a pistol in his turn. "I think it will be better to burn his brains instead," he said. "Stand away from him, madame."

Far from obeying that imperious command, Mme. de Plougastel rose to her feet to cover the Marquis with her body. But she still clung to his arm, clung to it with unsuspected strength that continued to prevent him from attempting to use the pistol.

"André! For God's sake, André!" she panted hoarsely over her shoulder.

"Stand away, madame," he commanded her again, more sternly, "and let this murderer take his due. He is jeopardizing all our lives, and his own has been forfeit these years. Stand away!" He sprang forward with intent now to fire at his enemy over her shoulder, and Aline moved too late to hinder him.

"André! André!"

Panting, gasping, haggard of face, on the verge almost of hysteria, the distracted Countess flung at last an effective, a terrible barrier between the hatred of those men, each intent upon taking the other's life.

"He is your father, André! Gervais, he is your son—our son! The letter there . . . on the table . . . O my God!" And she slipped nervelessly to the ground, and crouched there sobbing at the feet of M. de La Tour d'Azyr.

Chapter XV

Safe-Conduct

Across the body of that convulsively sobbing woman, the mother of one and the mistress of the other, the eyes of those mortal enemies met, invested with a startled, appalled interest that admitted of no words.

Beyond the table, as if turned to stone by this culminating horror of revelation, stood Aline.

M. de La Tour d'Azyr was the first to stir. Into his bewildered mind came the memory of something that Mme. de Plougastel had said of a letter that was on the table. He came forward, unhindered. The announcement made, Mme. de Plougastel no longer feared the sequel, and so she let him go. He walked unsteadily past this newfound son of his, and took up the sheet that lay beside the candlebranch. A long moment he stood reading it, none heeding him. Aline's eyes were all on André-Louis, full of wonder and commiseration, whilst André-Louis was staring down, in stupefied fascination, at his mother.

M. de La Tour d'Azyr read the letter slowly through. Then very quietly he replaced it. His next concern, being the product of an artificial age sternly schooled in the suppression of emotion, was to compose himself. Then he stepped back to Mme. de Plougastel's side and stooped to raise her.

"Thérèse," he said.

Obeying, by instinct, the implied command, she made an effort to rise and to control herself in her turn. The Marquis half conducted, half carried her to the armchair by the table.

André-Louis looked on. Still numbed and bewildered, he made no attempt to assist. He saw as in a dream the Marquis bending over Mme. de Plougastel. As in a dream he heard him ask:

"How long have you known this, Thérèse?"

"I . . . I have always known it . . . always. I confided him to Kercadiou. I saw him once as a child . . . Oh, but what of that?"

"Why was I never told? Why did you deceive me? Why did you tell me that this child had died a few days after birth? Why, Thérèse? Why?"

"I was afraid. I . . . I thought it better so—that nobody, nobody, not even you, should know. And nobody has known save Quintin until last night, when to induce him to come here and save me he was forced to tell him."

"But I, Thérèse?" the Marquis insisted. "It was my right to know."

"Your right? What could you have done? Acknowledge him? And then? Ha!" It was a queer, desperate note of laughter. "There was Plougastel; there was my family. And there was you . . . you,

462

yourself, who had ceased to care, in whom the fear of discovery had stifled love. Why should I have told you, then? Why? I should not have told you now had there been any other way to . . . to save you both. Once before I suffered just such dreadful apprehensions when you and he fought in the Bois. I was on my way to prevent it when you met me. I would have divulged the truth, as a last resource, to avert that horror. But mercifully God spared me the necessity then."

It had not occurred to any of them to doubt her statement, incredible though it might seem. Had any done so her present words must have resolved all doubt, explaining as they did much that to each of her listeners had been obscure until this moment.

M. de La Tour d'Azyr, overcome, reeled away to a chair and sat down heavily. Losing command of himself for a moment, he took his haggard face in his hands.

Through the windows open to the garden came from the distance the faint throbbing of a drum to remind them of what was happening around them. But the sound went unheeded. To each it must have seemed that here they were face to face with a horror greater than any that might be tormenting Paris. At last André-Louis began to speak, his voice level and unutterably cold.

"M. de La Tour d'Azyr," he said, "I trust that you'll agree that this disclosure, which can hardly be more distasteful and horrible to you than it is to me, alters nothing, since it effaces nothing of all that lies between us. Or, if it alters anything, it is merely to add something to that score. Any yet . . . Oh, but what can it avail to talk! Here, monsieur, take this safe-conduct which is made out for Mme. de Plougastel's footman, and with it make your escape as best you can. In return I will beg of you the favour

463

never to allow me to see you or hear of you again."

"André!" His mother swung upon him with that cry. And yet again that question. "Have you no heart? What has he ever done to you that you should nurse so bitter a hatred of him?"

"You shall hear, madame. Once, two years ago in this very room I told you of a man who had brutally killed my dearest friend and debauched the girl I was to have married. M. de La Tour d'Azyr is that man."

A moan was her only answer. She covered her face with her hands.

The Marquis rose slowly to his feet again. He came slowly forward, his smouldering eyes scanning his son's face.

"You are hard," he said grimly. "But I recognize the hardness. It derives from the blood you bear."

"Spare me that," said André-Louis.

The Marquis inclined his head. "I will not mention it again. But I desire that you should at least understand me, and you too, Thérèse. You accuse me, sir, of murdering your dearest friend. I will admit that the means employed were perhaps unworthy. But what other means were at my command to meet an urgency that everyday since then proves to have existed? M. de Vilmorin was a revolutionary, a man of new ideas that should overthrow society and rebuild it more akin to the desires of such as himself. I belonged to the order that quite as justifiably desired society to remain as it was. Not only was it better so for me and mine, but I also contend, and you have yet to prove me wrong, that it is better so for all the world; that, indeed, no other conceivable society is possible. Every human society must of necessity be composed of several strata. You may disturb it temporarily into an amorphous whole by a revolution such as this; but only temporarily. Soon out of the chaos which is all that you and your kind can ever produce, order must be restored or life will perish; and with the restoration of order comes the restoration of the various strata necessary to organized society. Those that were yesterday at the top may in the new order of things find themselves dispossessed without any benefit to the whole. That change I resisted. The spirit of it I fought with whatever weapons were available, whenever and wherever I encountered it. M. de Vilmorin was an incendiary of the worst type, a man of eloquence full of false ideals that misled poor ignorant men into believing that the change proposed could make the world a better place for them. You are an intelligent man, and I defy you to answer me from your heart and conscience that such a thing was true or possible. You know that it is untrue; you know that it is a pernicious doctrine; and what made it worse on the lips of M. de Vilmorin was that he was sincere and eloquent. His voice was a danger that must be removed—silenced. So much was necessary in self-defence. In self-defence I did it. I had no grudge against M. de Vilmorin. He was a man of my own class; a gentleman of pleasant ways, amiable, estimable, and able.

"You conceive me slaying him for the very lust of slaying, like some beast of the jungle flinging itself upon its natural prey. That has been your error from the first. I did what I did with the very heaviest heart—oh, spare me your sneer!—I do not lie. I have never lied. And I swear to you here and now, by my every hope of Heaven, that what I say is true. I loathed the thing I did. Yet for my own sake and the sake of my order I must do it. Ask yourself whether M. de Vilmorin would have hesitated for a moment if by procuring my death he could have brought the Utopia of his dreams a moment nearer realization.

"After that. You determined that the sweetest vengeance would be to frustrate my ends by reviving in yourself the voice that I had silenced, by yourself carrying forward the fantastic apostleship of equality that was M. de Vilmorin's. You lacked the vision that would have shown you that God did not create men equals. Well, you are in case tonight to judge which of us was right, which wrong. You see what is happening here in Paris. You see the foul spectre of Anarchy stalking through a land fallen into confusion. Probably you have enough imagination to conceive something of what must follow. And do you deceive yourself that out of this filth and ruin there will rise up an ideal form of society? Don't you understand that society must re-order itself presently out of all this?

"But why say more? I must have said enough to make you understand the only thing that really matters—that I killed M. de Vilmorin as a matter of duty to my order. And the truth— which though it may offend you should also convince you—is that tonight I can look back on the deed with equanimity, without a single regret, apart from what lies between you and me.

"When, kneeling beside the body of your friend that day at Gavrillac, you insulted and provoked me, had I been the tiger you conceived me I must have killed you too. I am, as you may know, a man of quick passions. Yet I curbed the natural anger you aroused in me, because I could forgive an affront to myself where I could not overlook a calculated attack upon my order."

He paused a moment. André-Louis stood rigid listening and wondering. So, too, the others. Then M. le Marquis resumed, on a note of less assurance. "In the matter of Mlle. Binet I was unfortunate. I wronged you through inadvertence. I had no knowledge of the relations between you."

André-Louis interrupted him sharply at last with a question: "Would it have made a difference if you had?"

"No," he was answered frankly. "I have the faults of my kind. I cannot pretend that any such scruple as you suggest would have weighed with me. But can you—if you are capable of any detached judgment—blame me very much for that?"

"All things considered, monsieur, I am rapidly being forced to the conclusion that it is impossible to blame any man for anything in this world; that we are all of us the sport of destiny. Consider, monsieur, this gathering—this family gathering—here tonight, whilst out there . . . O my God, let us make an end! Let us go our ways and write 'finis' to this horrible chapter of our lives."

M. de La Tour considered him gravely, sadly, in silence for a moment.

"Perhaps it is best," he said, at length, in a small voice. He turned to Mme. de Plougastel. "If a wrong I have to admit in my life, a wrong that I must bitterly regret, it is the wrong that I have done to you, my dear . . ."

"Not now, Gervais! Not now!" she faltered, interrupting him.

"Now—for the first and the last time. I am going. It is not likely that we shall ever meet again—that I shall ever see any of you again—you who should have been the nearest and dearest to me. We are all, he says, the sport of destiny. Ah, but not quite. Destiny is an intelligent force, moving with purpose. In life we pay for the evil that in life we do. That is the lesson that I have learnt tonight. By an act of betrayal I begot unknown to me a son who, whilst as ignorant as myself of our relationship, has come to be the evil genius of my life, to cross and thwart me, and finally to help to pull me down in ruin. It is just—poetically just. My full and resigned acceptance of that fact is the only atonement I can offer you."

He stooped and took one of madame's hands that lay limply in her lap.

"Goodbye, Thérèse!" His voice broke. He had reached the end of his iron self-control.

She rose and clung to him a moment, unashamed before them. The ashes of that dead romance had been deeply stirred this night, and deep down some lingering embers had been found that glowed brightly now before their final extinction. Yet she made no attempt to detain him. She understood that their son had pointed out the only wise, the only possible course, and was thankful that M. de La Tour d'Azyr accepted it.

"God keep you, Gervais," she murmured. "You will take the safe-conduct, and . . . and you will let me know when you are safe?"

He held her face between his hands an instant; then very gently kissed her and put her from him. Standing erect, and outwardly calm again, he looked across at André-Louis who was proffering him a sheet of paper.

"It is the safe-conduct. Take it, monsieur. It is my first and last gift to you, and certainly the last gift I should ever have thought of making you—the gift of life. In a sense it makes us quits. The irony, sir, is not mine, but Fate's. Take it, monsieur, and go in peace."

M. de La Tour d'Azyr took it. His eyes looked hungrily into the lean face confronting him, so sternly set. He thrust the paper into his bosom, and then abruptly, convulsively, held out his hand. His son's eyes asked a question.

"Let there be peace between us, in God's name," said the Marquis thickly.

Pity stirred at last in André-Louis. Some of the sternness left his face. He sighed. "Goodbye, monsieur," he said.

"You are hard," his father told him, speaking wistfully. "But perhaps you are in the right so to be. In other circumstances I should have been proud to have owned you as my son. As it is . . ." He broke off abruptly, and as abruptly added, "Goodbye."

He loosed his son's hand and stepped back. They bowed formally to each other. And then M. de La Tour d'Azyr bowed to Mlle. de Kercadiou in utter silence, a bow that contained something of utter renunciation, of finality.

That done he turned and walked stiffly out of the room, and so out of all their lives. Months later they were to hear of him in the service of the Emperor of Austria.

Chapter XVI

Sunrise

Andé-Louis took the air next morning on the terrace at Meudon. The hour was very early, and the newly risen sun was transmuting into diamonds the dewdrops that still lingered on the lawn. Down in the valley, five miles away, the morning mists were rising over Paris. Yet early as it was that house on the hill was astir already, in a bustle of preparation for the departure that was imminent.

André-Louis had won safely out of Paris last night with his mother and Aline, and today they were to set out all of them for Coblenz.

To André-Louis, sauntering there with hands clasped behind him and head hunched between his shoulders—for life had never been richer in material for reflection—came presently Aline through one of the glass doors from the library.

"You're early astir," she greeted him.

"Faith, yes. I haven't been to bed. No," he assured her, in answer to her exclamation. "I spent the night or what was left of it sitting at the window thinking."

"My poor André!"

"You describe me perfectly. I am very poor—for I know nothing, understand nothing. It is not a calamitous condition until it is realized. Then . . ." He threw out his arms, and let them fall again. His face she observed was very drawn and haggard.

She paced with him along the old granite balustrade over which the geraniums flung their mantle of green and scarlet.

"Have you decided what you are going to do?" she asked him.

"I have decided that I have no choice. I, too, must emigrate. I am lucky to be able to do so, lucky to have found no one amid yesterday's chaos in Paris to whom I could report myself as I foolishly desired, else I might no longer be armed with these." He drew from his pocket the powerful passport of the Commission of Twelve, enjoining upon all Frenchmen to lend him such assistance as he might require, and warning those who might think of hindering him that they did so at their own peril. He spread it before her. "With this I conduct you all safely to the frontier. Over the frontier M. de Kercadiou and Mme. de Plougastel will have to conduct me; and then we shall be quits."

"Quits?" quoth she. "But you will be unable to return."

"You conceive, of course, my eagerness to do so. My child, in a day or two there will be enquiries. It will be asked what has become of me. Things will transpire. Then the hunt will start. But by then we shall be well upon our way, well ahead of any possible pursuit. You don't imagine that I could ever give the government any satisfactory explanation of my absence—

assuming that any government remains to which to explain it?"

"You mean . . . that you will sacrifice your future, this career upon which you have embarked?" It took her breath away.

"In the pass to which things have come there is no career for me down there—at least no honest one. And I hope you do not think that I could be dishonest. It is the day of the Dantons, and the Marats, the day of the rabble. The reins of government will be tossed to the populace, or else the populace, drunk with the conceit with which the Dantons and the Marats have filled it, will seize the reins by force. Chaos must follow, and a despotism of brutes and apes, a government of the whole by its lowest parts. It cannot endure, because unless a nation is ruled by its best elements it must wither and decay."

"I thought you were a republican," said she.

"Why, so I am. I am talking like one. I desire a society which selects its rulers from the best elements of every class and denies the right of any class or corporation to usurp the government to itself—whether it be the nobles, the clergy, the bourgeoisie, or the proletariat. For government by any one class is fatal to the welfare of the whole. Two years ago our ideal seemed to have been realized. The monopoly of power had been taken from the class that had held it too long and too unjustly by the hollow right of heredity. It had been distributed as evenly as might be throughout the State, and if men had only paused there, all would have been well. But our impetus carried us too far, the privileged orders goaded us on by their very opposition, and the result is the horror of which yesterday you saw no more than the beginnings. No, no," he ended. "Careers there may be for venal place-seekers, for opportunists; but none for a man who desires to respect himself. It is time to go. I make no sacrifice in going."

"But where will you go? What will you do?"

"Oh, something. Consider that in four years I have been lawyer, politician, swordsman, and buffoon—especially the latter. There is always a place in the world for Scaramouche. Besides, do you know that unlike Scaramouche I have been oddly provident? I am the owner of a little farm in Saxony. I think that agriculture might suit me. It is a meditative occupation; and when all is said, I am not a man of action. I haven't the qualities for the part."

She looked up into his face, and there was a wistful smile in her deep blue eyes.

"Is there any part for which you have not the qualities, I wonder?"

"Do you really? Yet you cannot say that I have made a success of any of those which I have played. I have always ended by running away. I am running away now from a thriving fencing-academy, which is likely to become the property of Le Duc. That comes of having gone into politics, from which I am also running away. It is the one thing in which I really excel. That, too, is an attribute of Scaramouche."

"Why will you always be deriding yourself?" she wondered.

"Because I recognize myself for part of this mad world, I suppose. You wouldn't have me take it seriously? I should lose my reason utterly if I did; especially since discovering my parents."

"Don't, André!" she begged him. "You are insincere, you know."

"Of course I am. Do you expect sincerity in man when hypocrisy is the very keynote of human nature? We are nurtured on it; we are schooled in it, we live by it; and we rarely realize it. You have seen it rampant and out of hand in France during the past four years—cant and hypocrisy on the lips of the revolutionaries, cant and hypocrisy on the lips of the upholders of the old régime; a riot of hypocrisy out of which in the end is begotten chaos. And I who criticize it all on this beautiful God-given morning am the rankest and most contemptible hypocrite of all. It was this—the realization of this truth kept me awake all night. For two years I have persecuted by every means in my power . . . M. de La Tour d'Azyr."

He paused before uttering the name, paused as if hesitating how to speak of him.

"And in those two years I have deceived myself as to the motive that was spurring me. He spoke of me last night as the evil genius of his life, and himself he recognized the justice of this. It may be that he was right, and because of that it is probable that even had he not killed Philippe de Vilmorin, things would still have been the same. Indeed, today I know that they must have been. That is why I call myself a hypocrite, a poor, self-duping hypocrite."

"But why, André?"

He stood still and looked at her. "Because he sought you, Aline. Because in that alone he must have found me ranged against him, utterly intransigent. Because of that I must have strained every nerve to bring him down—so as to save you from becoming the prey of your own ambition.

"I wish to speak of him no more than I must. After this, I trust never to speak of him again. Before the lines of our lives crossed, I knew him for what he was, I knew the report of him that ran the countryside. Even then I found him detestable. You heard him allude last night to the unfortunate La Binet. You heard him plead, in extenuation of his fault, his mode of life, his rearing. To that there is no answer, I suppose. He conforms to type. Enough! But to me, he was the embodiment of evil, just as you have always been the embodiment of good; he was the embodiment of sin, just as you are the embodiment of purity. I had enthroned you so high, Aline, so high, and yet no higher than your place. Could I, then, suffer that you should be dragged down by ambition, could I suffer the evil I detested to mate with the good I loved? What could have come of it but your own damnation, as I told you that day at Gavrillac? Because of that my detestation of him became a personal, active thing. I resolved to save you at all costs from a fate so horrible. Had you been able to tell me that you loved him it would have been different. I should have hoped that in a union sanctified by love you would have raised him to your own pure heights. But that out of considerations of worldly advancement you should lovelessly consent to mate with him . . . Oh, it was vile and hopeless. And so I fought him—a rat fighting a lion—fought him relentlessly until I saw that love had come to take in your heart the place of ambition. Then I desisted."

"Until you saw that love had taken the place of ambition!" Tears had been gathering in her eyes whilst he was speaking. Now amazement eliminated her emotion. "But when did you see that? When?"

"I—I was mistaken. I know it now. Yet, at the time . . . surely, Aline, that morning when you came to beg me not to keep my engagement with him in the Bois, you were moved by concern for him?"

"For him! It was concern for you," she cried, without thinking what she said.

But it did not convince him. "For me? When you knew—when all the world knew what I had been doing daily for a week!"

"Ah, but he, he was different from the others you had met. His reputation stood high. My uncle accounted him invincible; he persuaded me that if you met nothing could save you."

He looked at her frowning.

"Why this, Aline?" he asked her with some sternness. "I can understand that, having changed since then, you should now wish to disown those sentiments. It is a woman's way, I suppose."

"Oh, what are you saying, André? How wrong you are! It is the truth I have told you!"

"And was it concern for me," he asked her, "that laid you swooning when you saw him return wounded from the meeting? That was what opened my eyes."

"Wounded? I had not seen his wound. I saw him sitting alive and apparently unhurt in his calèche, and I concluded that he had killed you as he had said he would. What else could I conclude?"

He saw light, dazzling, blinding, and it scared him. He fell back, a hand to his brow. "And that was why you fainted?" he asked incredulously.

She looked at him without answering. As she began to realize how much she had been swept into saying by her eagerness to make him realize his error, a sudden fear came creeping into her eyes.

He held out both hands to her.

"Aline! Aline!" His voice broke on the name. "It was I . . ."

476

"O blind André, it was always you—always! Never, never did I think of him, not even for loveless marriage, save once for a little while, when . . . when that theatre girl came into your life, and then . . ." She broke off, shrugged, and turned her head away. "I thought of following ambition, since there was nothing left to follow."

He shook himself. "I am dreaming, of course, or else I am mad," he said.

"Blind, André; just blind," she assured him.

"Blind only where it would have been presumption to have seen."

"And yet," she answered him with a flash of the Aline he had known of old, "I have never found you lack presumption."

M. de Kercadiou, emerging a moment later from the library window, beheld them holding hands and staring each at the other, beatifically, as if each saw Paradise in the other's face.

THE END

About the Author

Rafael Sabatini (1875-1950) was born in central Italy to an Italian father and an English mother. His birthplace, the medieval walled town of Jesi, was one of decaying palaces and ancient churches; it was this, perhaps, that inspired his lifelong passion for history. He studied in Switzerland and Portugal and traveled widely, settling in England as a young man. He mastered six languages, though he chose to write exclusively in English.

Sabatini's fictions, although not well-received by critics, proved immensely popular, and several of them were later made into films. Despite Sabatini's love of history, he had no more faith in the accuracy of historians than most historians had faith in the accuracy of *his* work. He cited such legends as William Tell, the Man in the Iron Mask, and some of the more outrageous claims made against the Borgias as examples of stories that had crept into history through bias and error.

In addition to *Scaramouche* and *Captain Blood*, both available in Common Reader Editions, Sabatini wrote over forty volumes of fiction (both novels and short stories) and non-fiction.